THE SOCIETY GAME

OLIVIA HOPKINS, THE UNRELIABLE WITNESS

H. LANFERMEIJER

Matador
9 Priory Business Park,
Wistow Road, Kibworth Beauchamp,
Leicestershire. LE8 0RX
Tel: 0116 279 2299
Email: books@troubador.co.uk
Web: www.troubador.co.uk/matador
Twitter: @matadorbooks

ISBN 978 1789015 317

British Library Cataloguing in Publication Data.
A catalogue record for this book is available from the British Library.

Printed and bound by CPI Group (UK) Ltd, Croydon, CR0 4YY
Typeset in 12pt Minion Pro by Troubador Publishing Ltd, Leicester, UK

Matador is an imprint of Troubador Publishing Ltd

To my family, you are all I need to love life.

CHAPTER ONE

JASON

Eight months ago

'The devil walks amongst us. You can't see, hear or smell him but you can sense his presence and when you do, run.'

Aunt Olive said this to me twenty years ago when I was fifteen. At the time I just thought she was nuts so I replied with a nod and continued with X-box.

I hadn't thought about what she'd said until the day I heard my uncle's name on the ten o'clock news.

I can't say I knew my aunt particularly well; she was the skinny, manicured, up-tight relative who once declared to Mum that she would never have married Dad.

'I wouldn't even look at a man without a six-figure salary let alone one who thinks battered trainers with stone-washed jeans is suitable attire to be seen in public. Honestly, Janet, he shops in C&A and drinks bottled lager.'

'Pretentious cow,' Mum used to mutter under her breath.

My aunt came back into my life on a wet Tuesday some months back when a letter from her arrived on my doorstep. I say letter, it was more of a manuscript for an epic film. It lay there, slightly damp from the rain, waiting for my return from work. The manila envelope was ragged at the edges and straining against the imprint of the brick of paper that was secured within it. I wanted to breathe in its contents instead of forfeiting my short evening to reading it, so I dodged my aunt until I crawled into my bed at ten after a supermarket meal for one, washed down with a pint.

Normally my enthusiasm to read in bed is demonstrated by a pile of intellectual statement books on my night stand. They lie on top of one another, often added to and occasionally dusted but never opened. But I'd known this letter was coming to me and I couldn't find a suitable excuse to ignore it any longer other than exhaustion.

Mum and I think one other person received a similar letter. I didn't want to be one of the 'chosen'; I wanted to bin it and not return to the crap my aunt brought on my family.

Mum received hers a month before mine. I understand why Mum refused to speak to me about its contents; it was too painful. I did try many times, as I wanted to support her, but she just changed the subject to trivial rubbish about her arguments with the gas board or asked about my day at work even though it's a job I hate and a career that has stagnated for years. Diversions and frustrations; however, here it is, my Aunt Olive's letter.

OLIVE

'Dear Jason, my dearest Jason,

I'll assume, as you read 'my dearest', you're uncomfortable at my affection for you? Maybe you're sceptical and wary that I've written? We haven't properly seen or spoken to one another in so very long. But I beg you to believe me that whenever we met I was thrilled and that excitement never waned over the years.

Your mother once idly commented, 'Jason has the same outlook on life as you – you are both dreamers, more interested in fiction than life.' From those few words, I felt ownership: my boy, my fellow dreamer.

Our meetings became sparse as you grew and I blamed your mother for that. However, if I'd known how my angry words served no other purpose other than to increase the time between your visits, I would have savoured the few I had and humbly begged your mother kindly, sweetly, for just a little more access. Sadly, like so many of us, I was born with the sin of pride and I protested with apathy.

Now I suspect it didn't bother her that I appeared not to care that she was never available to see me, and I know it couldn't have affected you that I was rarely around. I'm certain my absence steadily chased away my claim of family attachment and I assume I morphed from Aunt to acquaintance. The only person who was hurt was me.

Today I savour the memories I have: from the tiny baby, compact and asleep in your babygrow, then the explorative toddler shuffling around my feet, to the excitable and giggling young boy pulling on my hand to play just one more game of football, then the teenager who boasted of his achievements in hockey. Now you are the handsome working gentleman travelling to the City of London to carve your name in the financial markets.

I revisit these memories and occasionally I can feel the joy your being in this world gives me. They are my movies, which I can rewind and play whenever I wish and I thank you for playing in them. So, to me Jason, you are my dearest Jason.

And for that I need to tell you why I've arrived where I am today; to let you know there are always choices in life and maybe my choices can influence yours.

So where to begin my tale? Perhaps with my typical day from not too long ago.

That day comprised of waking at whatever time my body chose. There were no rude interruptions from bells, no strict timetable to follow and no boss to dictate my hours.

Nevertheless, I still had a collection of decisions to make from the moment I woke.

The first was what exercise to start the morning? Either I had a personal trainer who came to the house gym or I traipsed down our garden, beyond the willow trees, past the summer house to our heated outdoor pool.

Then what to wear? Which designer? Where was the venue? But by around one thirty I would be ready to leave for my lunch date with the girls (or shopping, as obviously I was not tied to only one event).

An easy life perhaps?

My dear Jason, to those who did not know me, the people who took a second look, the strangers who stared at me in the street, I was a beautiful, wealthy woman who encapsulated all that glamorous society should be. I was the lady in the best magazines who photographers tried to mimic with a prepubescent child model and the latest designer wear.

But, justice isn't made from one still, it's made from twelve people listening to two barristers, interpreting that picture of a perfect woman in a perfect life. A quick glance at the image then the first interpretation may be of greed, unfair luck bejewelled on one person laughing at the common woman who couldn't afford the shoes she walked in. But stare a little longer and the other, secret, silent interpretation is a desperately sad woman controlled and broken by the life that she had prostituted herself for.

So, my darling Jason, justice is the lawyer who can shout the loudest about one picture in a biased society.

CHAPTER TWO

Olive

Many, many years ago

My first memories were of indulgent cuddles from my mum and dad amidst the sullen tantrums of my older sister, your mother, Janet.

I have a photograph from when I was about three years old. I have red hair with large curls wrapped around my chubby, happy face. My blue eyes are framed by long eyelashes, my cheeks reddened from playing and my pink lips stretched by laughter. If you wish to take a look, I know Janet has a copy of the photograph I'm holding. It shows her cuddling me with a bored expression on her face, and she is being cuddled by Mum and Mum is being cuddled by Dad. As I recall, your mother's copy is framed and hanging in her stairway, next to the oval mirror. I'd like to think it's still there but I understand if it's been discarded.

By the time she was fifteen and I was eight, your mother created a thunderous atmosphere, oppressive and heavy.

Eventually, Janet abdicated from the family. She left with your father to a flat near Woking.

In the years that followed, I saw little of her. Instead I watched the decline in my parents' health and it was me, as a naïve scared child, who had to watch them age. In the case of your grandad, I witnessed him shrivel up and wither away. I could no longer seek sanctuary in the safety of his lap. Instead, I stood frightened as Dad was slowly tortured to an early grave by pancreatic cancer. His last days and my last memories of him, when I was barely thirteen, were as a skeletal man forcing a smile for his daughters.

You never knew your grandad and he never knew you, but if you had, then your life would be richer for it.

I didn't hear my Mum cry on the day he died, I didn't hear her cry during the funeral and I don't think she heard me cry. Instead, I would listen to her muffled sobbing at night after she had gone to bed, lying alone in the spot Dad used to be in. But still Janet rarely visited and the house remained quiet throughout the remainder of my teens with me going to school, Mum off to work, and us returning for dinner before East-Enders then bed. Gradually the sobbing stopped and an outwardly benign life continued.

I confess I daydreamed of my future throughout my school life: I dreamt of a wardrobe full of gowns for all the evening functions I would attend and stunning suits to wear to the office for my dazzling career where I would meet my wealthy, handsome and successful husband.

I wouldn't be like the girls in class (as fate predicted), trudging through scripted pre-lived lines whereby they met some bloke from school or some club in town. Married by twenty-three, pregnant by twenty-five, in a two-bed semi and divorced by thirty-five with three kids. My parallel life would eclipse anyone I knew, as payment for how their lives had eclipsed mine at school.

It was then that you were born, just after my A' level results. Your father was an adolescent crush who refused to go away. He was from Janet's school and worked as an apprentice plumber until he was sacked for consistently choosing his bed over working. I know you don't see your father these days but may I reassure you that you are not missing anything; I merely pity the gullible women who took him in during and, subsequently, after Janet.

I still smile recalling the day I met you, two days into your life. You were wrapped tightly in a white swaddling blanket within a perspex hospital cot. I had an overwhelming urge to free you from those confines, but instead I mimicked your grandma in my hyperbolic: 'Ahh, he's gorgeous, beautiful. Well done!'

From that day, I rewrote my script to include ultimately finding the perfect man and having a child as precious as you. Though, in my film, I would have my child in a private hospital in London or maybe New York, not Woking General NHS hospital. And I would be dressed in a midnight-blue, silk nightie whilst smiling serenely to my guests – not sobbing discreetly to any visitor, dressed in a blood-stained flannel gown given to me one Christmas ten years earlier.

Your mother was overjoyed to have you but naturally frightened to be a new mum with no income and a man who was there in spirit but absent in support of any kind.

Everyone around her pandered to her demands; your grandma, at that moment, was no exception and for the first two months she went to help every day in whatever way she could, right up to the day another argument erupted over some trivial matter (I think about number of feeding times), and the visits fizzled away.

Mum was distraught. 'I didn't bring my children up to squander their education by scrounging from the state,' she said over breakfast one morning. 'Neither parent works or contributes anything to society. They merely expect and accept all their living needs from the taxpayer. Janet lives in a far better flat than most hard-working parents can afford!'

'And what of the father?' she lamented whilst scrubbing the kitchen floor one afternoon. 'He lounges around his free accommodation watching Sky television or the like. The last time I was allowed to enter their 'free abode', he could muster only a nod of acknowledgement to me.'

'He's not at all ashamed or embarrassed that he does less than a parasite without a host', she spat one evening during a re-run of Antiques Roadshow. 'Instead, he just grunts to those who have worked all their lives to support their family and sleeps on a settee I paid for!'

She hadn't paid for it as it was a wedding gift to my parents over thirty years prior and it was either going to charity or to Janet, but I understood the point she made.

Thankfully, it wasn't long before your father disappeared. You were less than one year old. I was not surprised; he was merely following what was laid out in his personal script, written before he was born. This particular scene was entitled, 'the typical, lazy, out-of-work man runs from responsibility to allow others to take care of his past failings'. It's an example of the 'responsibility scale': if we were all to be placed in a virtual line from most caring and understanding all the way down to useless bum, your father started two thirds of the way down with aspirations to fall lower in the scale. I am aware of my lack of sensitive diplomacy surrounding your father but I'm reflecting many years of dinner-table discussions, of which you were a part. I also know that you may have inherited his nose and auburn hair, but the lazy gene bypassed you in favour of the more dominant accomplishment gene. Your father, in contrast, has achieved the bum scale.

During this time the equilibrium of Mum's body altered

subtly. She was permanently tired and had severe shortness of breath. I regret merely listening to her diagnosis of acid reflux because one Tuesday, in the summer of your second year, I came home to an ambulance and Jean, from across the road, tugging at Mum's lifeless arm. She was rushed to hospital and diagnosed with heart disease. She was fifty-four. Although she survived, her life was stripped to a wheelchair, with easy access railings everywhere.

I was now twenty years old. I didn't go out; I didn't even try, I just melted into the walls of our house and waited on Mum who was slowly shrinking away into her wheelchair.

Jason, I've relived my life and wondered where it was that led me to today? Which bank did I jump from to slide down the stream that brought me here? Maybe it was the loss of my father, maybe losing my sister to your father or maybe it was the 11th of April of my twenty-first year.

That spring day my mum was shipped off to hospital where I took up vigil; and May 8th she died. And I was alone except for Janet and blessed you.

A few days after saying goodbye to Mum, I was summoned with my sister, to a solicitor's office to discuss Mum's will.

In Woking, opposite a sixties' bland concrete fountain, was Thomas & Lewis. The office was on the third floor of the last remaining Elizabethan building in the town. Its façade stuck out like a groomed lady in a brothel surrounded, as it was, by faded, exhausted, breathless buildings.

I was five minutes early for my appointment in the office on the third floor so I sat down in the waiting area. I looked at the pimpled plain receptionist opposite me and I smirked that even in my grief I had bothered to wear make-up.

Janet arrived less than five minutes after me.

'I thought I was going to be late. The babysitter didn't turn up on time then I missed my bus and to cap it all I went to the wrong end of town as the bus driver swore Raynor building was that end.' Janet humphed as she slumped into the chair beside me.

'And hello to you too Janet! I've been here ages, absolutely ages. And don't worry, I've signed us both in. I would have appreciated a phone call, something to let me know where to meet – I just had to assume it was here. And should you be interested, I had difficulty getting here too – the taxi driver had no idea where this was either but I managed to get here on time.'

Janet's slim face rolled my way.

'Don't start Olive. I'm still early and just because you're earlier than me just means you're wasting more time than me. Plus, I have a few more things to worry about than how my hair is to be worn today.'

Her face rolled back so I could get a glimpse of her dark hair shoved into a misshapen ponytail.

'You're not even wearing tights, Janet.'

'Seriously, shut up!' Janet lurched her face towards mine, forcing my neck back against the metal bar of the chair. 'And with what money do I buy tights? Nappies and little things called food use up all my money. You, on the other hand, don't have any of these inconveniences.'

I would have retaliated and reminded her of the sacrifices I had made in my life to look after Mum but my defence was interrupted by Mr Thomas opening the door to his office to invite us in. He was a large man dressed in a linen sky-blue suit which was crumpled around his bulbous waist. His tan shoes were scuffed about his toes and his tie hung like a loose noose around his neck. His face slumped around a mouth which had given up the strain of holding a smile long ago; now there was an etched frown from the corners of his mouth all the way down to his triple chin which sat squeezed above his collar.

The office was dark and smelt of dust and stale air. Bright beams of light squeezed through cracks in the window shutters, forcing me to squint as I edged my way to the only available seats in the office.

'Er, welcome and I'm sorry to hear of your loss and so forth. Anyway, it's very unusual to actually read a will,' Mr Thomas began, 'in fact, I've only done it once before. Legally, all I need to do is pass you both a copy – which I can do if you wish to read it alone elsewhere? The reason— oh please mind that pile, just step over it, I really need more cupboard space. Anyway, the reason I called you in was just to reassure you the changes that were made in your mother's will were done more than six months ago. All is legal and above board as they say. Yes, do sit there – a favourite of my cat so please excuse the stray hairs – but be warned she may come in and sit on your lap.'

I sat next to Janet, though my mind was straying to the comment she'd made earlier about my hair.

'Would you like me to read it or do you want to take the copies away with you?' continued Mr Thomas. He released the folded documents and then wiped his forehead with his hand and, with his wet fingers, he picked the papers up again and gestured for us to take our copies.

'No, no, it's fine. Please read what it says,' Janet and I chimed in unison. Mr Thomas squelched his neck further into his collar, 'As you wish.'

I remember the tingle in my chest, which felt inappropriate for the reading, but I also remember my gasp as Mr Thomas continued to read that the woman who abandoned us, who concentrated on her life regardless of the difficulties I was facing caring for Mum; was to receive everything. Mum even sweetened the prize for Janet by describing how Janet had lit her life for so many years:

'...Thank you for my grandson, thank you for your love and thank you for being my beautiful daughter. Please believe me, you are my loved little girl...'

The grateful dripping tears from Janet's face should have been mine. Instead, I felt the sting of hearing that the house I grew up in was to be given to Janet to bring up Jason.

I marched out after a dignified goodbye to Mr Thomas. I contemplated the possibility that it was a scheme constructed by Janet and her new lover, Mr Thomas, but I rationalised these would be extreme measures even for her.

Outside was a sharp, fresh day. The rain had washed the streets and the sun was dutifully drying the pavement. I squinted in the sunlight and stared at Janet. She was still whimpering, her lips shivering and her eyes dragged down to her cheeks.

'She's really gone. We'll never hear from her again, we'll never be hugged by her, we'll never have her scones and jam. Nothing, she's gone!' Janet whispered to herself.

'At least you'll never have your arguments,' I spat.

'We didn't argue? Why are you saying that? She was my Mum and I want her with me. Ah, poor Jay, he's not going to know her,' she paused and looked at me. 'You okay? You look irritated. Are you sad? What's the matter?'

'£11,000, that's it. I've lost my home and I have nothing to show for it...' I began.

'No, you have half her savings plus half of the house? What are you on about? She said we all live there but it is not to be sold until Jay is eighteen.'

'So, because I don't have a baby, my life is on hold? And her exact words were that Jason was to receive a share of the house which you keep in trust, so it's not half is it?'

'Okay a third, but oh my God! Is that it? It's all about money? You weren't moved by her loving words to you? '...my sweetest baby girl... so beautiful, my gorgeous dreaming girl...' Jeez. What did you want Olive? What did you expect? What is wrong with you? We've lost Mum! It's just you, me and Jay! You have a home with us, always. You have half her savings, you have her memory and you have a testimony which recounted how she treasured you to her last days... Olive she's gone!'

'...I do know she's not here, I also know how I was always with her, how all you two did was argue but just because you have Jason, you're her 'special little girl' and you get everything.

I gave up so much of my life to care for Mum – dressing her, feeding her, getting her to the toilet, wheeling her around the park in between cleaning the house and giving her her medication. Is this what a woman my age does? Not going out, not shopping for me or partying? No. I forfeited my life for Mum and I'm thanked with a third!!'

I moved aside for a passer-by who stared at us. I then walked to the fountain where the taxi ramp was.

'Wait! I'll get a taxi with you...'

'Well you can afford it now, can't you – perhaps it should be me getting the bus or maybe I should just walk – you'd like that as you drive by!' I twirled around to join the queue.

'Where are you getting this? I loved Mum! She was the woman who kept me going these last few years. She was the woman who reminded me my life wasn't completely rubbish. I'm sorry I didn't do as much as you, I have Jay remember? but I still miss her. I no longer have our daily chats and I'm sinking. I'm not coping.' I could see Janet's lip quiver; she looked up at the sky to calm herself, 'Okay, I'll assume you are just missing Mum so instead of slapping you I'll remind you we have each other and we can be a family just as Mum said in the testimony. Please Olive, right now we need each other.'

Janet's dishevelled fringe flopped around her sad face.

'I'm getting a taxi home,' I screeched.

Janet leant forward and sharply said, 'You live alone in your head Olive. Mum loved you and wanted us to be sisters again. That is all that happened. You're a selfish, self-centred, egotistical dreamer.

What's worse, Olive, you don't recognise who loves you. Instead, you bury your head in magazines and dream of a day that you can be one of those materialistic, vain women that prance about on each page. Get a grip, Olive, life isn't about money and clothes, it's about family. Mum served you tirelessly; her life was dominated by making you happy. But for once, Olive… jeez don't ignore me, I'm trying to help you…'

I slammed the taxi door and urged the driver to speed away. As he did so I looked at Janet standing alone. I reassured myself that I wasn't a dreamer, I was a realist. Go get life, I thought. Maybe go to Australia? I had always dreamt of that and how jealous anyone who knew me would be, especially Janet, stuck in my home. She could have it. I was going to grab life and enjoy it from now on! I'd go travelling to the party country without Janet, without Mum and without anyone.

CHAPTER THREE

JASON

This self-righteous crap had taken me to one in the morning. She went on about how life was passing her by, how she had needed to escape the house that my mum now owned. I couldn't get my head round what she was drivelling on about with the house. This 1960s bungalow was in all our names and it was eventually sold seven years ago; it paid off my parents' mortgage, gave me a deposit for my house and the final third morphed into my aunt's bank account.

My night had been cut short to a cat nap and, as I lay awake in the dark, I thought of my earliest memories of Aunt Olive but they were clouded by recent events. I couldn't see her or the picture she'd spoken about; a picture I've passed loads of times without acknowledging it as anything other than another memory on the wall.

She did have a point about me. Like her, I loved books, plays, films. I used to want to be a screen writer. But that road was too thorny to follow and instead I chose the easy money path. So, after leaving university I followed the financial railway tracks into the city. A train I'm still catching today.

My alarm shook me awake. My eyes begged me to stay shut for a few seconds more. But the reality of a breakfast meeting yanked them open and my brain kicked me out of the warm bed to a cold sharp slap of my bedroom air. This was my usual morning, which began too early for my health and too suddenly for a comfortable ease into the day. Unlike my aunt's day, every part of my morning routine was timed to get me to my desk with the least amount of time and effort for just a few extra precious moments in bed. It's a strategy which has never let me down but I still don't wake and function coherently until just after nine – everything before then is a daily blur.

On the train to work I stroked the rough edges of my aunt's envelope. I looked around at the other passengers. They were duplicates from the original mould of the city work force; tired and ragged in pin-striped suits. I wondered what they did to pay their mortgage. Whether, like me, they spent their life hours rushing from one unfinished project to the next in pursuit of promotion.

My breakfast meeting consisted of deflection of faults to delegation of tasks from one department to the next. It was the usual roundabout that I'd sat on since the day I started at Morgan and Price. That morning, I left deflated that the work I had slaved over for the last two months was rejected as it no longer fitted into the working model of 'today'.

'Nothing changes, Steve.' I said. 'Same crap, different arse.'

Steve was one of my team and he had his eye on my job. I didn't care; I had my eye on my manager's job. The whiff of promotion was in the air and we were all pushed to give more of our lives to the office in the hope we would slide up hill.

'What changes, mate, is the weather, that's all you can count on. By the way, where were you last night? We all ended up at the Hog's Head for lock-in, but no Jay!'

One thing about Steve, his daily routine doesn't include sleep.

'Sorry mate, I was knackered. Needed to be in for this meeting and, after last week, I needed sleep. Seriously Steve, I don't know how you do it. I'm up every day at five-thirty for the piggin' 6.17 train. Why can't a day start at ten? Worked for my aunt.'

'Know what you mean, slept for twenty minutes on the lav yesterday – longest sleep I've had in ages.'

I picked up the manila envelope and showed it to Steve.

'Well it's here,' I said.

'That's either the yellow pages or Aunt Olive's famous tell-all gossip,' Steve clapped his hands. 'Mate, give us the lowdown.'

'I read it until one in the morning.'

'Damn! Nice going, Jay-boy. So? Was it worth missing the beers with the boys?' Steve said.

'So far, it drones on about her start in life and how she was cheated by everyone she knew, how life was hard as a poor girl living with her mum, who died when I was born. Then she inherited money but somehow Mum was the cause of all her misery – I didn't get very far and I think I've got to her buggering off to Oz leaving Mum on her own.'

'You look pissed mate.'

'Not really,' I said, 'didn't really know her that well so don't care. You know how it is.' I threw the letter on the desk.

'Yeah, yeah. See what you mean, Jay. How is your mum? If you don't mind me asking?' he asked sheepishly.

'Mum's bearing up as best she can. She still jokes that it's another drama in Olive's life and there'll be another around the corner, but I know she's finding it difficult.'

Steve lent in and almost whispered, 'And your Aunt Olive? How is she?'

I backed away to check if I had any messages on my phone and reluctantly replied, 'Dunno, same old I guess. Her letter is all I can go on. Weirdly, she tells me how much she loves me, but I don't really know her and reading this, so far, I don't really like her. I don't know why she's telling me about where she grew up, arguments she had as a child and all that bollocks. I don't get it mate.'

Steve then stood up to face me.

'We're all born and we'll all die, no one can change those facts about us, but it's the life we lead in between these dates that we are allowed to manipulate to make the beginning and the end worth our while,' he said.

'Mmmm, not sure what relevance that has to my aunt? But thanks.'

Steve continued, 'You may not like her but maybe you can understand her, you know, where she started? Ah, don't laugh Jay, just thought you should know like.'

'Right, yeah, thanks. Seen Peter's new Audi R8?' I replied.

'Yeah, sweet. Jammy git!' Steve smiled and returned to the audit he was working on.

It was past ten o'clock when I finally left the office. Admittedly two hours of my office time was spent in the Fox Tavern but, thanks to the late hour, my company paid for a taxi back to my house. The drive home afforded me a little more reading time in an attempt to calm down from the day at work:

Olive

'Jason, our ideas for our life are often easy to formulate yet nearly always impossible to execute. Sometimes it is easier to delegate plans to the dreams' department. My dreams knocked at my daily thoughts and kept me happy as only dreams of a promise of better times can.

One consolation of my sister moving into my house was being with you every day. I remember how you learnt to crawl by first shuffling backwards then progressing to an army belly-pull using just your arms to propel yourself around the room. I was mesmerised by how you were able figure out your world around you and how at age three you gabbled away about everything you saw and touched; so, it was probably you and your charm that stopped me from entering a travel agent's shop and buying my ticket to Australia until I was twenty-two.

The catalyst to walking into the shop was Janet; she dared me, gently at first then with a bit more vigour until the taunting began. She claimed I would never leave, that I would sit around the house irritating her until I was grey-haired, owned a brown sofa and cuddled my cats all day. 'No life and no hope,' she would tease.

I didn't deserve the taunts from Janet or the pitiful looks from the neighbours and I didn't deserve the gossiping from past school pupils. Admittedly, nothing was ever directly said to me but I heard them daily via their sly secretive glances, their strained smiles as they passed me and their covered chats to one another. Conversations I could still hear as I lay in bed or prepared the dinner or when I walked pass the travel agent's shop.

'Pathetic,' they would gossip, 'still living at home.' 'She needs to get a life,' was another taunt, 'thank god I'm not her.'

'You're paranoid.' Janet said one afternoon in the high street. 'Nobody is saying any such thing about you and, even if they were, why should you care?'

'You would say that, you're not the one broke without a future – I'm twenty-two and I don't have a job, a boyfriend or a life,' I cried.

'Well get one, as I keep saying to you time and again.' Janet replied.

'What a boyfriend?'

'No, a life. In fact— ooh, look where we are! How convenient.'

I looked around to what she was referring to and felt the nudge on my arm pushing me into the travel agent's shop.

Janet spoke on my behalf about where I was to land in Australia, the internal flights I was to take and how long she wanted me away for. Janet had planned everything.

'If I didn't do it, Sis, then your sulky face sure as hell wouldn't. But regardless, everything is negotiable and changeable apart from cancelling. So, you're going and it's happening in less than one month.'

I turned and looked at Janet.

'You look shocked,' she said, 'but take heart my sweet Olivia,' she continued, 'one of your personality traits is that you're easy to push and pull around; maybe a disadvantage in your eyes, but for me, it has meant I can send you off to Oz without a quibble. So now, my beloved, stop obsessing about what people think of you and grab your life. Can I have a smile, and maybe a thank you to your sister who just wants you to be happy?'

Instead, I just nodded and I kept nodding whenever anybody asked me about my trip and how excited I must feel. All I could muster was a, 'Yeah, very excited, thanks'.

'So exciting!' said my neighbour, 'Where do you start first? Your sister said Sydney. Where are you staying? Oh, you must be so excited; oh, and after everything you and your sister have been through! It's about time life turned around for you both. How exciting. I was chatting to John only yesterday...' John, her husband, who doesn't know me and undoubtedly didn't care. 'We were just saying how excited we are for you, how excited you must be. So pleased, how exciting...'

I hoped my excitement would grow to match hers. I hoped it would bubble from my stomach to snatch a breath and give involuntary giggles as I thought of my journey to Australia. Instead, I felt permanently nauseous as fear gripped my throat and churned my stomach. I fidgeted from one sleepless night to another right up to the day Janet accompanied me and my 70-litre rucksack to the airport.

After twenty-three hours sitting in the same cramped conditions on a Boeing 747, I landed in Australia. I walked through to the arrival hall laden down with my rucksack, which felt like a huge lazy bear on my back.

(In years to come, I discovered the maximum rucksack size for my height and weight was 55 litres and not the 70 litres I lugged around with every available crevasse and corner rammed with 'just in case' clothes. At least my future chiropractor will be pleased for my vanity. For those about to embark on a tour of down-under all you need are two pairs of shorts – one smart and one for the day, three tops – which can be smart or casual, one pair of flip-flops, one pair of trainers and one hooded top; you certainly do not need to take two sets of bed-linen as I had done).

I found an information board at Sydney Airport that detailed all the different back-packers' accommodation in and around Sydney. I picked the Kings Cross backpackers' 'hotel' as they offered a free pickup and the accompanying pictures were of happy travellers in a bright and colourful dorm. The reality was I had to make my own way there and the hostel was above a sex shop with a filthy door to an equally filthy reception. I mused that at least I wouldn't get lost in the city as my 'hotel' had a huge luminous neon-lit condom reaching to the third floor and could be seen from most parts of the Kings Cross district.

My first night was spent hugging my rucksack for fear those around me in adjacent bunk-beds would steal my clothes and shoes (of course in hindsight, I should have been grateful as that may have saved my back). In the morning I calculated that there was no shame in returning straight back home on the next available flight I could get. However, to this day I smile at how on my very first day travelling, the very first person I spoke to was Carolanne.

'Wow you look like you've been slapped with an iron pillow. You've either lost all your money, lost your passport or discovered you're not in Oz but back home in Wormwood Scrubs?'

Carolanne was petite, blonde, toned and tanned. She was the type of woman who could model for Mattel as Malibu Barbie.

She was confident and had a warm inviting smile. She also had an enviably small rucksack.

'Oh er, no, I'm fine thanks.' I broke a smile just to reassure her I didn't need reassuring.

'You're not in Wormwood Scrubs, you know that? You are in Oz in the Kings Cross 'hotel'... though Wormwood Scrubs would probably be cleaner and more comfortable – but at $12 a night you really can't complain.'

She was wearing pyjama shorts and a red vest top, effortlessly sexy and the opposite of my attire of a long nightshirt and socks. My red hair was pulled back into a tight knot to hide its unruly, fuzzy nature. Carolanne's in contrast was long, smooth and bouncy.

She was an instant friend and I followed her around Sydney going wherever she suggested (which was invariably another bar to chat to men who always bought her and me our drinks for the afternoon and night). Even though I had a rucksack full of clothes, I too bought silver hot-pants similar to the ones she wore. I was a faithful companion by perfecting my broad smile, tilting my head seductively to one side and allowing Carolanne to do all the chatting. Eventually, Carolanne would summon me to go, when she was bored of their company, and we'd leave for either another bar or back to the luminous condom we called home.

In the spirit of travel, we both decided that Australia offered more than Sydney and it would be appropriate to at least attempt to venture beyond the city boundary. After two months we picked up our rucksacks and took the train to the Blue Mountains just outside the city.

As any good sheep dog would testify, my best feature is my ability to obey instructions. Carolanne herded me to a caravan park she'd heard about. She sat on the 1970s sofa cushions in our tired and weary trailer and said, 'I told you, it's great. We're going to have a good time here. All the caravans are full and did you spot the blond bloke going into the one about two doors down? You should have – he was gorgeous! I haven't seen any other women around – though there usually is one sniffing about. I vote we go over as soon as we can and see if they've got any alcohol on them. They should, he looked like a laugh.'

The 'blond bloke' opened the door and a waft of stale beer, cigarettes and body odour surrounded us. Carolanne was not put off as she fell into her giggling, sexy, femme fatale that could snare any male. We entered a typical male domain that had produced the smell and I sat at one end with Carolanne holding court the other.

'Fancy a VB? It's beer, but only by Ozzy standard – I'm afraid I've got nothing else to offer you.'

A thin, long man held out the can, which I accepted.

'Mind if I smoke?' he asked as he was about to light a cigarette.

His head was cocked to one side and as he drew the initial glug of smoke his cheeks hollowed and his jaw bones sharply jutted out revealing the shape of his skull.

'Please go ahead, I don't mind at all. Thanks for the beer, sorry I've not bought anything; we've just arrived,' I said, though I wasn't really sorry for the lack of offering as I've found a polite excuse has always proven to be an accepted substitute for manners.

'Hey no worries. Soo, I'm James, this is Tom, Chris, Monty and Rob.'

Each one turned their head to me as the register was called then promptly turned their head back to Carolanne leaving me with James.

'I'm Olivia, Olive or Ol, whatever you choose. I respond to any form of my name.'

'Nice to meet you, Olivia.'

We both smiled our introduction smile. James' smile drew his eyes in on the act. They were embracing and momentarily distracted me from the shine of oil over his face. Around his hairline and around his hollow cheeks was a rash of spots; his acne had also migrated to his shoulders as I could see fierce spots with white mountain peaks poking out from his t-shirt, they tumbled down his back which was slightly displayed as the neckline of his top sat away from his thin neck; a neck which housed a disproportionately large Adam's apple.

'So, what bought you to Oz, Olivia, Olive or Ol?'

'My sister decided it was time I went; she wanted her own space under her rules, so I didn't fit in anywhere in her perfect little life.'

'And you do everything your sister says?'

'Usually.'

'Well as I see it, your sister's a wazzock. She kicked you out of wherever to live in Oz. It's paradise here girl!

Another beer? There are some more somewhere. If not, you can top up with the dregs from the bottles around me… I know what you're thinking, I really need to dust this armpit of a caravan, but I'm a bloke from Sevenoaks so I get away with this crap-hole thanks to my own gender thinking dregs from a bottle is a suitable substitute for a drink to offer a lady – sorry!' He winked.

I learnt he was from a small village and that his ambition was to be a carpenter but he was a gardener instead as it was available work. I informed him he was wrong, they are both laborious jobs and he should reconsider his options to a warm cosy desk somewhere. He then asked what I did for a living?

'The same as you – I'm avoiding it all, I'm travelling.' James laughed and each time he did his bulbous Adam's apple bounced up and down his long neck.

'I'll be a carpenter one day but the course fees are proper high. My Dad has promised to invest in the tools I need as soon as I start. I'm pretty lucky. I just really enjoy making stuff with my hands, seeing the things in my head come to life and all just from the tools God and genes gave us. Hopefully what I will make will stay on this planet longer than me. I just love it, especially the wood.

I sometimes wonder where it's come from before I get hold of it. Maybe the wood I use once protected a person from the rain and they're no longer alive today, but for that moment the tree loved and cared for that person. Then a cutter comes and I get to create something, anything, just to show off the wood. Ah, I bet you think us a right wazzock?!'

He was holding his hand in a bowl shape as he was telling me this.

'Have you ever sold anything?' I asked,

'Twice; my friend has a glass company and tours around England following the craft markets and she agreed to sell my pieces for us. So far, I've sold a salad bowl and a chopping board. I can do more than just that and it's good money when I do. I don't have the equipment for it yet but I will one day. Aah, watch out Rob, you wazzock!' he said, as he broke his bowl and placed his arm across me to shield me from Rob, a large man made larger by being drunk and in charge of a body. As Rob manoeuvred around me his arms hit me in the chest.

'Sorry, I was just trying to grab a lighter that's behind you… Sorry, sorry…' Rob attempted a salute then fell back to his original position on the floor beside all the other, now very drunk, men.

'Would you like to go for a walk?' James asked.

It was not the walk that concerned me or even James, but it was the fear of other people thinking I may be going on a romantic walk with him; it was also the fear that James may think I was going on a romantic walk with him

'I'm not sure, only because it's hot in the caravan. Only a short walk if that's okay? Sorry but, er, okay. Just a small walk for air only.'

As we left the caravan I could hear sniggers and laughter. I looked back at the crumbling cave.

'Relax, I don't bite. You just looked uncomfortable and I thought fresh air would be good. If you're worried, no one has noticed – they're too pissed to notice their own feet let alone anyone else coming and going.'

'Oh, I don't mean that. I don't care what people think and anyway Carolanne would put them straight, so don't worry.' I hurriedly said.

'Oh right, thanks, nice,' James whispered.

He towered above me like a council block of flats; tall, thin and tatty. His clothes were designed purely to dress this great structure as economically as practical.

We continued to chat about who we were and then what I liked and what I wanted. He listened intently to everything I said and he didn't interrupt me or try to contribute examples of his own life to corroborate my stories. He just listened, learnt about me and smiled.

When we returned sometime later, wolf whistles and laughter erupted around us.

'Where have you two been? Ha, didn't take you long James!!!'

The blond, good-looking one laughed at us and smothered me in humiliating sniggers. I protested my innocence but it was thrown out of court so I used an alternative tactic of sitting apart from James and purposefully looking anywhere other than in his direction. James accepted my rebuttal and, as a gentleman, he sat next to Rob.

'Ol, we're off to see the Blue Mountains... that's right, isn't it? I'm sure something is blue. Anyway, we're going to see them. Going to be amazing, really spiritual I hope,' Carolanne declared. She then swivelled in her chair to face James.

'You're coming James... James?' she swivelled back to confirm his name from others around her then swivelled back.

'Yes, you've got to come as Olive needs a hand, this little pretty lady needs looking after and you can do it.'

She didn't wait for a reply but swivelled on a smile and winked to all her jesters. Her performance made me squirm but I mainly felt dejected that anyone placed me in a category of women who would have accepted the advances of someone like James.

The matchmaking continued for our walk into the Blue Mountains. Regrettably, I couldn't fully appreciate the views of the purple hue from the eucalyptus trees across the vast expanse of wilderness, with its deep forested gorges and precipitous cliffs, as I was too preoccupied with proving to others that I had no interest in James whilst making sure James didn't notice my rejections of him.

'Is there something wrong? James is soooo sweet. I really feel his spirit – it's pure and I think he's cute,' Carolanne said that evening.

'I wouldn't call him that,' I said. 'He is lovely as a person but that's all.'

I stopped short of admitting that I measured myself to be at Major level in the social army, and many ranks above James.

'Shame,' she sighed.

I slumped further in the deckchair that I'd been sitting in for the last hour. It was my retreat outside my caravan as it overlooked the camping area and the communal fire-pit. Each caravan had their windows and doors open to let in maximum cooling air, albeit at the expense of more flies.

I pondered, whilst watching Carolanne being entertained by her male fan club; perhaps I was deluded and everyone else was just showing me that I should be grateful for what I could get and that was James – sweet on the inside but spotty on the outside.

I didn't stay in the Blue Mountains much longer as Carolanne wanted to move onto Melbourne. We left together, thankfully leaving all sniggers behind me.

Melbourne felt European with a hint of '1920s American Al Capone city' about it. There were trams that railed around small uniform tree-lined open parks and through streets with tall brown buildings and black iron-windowed bars. All of this was seen through squinted eyes as it rained most days whilst I was there. It was an easy stay of avoiding the rain and going out for occasional coffees but I could feel the restless twitching from Carolanne.

'Captain's Corner followed by the Gateway, yep we'll start there. Geez does it ever stop raining here?'

Carolanne head-butted our room window, 'That Susie girl, the short one with the big bum, declared Melbourne was better than Sydney! So far, I'd say she's conned us – it is dull, Olive! I said it's dull here, don't you agree?' She stared at me and I nodded.

I was on page thirty-two of my magazine, stuffed full of perfect lives seen through the eyes of perfect women with perfect wardrobes. On this page the Countess 'whomever' was standing in a ball-gown on the slopes outside her Alpine lodge looking rich, serene and cold.

'Awwww! Why do you waste your money on these magazines? You're always buying them. But you know what I've got to say? Don't look at their pictures. These women are all airbrushed just to sell you an image. It's fake, not real.'

She stopped and grabbed my magazine.

'Seriously, look at her on this page – the model advertising coffee, she's pouting over her morning mug. Who does that? She almost looks aroused as she puckers up to take a sip. Creepy! Ol, you need to see that now is real; this room with your smelly trainers and questionable taste in luminous sports socks is real, and it's worth far more than the way a designer wants you to look at that moment.

You know what, sweetie, my mum used to say, 'Hold your head up and enjoy the day otherwise, you'll be attached to someone else's fantasy life and become detached from your own', it's only now, in Oz, that I get her words. Ol, do the same, feel the spirit of now and then you'll feel the spirit of you and others around you.'

'Not a clue what you've just said, Carolanne, but all I know is I want to be that woman pouting over her coffee looking gorgeous.'

'You don't like coffee.'

'She's persuaded me to start, speeds up my metabolism. That's the spirit I want.'

'You should read the book – '*The Spirit of Life and How to Touch It*'. I'm reading it right now and I'm already feeling it. I will be free of the chains we bind ourselves with.'

'Mmmm, I think I'd rather feel the now the way my magazine shows me, but thanks all the same.'

There was a knock at our room door. Doing nothing all day infected my ability to enthuse about anything, including merely opening the door to, undoubtedly, the owner claiming our rent was due or checking we were okay – a ruse to see Carolanne. I expected to see a grinning, short, fat, sweaty man and instead I opened it to a tall, thin man who startled me:

'James! What are you doing here?' I said, whilst frantically straightening my hair.

Carolanne bounded over to James to give him a hug.

'Wow, you're a welcome surprise! Where's Chris? We were just talking about tonight and now you've helped us decide: wherever you two are, we'll be!' she said.

The inevitable question of whether Carolanne could travel to Cooper Pedy with Chris, alone, arrived within a week of their arrival. Cooper Pedy was an opal mining region with underground cave homes; it sounded interesting but far too hot for me and the way the question was phrased, by Carolanne, it was a region I was not invited to. I bowed out and agreed to further explore Melbourne with James.

They disappeared on the Tuesday and by the Wednesday we had planned open air cinema, evening strolls, tours of the coffee shops and various long days on the beach between rain showers.

By the end of the following week we decided we wanted to continue on to Adelaide. It was the town of churches but I was more interested in the fact there was a free concert by Crowded House in the centre of the city on the following Friday.

'I can't say I'm a huge fan of Crowded House; I thought they'd split?'

'It's free and they're great. Just think, everyone would want to be there and we get that chance for real – be excited,' I commanded.

'Don't care what other people think. Either way though, I'm made up to be going to the concert with you. You know what, Olive, you're alright!'

'I'll take that as a compliment but take that wry smile off your face; friends, remember?'

'Yes, Olive, just friends.'

Our intention was to arrive early as we were aware that it was not a private concert for us with a concert hall consisting of two lounge chairs and a bottle of wine but that others from around Adelaide would be joining us. What we weren't prepared for was the rest of Australia and beyond invading this concert.

When we arrived, we were directed to various different vantage points by the police, unfortunately, we discovered this was not to see the band on stage but to be in a spot to look up at huge screens.

'So, we arrive two hours early to sit for two hours to watch a piggin' TV screen for a further two hours. Somehow, this doesn't seem a particularly clever plan when there's a TV in our hostel showing the concert, with a sofa and beers, but maybe I've got this all wrong?'

'But we have to be here. Everyone would want to be in our shoes. I did say we should've left earlier,' I said whilst trying to squeeze in between other duped people in the same position as ourselves. 'I hate our position, I bet there's a VIP section. Where's Carolanne when you need her?'

'Who cares? There's no point fighting it Ol, we're stuck here… Sorry mate, can we sit here?'

James ignored the answer from a person leaning against his girlfriend trying to fall asleep and just sat down.

'Sit here James, next to me – actually no, bugger off. I'll save our places whilst you go and get the drinks in from that kiosk over there.'

'We have beers at home already paid for so avoiding that eight-hour queue.'

I sat down in the heat and rolled up my jumper into a pillow to indicate I wanted to lie down.

'Beers it is! I'm off to queue, enjoy your snooze and I'll be back as soon as I can which is, hopefully, before the concert starts or at least before it ends.'

He was surprisingly quick, especially as he emerged with a dozen cans. I didn't have the heart to tell him I still hated beer and instead opened the first in the hope that my thirst would disguise the taste. It didn't, but I managed to finish one can in between bottles of water by the time the concert was finished. James gave away a further two to the couple next to us and he finished the rest over the course of the concert.

So, by the end, James was drunk and he wanted to tell everyone how great life was:

'Isn't it great? Olive, Olive, life's great and you're propa sweet Oliviahhh.'

'You're drunk and we need to get home.'

I was sober so it was down to me to figure out how to get home amongst the throngs of people enveloping us. James was unaware that he was walking into people and when they made a gesture for us to get out of their way, he told them I was lovely and so were they; remarkably, this worked on everyone he barged into.

I was James' walking stick on the initial stages but, the further out we got from the town centre, I became his walking wall as James slouched over my shoulders as a dead weight, dragging his feet behind us.

'Try and stand straight. I can't carry you all the way back. Seriously James, one leg in front of the other... Oh, and a warning: don't pee please, I mean it, don't pee as I'm not clearing you up. You'll stay in your trousers until your sober-self realises you wet yourself.'

I was now staggering from side to side bouncing off people like a gumball machine.

'I know I'm proper leathered but you're proper sweeeeet!... Look everyone at how great she is,' he shouted. 'You, Oliviaahhh, you're awlright!'

'Shut up! Everyone is looking. Look, everyone is staring, it's embarrassing.'

'I don't care and you are beautiful, really beautiful.'

'No I'm not, I know I'm not. I have orange fuzzy hair.'

'Nooo, you're great and sweet. I love yer hair, it's zingy – you're zingy like the fruit. You're a fruit, a tasty zingy sweet zingy fruit.'

'Great my stamp on the world is I'm a fruit.'

I tugged at his limp legs to remind them to walk.

'You're more, Olive, you're beautiful. But the most incredible things about you, are your eyes; your eyes twinkle, there's something amazing about your eyes. You're perfect, girl.'

The crowd cheered and I felt the beautiful showgirl.

'You're a romantic, thank you.'

'You're the most beautiful woman I've ever met,' he whispered in my ear, making my heart tickle.

He rested his head on my head which made him heavier. I strained to keep him close to the side as I could hear a car beeping its way through the crowd.

'You know I'm not Carolanne, but thanks anyway… seriously we need to move to the side, a car is almost behind us.'

'Olive, you're perfect. You mustn't look at anyone else. You're natural and sweet. Don't go changing. Noooo, don't change anything about you.'

I tried to pull him back over to the curb but he broke free. He stood in the centre of the road illuminated by the car that was now crawling behind him, with his audience along the curb. The car headlights were his stage lights and the road his platform, he raised his arms above his head and shouted.

'This woman is perfect the way she is. She's stunning and I love her, I love her!'

His audience cheered at his drunken love for me as he stumbled into the middle of the road but as he did so his trousers had loosened themselves to around his bottom line. He tried to grab them but missed and instead stumbled on further up the road. The car behind him was no longer beeping and its occupants were laughing. His trousers slipped further and were now around his thighs and again James tried to grab them and again he missed, so he stumbled on further until his trousers, which had taken his pants as hostage, were now around his ankles. At which point James stopped, the car stopped, and the hundreds along the roadside stopped as James tried to reach for his trousers and pants by bending over displaying his full glory in front of the floodlights for an Adelaide audience. I rushed over to help when all his efforts to rescue his trousers and pants failed. Everyone around us was laughing, including me.

'I love this womaaaan. She's perfect,' he shouted to his appreciative audience, still with his pants around his ankles.

I dragged him to the side then I hauled, pushed and rolled him home. It had been a long day and an embarrassing night but as I lay awake next to a snoring James in the recovery position, I realised I had never felt as beautiful and happy as I did that day.

A day I relive as often as I dare.

CHAPTER FOUR

JASON

It was raining in the UK. The whole of the country was soaked. Europe was enjoying a bumper ski-season, Canada and the USA were also experiencing huge snow falls albeit in sub-zero conditions. And even though the extreme cold was proving hazardous over there, I was jealous of their far more interesting weather in comparison to this bland, boring rain, rain and more rain falling on my head. However, the country I was really jealous of was Australia; they had beer-drinking sunshine and, as my newspaper tortured me with every day, the pictures zooming in showed the average Australian enjoying the surf, beaches and beer as if the country was one big luxury spa hotel.

I stepped off the train and felt a vibration from my phone; I knew it was Sandra, a woman I'd been dating. Unlike James and my aunt's relationship, every friendship I have with a woman is tainted with boredom of seeing the same sights in my life, be it my work or my house or the pubs I go to. Nothing changes except the face in front of me. Sandra was no exception. I couldn't be bothered to answer her message or even take it out of my pocket.

As I figured, if I saw her without having read it then I could legitimately say I hadn't received it. But as I walked through the train barriers I felt the phone vibrate again, this time I ignored it in anger. I switched my mind to Australia, to try and forget that my job was eating me alive; my manager stretched every hour to squeeze more reports from me. I was pulled from one project to the next by every limb that he had a firm hold of, and there was no give. So, my spare time was not going to be wasted by a woman whose only interest was herself; Bastard maybe, but an honest one.

It had been a week since I picked up my aunt's letter. The last I read, she and James had travelled together from Broome to Cairns.

In Cairns, Aunt Olive had learnt to dive. She wrote how James had persuaded her to sign up for the course and how he had coaxed her into taking her first breath under water in the swimming pool. She had been terrified of the subsequent three-day boat trip to accomplish her Padi course because, like me, she suffered from sea sickness. James held her hair whenever she was feeding the fishes and stroked her hair whilst she slept on his lap, as the boat bobbed and bobbed and bobbed her fragile stomach up and down.

He read all the notes so she could pass the written tests and eased her into the water each time she began a new dive. Slowly, her love for this under-water home grew until her enthusiasm for swimming with the Australian fishes surpassed her loathing of the dive boat.

After the trip, they professed to each other how they were converted divers; how they were going to become dive instructors and open their own dive shop. These plans lasted from Cairns all the way back down the East coast and back to Sydney. Olive wrote she was excited for her future and enjoyed studying for her next diving course. When they returned to Sydney, they found a back-packers' hostel in Manley Beach just west of the city. Together they completed their advanced diving course. Olive wrote how:

'...time had slowed down to lazy, sunshine days of reading about where we would dive in the world, what we would see under the water and how all of the secret water gardens would be experienced with my friend whom I had grown to treasure...'

Olive had forgotten what day, week or month she was enjoying as she lay on the beach or went for another beach dive. But time was ticking and her return date was creeping up behind her. It rudely tapped her on the back when Carolanne re-emerged in the wings at the promised, scripted time:

OLIVE

Carolanne sat on her rucksack in the hallway of our backpacker hostel looking tired and dishevelled.

'Olive!' she squealed. 'Oli, I missed you; I'm so sorry I left you alone but please tell me you had a great time, please! I felt so guilty, especially as I left you with James and yes, I know you told me you weren't interested blah, blah, blah, but seriously, I wouldn't have left you if I thought he didn't have a beautiful spirit and wouldn't look after you. Anyway, I had a great time, ah, I hope you had a great time? How long have you been here? Are you on your own as I'm here now and we can check out Sydney together. Jeez I'm tired, where do I book in?'

She flopped her head on my shoulder mid-flow of questions. I hugged her and looked around to check James hadn't heard my original thoughts about him.

'All is good, Carolanne, I learnt to dive and I saw turtles, Hammer-head sharks and...'

'I'm so pleased – did you dump James then? I'm sorry, and if it's any consolation I dumped the cock that I'd decided to dump you for so, again, I'm sorry.' She then looked up.

'Oh James... Hi!'

James beamed his bright welcoming smile with his arms outstretched to grab a hug from Carolanne.

'Oh James, I'm so pleased to see you. I was just saying that you would have looked after my Olive and you have. Oh thank you, thank you!'

'Don't worry, Caz, Olive can care for herself,' he said with a slight irritated tilt in his voice, 'she's a grown woman. I gotta go, do you need anything, Caz?'

He nodded a goodbye to both of us and I watched him walk out to buy some more bread and milk for the two of us.

'Are you two together?' she whispered as if asking about a state secret.

'No, sweetie, no,' I said firmly.

I pointed to where she could dump her bags in my room and where she could lay her head on the spare bed. She gratefully took up the offer. Her eyes were heavy but she ploughed on with her questions about James until she was satisfied he was just a friend. I left her to sleep and went to find James but he still hadn't returned from the shops with bread for my toast. After an hour I abandoned my look-out post and checked on Carolanne. She was just waking when I walked in.

'I'm pleased you had James with you. I genuinely felt guilty about buggering off. I thought Chris was a pure soul but he wasn't, he was just another cock in a whole line of cocks.'

'It doesn't matter. We arrived in Oz alone and we'll leave alone, so what and where we go and do is not a problem; I really didn't mind you going.' I stroked her hand and smiled but she seemed sad,

'Don't say that, I love being with you. I want to be friends with you always, regardless of where we are, and I hated being with 'numb-nuts' instead of you.' She rubbed her sleepy eyes. 'Please stay as my friend, don't go anywhere. Ooh, I didn't take my mascara off; it's on my hands now. Is it down my face?' I nodded and passed her make-up remover. 'Thanks and you need to know, Olive, you're too fragile to be on your own; you're someone who needs to be cared for. You're like a beautiful china doll.'

Her eyes looked into mine and I replied, 'Thank you and don't worry I'm not going anywhere, I promise. So, what happened to Chris?'

'Aah don't say that cock's name. He was such a bell-end. He left me in the middle of Alice Springs for some other girl. When I caught up with him he said I was crowding him and he turned his back on me in the bar he was in – he turned his back! I had only gone there because he wanted to, but I didn't have the money to get back as I'd spent it on a tour to Uluru or Ayres rock as it's called now – on his insistence.'

Carolanne leant in to me. 'By the way, unless you're a lemming with a suicide wish, don't attempt to climb it, except if it's your only escape from the flies surrounding the rock or the cock Chris at the bottom! I got some good pictures to show off at least.'

She held my hand and her eyes lifted. We chatted for about another half an hour but my mind kept wondering off to where James could be.

'He'll be back. He'd never leave you, Olivia.' Carolanne said softly, then she turned on her side and rested her head in her left hand.

'So what is there to do here in Manly Beach? I met some girls who are leaving at the same time as us, in three weeks. They're really cool and they said there's a beach party tonight. They're meeting at Steyne bar. Let's do that tonight. We can ask James as well if you want him to join us? Where's the Steyne bar anyway? It doesn't matter, we'll find it. Oh, Olive, you have no idea how good it is to have you with me again. Hurry up and get dressed. We'll leave a note and meet James there.'

I prolonged the time it took for me to get ready for as long as I could in the hope of catching James. As we left the hostel behind

I hunted up and down the road. I discreetly kept searching until we reached the bar. When there, I kept close to the bar door so that I could be the first to grab him and rebuke his tardiness at not coming back to me as soon as he'd promised. There was no sign of him and worry was circling around me.

Carolanne was annoyed with me as I wouldn't head further inside the crowded bar. It would have been easy to get to the bar as Malibu Barbie could part any crowd as long as the occupants were men. She didn't have any money on her so she needed to slowly make her way through to catch and reel in an unsuspecting wallet attached to a gullible man.

'He'll be here, he's probably already inside. Please Ol, I promised we'd meet some girls I'd met. You'll really like them I think we have the same spirits.' She was staring inside the bar as she was speaking to me.

'Why don't you go in and I'll wait here for James. If he's still not here by the time you've found them, then come and get me,' I offered.

'I shouldn't leave you on your own, but okay.'

And off she darted into the crowd. No more than five minutes later she re-emerged with a beaming smile smothering her face.

'I found them and we're all leaving for the beach now. They've managed to pick up some blokes who are bringing the beers so we're all sorted.' She grabbed my hand and pulled me from the bar entrance just as a group brushed past me heading for the beach.

I sat on a rock in front of a beach fire next to a woman called Tatiana, drinking from a carton of wine.

'You don't seem to be enjoying the vintage? Only joking. I'm a bit disappointed as they were supposed to have bought bottles but this is the rubbish they brought along. Uh, it's cheap – but at least it's alcohol,' she began.

Tatiana swigged from her plastic cup and surveyed her party. Her hair was long and straight and she stroked and tossed it from side to side every time she moved her head to scan the clientele around her. If her eyes rested on anyone looking her way she would include a ruffle of her mane, and if that person happened to be male, then her straight red mouth would pout. However, if this man was not to her taste then her eyes would dismiss his obstinate gaze by purposefully looking in the opposite direction, but if they were to her liking then she pouted a little more. It was an effective dance which brought many lucky men drooling towards her over the many years I would subsequently know this lady.

Tatiana had long, slim, brown legs which ended in stiletto mules. I was curious as to why she'd be wearing them on a beach, let alone why she would have even packed them to go travelling, but they complemented her limbs and exaggerated their length so my question was answered before it was asked.

'Sorry, it's not the box of wine, thanks anyway, but I was supposed to be with a friend of mine who hasn't turned up,' I replied.

I hid my inferior shoe-wear from sight; by now all I had left for my feet were trainers and a pair of well used black flip-flops.

'Aah yes, Carolanne, or Carebear as I will call her, mentioned about James but if he can't be bothered to turn up then you have to dump him, friend or not. Only joking. Anyway, look around, there are loads of guys here and you know what, little lady, you're really pretty, so don't feel bad that some loser guy has dumped you. Instead feel good that you're pretty and you can replace him.'

Her pout had turned to a rigid insincere grin; it didn't last long before it sank back into a pout. I felt honoured by her appraisal, causing my mouth to involuntarily pout in gratitude.

'It's not like that; he really is a friend. We've travelled most of Australia together and he's my dive buddy. We hope to one day open a dive shop together. I'm not sure where yet but at the moment we're thinking about Egypt...'

'Uh, little lady, stop, I don't dive. I did it once and the instructor said I was really good, a natural even, but I don't see the point – plus, it's really bad for your hair and you have gorgeous red hair, which you don't want to ruin. Seriously, I know for a fact that the deeper you dive the greater the salt content of the sea and salt dries your hair out. If I took up diving I think my hairdresser would have a fit and insist I gave up.' She fluttered her hair and continued, 'Plus, all the fishes live near the surface so it's better to go snorkelling. That's what we do most days just over there by that hut with the sign 'snorkelling gear for hire'. You can join us tomorrow if you like? You don't need to go diving anymore, plus, I think it's too boring for you anyway and remember 'no – no for hair'. So, yes? You'll come? Good, all sorted. Aah, there's Sandy, Hi Sandy!'

The beach we were on was a sort of beach cul-de-sac. It was at the far end of the sea-front. It was small and enclosed by pine trees. The sand was still warm from the scorching day, the sun had long left this side of the earth and the moon sat proudly just above the horizon. It shone like a florescent torch illuminating everything it touched in a silvery grey. Everyone around me was chatting or laughing. I could smell the warm ash from the camp fire and I felt privileged to be there.

Tatiana lent back on her elbows, the tips of her long hair touching the sand and her long legs crossed displaying her high stiletto shoes; she had elongated her body by just a change of pose. I attempted to mimic her but I couldn't stretch out my legs as I had calf cramp from hiding my flip-flops beneath me.

'Seriously, little lady, you can come if you want. Carebear says you're okay and she says she feels really guilty about leaving you, but you were fine as you were with some bloke who looked after you. Are you seeing him? What's he like? Were you okay?'

Tatiana then redirected her gaze from looking at anyone in the party to looking straight into my eyes. She said, with spite in her voice, 'Oh my God, what a cow for leaving you though, I've not known Carolanne long but I can see it in her eyes that it's all about her and this just confirms it for me. Don't you agree? I'd never do that to a friend – ever.'

She then looked back out to the crowd disinterested in my answer. Instead Tatiana bolted up onto her heels and squealed to someone else.

'OMG. I'm sooo buzzed to see you!'

Without saying goodbye, she walked away from me by awkwardly lifting her feet high above the sand with each step to protect her heels from disappearing into the sand.

The night continued and more people approached me, thus pulling me into their scenery. I began to feel part of the night and I even started flicking my hair from side to side. Close to midnight I had forgotten about the whereabouts of James. I was temporarily no longer the girl who read dive books until 9pm snuggled up with James; instead I was a party girl, dancing on the beach with strangers who professed to being my best mate after knowing me for as long as a wave-break.

Carolanne and Tatiana came over to me again. I hid the tickle of laughter I had in my throat at watching Tatiana walk like a giraffe on sand.

'So you're coming with us tomorrow? Aah, Oli, I'm so pleased you're coming with me.' Carolanne beamed.

'Yeah, Oli, we're all going together, you'll have such fun, trust me, and don't worry about swimming with the fishes, you'll be fine,' Tatiana said.

Even though Tatiana was talking at me she was still looking past me to everyone around her; it was as though she was surveying her territory and checking all her maids were working well. I smiled and cocked my head in all directions to recapture her gaze, but as I did I caught sight of James and Chris in the far distance coming towards us.

I wasn't relieved or even pleased to see him. Instead, my throat constricted and my heart beat faster. I grabbed Carolanne and subtly nodded over to their direction. She looked around and unsubtly said, 'Aþ, the nerve of him! I can't believe he has come here; there is no way I'm talking to him, no way! Olive, you have to protect me,' Carolanne declared as she flirtatiously shuffled her head from side to side. Thankfully, Tatiana disappeared by the time James and Chris arrived.

'I'm sorry for the confusion today, Olive, I thought I'd told you I was going out and then I got caught by Chris. We went for a beer and by the time I'd got back you'd gone and I didn't know where. I'm sorry.' James glanced a 'Hi' to Carolanne then looked back at me with a worried tone in his eyes.

I smiled to reassure him that I didn't mind his absence then searched the beach as to who might be looking my way. As much as I searched, no one was looking. So, at an opportune moment I tried to prize James from Chris to a secluded corner of the beach. By now Carolanne and Chris were engaged in a quiet but absorbing argument. They were not interested in us, in fact, I don't recall Chris even saying hello to me, but then I don't recall saying hello to him; it was mutual ignorance of one another.

I pulled James to a tree log in a dark patch of the party. The waves softened, the grey noise of giggles intermingled with the odd shout for beer or a rhetorical innuendo from someone to somebody.

'Don't worry about today, it's fine. I'm probably going soon anyway. Do you want to come? No? Yes? You won't like it here. I'm bored, I need to get back,' I gabbled at James whose face retreated slightly as if I was blowing into his eyes.

'Er, whatever you want, I promised Chris I'd find Carolanne and that's done so I can walk you back or buy you a drink somewhere, if anywhere is open, or just keep you company?'

'Going back,' I snapped. 'Sorry, it's been a long night; I'll grab my jacket and say good-bye to everyone. You stay there, don't move.'

I hurried off to the pack of new friends, most of whom still hadn't seen us as they were engaged with their own interests; either girls giggling, men drinking or men preying on giggling girls. I nodded a 'bye' to Carolanne and grabbed my jacket which was precariously close to Tatiana who expertly cornered me when I got close to her:

'Olive, who's that?' her face was tilted into a question mark with her eyes raised in a curve and her mouth open like the full stop.

'Oh that's just James, only James, he's a friend of mine, just a friend that's all, just a friend,' I flustered.

'A good friend?'

'Oh, not really. He's the one I spoke about, the one who likes diving and we went diving together.' My voice raised an octave as I continued, 'Just a friend, that's all'.

'How sweet.' Tatiana tilted her head back so her eyes were forced to look down on me.

'Are you more than a friend to him? Come on Olive, you can tell me.'

'No no!' I replied, 'definitely not. I don't really know him' I screeched another octave higher than before.

'I thought so; he doesn't look your type. Do you think he likes you more than you think? How funny that would be!' Her voice was now slow and mine was quick to deny James for the third time.

'No, Tatiana, he's just a friend who is walking me back that's all, nothing more and even if there was, which there isn't, then I'm not interested.'

'Good I'm pleased. But how sweet a friendship! Always useful to have sweet friends like that; lucky you. Now don't forget snorkelling, I'll see you tomorrow, bye for now.'

Tatiana kissed the air around me then turned on her heel and I scuttled back to James who seemed a little disgruntled at being shoved in the corner. I whisked past him and gestured that he follow me back to the hostel.

I slipped into days of either avoiding James when I was with my new friends, to engineering moments we could spend together that appeared to James as a genuine special appointment just for him.

When free of James I followed Tatiana and Carolanne as though they were my nemesis. When my friends were busy, I would recount the previous few hours or day I'd spent with Tatiana and her company to James. He would laugh and I found my strength to rebuke him for his judgement of them. It was a strength I didn't have with Tatiana but, instead of questioning my capricious nature, I ignored it and merely enjoyed the perceived authority I had from the considered superior beauty passed to me as an employee of Tatiana & Co. But in contrast, I also enjoyed the relaxed ease I felt when I was off duty, with James.

The last part of my stay in Australia was interrupted by a niggling worry that began to surface quietly and stealthily from innocent chats about different careers, to jobs we wouldn't like to do, to jobs we had lined up. As the menacing final day approached this concern turned to nausea as I knew I had nothing to return to apart from my sister and a house I grew up in. I had never worked, I was twenty-three, with few qualifications, and I had never broached the subject of how to make my own way through life until now. James was comforting and came up with many suggestions but these all involved beginning with studying. This was a prospect I couldn't face; I feared returning to school as I didn't want to turn backwards in my life.

Recently, Jason, my dear reader, I learnt about 'Existential Anxiety'. We are not told how to live our short existence to the greatest, to ensure we don't waste a drop. We are not told how a fulfilling, fun and frivolous life should look. Instead, we muddle through a collection of possibilities as to what could offer the 'life best spent' if we just took this ride or that ride or another ride down life's river. It's like a gambling table where the game is our life, the dealers are those around us and the cards are the choices we are thrown. If we gamble well then we get to make the most of our existence but if we take the wrong hand then the table wins and we must live with the consequences of an unfulfilling life.

The night of gambling is short, from dusk till dawn, but it could be even shorter if the decisions we make are particularly poor and we are dealt out of the game before the sun has set. We have only a short time to play and we play without knowing the rules as these are revealed the more we gamble and understand the card game. More often, this expertise comes at a time when dawn is soon to break and the table is to be packed away. Accelerated learning is a consequence of playing a poor hand.

But how do we decipher the best hand to play until after we have played? The night is slipping away and the gambling money pile is getting smaller and smaller. Thus, we live in a permanent state of anxiety that our hand is poor and our decisions are worse. It is part of our innate sense of survival that we migrate towards the wisdom of others, giving us hints as to how we play our hand without losing our chips. It is why we join a queue when queuing is not necessary or why we accept the teachings from a weekly magazine astronomer whom we have never met but who knows all there is to know about us from slipping us into one of twelve bags.

I was a young girl influenced by popularity and beauty and so the only person whom I naively perceived to understand me then was Tatiana and she was the one I chose to throw my chips onto my table. She encouraged me that getting educated was a backward step and it would only serve to add one line on a resumé but getting a job would show more commitment. It also meant I'd have money to start living the way I wanted to live. I knew she was idealistic in her view of the job market but it was easier to listen to her than face the prospect of studying for the next three years.

'Seriously, no one bothers looking at the section on

qualifications, what they want to see is a commitment to the job you choose, so burying your head in books is diverting you away from learning about the job. It shows far more commitment to your career if you're willing to work than just study. I'm going to work in the city anyway, my cousin has a friend who can get me into Ernst Young soooo...'

Tatiana had a smug smile as her statement trailed off after the word 'so', as if that replaced a full stop in conversation.

'Do you think there are other placements there for me?' I delicately explored,

'I doubt it but I'll ask for you. Don't get your hopes up as they're a hard company to get into, so I'm really lucky.'

I didn't pursue it further as she turned away but then sharply turned back at me with a forceful determined expression. Her lips were straight and thin and her eyes cornered mine so they couldn't escape without a tug of war.

'Why do you need to have a career anyway? I don't want one, I don't need one. Olive, trust me, there are easier ways to make money in life without working.'

We were sitting on a bench on the promenade above the beach. Tatiana didn't want to walk on the sand as she claimed it irritated her toes and she wanted to protect the skin on her feet, so we sat on this bench overlooking families playing together in the sand and in the sea. It was late afternoon and the fathers were home from work and these men were out taking their beloved wives and children to the beach for the remainder of the day. Each pocket of people was a family; they were there to share their lives at that moment in the sun with no one else but each other and they were all laughing and building memories to enjoy again whenever they chose; perhaps when their children had grown up and found a family to play on the beach for themselves.

'Work in the city is fine but you're there to find a credit card attached to a man. The man works and you get to stay at home doing whatever you want.'

'I doubt it's that easy,' I replied.

'Yes, it is! and that's the point of being pretty; don't waste it on ordinary men or on an ordinary life working at a career that isn't worth anything to anyone. My sister, Carrie, works every day for a job which requires her to get up at six in the morning to earn money for other people and in all the years she's been there she's had only two promotions. She's a lawyer who is not married, she lives on her own and most Saturdays she's crying down the phone that she's lonely. She does nothing about it and time is whooshing past her and taking her looks away with it. She's thirty-three and doesn't even have a boyfriend and she doesn't have the time to even try to find one, so the probability is she'll end her days alone.'

Tatiana shook her head with pursed thin lips.

'Carrie is like an old lady in a motorised wheelchair that is stuck in the middle lane of the motorway; she can't get out, she can't pull over; she just has to push the button and hope that somehow she'll speed up and join the fast cars around her and if she can't, she prays she isn't run over by a huge truck.'

Tatiana grabbed my arm with her long fingers.

'Is that what you want? Or maybe you'd rather take the sweet true love approach in life, such as my other sister Louise who married at twenty-four and had two children? They had no money but supposedly she was content with her two-bedroom terraced house and working long hours for a local computer repair shop as their bookkeeper. She bought up his children and forfeited holidays, new clothes and even nights out with her friends to ensure her family were well cared for. Rob, her husband, also worked long hours and even longer hours when he was cheating on my sister. Eventually Louise broke down and got rid of him as she couldn't face finding out about another affair he'd had. She, like me, had spent her young life learning about affairs as we grew up with a cheating father who eventually left us when I was thirteen years old. All men cheat – all men –

and they're the ones who drive the fast cars pushing the likes of my sisters off the road. There's no exception to this rule, all men cheat and if they don't it's because they didn't have the opportunity to cheat – but they all aspire to it.'

Tatiana nodded at me and released my eyes from her grip.

'My dad didn't cheat I'm sure,' I said as a defence,

'How do you really know? Ever asked him?'

'He's dead.'

'So he left without being discovered.' She swung her head to the sky, 'Sorry, but all men cheat.'

I tried again but this time with a stronger line for the defence.

'These men here aren't cheating; look at the man in the blue trunks hugging the woman with the brown bobbed hair. He kisses her every so often; it's tender, between two loving people.'

'He's about twenty years older than her and clearly she is his mistress. His wife is at home waiting for him to stop kissing this woman and return to her and their humdrum life.'

Her case for the prosecution was strong as, although they were tactile with each other, he was greedy for her affection but she looked as though she was being bruised by the embrace of her fifty year old boss and wondering if her pay rise was really worth it.

I tried again and bought in more witnesses.

'Okay what about that man there playing Frisbee with his two sons, there's no mistress in sight there?'

'There's also no wife and this means he's divorced because he cheated and it's his afternoon with his kids.'

'The man over there then, he's definitely with his wife and kids and having ice-cream with his children.'

'Again, he's having ice-cream with his kids but not his wife who is paying attention to her children but is also making a show to ignore her husband. She knows he's cheating and he knows she knows he's cheating; the afternoon is a façade for their kids but ultimately he'll be the same as the previous man and buying ice-cream alone.'

Tatiana rested her case, but I had one last witness to present – if you'd permit, m'lud. 'James. He'd never cheat on his wife.'

'First of all, please say you're not thinking about being his wife or even his girlfriend and secondly, maybe he would be the exception, but if you were his wife, you'd spend your days knitting jumpers to keep out the cold in your wooden cottage whilst he cheated on you with a fishing rod under the pretence that he's trying to catch dinner; plus he'd cheat you out of having a life.'

My defence crumbled due lack of evidence and so men across the world were found guilty of cheating.

'So, what's the alternative for me then?' I pleaded.

Tatiana once more grabbed my gaze in hers and said slowly and quietly as if she was telling a ghost story and trying to build the tension; 'You accept men cheat and you marry them anyway but the trade is their credit card. They can cheat all they like with anyone willing to massage their flagging ego, whilst you spend the money that they earn on yourself. Anyway, the only point of men is to have babies and when you do, these babies will grow up and go. You're on your own either way.'

She looked back up to the sky to absorb the sunshine having triumphantly revealed her great mystery to happiness. She continued, 'Come and live with me and Carebear in London. You'll do well with me, I promise.'

The cards were thrown and I accepted. I would be living with my two best friends, which included fun as part of the package. I didn't have to worry anymore at piecing together a plausible future as this amazing lady sunbathing on the pier in front of a crowded beach of cheating men had crumpled all my anxieties away by handing me a new deck of cards to play with.

The final days were spent in a daze of excitable planning about where we were to live; it transpired that Carolanne had access to a flat in Baker Street through her father. It was occasionally used by him during the week whilst he was working in London but he was taking early retirement and he was nested in his bungalow in Eastbourne with his third wife.

My stomach no longer lurched with nerves but it churned with excitement. I was now eager to return to England and I promised myself I would start fresh with a diet and new clothes. I was confident a job would be easy to find as my perspective had altered and now a job was secondary to my lifelong needs. I didn't want to work and the job I got would serve to finance the appropriate investment in me, so I was able to hunt for the appropriate boyfriend which, according to Tatiana, was easy to catch. This was my new job; to find the right man who would treat me to an exciting, fun and frivolous life, but for this position I would have to look the part.

I needed to slim down considerably; my bottom was far too large, my legs were too cumbersome for their purpose of placing one foot in front of the other. If I stood with my legs hip distance apart they did not meet for the first time at the knees but instead moulded together like a mono-leg. I calculated I needed to lose at least half a stone to look as elegant and beautiful as Tatiana and Carolanne. The revenge attack on my pear-shaped body started in earnest and it would continue for the rest of my life.

James was opposed to me losing any weight, claiming that I was already too slim. I ignored his gentle pleas especially as I felt strong at the control over my body shape by just denying it food. It proved to be a cheaper option as I did not need to buy any groceries but unfortunately, this was the only immediate benefit of only eating toast in the morning and then water throughout the day with a reward of toast in the evening.

The immediate disadvantage to my radical plan was obviously hunger. However, starvation is beyond hunger – it's a constant pain. At the start, my brain screamed at me to prescribe food; any food. It didn't matter what. I would obsessively watch others eating, as if their chicken sandwich with juicy tomatoes and lettuce all dripping in mayonnaise would telepathically arrive in my mouth. I found myself involuntarily licking my lips then actually chewing my tongue as I watched a sugary doughnut being eaten. Each night I would be uncomfortable as I lay on my side trying to think about anything other than food. I would wake from a disturbed night's sleep excited at the thought of my toast or one bowl of cereal that I allowed myself in the morning. As the days passed I progressed from just pain to feeling tired to then owning a constant state of lethargy and apathy to everything going on around me. Eventually I was rewarded from the sense of achievement each day at overcoming cravings and controlling my body and watching my casket slim down to the shape I wanted.

I never quite reached the haven of my perceived ideal shape but I liked seeing my clothes become baggy and no longer fit me anywhere. This meant I could slip into the type of clothes that flattered Tatiana whose legs were stolen from a giraffe; they did not meet at any point from groin to toes.

I also wanted to be a reflection of the models in the magazines and I wanted to believe that I had stumbled across the secret to happiness as all I needed to be was slender and beautiful and my life would effortlessly fall into a glamorous world where others admired me. I would be that butterfly emerging from the chrysalis of an awkward childhood, or I could become the Barbie doll I used to play with as a twelve year old instead of the chubby baby doll girl I initially cuddled. Surely, life would be simpler, easier and happier if I was thinner, much thinner?

My friends were supportive of me, especially Tatiana. She encouraged me to skip meals and continually warned me of the calorie content of foods. She helped me to ignore hunger pangs by diversion tactics, such as cleaning my teeth or deliberately starting a conversation with anyone around. She also taught me phrases to live by such as; 'will a second bite taste any better than the first?' or 'chew food thirty times before swallowing'. I can't say it was particularly helpful in stopping my brain from obsessing about food but it bought me time so that I escaped the temptation of picking up a biscuit that was calling me, shouting my name and telling me it was just 54 calories so what harm would eating it be? Every time I resisted was like a victory for my future happiness, but when I ate the illegal food it felt like a deep defeat and I loathed myself and what I was and what I could potentially become if I don't control my life by controlling my appetite: a pathetic overweight girl living in her childhood home, who no one could possibly like.

On the penultimate day in Australia I was approaching my goal of existing on 500 calories a day. I knew that my extreme lethargy was due to my lack of food but I wasn't going to abandon the dreams of the stunning clothes I would be able to wear or having legs that could not touch each other. I could see the trousers I would wear to show off my figure, with high heels that elongated my legs even further. I would appear to glide wherever I went and I would be accompanied by envious looks and songs of 'Ooh, isn't she gorgeous!'

'You look proper sick,' said James. He had sneaked up from behind and sat down on the beach beside me. The sun was starting to set and the air turned an orange colour, which discoloured all the anchored boats touching one another like clinking wine glasses.

'I'm okay, just a bit under the weather at the moment.'

I kept staring ahead at the people who had arrived to start their evening on board their yachts,

'I haven't seen you in ages. Are you avoiding me? I'm getting worried about you.' He playfully nudged my elbow.

'C'mon, what's up? You're not yourself,' he persisted.

'I said I was fine, so why are you asking me again? I'm just a bit tired that's all,' I spat.

I kept staring ahead at the people who were now on the deck of their boat and opening their bags to reveal bottles of wine and long French sticks which would, most likely, be eaten with soft brie or pâté and cucumber. My mouth started to water and I imagined they must be wealthy and happy people because their life was easy and fulfilling thanks to their bank balance that afforded the boat the pretty women could party in.

'You're not fine Ol, you're miserable! Please look at me Olive, not them, and tell us what the matter is.'

The women were now laughing with the men who had accompanied them on board; they were undoubtedly, rich and successful.

'Olive, what is wrong with you?'

'What do you want me to say James? I tell you I'm well and still you have a go at me! I'm just a little tired.'

'Try eating then and maybe you won't be so tired!'

I knew I was being irrational but his last comment dragged out tears; tears I didn't want or need and tears I was embarrassed by and yet, there they were.

'Olive, you can tell me anything. Please, just talk to me.'

It was tempting; I knew it would be therapeutic like rubbing cooling cream on a burning rash.

'Don't you want to be like those people on the boat? James, I go soon and I have nothing, nothing to go home to,' I sobbed.

In the dusk I noticed that James' skin was clear of spots and the setting sun shaded his face in parts to make him look rugged and almost handsome. I wanted a warm, gentle hug but instead I looked back at the bobbing boats.

'Look at them, they are clearly having fun,' I continued. 'The woman in the red, sheer, tight top, she's stunning, and the blonde woman, you can tell she's rich just by looking at that dress; that's a dress that I wouldn't be able to find at the local market; no, that is an expensive dress. And look how great their night is going to be on that boat, eating and drinking and soaking up their evening to its max. I doubt they're looking my way wishing they were me!'

'Well they should, Olive. You're beautiful and you'll have a rich life; maybe not one filled with boats and champagne and the like, but a happy one if you let it.'

'No, James, it's not fair, it's not fair! I want what they have, I want to be as beautiful as the woman in red and I want to be drinking champagne on a boat.'

Envy harpooned its way towards me from the yacht, yet I couldn't look away from them to James.

'Jeez, Olive, you're better than any of those hags especially the one in red. Seriously Ol, when I look at her I just want to ask if she'd like a sandwich, chocolate, anything – just eat woman, you look proper skinny!'

James stroked my hand and then let it rest between his.

'You don't need any boat, Olive, and you don't need to lose weight. Olive, you can look at them and think 'good for them', but then you need to remember you're naturally beautiful, and when you laugh it's infectious. You're intelligent and kind. You've got it all.'

'I may not need a boat or champagne but I want them,' I whispered.

'Please just be you Ol, cos you're who I love.'

James' words stung me and I swung round to stare at him, so he continued.

'I love you Olive. You're not the woman on the boat but you're the woman who travelled around Oz with me, laughed at my crap jokes, went diving with me in between feeding the fishes, made me laugh until my sides split. You know I love you and I don't know how I'm going to cope with my last two months here without you beside me. I know I'll just be counting away my days until I can get on a flight to be close to you.'

I stared at him wishing I knew how to migrate this conversation back to talking about me wanting champagne with handsome men.

'I love you Olive, if you'll have me?'

Jason, if there's a moment in our lives that we could return to and change anyway we liked then that single moment, sitting on the beach under a warm sky surrounded by laughing people and a gentle breeze that stroked my hair across my face, would be one of the moments I would run back to – just then, just after James confessed he loved me. Once there, I would slap myself as hard as I could or I would shake myself until my shaking head made me dizzy. Then I would sit myself down again and tell me to stay quiet, say nothing, just be.

Unfortunately, a moment is only lent to us, for us to either enjoy or for us to ruin like muddy snow.

'Ah,' I snarled at James. 'I'm not interested in you, I never will be! I told you that I'm not interested, I told you that from the beginning and that was one of the conditions of our friendship, why destroy it all?'

'Okay, you've made your point.' He looked away from me.

At least I should have stopped there, when James dropped my hand and faced forward, his smile gone and his head bowed. I should have, but I didn't.

'Who do you think you are?' I continued. 'I don't fancy you, I never will and even if I did, we have nothing in common – I want a life of champagne and yachts and you want to be a carpenter, brewing beer on the side.'

'It's a great ambition and I'm good at it,' he said,

'So what?! I'm not going to waste my life as a carpenter's assistant or, God forbid, a carpenter's wife – why would you even think that?!'

'Ol, where've you gone? Since getting back to Sydney you've changed. You're two women; one perfect, who I think of all the friggin' time. Literally no other thought gets in my head; I forget where my hostel is when I'm walking home cos you're stuck there rubbing out my directions. I don't sleep, I don't eat.

'And then there's the woman, sitting here on the sand. Jealous of a skinny, posh bird just cos she's sitting on a yacht. The Ol I love wouldn't care, or so I thought; she also wouldn't be so cruel. Thanks, I feel a proper wazzock because I actually thought you could love me back.'

'Seriously? Not a hope!' I retaliated with a cruel snigger.

'You know what, Olivia, this morning I couldn't imagine a day without you, but I see you can't imagine a day with me in it.'

At that point James got up and started to walk away. After a few steps he turned back.

'Ever since you got here you've done nothing but hate yourself. You're this timid mouse who wouldn't dare say boo to your mistress Tatiana. Grow some, Olivia, and when you have, look me up. Maybe we can be friends again. Until then, enjoy your life. I'm done.'

I watched his strong lanky body be whisked away by his long lanky legs and I sat rigid to the sand. I can still see him, even today, walking away from me. I still yearn for him to turn around, just once more to look at me, as maybe I would have shaken my head and rebuked my thoughts and run after my friend. Instead I sat sobbing whilst woefully watching the bobbing boats. I had forgotten I was hungry but its effect was still there as I was too listless to attempt moving from my position.

It was my last night in Australia and it was time to say goodbye to this section of my life and to start afresh with Tatiana and Carolanne. Perhaps if James had returned then, maybe, he would have steered me away from the next section but he continued walking and he didn't look back.

CHAPTER FIVE

JASON

I visited my mum the following weekend for a Sunday roast. I was grateful as my work schedule doesn't permit me to keep track of a government recommended high nutritional diet; I'm either grabbing a full fat sandwich from some dubious middle eastern deli shop or I'm entertaining clients with cocktails washed down with beer before grabbing a burger at 11pm from Waterloo station.

I can hear the rumble of my stomach straining at the sides and threatening to bulge to a thirty-something paunch as soon as it deems I've reached that apathetic life stage where I'm too tired and lazy to do anything about losing weight. That apathy is closer than I'd like to admit as Saturday football has given way to catching up on emails whilst nursing a hangover.

Mum had cooked lamb followed by jam sponge with custard. Colin, my step-dad, or just Dad, was asking about work; he got the hint that it was a conversation I didn't want, from my monosyllabic answers, so he changed the subject to the fact he's planted the runner beans and as soon as they're ready he'll come by and re-plant them in my garden. I reminded him that last year's crop died as I didn't, and still don't, have the time to water them, but he was adamant as they're a hardy plant and apparently they were my favourite vegetable when I was a child.

I sat next to Dad whose round stomach was embraced many years ago when he abandoned his love of playing cricket. He's known me since I was six years old. I remember sitting on the beach, on any one of our summer holidays as a child, teasing him with Mum about the fact that his stomach looked like he was heavily pregnant. He would join in – claiming he was nursing a beer baby that any Englishman would be proud of.

My dad is a great bloke with a square face and a thick line of hair around the back of his head, as if his head had grown a hedge to keep his neck warm. He's a retired history teacher and now spends most of his time content and happy in the garden or at the local history club.

'So, what was the outcome of your recent appraisal?' he began. 'Did you remind them you are not a slave and everyone deserves time away from work and when you joined you only wanted to work there – you hadn't planned on moving in!' Dad chuckled and to my disappointment he continued, 'You told me there are showers there so why not go the full hog and install a lounge, kitchen and bedroom?'

'There are showers as people cycle in or go to the gym during their lunch hour. There is a kitchen and there is a lounge but no Dad, ha ha, there's no bedroom. My appraisal was last month and I mentioned it to mum but to summarise yet again, I'm doing fine but promotion could not be discussed as there is an announcement soon by the company so, yada yada yada – who knows?! But then who ever knows?'

Before Dad or Mum could prolong the career talk about a career they knew nothing about, I pounced in.

'What was Aunt Olive like when she came back from Oz?'

Dad shook his head, 'Didn't know her then, er, Janet?' He

looked at Mum, placed half a roast potato in his mouth and settled back for a story.

'You missed nothing Colin! She came back slimmer, moody and moved in to a flat in London with a very skinny and equally moody woman. We called her Pariah.' Mum smiled to herself. 'Irritating woman who I think has muttered the total of five words to me in all the time I've known her.'

Mum paused to pour more gravy over her dinner and nodded as she did this. 'Yes, strange woman but Olive was still my sister and I endured Pariah to be with her. You won't remember her Jay as you were just a toddler but Australia had definitely changed your aunty. She had grown but shrunk in size. Travelling should influence a person in positive ways but instead she remained a tempestuous teenager who took her frustrations out on me.

'Apparently, life was inadequate back at your nana's house so she needed to break away and spread her wings.'

Mum's voice raised to a dramatic high and her arms raised above her head as if addressing an operatic audience.

'To grab all that life had on offer and to conquer her greatest dreams and be all that she could be!' Her arms dropped. 'So, she left home, got a job in Boots and shared a horrible little flat above a carpet shop.' Mum huffed her contempt.

'Soooo pretentious! Oh, and her scathing remarks to me – I was a single mum struggling to raise my gorgeous boy and train as a teacher and I'm extremely proud that I achieved a successful teaching career and raised my boy to be a gentleman. Oh, but that's just not good enough apparently in the world of your aunt!'

Mum grabbed my hand from across the table, 'But you're worth it my gorgeous baby boy. Anyway, it was the start of all this mess, I really mean that. She never ate and instead spent most of her time engineering ways to get money from various people to get new clothes. Admittedly, she always paid me back but she was like an artist trying to sculpt and then re-sculpt her appearance. It was never good enough. I never saw her wear anything twice or be satisfied with herself. She would obsess about the most irrelevant aspects of her outfit and try and retry different tops to trousers or different skirts with tops or different dresses with different shoes. Ultimately though, her decision was based on the time Tatiana would summon her to go out.

I hated going over there but I wanted to see Olive and I wanted her to see you, Jay. She really sparkled when you were scuttling about that dive of a flat – though I used to have you on my lap most of the time as I was worried about what you might step in.

Tatiana used to smoke, incessantly forming smog around her. She'd look for various ashtrays dotted about to deposit another butt. It used to remind me of stone piles on our rambler walks – whenever Colin and I pass one in the Lake District I always mention the ashtrays in that flat, don't I, Colin? Colin, don't I…? Ahh, deaf as a post.'

Dad shook to attention nodding and repeating the last sentence, 'Ashtrays, stone piles, yes dear.'

'Anyway, in those days, like I said, I was studying to become a teacher. I was working full time and caring for a bubbly four year old, so when an offer of a night out with Olive was offered, I'd always agree. It was ludicrous really because I don't recall ever having a good night.

'It started by greeting my babysitter and promising I'd be back before one in the morning. I'd arrive at Olive's flat and sweet, gorgeous Carolanne would open the door. Carolanne was always ready on time and calmly waiting for the others on a nicotine-stained yellow armchair with magazines strewn around her feet (which I suspect was to hide the dusty, manky, yellow carpet which matched the nicotine-stained yellow painted walls). Opposite this chair was a dishevelled navy corduroy settee which had Tatiana's oblong packs of 200 cigarettes all around and piles of cheap romance books. The windows were brown and again stained with nicotine (apparently Carolanne's father was a chain smoker as well so the flat didn't get a break from the chemical). The flat was like the lungs of an old smoker with asthma.

'On these nights, I often tried to wait whilst standing as I hated sitting anywhere in case I sat on something, but my decision to take the chance to sit was based on the stage of dress Tatiana was in; if she had her makeup on then I knew I wouldn't be waiting for long, but if she was still wrapped in a towel and huffed passed me without acknowledging my presence, then I knew I was paying for at least one hour of unnecessary babysitting. Eventually Olive, then Tatiana, would emerge just before I made my decision to leave in frustration.

'Anyway, both were smothered in makeup, in particular Tatiana's makeup was heavy enough to paint walls, though it didn't disguise her disgust of anything, something, I don't know, but in those days, I assumed it was me. The only person who didn't laden her eyes down with false eyelashes and mascara or have huge back-combed hair sprayed to cement stiffness was Carolanne, just effortlessly beautiful.

'Oh, but Jay, the foundation Olive and Tatiana wore made their skin look as if they were corpses ready to be presented to the funeral procession. And their lipstick was a high gloss beam that made their lips stick together when their mouths were closed so that a sentence from either one of them always began with a momentary delay whilst they peeled their lips free.

'Don't look at me that way Colin, or you Jay – okay, okay, I'm being harsh as actually they were stunning and when we finally reached the club men would literally part like the red sea to stare at these three women walking in like Moses and the Israelites. I would take advantage of the space it created as if I was a three-wheeler transit van following a police car in a traffic jam.'

'Janet, you're gorgeous and my lovely lady; I'd have been staring at you.' Dad sweetly interjected with a supporting grin.

'Thank you darling, aren't you trained well. But trust me, I really didn't care. I was just pleased to be out. In fact, going out then was like some sort of prescription drug. I would crave a night away to escape the intense concentration of rearing a child, (as much as I loved you darling) plus studying, but I was always so tired and by the time I arrived I was already wishing I was home. I would persevere hoping for a high inside but actually, what came instead, was the draining sense of boredom and frustration.

'Boredom, as in these clubs it was too crowded to chat and catch up with Olive so I spent the night nodding: nodding to reply to Olive's attempt to say a sentence, then I'd receive a nod whenever I reciprocated a sentence to Olive, which again was greeted with a covering nod of agreement.

'And frustration which started at the queuing stage; whether it was the queue to get in or the queue for the cloak room (it was only me who had a coat even in the depths of winter) or, worst of all, the queue for the drinks. In that particular queue I would be shoved from side to side as I shuffled forward for my eventual turn. I'd pay an extortionate amount of money for four drinks then weave my way back to Olive and an ungrateful Tatiana. Sometimes Carolanne was still waiting for her drink but usually she was chatting to friends or some good-looking man was chatting to her which meant I got two drinks (this was actually an advantage as I didn't have the money for another round and Tatiana never offered; Olive sometimes did but it was rare).'

'So why did you always offer first? Why didn't you just take it in turns?' I said.

'Olive didn't have any money but offered when she could, Tatiana was far too protective of her own money and never offered and she would look for anyone else to pay for them and Carolanne always had someone buying her drinks without trying. I suppose if I waited for someone to offer I would have gone thirsty, plus it broke up the monotony of the evening to queue for drinks.

'Apart from this, I'd stand for hours as there was never anywhere to sit so, even in my twenties, I'd ache like old lady. But the worst part of the evening was the feeling that I was on some sort of shopping channel run by judgemental women for a slobbering male shopping audience:

'There was a distinct ritual to it all that I never really got into. It would start at the 'walking in stage': we were presented and eyes would scan the goods. Then the second stage was the drinks ritual: I would hand the drinks out to my sister and co. who would be looking anywhere except at me to say thank you. I would attempt a conversation but, although there were nods and 'ahas', their eyes were not looking my way but instead scanning the room for a captive buyer. Should there be a catch, then the next stage was: the girls giving an animated laugh followed by the catch phrase, 'Ahhh I love this song' and they would sing to one another. This was the buyer's cue to reel in and try to infiltrate the girls' net. I would stand back and just watch as Tatiana would assess whether they had the purchasing power.'

'Purchasing power? You mean they got their wallets out? What sort of club was this?' I questioned,

'Oh no, nothing as direct as that, far less honest. Tatiana trained both Olive and Carolanne to notice the subtleties of a successful man's financial emblems – wealth tags if you like. For example, shoes; brogues or fashionable designer footwear and the like – strictly no buckles or old tatty black shoes. However, the main wealth tag was the watch. To this day, I can distinguish between a Breitling, a Tag or a Rolex and a cheap high street watch.

'If they failed any of her tests then she would pull the net in and the men duly skulked off, but if they were successful then stage four of the buying ritual commenced and these candidates would say some inane comment like, 'You're far too beautiful to be dancing alone, so here I am.' And the girls would giggle and basic flirtation would begin which allowed for the men to ultimately pair with their chosen girl. This stage was the only time I saw Tatiana smile, normally her expression was an aloof stare, as if she had discovered you'd behaved badly and she knew and she had every intention of bribing you with her solicited discovery.

'The final stage: the breaking away from the group. This was the purpose of the dance floor. Even though the music was mainly a beat and no rhythm, it just meant that they could finalise the transaction away from other people watching.

'This was the worst part of the evening as it meant that I was now alone to wander round and round the same dark, small space again and again searching for somewhere to sit and clock-watch until a decent hour came for me to find Olive and tell her I was catching the last train home. In summary Jay, dull, boring, dull!'

'Why didn't you meet anyone? I've seen pictures of you when you were younger and I think you weren't bad, in fact, alright-looking for a mum.'

'Alright looking for a mum!' All the sincere encouragement a lady needs to hear, I think I was more than alright looking – don't you agree Colin?'

'Yes of course, beautiful dear – well I married you so I thought you were alright.' Dad ruffled from his Sunday afternoon trance.

'Oh, the sweet compliments are flying in! Well in answer to your question, I was and I was chatted up by many men.'

Mum smiled and stroked her curled hair; her hair still had the indentation of the curlers she'd used a few hours earlier.

'Well, my happiness was a little boy tugging at my ankles and snuggling into my arms and so I really didn't care or need being chatted up by drunk men. That said, I was pretty – as were most of the women in the club – but the men certainly weren't handsome. If I ever came across someone I liked, whom Tatiana approved of, then their brash, patronising, insincere personality eroded away any initial attraction I may have had.

'I often wondered whether these men all owned the same book on, '*How to Influence Women*.' Chapter One was a sleazy line congratulating a woman on being pretty; no matter how the woman is dressed tell her she is the prettiest in the room. This was a short chapter so that they could quickly get to Chapter Two. This chapter was about them; how they worked in London but they are soon to get a promotion which means an overseas detachment, thus trebling their salary – a salary that is so vast they struggle to know what to spend their money on. At this page of Chapter Two, there are a few suffixes, such as: tell the lady she must have a ride in their new Porsche, or they must try out the amazing restaurants they dine at which are exclusive only to them and what a privilege it would be to experience such fine dining. If this didn't work then they went onto the next chapter; their sporting prowess. I met many men who told me how they could have been a professional tennis player. In fact, if you want to know why Wimbledon tournament is not dominated by the British then it's because they all work in the City of London or New York and they just don't have the time to compete.

'Should any of this hypnotise a woman onto the dance floor then it was onto Chapter Four: buying as many drinks as they could shove down their prey until they stumbled into a taxi with them.

'However, should any of this not be successful then the book instructed these men to revert to Chapter One then Chapter Two and so on, in a cyclical whirl for the woman in question, until either she gives in or the man spots a more willing candidate and abruptly abandons his shopping cart for another.'

'Wow, we're just all transparent bastards aren't we... Did it ever work on you?' I winked.

'No it did not!' Mum replied curtly. 'And in any case, I soon met your dad at a teacher training day.'

'And that was the end of it?'

'And that was the end of that. But it often worked on your aunt.'

Mum giggled to herself as she cleared the plates away to make room for the roly-poly jam sponge she had been steaming for the last two hours. The steam from the pudding fogged her glasses and she wiped them clear with her oven glove.

'I can't see it in Aunt Olive, she's too, I dunno, up-tight, prudish maybe?' I said.

'Oh, I have a few stories about your aunt. Would you like custard or cream?'

She had already poured the custard into the family Sunday roast jug; an old jug covered in roses, burnt custard stains from past Sundays, complete with chips on the handle.

'I have some cream in the fridge from yesterday's pudding, a gooseberry pie – gooseberries picked from the garden by your father, there are some left if you'd prefer that?' Mum was standing with one hand holding the custard and the other poised to grab whatever we desired for pudding.

'Custard and no to gooseberry pie, but finish what you were talking about,' I said impatiently.

'I can't tell you darling it would embarrass you,' she sighed at her memories.

'He's thirty-six Jan,' Dad said, 'I think he'll cope – and cream for me and if there is gooseberry pie then I wouldn't mind that as well – it was a good pie don't you think? A great gooseberry crop this year.'

'Then get it yourself Dad. Mum, sit down and finish.'

Mum swivelled around, grabbed the cream and sat down.

'It started slowly at first with just one weekly night out. All Olive's wages were spent on her dress, which certainly followed fashion but didn't follow taste. I often wonder whether fashion designers get stumped for fresh ideas, so create designs that only a model with good lighting and a clever photographer can pull off. These unflattering designs seep down into the general public who the designers rely upon to buy under the guise of 'following fashion'. Olivia, my sweet sister, was one of them. Her dresses became shorter and tighter but even though I balked at the daring length of them they, nevertheless, achieved the desired effect.'

'Yeah, and?' I said.

'One particular dress had a see-through top and Olivia would wear a half cup bra with it. It was actually passible some years ago as it was well before her first boob operation but it still gave men a creak in their neck.' Mum giggled to herself again as she watched this particular memory.

'In her letter she said she was on a diet to lose weight; was she very skinny?'

'She idolised Tatiana and tried to copy everything she did but when she first came back from Australia she was still quite plump. It took a while for her to really slim down.'

'When I first met her,' interjected Dad, 'she was quite voluptuous, with flaming red hair. I have to say she was a looker and she should have stayed that way. I'd say she had the Marilyn Monroe style and I can't understand why that isn't good enough for you women. After all, Monroe was an iconic beauty.'

'A beauty who died having led a tragic life. But even so, Olivia just wanted to look like Tatiana; thin, ironed-straight hair and a permanent look of disgust,' replied Mum.

Mum and Dad shook their heads; Dad took a bite of his jam sponge.

'Complete waste of God's wrapping paper if you ask me,' he said between bites.

'So, apart from her being a misguided groupie of Tatiana, what was so dangerous for my ears?'

'As I said, she spent every penny she earned on clothes, makeup and hair styles and her demeanour became slightly slutty as she progressed through the ranks of nightclub connoisseurs. I eventually stopped going so frequently as, whenever I went, I would be abandoned by all three by at least midnight and I would walk endless laps of the club we were in, desperately trying to find my sister to angrily tell her that I was leaving and thanks for another awful night.

'Olive would call me the next day to apologise for her disappearing act, however, it was merely an excuse to tell me about the amazing man she had met the night before; how he lavished her with champagne and, because he had bought a particular bottle, then they had a private booth. I'm fuzzy on details as I never got to sit down in these places; the clubs we went to, well, they were just walking gyms to me by the end.

'Olive was affected by the flash arrogance of these men. She never tired of their boasts even though each man had the same story to tell and the same catchphrases to woo a woman into their bed. These slimy, sycophantic snakes had a shelf life and that was about five minutes after feeding off my sister and then she was no longer the goddess they professed she was. These men always had a busy day or breakfast meeting, so she needed to leave as soon as they had slept with her, but they would call her very soon, all untrue. Alas she never saw it. Instead she focused on the lavish lies and promises of a call. On one occasion she convinced herself that this man was a genuine perfect prince who had fallen in love with her because after the deed he paid for a cab for her to return to the club he had picked her up from!

'Unfortunately, my attempts to explain to her that these men were fake and please leave them in the pond she had scraped them up from, was met with anger and defiance. She would tell me I was jealous and I couldn't handle the fact she had met someone amazing and I was stuck with Colin, who wasn't rich or cavalier enough to ever buy me champagne; the fact he was an intelligent, kind and genuine human being was an insignificance to her as he was just a trainee teacher who couldn't possibly afford the exciting life she wanted.'

Mum sighed and looked down at the table. Dad grabbed her hand and she squeezed his hand in return.

'You were a good sister, Jan, and I'm sure she knows that now and I'm sure she knew that then, she just couldn't deal with someone telling her the truth,' Dad said.

'In summary then,' I said, 'you're revealing that Aunt Olive was a slapper.'

'Jason, that's not nice to say about your only aunt.' She paused, 'Okay it is true, but at least stop that dirty snigger and pass me your bowl, if you've finished?

'Anyway, she was very pretty and actually she had many boyfriends – at least these were the ones who rang the next day. They took her out on extravagant dates but these relationships had a shelf-life of around three months. It was the same pattern over and over again: in the first month she was their princess, a woman whose beauty and grace they were entranced with and she was treated to expensive restaurants and showered with gifts. In the second month, their relationship slipped into a standard dating scenario where they chatted about life over dates of dinner or walks, it was this month she was happiest and most hopeful but unfortunately, by the third month, the calls diminished, the dates dried up to meetings in his local pub and then he would just disappear from sight. There wasn't the courtesy of a call or even a note to tell her she'd been dumped. As there were no official partings I'd often tease her that technically she's still dating some of these obnoxious men.

'Sadly, and I mean sadly in the deepest sense this word can convey in any sentence it has ever been used, sadly, she eventually met Mark.

'Marksman as we referred to him. He oozed every loathsome characteristic I'd ever come across in these clubs, though I confess, at first, he was charming and extremely handsome.

'He disliked me and he disliked Colin, so of course your sister and I slowly drifted apart from one another. I shouldn't have allowed it but I was living my life and I was happy. I didn't want my sister to upset me the way she did, so I went my way and she went hers.'

Mum sighed and quickly shuffled out of her trance to start loading the dishwasher before making the coffee.

CHAPTER SIX

Olive

About thirty years ago

Janet visited whenever it was convenient for her to escape the tedium of studying but I always felt she was eager to leave as soon as she arrived. She would sit on our sofa and say very little other than a series of huffs and ahs. When I would challenge her as to what she meant by her splutters she would reply with; 'Nothing, it's fine. Just hurry up and get ready,' or 'I have a babysitter waiting at home for £3/an hour don't you know?'

The flat I was living in was a typical girls' flat with magazines everywhere and clothes strewn about the hallway waiting their turn to be washed and so, admittedly, it was not ideal for visiting guests. But it was in the centre of London and perfect for living a young life of work, coffee shops then clubbing.

Janet used to moan incessantly about how overwhelmed she was with training, working and keeping a household going for a young boy who was now smashing his trains and cars into freshly ironed washing or climbing trees and then not being able to get down. I sympathised, especially at her having to get up at 7am on a Sunday just because her son had not yet learnt about lie-ins.

By now you were about four years old and when you came to see me, or me to you, I couldn't resist grabbing as many as possible of the consuming hugs you gave. I knew your mother had little money so I always bought coffee and only occasionally would I allow Janet to buy drinks at a club she had joined us to. I didn't mind, as at the time I was earning more than Janet.

Carolanne had got a job at Liberty of London thanks to her father who had connections with recruitment. It was not long before Carolanne had found me a job there, after I was dismissed from Boots for being late twice. I wangled my way into Liberty's as they needed Christmas staff, in particular someone to wrap the baubles in the Christmas department. I admit I had greater aspirations back then and I dreamed of becoming a CEO of a company, but desperation for money dampens any ambition to the 'whatever is available' dream.

I worked hard that season and I was the only one kept on after the Christmas period out of twenty temporary staff. I remember that boost from my manager, Clive. So, my ambition was renewed and I quietly dreamt of becoming the first chairwoman of Liberty of London.

Tatiana pointed out that I was now '…a permanent shop assistant and one of hundreds in a store of many stores in this city. So, if you aspire to be a great business woman, then answering inane questions from ignorant tourists is not going to get you to any boardroom.'

Her evidence was based around the fact Carolanne had not had a pay rise in the time she had been there and I had merely been shuffled from the Christmas department to the Rugs and Carpets department, whereas, she had already received a three per cent increase and a promotion and she had been with her brother's accountancy firm for only six months.

On reflection I didn't care too much. I was finally being paid a reasonable wage and I loved working in a vibrant iconic British store. My working week was based around a shift pattern. I opted for later shifts as I liked to sleep away my mornings, but this meant I often worked late; stock keeping and basic administrative work after the shop had closed.

There was a buzz about Liberty's. I remember the first day I returned to this store after Christmas. I entered at the staff entrance at the back where I checked in with Cara, a middle-aged lady who had been with the company from the age of sixteen and had worked her way downwards to the reception desk (which suited her as she did not like people and so didn't want to have to deal with foreigners, especially those who didn't speak English). She had yellow hair which clashed with her grey roots which clashed with her green splodge of eye shadow smudged over her eyelids, which also clashed with the faded lilac walls of the stockroom. She was famous throughout the store for her moaning but I recall her with fondness as she was the gate to Liberty of London.

From Cara, I weaved down the hallway crammed with storage boxes filled with everything from foreign antiquities to cosmetics. I would then open a side door and emerge into the tranquil gentility of the store. Elegance and wealth wafted throughout the Elizabethan building. It was like a wise old English gentleman who sat in tweeds and surveyed his vast estate from within his English country manor; content that everything was in its place and everything was just so.

Each floor overlooked another and was dominated by an atrium which had a domed window at its summit, spilling light onto every floor. The department I worked in was on the third floor next to lamps and general objets d'art from around the world (mainly Marrakesh, or so it seemed to me), and it was also just before the Modernist Art department with paintings from around the world (but mainly America, or so it appeared to me).

The room I worked in was filled floor to ceiling with silk rugs, whose pile moisturised the hand that stroked them. I was trained to understand how each rug was made, which village they came from and, at times ,even whose hand had woven the rugs. My favourites originated from the hands of women in the Atlas Mountains, as their designs were a little more intricate and the colours more vibrant.

I enjoyed my job and I was proud to work there. I especially loved the people I worked with who were all passionate about the products they sold. My manager was a man called Clive, he was tall and slender. Together we would watch the customers come into our corner of the department store and try and guess where they were from and whether they would buy a rug that day. Work was not a chore but a place I was willing and happy to spend my time.

I used to watch customers and on most days I would become fixated on the one exceptional, wealthy woman who glided through the store. She was the woman who was exquisitely and expensively dressed with manicured hair and nails. Her makeup was delicately, yet effectively, applied to enhance her deep red lips or her deep rich eyes. Her age ranged from thirty to eighty but she never failed to entrance me or others in the store. It did not matter who these women were, there was always one a day. I yearned to be one of them, perusing the store wondering what to buy to fill my grand house whilst wearing stunning designer clothes.

After work I would meet with Carolanne and we would walk home together. It was our chance to talk alone, away from customers or managers and also away from Tatiana. I confess we gossiped relentlessly about her; for Carolanne, she gossiped to transfer her annoyances and general dislike of Tatiana. For me, I gossiped to try and understand her.

'Does she ever smile?' it would begin.

'I think life just irritates her,' we would continue.

'And she has a bitchy comment about everyone she meets,' I would say, 'This morning, she even commented, "I know they have to find witnesses for the murder report on the news but do they really have to choose fat ones?" So ignorant!'

Despite my gossiping, I remained a convenient and subservient coat for Tatiana, to shield her from the cold social faux pas of going anywhere by herself. Those evenings were far easier when Carolanne didn't have a date and she would join us. 'I'm only coming to be with you Olive,' she would mutter as we left the apartment.

We went to clubs across London. The one we went to the most at the beginning was called The Zoo. I'm not sure how, but we had managed to get on the VIP list. It meant we didn't need to queue and freeze with everyone else as we didn't want to bring a coat to save time queuing for the cloakroom or to save money to pay for the cloakroom. This was the only advantage as inside we still needed to scramble to get access to a booth.

My dear Jason, as an aside, I have observed whilst growing up that I am at a disadvantage due to my gender. From an early age I was taught by society that I am weaker than my male social colleagues and to aspire to be stronger means abandoning girlish traits and harnessing the power of boys. When I was small I attempted to 'not' throw like a girl or cry like a girl or giggle like a girl or fight like a girl. Instead, my natural physique and temperament should be quashed if I was to progress as a person and I should accept the phrase 'like a girl' as an insult and not a fact of my gender.

In my teenage years I had a brief respite from my social weakness as I was academically far brighter than my male classmates, but it was only a brief respite as I had to nurse my parents and thus abandon any chance of a university education to gain a certificate to declare that I was an intelligent woman and not 'just a girl'.

In my twenties, I slipped into accepting I was 'just a woman';

powerless, with little prospect of catching up with other women my age who rejected the word 'just' and sailed down their own stream of an educated woman. They commanded a city job and demanded respect from a male society. I perceived it was too late for me, so I resided in the muddy banks of society's river and watched successful women sail by.

But, in nightclubs, such as The Zoo, I was more than 'just a girl'. There I was a powerful woman. I had slobbering men clambering around me. I fed from their subservience and they fed from my compliments, which massaged their flailing egos. I grew in stature every time a man professed his deep admiration. I could feel their eyes following me as if they had leashes around their necks that I could pull towards me at my will. I did not pay for drinks in any club and eventually I learnt what type of man would eagerly buy bottles of expensive champagne to ensure we had a booth to sit down in.

I was sailing on the richest social river in these clubs and occasionally a city working woman would appear in my domain and then it was their turn to sit on the muddy bank and watch me sail by.

I confess I met many men, to the disgust of my sister. Janet would rarely join me out and when she did then she moaned how hot and bored she was or constantly asked how much longer was left of the night before she could catch the night bus home. It was a shame as, when she was with me, I never left her side and I always made sure she was as happy as my miserable sister could be in a London club. When we progressed to The China Club, Janet stopped coming out with us altogether.

The China Club was just off Soho and, in those days, it was where the most successful men were; they bought champagne the way most men bought beer. There was a slight downside, which was the escorts who were employed by the club to keep these men happy. They were not advertised and only men who openly displayed their wealth, were introduced to these women.

Fortunately, Tatiana and Carolanne were able to block them, gaining these men's interest before the escorts had a chance to sit down.

The other downside to The China Club was the amount of cocaine that was snorted. I knew it was used elsewhere but here it was inhaled as freely and openly as sipping on champagne or cocktails. I missed the discreet use of cocaine. Prior to The China Club, the people we met merely disappeared to the toilets and when they returned they were rubbing their noses as if they had a cold, they also emerged as people who now laughed inanely at the most trivial of events. I once abandoned a soap actor who thought the person behind me looked like Bruce Forsyth. He thought this comment to be both funny and insightful. Neither was true, particularly as the person was a woman in her twenties with a blonde bob; if he'd likened the twelve o'clock shadow on her upper lip to Bruce's moustache then it may have triggered a smirk, but instead he repeated a cycle of poking her and saying, 'Nice to see you, to see you nice! I said, eeeee nice to see you,' followed by laughing in my face or on my lap as he'd lost his sense of balance and used me as a prop. After a while of soaking up the admiration from others that I was sitting with an almost famous person, I pulled away from him and allowed his face to bounce on the table. I then wandered off into the crowd again leaving him laughing at the mirrored table surface.

The advantage of meeting wealthy men was they were able to fill the gap in the evenings when I was not at a club. Tuesdays and Wednesdays were invariably date night, as after meeting someone on Thursday or Friday or Saturday in a club, Sunday was a rest day with negotiations of the forthcoming date occurring on the Monday. So that, come Tuesday and sometimes Wednesday, I was treated to elegant evenings across London. My favourite still remains Quaglino's, just off St James Palace or the Wolsey, next to the Ritz. Unfortunately, most dates were disastrous; when I met them again at the restaurant they always seemed smaller and fatter than I remembered them in The China Club. In most cases, they were also older and duller than the dim lights of the club allowed me to see.

I was grateful for the night out at these places but over dinner I would look at my date wondering who they were. They babbled into their meal and spewed forth what I thought were inaccurate and ignorant theories on business and politics. I would smile and nod my head, but I wouldn't challenge them even though I knew they were wrong in their opinion from all I had read of current affairs. It was always easier just to chat to myself; *the restaurant is wonderful; it's just a pity about the date.*

Carolanne usually laughed as I escaped through our flat's front door, exclaiming, 'Another date where you need to call the fraud squad? My gorgeous Ol, has someone stolen your date from three days ago and replaced it with the creep standing outside?'

As he talked I would nod and at times exclaim, 'Wow you're amazing'; he didn't catch my sarcasm but then I suppose he was talking to himself and he wasn't thinking he's full of crap, so why would he catch my hint that he was full of it?!' I giggled over a glass of wine.

The evening would end with our dreams of meeting a man who was handsome, intelligent and kind. For Carolanne, the list also included funny and fun to be around but for me, my list ended with rich and very rich.

The conversation of meeting these golden men, crafted by angel hands and polished by cherub wings, renewed our hopes of finding them while we trawled through the men crafted with a meat cleaver and polished with a bloody rag. Eventually our angel would find us and hold our hands, leading us away from the cliff edge of society's conceited and tempestuous offerings. If I stopped looking then I would fall off the edge and land at the bottom of 'nowhere special and stuck where I land'. So, my week started again with waking on a Thursday, going to work and clubbing each evening until Sunday.

CHAPTER SEVEN

Your mother stopped coming out the moment she met your father, Colin. He was much slimmer when I first met him but other than his size very little has changed about him over the years. I liked him then and I like him now.

For three years I lived the same week over and over again interspersed with occasionally being taken somewhere new on my Tuesday nights. By the time you were seven or eight, I had been on countless dates with the same mould of man but at least I had been promoted to assistant buyer. I was extremely proud to be promoted; finally, I was recognised within the store and I received a small pay rise.

Shortly after I received my prize of a new name badge with my title on it, James walked back into my life by wandering past my department. Clive had left that morning on another trip, leaving me in charge. I had my head under the counter looking for the company contact book to call someone to answer a question for a customer about removing a blood spot on her rug, bought from us in the spring of the previous year.

When I popped my head over the top my eyes rested upon a man in a beige duffle coat, he was tall with unkempt curly hair.

He was distinguishable from all the other customers as he was neither a wealthy shopper nor a tourist gazing at the wonders in the store. My heart fluttered as he sauntered past and I breathed in my call to him. Nothing came out and I watched him pass me and amble into the modern art section where he stopped to look at the paintings.

'You need a professional cleaner to remove the stain otherwise it will be permanent,' I hurriedly told the lady who had monopolised the last hour of my working day.

'You say that dear, but as I said…'

'Then try salt and elbow grease…'

I darted out of my department and stood in the entrance of the next section watching this lanky man peer into a painting of multi coloured dots. I stood behind him trying to catch an opportune moment to say hello, but James was too absorbed in his thoughts to notice my lightly flapping hands gesturing I was here.

After a length of time, James turned and peered directly down into my eyes. For a moment his expression did not show he recognised me, and I feared I was mistaken and this was just a stranger in a duffle coat that I had been waving to.

'James? It's me.' I whispered and James continued staring at me quizzically.

I stared back into his deep green eyes waiting for further instruction from them that he recognised my blue eyes.

'Olive? Olive!' He said softly.

It had been years since I had last seen him, running away from my rejection. He had every right to politely acknowledge me with a nod and cursory, 'Lovely to see you again, I hope all is well but I must be off to anywhere but here. Good bye.'

Instead, his arms wrapped around me and I squeezed him back. The memories of his hugs remained accurate and the happy peace they gave me was like a drug I had gone cold turkey on, but I remained the ever-faithful addict.

'You've made a dull shopping trip with my mum worth the sacrifice of a Wednesday.'

He then looked down at his feet and shuffled awkwardly to one side and the other. My mind was vacant for appropriate conversation that would fill the gap of the three years that we had been apart.

'Oh, how nice, a shopping trip with your mum. Is she here for anything in particular?'

'Er, my sister is getting married and Mum's looking for shoes or a hat or handbag or something like that.'

'Nice, nice. Er, she has an outfit already to go with the hat and shoes and handbag she's looking for?'

James paused and resumed his look my way, locking his eyes once more with mine. His lips were the same lips I remembered but they were now snuggled within a ring of stubble which caressed his gentle smile:

'No idea, I really don't care. We've been in and out of various stores for TWO hours and she's succeeded in losing me here. I say succeeded, it's more of a mutual parting so she can pick up bags one by one and shake her head but then go back to the same one at the beginning of the line and repeat the process. Why do you women do this? Pick a bag or shoes or whatever and stick to it.'

'It's genetic,' I chuckled. 'It comes from our time in the Sahara desert. From an evolutionary stand point we needed to check the minute detail of the berries we picked; could they be eaten or were they poisonous and thus could only be used to decorate our cave? We haven't lost that sense of detail and over many thousands of years this comes out in how we shop for accessories!'

'Really? Cos you don't want a poisonous handbag? Wow, who knew?!'

'Social suicide!'

'Coffee?' He said. He grabbed my right hand and it fell snugly within his.

'Ah, I work here so I can't leave but I've been on an early shift so I finish around four-ish. My colleagues, Suzannah and Jake can cover when they get in.'

I pointed over to the pile of rugs to reinforce where I spent most of my days. A pang of pride welled up in my throat and I gushed, 'I'm the assistant manager. I really enjoy working here and surprisingly I know more about rugs than I do about myself and I want to learn more. I know, I know it's daft and most find it dull but I enjoy it. I could show you around in the meantime whilst Jake comes in. I'm not sure how long Suzannah will be. I'm babbling I'm sorry.'

James squeezed my hand again and his duffle coat sleeve tickled my wrist.

'I'd love to see around and I'm so pleased you love your job, really pleased, but how about I find my mum who is probably knee deep in shoes or bags and I tell her that I'm abandoning her for you? This will make her very happy, I promise you; mainly because she gets rid of me and my moaning. I'll come back here for four or earlier? I can look around then maybe?'

'Earlier, earlier say three? I won't bore you with showing you my rugs but instead we'll go for coffee and I'll bore you then with my scintillating conversation on the art of rug-making. Fascinating I promise!'

'I'll be here for three and trust us, you could never bore me.'

James started to walk away, then his tall, towering body turned back to tease me.

'Stun me and surprise me, yes, but bore us? Never.'

James turned and strode off. I watched him go but this time grateful for the anticipation of his return in one hour and seventeen minutes.

James returned earlier than three. He took me to a generic corner café; the type whose individuality had been stripped away by a coffee chain. We sat on stools at the window with a bar table which stretched the entire length of the café wall. I drank my coffee slowly and refused a poppy seed muffin (I had already eaten 893 calories that day and the coffee was another 27 calories, so with a muffin I would have exceeded my afternoon calorie allowance).

'Still dieting? You look great, so personally I would suggest you enjoy the five billion calorie bun.'

'Shut up and, instead, tell me all about you and your life. Are you working as a carpenter? Where are you living? Do you still see the Oz crowd? Tell me, tell me.' I hugged him again, 'And I'm sorry. Sorry for everything.'

James smiled. His spots had diminished but his long thin face still glistened in the sunlight. He wore a blue cable knit jumper which was slightly baggy around the neck. His Adam's apple protruded above the collar of his white shirt. I remembered his neck from Australia but this time I felt reassured that there was a beautiful consistency about him; his body would always be tall and lean, his neck would always be long with a huge Adam's apple.

'Life is good, I'm working for a firm in Wimbledon that builds stage sets, mainly for West End shows. They're also training me on the job as I couldn't afford the course I wanted, but this way I'm earning whilst learning. I have my own flat in Norwood which my mum invades but she's great as she does all my washing and ironing... I insist she doesn't do it, really Olive, I whisper under my breath: 'Mum stop please, I can do it,' but she just doesn't hear me. Ah, don't look at me like that; it makes her happy! And yes, I see Tony, Rich and all the others from Oz. You? Please tell us you kicked that Tatiana into yesterday?'

'Er no, sorry!'

I was embarrassed, so the conversation was swiftly swerved round to talk of diving and how I longed to go again. By the end of our coffee we had planned a holiday to Egypt to go diving together. We also swore that we would try and see each other whenever he was in London on his work trips, which happily, was on a weekly basis.

I left the coffee house elated that I had found my friend again but by the time I had returned to my flat I was deflated. I knew Tatiana would tease me for sharing a coffee with lanky James but I also feared the disappointment from Carolanne. I elected not to tell them and I decided that it would be easier if I glossed over my day in favour of hearing about theirs.

Carolanne was waiting for me with a glass of white wine, handed out as I crossed the threshold. I stepped over Tatiana's pile of cigarette cartons and magazines and slumped into a dusty sofa. I grabbed my wine and smiled into the glass and said my rehearsed lines, 'Ahh good to be home, dull, dull day, what are you up to tonight? Anything interesting?'

'Jake told me you left with some tall bloke! Who was this?' Carolanne leaned over her arm rest and grinned in anticipation for a story.

'Oh that, er no one special.' In my reluctance to speak my voice cackled, 'Er, do you remember James?'

'James, James. No… oh, was he the one two weeks ago? The producer man? You're nodding no, so er ooh! British rail manager, no he was Graham – I remember him as his name suited him. Now you're looking weirdly at me, but either way, it's not him… James… James, now you're looking worried aww, not James from Oz? Now you're nodding! So it is! It's Ozzy James, ahhh, he was sweet!' she squeaked.

'Don't be embarrassed Ol, he's sweet, I really liked him but there is nothing between you is there? You said all along you weren't interested in lanky James?' She paused, 'I'm not being rude sweetie, but really? You and James? I don't really know him but he's so thin, I'm not being rude, honestly I'm not.'

Of course she was being rude and of course I didn't correct her. Instead I emphatically denied any involvement with James.

'He's my friend, really he is. I probably won't see much of him anyway but if I do see him then obviously I can't be rude and ignore him. Today for example, he had come to say hello to me, I couldn't hide so I had to chat and in some ways it was nice to find out what he was getting up to. So yeah nothing really. Tea? Do you fancy Lady Grey or Lapsang?' My voice trailed off at the end and Carolanne winked to indicate she knew that I wanted to change the subject.

'You know what, I take what I said back. I think he's sweet and good for you. Ignore me; who am I to judge? I date coke heads who can't string a sentence together so if you like him then ignore me, us and everyone, especially as he's one of life's gentlemen. In fact, you know what, feel his spirit, that's more important than looks.' She smiled.

'He's only ever going to be a friend.'

'Whatever you say honey and I'll have builder's tea.'

Tatiana did discover I was friends with James but her reaction was to snort her disapproval; she seemed satisfied that we were only friends and eventually her disinterest in other people meant she ignored the occasions I was out with him.

It began with coffee after work when he was in town and progressed to seeing each other most Sundays. I looked forward to these days as there were no expectations of what the day could offer me. We would meet for morning coffee at a corner pub and read the Sunday papers. The pub had a large sofa and we would sit in peaceful silence, occasionally commenting about an article we were reading. Afterwards we would take a stroll and talk about anything and everything. There were very few pauses in our conversations but when there were, I would just enjoy looking at the sparkling river or the pink candy floss blossom on the spring trees or the passing clouds bumbling about the sky over our heads. Scenes I didn't appreciate when I was alone.

I didn't talk of my time with James and after a while, I became two people: one glamorous and sexy, foraging for exciting nights at clubs and wine bars, and the other was a break where I relaxed with James. The two lives were kept separate like work and play and should either of them mingle then I was vague with any enquiry about one life to the other. I even began to dress differently: with one life I wore a uniform of fashionable clothes and the other I wore jeans and trainers; as if I was coming home after a long day at work and snuggling into my dressing gown on the sofa.

Six months after meeting James, my schizophrenic lifestyle was intensified when I met the second man in my life, Mark.

CHAPTER EIGHT

That Thursday afternoon, in late August, was damp and chilly. It was a year that the month of August had not read its brief on what weather it should be offering the British people. Instead of hot, bright sunny days leading to warm evenings with an orange sky at dusk and a clear sky at night, there were rainy days and nights. Throughout that year, the weather was autumnal with damp mornings leading to wet days and wetter evenings. The land was drenched and the whole of England was tired of the mundane, predictable rain. We had been cheated out of our summer as spring had leapt head forth into autumn. However, on this particular day there was a glimmer of hope that Noah's ark was not in the process of being constructed, as the nation feared. On this day, there was merely damp air with only the threat of rain above our heads. The evening saw windows opened for the first time and pubs spilling their outdoor furniture onto the London pavements to rejoice that maybe summer was peeking its head around the corner. A timid buzz from the anticipation of seeing the sun and a white dove followed all Londoners; and this bird of hope followed three girls into The China Club.

We had not been to this club in a little while as Tatiana wanted to try other places. The truth was she had been avoiding a girlfriend of a man she had been seeing. She confessed she knew he had a partner but she loved the thrill of claiming an unattainable man. But this girlfriend guarded her possession and threatened to attack Tatiana. She emphasised her threat by pouring a jug of beer over Tatiana's head. Tatiana ran out of the club in anger and I had trailed after her (with a wry smile) before comforting her by telling her that her aggressor was; '...ugly and she's just jealous of how pretty you are... but maybe it would be good idea to avoid this woman's boyfriend in future?'

(Incidentally, I do not recall ever placing any blame on the shoulders of the girlfriend's man, especially as it was his jug of beer that he had bought for himself to accompany watching the spectacle of two women fighting over him.)

Tatiana seemed nervous as she jerked her head around at anyone that passed her then jerked it back again when she had confirmed she didn't know them. Her arms were folded and her lips pursed in readiness.

Carolanne and I stood in the queue for The China Club with Tatiana cowering behind us. I was enjoying soft gentle fingers caressing my head from the light evening breeze. The moon was full and low in the sky; it looked like it had been polished to a high shine as it shone across the city lighting up all the puddles until they glistened. I cocked my head to one side and tucked my arm into Carolanne's.

'James needs to be here to see the moon. It's so large tonight, I wonder if it's moving in to steal a kiss from the earth,' I whispered.

'You're a romantic in your heart. Where is James? Why don't you invite him along? You never know, he may bring some good-looking friends? Ooh, we're moving closer to the front. It shouldn't be too much longer.'

Carolanne hugged my arm and rested her head on my shoulder.

'He doesn't like clubs and he doesn't have any good-looking friends, believe me; plus they're all carpenters and so all broke.'

'I bet they're sweet. I'm tired of pushy, rude, arrogant, egotistical men who just want to bounce me around like a tennis ball to hit from one side of a court to another,' she sighed.

'Now who's the romantic thinker?'

'It's beginning to hurt, sweetie. I don't want to be emotionally bashed around anymore. Who cares about rich? I care about being cared for.'

'How about kind and rich?' I said.

'You know, my friend,' Carolanne replied, 'there is a Bantu word 'mbuki-mvuki' which means, 'to dance naked with wild abandon.' There is no equivalent English word because very few know how to dance with wild abandon. In there I don't dance because I'd be dancing to someone else's beat. I don't want that in life anymore, Ol, and neither should you. Don't you think it's time we escaped? There's got to be something better.'

I didn't answer instead I pulled her into the red entrance of The China Club for the needed boost of power. I was like a rechargeable battery which had become depleted of energy throughout the day.

Since we'd been there last, the club had a slight renovation: the light was purple with shaded areas of red from the booths. In each booth the same white leather sofas with diamante studs welcomed customers but now hung an oval chandelier with droplets of crystals surrounding a central white light, which shone onto mirrored tables with one red glass lamp at their centre. The atmosphere oozed a lascivious air into the nostrils of all those who walked through the doors of the club. As I entered the main central area, my breath was caught by a man sitting in one of these booths.

His companions were boisterous and shouting at one another but he was turned with his back to the group and his body facing toward the dance floor. He looked controlled and appeared to peruse the area as if he was a woodland stag policing his territory. He was sitting on the corner leaning over with his elbows on his knees. In his left hand he was twirling a brandy glass and staring at his cognac. His tie had been loosened and hung around his neck like a noose. His white shirt was undone down to below his Adam's apple and just a peek of toned chest teased its way through.

He looked like a bored headteacher in control of an unruly class. His jaw was square and jutted out from his face which smouldered contempt for anyone who would dare to contradict him. He did not smile and he did not look up but the whole club stared at this man who sat at the top of Darwin's evolution scale.

I sensed him before I even saw him and when I did, I too joined the masses of women who discreetly stared his way.

It is a primeval flush of hormones that drenches us when we see a person we are attracted to. Apparently, this lustful hormone stays with a person for nine months; just enough time for a baby to be conceived and born – Mother Nature is a cunning croupier who deals cards to an unwilling gambler in a card game of love. When I was handed my cards on a damp August evening there was little I could do with them other than to play.

This hormone caused my heart to beat faster, my mouth to turn dry and the power I had happily harnessed and unleashed on other men was rendered useless as I became a shy elf, struck with nerves by the person at the other end of the room.

'That is Mark, I can't believe it,' Tatiana squealed. 'That is Mark from CBS bank, he's one of the youngest senior hedge fund analysts they've ever had and he also has his own dot. com business – I think. At least that's what the girl over there said, but whatever he is, he's loaded and gorgeous to go with it. And the other woman over there, the one in the cheap red boob tube, told me that he's just returned from New York and broken up with his American girlfriend and so definitely single.'

She blurted all this into my ear then started looking around like a hit-man searching for his target.

'Carolanne isn't here is she? Good she's so controlling and pushy; a man like Mark can't stand women like her so if you see her let me know okay? The last I saw of her was about ten minutes ago and she was chatting to her itsy bitsy friend Lisa – can't stand her, she's really annoying as she thinks she's better than everyone else when she isn't. Anyway, shadow me as I'm going over to talk to him. I look good, yeah?'

Tatiana straightened her silver slip dress and pouted at the mirrored wall behind me. She then ruffled her hair so that it fell slightly thicker around her shoulders. She lifted one shoulder and pouted into the mirror again before once more looking at me.

'Yes? I look good?' she said and I nodded in compliance. 'So you'll follow me over?' Her voice was still in a high-pitched squeal.

'You look good as well Ol – love the red heels. Anyway, all you need to do is come over with me and, if needs be, talk to his mates – you can do that right? Good, let's go.'

She turned on her silver stilettos. My heart was now thumping wildly inside my chest and I breathed out a pleading 'no!' But I followed, as I was a good lap dog, even when I was facing an imminent slap of social embarrassment from Mark and his lair.

Tatiana artfully walked past his table whilst pretending to talk to me, I tried to act but all I could do was smile, she then turned and walked past his table again but this time looked their way then returned to the bar we had been standing by before she had left for her catwalk.

'That should do it for now. Is he looking my way?' Tatiana

was slightly out of breath. 'No, don't look over! It's so obvious, Olive just step that side; now can you see?'

I tilted my head and I caught the full view of his strong face. He was looking our way and when I caught his eyes looking at us I jerked back as if to hide from a firing range.

'Er, yes, he's looking your way.' I could feel that my neck had stiffened and I was aware I was squeezing my purse tightly as the buckle was digging into the palm of my hand.

'Okay Ol, order me a drink and we'll go outside onto the balcony. When he comes out wait for about five minutes then go back inside saying you're cold.'

Tatiana's cheeks were flushed and she had developed a pouting twitch which meant everything she said was accompanied by a flick of her hair and a pout.

I did accompany her outside and I did get cold waiting for Mark to open the door to the balcony. After twenty minutes of huddling together over a glass of champagne, Tatiana conceded defeat and re-entered for another strike. However, Carolanne was now sitting and laughing in amongst the men on the table. Mark was facing inward with his leg arched out. He appeared absorbed by the animated laughter of Carolanne. Her blonde hair was piled high above her head and she was the vibrant vixen that Tatiana hated.

'We can't go over now. Carolanne is so annoying. She thinks she's amazing, well she isn't. The trouble with Carolanne is she thinks she's amazing – amazing and funny and beautiful, well I don't think she is. Ahhhh that woman! Seriously, she is sooo annoying – who does she think she is?'

This time Tatiana looked in the mirror and pouted in anger. I sympathised, I too was looking into the same mirror and I wished I saw Carolanne as me instead of my snow-white skin under a mass of red curls.

We continued to watch from afar and I continued to listen to Tatiana ramble on about the evils of Carolanne. Tatiana created an acerbic atmosphere which was diffused when Carolanne came over.

'Come on Tats,' Carolanne said, 'take that miserable look off your face. For some reason he wants to meet you.'

'Who? Who wants to meet me?' Tatiana replied between pouts.

'Give up Tats, that doesn't wash with me,' she said.

As I approached the table my paranoid self screamed at me to do nothing other than to sit. I loyally complied and sat next to tiny Lisa who squeaked a giggle at anything the surrounding men said. After a while my cheek muscles began to ache from my forced smile, I stroked my face and looked up at Mark. I was impressed to see Tatiana had wrestled Carolanne away from him and was leaning over to talk into his ear. He still appeared bored but he had his right hand on her left crossed leg.

As the night progressed Mark's men peeled away. One of them left with Lisa who, comically, reached to the elbow of her night's companion. I was left sitting with my chin resting on my hand and stealing the odd glance at Mark who was now laughing with Tatiana. My mind drifted down to the mirrored table top.

'Ooh upside down version of me is not pretty,' I thought. 'I wonder how many mirrors they broke putting these in? Got to replace Carolanne's hand mirror, I think I took it to work yesterday? No, not there. Ooh I remember now, Betsy has it. I'll call her tomorrow. I'm thirsty, only upside-down bottles here. Is it rude to scrape out the champagne dregs? Best I didn't...'

'I've been waiting for you to talk to me. I'm sorry my friends are overbearing at times but now they're gone, maybe you could speak to me?' came a deep voice.

'Eh, what?' I said.

I looked up at the source and I was locked by Mark. His

unruly dark hair fell around his forehead. He had blue eyes that were so deep they looked almost black set against a tanned face, like Mediterranean pools on a beach.

Impromptu questions from a stranger may lead to a discussion or it may lead to the start of a wonderful friendship if the answer is a wise witty response. Unfortunately, all my dry mouth could muster was, 'Oh er yeah, sure, yeah definitely.'

I said this as I brushed my red hair away from a sweaty brow in an attempt to deflect attention away from the colour with the flush of red which had sprung up on my cheeks.

'Not too shy?'

I knew it was a rhetorical question designed only to bring a sly smirk upon his face but I didn't know how to respond and so, again, all my brain could offer to rebuke him was, 'Err excuse me? Not shy just sitting here.'

'It's okay, I like shy. You have a lot of red hair. Is it yours?'

'Er yes, it's my hair. Big hair I know and very red but it's all mine. Who do you think I'm borrowing it from?'

'Nice one red. Touché. Anyway, I like it, it's striking.'

He then winked, I then gulped, Tatiana then twitched and said, 'Ah my sweet little friend Olivia, Mark. She's the best of friends but you're right Mark, Ol is shy; wow you're such a good judge of character Mark; I love that in a person.' Tatiana turned to me in a position that blocked Mark. She pursed her lips and said, 'You're my little mouse but I love you anyway.'

Tatiana laughed and tugged at Mark's shirt sleeve to encourage him to laugh and sadly he did.

We enter battles when we know our army is strong, if it is weak then we fall on diplomacy to ease our way out of conflict. I knew I was weak against Tatiana; I was not confident to argue with her as her ammunition was sharp and it always cut her opponent. I had seen her fire out at others and I did not want to be defeated and humiliated in front of Mark, instead, I gathered my purse and smiled at Tatiana.

'Love you too Tats. You'll always be my gorgeous black cat. Enjoy your night. I'm off. Lovely to meet you Mark. Night.'

Carolanne caught up with me and suggested we go home together as it was now two in the morning and she thought it prudent to leave Tatiana and Mark together. I agreed and we traipsed home in a summer drizzle that hazed the previously perfect full moon to a white smudge.

Curiously, Tatiana was no more than twenty minutes behind us. We had only just sat down when she opened the door and smiled at us to indicate a successful evening.

'We're meeting tomorrow after work,' she beamed. 'What do you think of that Carolanne?' She winked at her and proudly walked to the kitchen.

'I couldn't care less,' Carolanne grimaced. 'Good looking and rich he may be but arrogant and rude he most definitely is. I'm sorry I left you with those men so soon after you arrived.'

'Why are you sorry? He was alright; I actually thought he was sweet. But Tatiana was her usual self, ignored me then told me I was a mouse – nice!'

'Ignore her. I do most days. She's now grey noise dumbing out the road outside. It's going to be the same for Mark.'

Carolanne rested her head on her hand and stared out the window.

'No dancing with wild abandon then. I'm sorry I left, Ol, but as usual one of them – Tom I think, short, squatty man, the one with the hairy mole above his left eye, remember? Looked like he had a third eye? Anyway, he suggested they should all take bets on which of you two they could sleep with first. When I said, 'You'd be lucky with Ol' and that you were my friend they just laughed, so when you came over (which I confess, was because of me and Lisa – sorry again but Mark had asked me to gesture you over, not Tats but you), I then left and I was so pleased you ignored them all. Sorry I've not been a great friend tonight but I'm pleased that the person the bet came up for was Mark who struck the jackpot with Tatiana. Good luck to him, as by the end of tomorrow I suspect he'll wish he had lost the bet!'

Carolanne had not been a loyal friend but I didn't mind as she had told me that Mark wanted me. Unfortunately, the insult that I was a horse to bet on had by-passed my young ears.

CHAPTER NINE

After that evening, the reflection in my mirror temporarily altered. I was the ideal woman, called upon over any other candidate. I was the woman others envied or desired. I was the woman scanned for guidance as to how to look, how to dress and how to snare the rich good-looking Mark.

But he didn't call or visit, there were no coincidental meetings nor was there any confirmation from others that I was the chosen one, and worse, he had started to date Tatiana; sexy, slender Tatiana. So my daydream did not last long and I began to scrutinise myself in the mirror and discovered to my horror a major flaw in my body. Over time, my chest had shrunk to a bland ripple. I hadn't appreciated this defect before. But there it was the obvious cause of my imperfection and this concern only intensified over the next couple of months.

'Seriously get over yourself Ol, there's nothing wrong with you,' said Carolanne one Saturday morning.

'It's her prerogative,' interjected Tatiana, 'to want what she wants. Personally, I think clothes hang better when you've got a bit more on top, like me for example. I can wear most clothes because they hang better.' Tatiana flicked her hair and looked in the hallway mirror. 'Just saying Carebear, to leave her alone.'

'Well we can't all be perfect like you and I'm not having a go at her I'm just pointing out there's nothing wrong with her other than paranoia,' replied Carolanne.

'That's so rude Carolanne. Ol, I don't think you're paranoid. I think you have a legitimate concern and if you think you're too small then I support you as that's what friends do.'

'Er, thanks, I think?'

'Take for example your new pink dress. Lovely, yes, but it definitely looks better on me, as I said, because I have a fuller bust. Just saying.'

'Don't listen to her, she's angling to wear your new dress Ol.'

'I'm not wishing to wear it! – although, if you're not wearing it then as you've made the suggestion Carolanne, then maybe I will – plus she knows I'm only joking. She's perfect, you know I think that eh?' I smiled. 'See she's fine and Ol, I see what you all mean about the dress, that it would be perfect for tonight, I agree, so just checking you don't mind if I wear it? Say if you don't want me to... Mark has promised to take me to L'Amour, Covent Garden and I can't wait!'

'Sure,' I said, but the injustice of my dress going out to L'Amour and enjoying the glamour of London's most fashionable restaurant without me or my bust was not lost on me.

'Wow, L'Amour, wow you lucky girl, what an amazing man and what an amazing place!' Carolanne got up from the table as she said this and animated her sarcasm by shaking her hands with mocking glee.

'Now who's jealous?' Tatiana said triumphantly and she too got up and mimicked Carolanne's' jazz hands then left the room to get ready for work.

That day I was due to see James in my lunch hour. I was looking forward to seeing him and just chatting.

'Do I have small boobs? Be honest, as everyone is repulsed

at the sight of them. Don't laugh James, I said, "repulsed", I'll say it again, repulsed by them,' I sheepishly asked.

'I mean this, mad woman, in the best way I can, to make sure you know what I think of that: Shut up! No don't start. I can see you about to open your mouth to ask us again. Shut up!'

I held his hand to stop him taking another sip of coffee.

'Please, I know I sound stupid but I hadn't noticed before and yes, it's vain, but now that it's been pointed out to me I just feel so self-conscious about them.'

'Give over! Who's been that rude and that indiscreet to say they are repulsed by your chest? And if there is such a person then who and what are they comparing them to? Is there a perfect size and shape? And if so, does that size suit everyone or is there the right size for one person? And if that's the case then well done, Ol, you have the perfect shape and size for you.'

'Tatiana. Well, not just her, but she's seeing this incredible man who laughed at me and the next day or so Tatiana commented about them. Well okay not commented, but agreed with me.'

'What a surprise! The woman who loves only herself. And why are you interested in the hypocritical beauty advice of a shapeless woman who herself, by-passed puberty?'

'I know, I know but...'

'Shut up, Olive, you know I think you're lovely and you know there isn't one single part of you I would change. Look at yourself and be happy.'

'Thank you, you're so lovely. You're my drug.'

James pulled his hand away from mine and caressed his coffee. He took a sip from the large white mug. Some of the froth stuck to his new fluffy moustache; he wiped it away with his right hand and with his left grabbed my right hand.

'You're such a romantic,' I said. 'You know, I'm jealous of your future wife.'

'I suspect you've ruined me for future women but I'll take anyone right now, especially as I have this new beard and moustache. What do you think? Stunning, yes? It makes us irresistible more than any Burberry male model, yes? Come on, own up Olive, see that woman over there? She's about to head butt the café window to get closer to the glory that is James Tanner!'

James did look better as the beard covered a line of adult spots that he had on his chin.

As predicted, the drug didn't last and by the time I came home from work my obsession about my chest had returned. Tatiana was sitting in the yellow corduroy chair dragging on a cigarette. Her hair was tied into a tight knot on her head, she was looking into three-dimensional space with her eyes narrowed to a slit. I sensed the angry aura around her so I looked for an escape route to my room.

'I have nothing to wear for tonight!' She exclaimed. Her red nails tapped her lips.

'I thought you were going to wear my dress?' I said.

'He's not taking me there! Can you believe that? He's not taking me there as he doesn't think it would be right to take me! What does that even mean? But oh, get this, he's happy to meet me afterwards about ten, but wait for him as he doesn't know how long he'll be and when I do see him I should look elegant for a change! What does that mean? What does it mean Olive?' Her red nails dug into her face.

'Sounds rude to me. Don't go,' I said.

'Don't go! And miss out? I don't think so. That's rude.'

'Why not? You're not his servant.'

She bent over in the shabby chair and yelled into her hands. My instinct was to back away as I hadn't encountered this emotion from Tatiana; the closest I had come was anger and embarrassment when the jug of beer was poured over her. So, I felt obliged to edge closer and place a hand on her shoulder. My other hand was searching for my new mobile phone as I felt it buzz in my pocket. Remember Jason, this was some time ago and phones had not long been in existence so it was a novelty to me and I was keen to see why it was buzzing.

'Elegant? Me? He's talking about me. Who does he think he is? Unless someone has been talking to him about me? Renka? Ah! She's always hanging around, sniffing after him. Yet what would she know about elegance? She thinks Burberry is the height of sophistication and did you see what she wore to Alice's – fat but nice – Alice's birthday? Seriously, I wanted to ask her if her Gran was missing her bedspread. Really, who is she to say: "Elegant for a change?"'

She paused and repeated 'for a change!' then she returned to her hands.

'But he's so sweet, it makes it worse Ol. Whenever he says stuff like this it's as if he's then putting himself out to be nice to me: "I'll meet you afterwards... I'll try and get away just for you so I can see you... but please gorgeousness, look elegant and stunning." He makes me think he's the one doing me a favour! Nope, it's not him, it's Renka, it has to be and I will say something to her.'

'Did you ask him what he meant by it all?' I said meekly as I tried to retrieve a text message with one hand.

'How can I have asked?' she yelled. 'He has some business meeting and he didn't think I would fit in... "It will be too boring for you, please understand gorgeousness." So, I'm not going to ask why, that just makes me look absolutely pathetic and ungrateful especially as he doesn't *have* to slip away early just to see me. As I said, I will say something to Renka, like, "excuse me but who are you to question my relationship with Mark?" and "elegant for a change? Try looking in the mirror first" – yes that's a good one, "Look in the mirror Renka before you judge me!"'

She returned once more to her hands and I read my text from Carolanne;

'Is Tatiana still angry? Just left the apartment,' it read.

'Beyond angry. Something about not meeting Mark and not dressing correctly?' I replied.

'I've just bumped into Renka, a friend of Mark's, and she's told me he wants to dump her!'

I read the last text then looked down at the heap in the shabby chair. Tatiana looked up at me again.

'What else am I supposed to wear? For example, your grey dress with the magenta pink twirls around the border – sorry I wore it on Saturday, but I did look amazing.' She returned to her hands and I returned to my text messages so I could hurriedly type:

'She has admitted it was her who wore my new grey dress!'

'I know she walked out in it and met Mark last Saturday, the first I knew about it was when she returned wearing it – apparently Mark went onto see someone else after seeing her that night!'

'What do we do with her? She's now really upset – come home!'

There was a brief respite in Tatiana's rants so that she could suck on her wet cigarette. I squeezed her shoulder.

'Maybe you could talk to him and ask him what he means by all this? That's what I'd do.'

She looked up at me and scowled. 'No way! I'm not that pathetic, maybe you are but I'm not!' I smiled my reply and returned to the buzzing phone and another text from Carolanne:

'Aah don't make me! The dumping is imminent and I'm trying to stay out with Renka to avoid the inevitable screams.'

'Where are you? I'll join you instead.'

'Coffee shop around the corner.'

I looked back at Tatiana, 'I'm sorry I've got to go out, you'll be fine. Wear the blue jumpsuit.'

Tatiana looked up at me, 'Wore that last Tuesday.' Her head flopped back into her hands, 'Life is sooo hard!'

'You left yet?' came another text.

'Maybe he's not for you?' I said.

'Don't be silly, have you met him?' There was a momentary silence broken by a whisper to herself.

'How can he not want me? Me, Ol?' She sighed and her head returned to the sanctuary of her hands.

I met Carolanne and Renka in the coffee shop and we indulged ourselves with coffee and gossip about Tatiana. The conclusion we came to was Mark was young, very handsome and he was enjoying life so why shouldn't he flit from woman to woman and what right did Tatiana have on him? She was demanding, difficult and she needed to start thinking about using mousse to bolster her hair as it was too straight and needed volume so, actually, the final conclusion was Tatiana had bought this on herself and Mark should not be blamed.

The winter was in full swing; the summer rain had been replaced with drizzle in the autumn then strong gusts accompanied with sharp cold stabs from the air by early January.

When we entered the downstairs communal hallway Carolanne and I laughed at our windswept appearance. There was a broken and tarnished mirror hanging above the apartment's letter-stacking shelves and I agreed with Carolanne that my cheeks were as red as my disorderly hair which had doubled in size. We shrugged at one another as it was Wednesday night and we had no plans to go out so it was only the television and the shower head that would see my hair.

I walked into our apartment behind Carolanne and kicked off my shoes but instead of being welcomed by Tatiana I was greeted by Mark. He was sitting in the same armchair Tatiana had sat in a few hours earlier. Without consciously thinking about it my hands were rapidly straightening my hair; like an army officer my heart beat to bark orders at my arms to straighten my suit and hide the bush on my head.

'Hi, sorry for the intrusion,' he said, 'but Tatiana was upset so I thought it best to come up.' He had risen from the chair and walked over to give a kiss on Carolanne's cheek. She welcomed him whilst I was cemented to the 'welcome' mat by the front door.

'How are you Mark? We've not seen each other since before Christmas when you came to pick up Tatiana for a works do or something like that?'

Mark looked tired and unhappy like a small child after a long hard day at school. His hair flopped about his eyes which were drooped down to his cheeks. His ears looked as if they had been struck by his angry mother and they too seemed to be slipping down his neck.

'Yeah. yeah, I remember.' Mark released Carolanne to look at me. I was still standing on our front door mat. He smiled and glided over. My heart barked its last orders in vain to straighten my hair, it then conceded defeat and wildly beat against its cage as Mark grabbed my arms and lent in to kiss my cheek.

I could smell his musk and the smoky barrel whiskey he'd had before coming up to our nicotine dive.

'I haven't seen you in months Olive. You seem to be out whenever I'm here. I always leave disappointed, but now I've caught you,' he said.

He still had me in his grip and I fluttered a form of reply from my dry mouth.

'Where have you been?' he asked softly, but instead Carolanne curtly replied for me;

'She's usually out with her mate James. He's a sweet lovely man, you don't know him.' She looked at me and smiled, 'They're good friends. Is Tatiana around?'

'I think she's getting ready.'

'You okay, Ol?' She edged towards me which broke me out of my paralysis. Mark let go of my arms and walked back into the room.

'Yes?' I was confused by her question and walked into the flat, finally closing the front door behind me.

'I'll go in and see her.' She walked towards the hallway and as she did she brushed next to Mark, she then looked back at me; 'I won't be long.'

I busied myself with taking off my name badge and placing it safely in my designated work drawer.

'James, eh?' he said and I turned to face him. His eyes had brightened and I could see the slight hint of a returning smile. My stomach was clenched and my brain was busy trying out possible answers and testing each one for level of intelligence versus level of credibility about my friendship with James. The bit test on answers produced a pitiful, 'He's a friend.'

'I can't believe any man would want to be your friend. I know I couldn't.' Mark's eyes released themselves from me and darted towards Tatiana's room, 'I know I couldn't be your friend.'

'Excuse me? I'm a nice person.'

'Sorry, I didn't mean it that way,' he brushed his hair from his face and looked sheepishly at his feet. He then looked up and stared through my eyes and into my head. 'I meant I would want more than friendship. Out of curiosity, does he want more than friendship?'

'Er I don't know. He's my friend he...'

'Fair enough, either way, he's a lucky man and I'm jealous of him.' And then he winked.

I opened my mouth as a gesture to offer a witty response but nothing came out as my brain had jarred shut. The only part of me that moved were my eyes, which followed Mark who had turned to greet Tatiana emerging from her room wearing my pink dress.

After they left Carolanne bounded out in her pyjamas with a bottle of wine in one hand and two glasses in her other hand.

'Girlie flick and girlie drinks, my sweet friend Olive.'

'I think Mark was flirting with me?'

'He likes the cutesy ladies and, Ol, you are a cutesy, even with your hair fuzzing away from your head – I literally think it has trebled in size.' Carolanne kissed my cheek then placed a video in the machine before jumping onto the yellow armchair.

'My hair – I looked a state, I looked hideous, he must have been teasing me, after all, why flirt with a woman who has wrestled with the wind and lost when he has Tatiana?'

'For kicks my sweet, for kicks. Enjoy the moment as he is gorgeous but I suspect he makes sport out of collecting women.' Carolanne looked at me and continued, 'Stick with James or if not James then find someone like James. Don't look glum just 'cos I said stick with James, He may not be Mark or look like Mark or have Marks' money but then Mark doesn't have James' loveliness or purity.'

I smiled and left the room to change from the day. I wish I could have settled my beating heart and calmed my brain but I couldn't. That night, all I was capable of doing was to shower, drink wine, watch a movie then stay awake all night recounting the conversation I'd had with Mark.

CHAPTER TEN

I experimented with boob enhancers from silicone bra inserts to sucking machines. The silicone inserts moved throughout the day and I was paranoid I was going to drop one from my bra onto the feet of a customer. I envisaged discreetly peeling off the sticky blob from their shoe so as not to distract them from buying a Persian rug for thousands of pounds.

I tried padded bras but the problem with these they were expensive and didn't fit me properly. They certainly pushed my breasts up but my own breasts would gradually spill over the top of the bra as the lining dug into my bosom. Within a few hours it looked as though I had four breasts that needed to find a line of piglets to feed.

The most extreme form of enhancement was a machine which sucked at my breasts. The advert had promised that within three months my bust would appear to have increased by a whole cup size. To reinforce their claim the manufacturers had a happy beautiful, well-endowed woman in a bikini top printed across the box.

For twenty minutes every day, I sat religiously with this machine sucking on me making a whirring noise. It was not only painful but painfully boring as I was confined to my room holding the suckers to my chest and staring at the wall. After three months I concluded there was ambiguity in the description of the results. I suspected if I had sued the 'Wonder Enhancer' company for fraud they would have pointed out that their only claim was: 'breasts appeared to increase but only in a certain light, time of day and if there was a full moon rising in the Azores and therefore, Ms Olivia, you do not have a cause for complaint'. Either way I had wasted £32 and thirty-five hours of my life staring at my powder pink bedroom wall.

The only thing that helped my confidence was seeing James, who would tell me I was, 'beautiful so please, for the last time, shut-up.' I was seeing him regularly and we even ventured outside London on holiday. I had little money so the holidays were not extravagant and James always made up my financial shortfall with loans at zero per-cent payback.

One holiday was just before seeing Mark in my flat. It was a weekend away walking in the Lake District. The village of Grasmere was serene: Jack Frost had lain throughout the village and crisped the January air. It frosted my nostrils with every breath. I could smell winter encrusted in the pine trees that lined the walking paths. The sky was a deep blue without any clouds spoiling the hills that gently rose over the village skyline. Our bed and breakfast was perfect to pick up any walking trail we chose and it was also convenient for James to pick up the Grasmere gingerbread biscuits which were freshly made each morning in the same shop to the same recipe since the 1800s. The smell of these biscuits filled my stomach each morning and on occasion I would allow myself a biscuit savouring every bite so that it lasted until at least halfway up a hill walk.

My concern about my body disappeared on these holidays mainly because of James battering me to shut-up, but it would always re-emerge as I approached London. Each time I said goodbye to James outside my apartment block I would confirm, then reconfirm, the next time we were meeting for coffee. He would then kiss my cheek and say, 'goodbye my Olive and shut-up about your boobs.' Then he would drive away leaving me behind.

As my key clicked in the door I would feel despondent at the prospect of re-entering my weekly cycle: Work beckoned each day, interspersed with nights out to clubs and meeting men who were inferior to the man I had briefly met on a summer's eve.

On this occasion I was unaware my depression would last just a few more days; just until I found Mark in my flat and he winked at me. Secretly, I replayed Marks words around my head and together with the memory of his dark, almost black eyes, I began a fantasy about his secret love for me. These fantasies were my new drug; they were far stronger than coffee with James or the feel of new clothes. I didn't tell James that he had been downgraded to mere paracetamol in favour for this new addictive medicine constantly swirling in my veins.

However, I did develop a new worry in life and that was the fear of actually meeting Mark again.

I knew he was rarely around as he travelled with work for most of his week and when in London he worked long hours in the office, plus his weekends were taken up playing golf at Weybridge golf club (I knew all of this as Tatiana was more knowledgeable about his life schedule than the diary Mark's personal assistant had.) Yet daily I pruned myself in case he would be in the flat when I returned from work, but this time I feared he would not wink at me or whisper for me to tease him; and then my drug would disappear for good and I would have to go cold turkey from my daydreams.

Some weeks later I was in the Pack Horse pub close to Richmond (it's the pub, Jason, you used to run up and down on the balcony outside shouting at the boats that sailed by whilst your mother and I sat under a willow tree with branches shielding us from the summer's sun). On this day, the winter rain had whitewashed the London streets overnight, the willow leaves had left the trees and the closed balcony was covered in crystal ice. It was a magical bright Sunday morning. The snow made London quiet as people slowed their pace, donned their warm winter clothes and headed for the comfort of an English pub with a roaring fire.

I was one of these Londoners, feeling cosy on a huge leather sofa with James. He was discussing the possibility of trying for our wreck diving certificate out in Taba, Egypt. The wrecks were not too far off shore with one shipwreck only a short swim away. I was listening and working up the courage to tell him I was wearing the deposit for this diving holiday and I was hoping that he would find my new white cashmere polo-neck (which was the perfect accompaniment to a snowy Sunday morning) an amusing alternative to a diving holiday.

'Don't worry! I will save again, but James, this was a bargain, an absolute steal. I saved nearly £110 and so, in a way, I made £110 by buying it!' I smiled and fluttered my eyelids at him as a comical apology.

'That's warped logic Ol, only you and all other women could come up with that. You know one day you will have to prioritise your money for little things like, I dunno, bills instead of clothes.'

'Never! With bargains like this jumper? How could I? After-all, who needs to pay for the trivial things like gas, electricity, water and food?'

James tried to hide his slight laugh and I knew he would be fine at a slight delay in me producing the deposit for our April dive. I sipped on my hot water with lemon and leant my head on James' shoulder as he drank his dark bitter beer.

'The wreck course goes someway to getting our master certificate, I think, but don't quote me on that. Anyway, we can then choose holidays based around what wrecks there are to dive. There's a book I want, but I can't remember the name – but it has all the world wrecks, plus history...'

As he was enthusing about all the diving holidays we would

take together, my phone beeped in my pocket. I reached for it and read the message on the face.

'So that's James eh?'

It was from a number I didn't recognise. I was confused by it and assumed the message originated from someone in the pub. I sat up away from James and looked around.

'You okay?' James asked. The phone beeped again before I could show him the strange message.

'Quiet now, you don't want to upset your boyfriend. Sit back.' I did as my phone told me but still I looked around, which prompted James to look around with me.

'What's up?' he asked.

'Oh, nothing, just… oh nothing. So where are we staying on holiday?'

James re-engaged with the sprawl of holiday paperwork on the table and again I looked at my vibrating phone.

'You look particularly beautiful today.'

I looked at the fire and then looked around and finally I spotted Mark standing at the bar surrounded by friends. He was detached from their conversation as he was staring at me. When our eyes locked he raised his beer. I nodded in reply and my cheeks rose in colour.

James interrupted me, 'Seriously what's going on?'

'James, do you remember me telling you about Mark? Tatiana's boyfriend? Really good looking and rich and successful…'

'Yeah, poor bloke.'

'Haa haa!'

'I was referring to dating Tatiana, but go on.'

'Well, Carolanne told me ages ago he's breaking up with her and now he's over there at the bar.'

'Is he the one texting you?'

'Yes, but I have no idea how he got my number and… don't look, he's coming over to us.'

Mark had left his party and was walking towards our table.

It was the first time I had seen him out of a suit. He was wearing dark jeans with a tight black V-neck jumper over a white shirt. His eyes were a piercing black and framed by his strong cheek and eyebrow bones. His black hair flopped around his face and as he got to a foot away from our table he combed it away from his face with his hand.

'Olive, it's so good to see you.'

He came behind my chair and leant down to kiss my burning cheek.

'And you must be James, perhaps?' Mark grabbed James' hand and shook it without looking at him. I noticed James' quizzical look as his hand was returned to him.

'I came over to say a quick hello and I'm sorry I can't stay otherwise I would join you for a beer,' Mark said.

'Hey, mate, stay if you can,' said James, 'we're not going anywhere as beer plus fire means I'm here for the duration.'

'Tempting but I need to go.' Mark's tone of voice was slower than James' which made James sound childish in comparison or alternatively, it made Mark sound patronising to James, I couldn't decide which way round it was though I suspect from James' snarl that it was the latter.

'Aah, leave the cold behind and join us,' James generously offered.

Mark cocked his head at James. 'It's so tempting, honestly James. I could think of nothing better than to stay in the warm with you and this gorgeous lady but unfortunately, I have a rugby tournament to train for. So, as I said, thank you, Jim, but I said no.'

'Er James… and okay.'

Mark nodded and he returned to join his friends who were also preparing to leave for, I assumed, a rugby training session in the snow.

'Wow, you couldn't mistake him for a ray of sunshine, I'm even feeling sorry for Tatiana now,' quipped James.

'Don't say that. He's just got commitments. I admire that sort of drive and determination in a person and Tatiana doesn't deserve him.'

'Steer clear Olive. He's interested in himself only and trust me, from what I've seen, Tatiana and Mark deserve each other; it's the order of things.'

We left the pub soon afterwards as I was irritated by James and James was too hungry to soothe my upcoming tantrum towards him. I was not interested in having lunch so we parted and I left for the cold walk to the station. It was not far and I wanted to enjoy the crisp winter's day snuggled in my cream goose-down ski jacket. Part of my journey took me along the Thames river path and as soon as I was walking along it I heard the fast paced sound of running boots. Instinctively I turned to face a potential attacker but instead Mark was running to catch me up.

His breath was frosted as if he was smoking one of his cigars. His black sports jacket collar was turned up around his neck, but the very tip of his ears were red as they were the only part exposed to the chilling air. He smiled and tried to catch his breath before saying in a hurried manner, 'I waited for you to leave and only saw your friend go, on his own, I then looked all around and finally spied you walking along the river so I chased down towards you, which is not easy as this path is icy. I almost fell twice.'

'Oh I'm sorry, this is just a prettier way home and my friend James prefers any homeward path that takes him via a burger van.' I smiled away my nervous joke which had by-passed Mark.

'I'm surprised he let you walk alone... but I'm here now.'

Together we walked along the Thames path. The sun shone as brightly as the snow on the ground and I watched his frosty breath dance as he talked to me about his life. He seemed to relax and on a couple of occasions laughed with me about my escapades with various customers.

'...Honestly Mark, I can tell the nationality of the person

by the way they ask for things or complain about London; for example, an American will always tell me that everything is done so much better in the United States of America, anyone from the Middle East tells me they know my boss so that I give them a bigger discount and anyone from Britain will moan – but would never complain – I could be showing them a ripped rug and they would tell me it's delightful but behind my back moan to each other how awful it is!'

'Ever thought about the diplomatic service? Not sure I could do your job – being polite to ignorant people isn't my thing... 'Madam, do you want this rug or not? If not then leave my department'. Do you ever get fed up with these people?'

'Not really, in fact it's part of my job I really enjoy. I get to meet so many interesting people and I just love people-watching and observing their joy in finding the perfect rug for them bought in a quintessential English store, and I'm part of that. I doubt they remember me when they step on their living room rug but maybe, just maybe, they do.'

'Oh, they'd remember you Olive.'

As we approached the entrance to the underground station for the final part of my journey home Mark turned to me.

'Do you mind if I don't take you to your front door and just to the station? I'm sure you know that I'm not with Tatiana any more. She was just hard work and... well, listen to your friends' version first but bear in mind that sometimes it's just not meant to be.

Afterwards, if you don't want to lynch me then maybe we could see each other again?'

He looked down at his feet then looked back to me, once more looking through my eyes.

'You make me happy. I like you Red.'

On the train home my phone buzzed as soon as I left the underground for the overground section of my journey. He had texted me three times:

'I want to see you again.'

'Let me know when you are free as I can't stop thinking about you.'

'Remember to let me know you are home as you agreed.'

All three messages twirled my stomach into excited knots and froze my brain to think only about him.

For the next few months I met him in secret. He took me to rooftop restaurants, to restaurants in London parks, to restaurants that were only lit by candlelight. We met on his lunch breaks and we met after work – just to 'brighten his day.'

'Tell me what you're up to today,' he would begin with at our morning phone call. I was usually in bed when he asked this and he was usually just out from a breakfast meeting having been at work for at least an hour.

'You ask that every morning.'

'I know, I'm sorry but I just like to picture you in my head, what you're wearing, what you're doing, who you're seeing. Silly really but it makes me feel I'm with you.'

'That's sweet. Well it's Tuesday so it's a late shift. I'm not due in until midday so I'll eventually get up.'

'Get up? it's 8.40am, I've been up since five! Get out of bed lazy lady!'

'As I said at some point I'll get up, go to work. Probably have my dinner break about five. I'm due to see James today for my break so...'

'No, no, no, you're my girl. I've not seen you since yesterday and that was only for a thirty-two-minute lunch break – not that I'm counting. No, tell James a rug emergency has loomed and you have to fly out to rugs-R-us world to sort it out. Then meet me and I'll take you to Quaglino's for cocktails...'

'Mmmm, working til eight with a thirty-minute break but nice idea. Sorry, but I promised James. How about after work?'

'Busy – I can only do five.'

'Mark don't be like that. Yesterday you said you weren't free all day so I made plans.'

'Gotta go. Meeting in five. I'll see you sometime.'

I put the phone down and felt too agitated to stay in bed. This agitation morphed to anger by the time I got to work.

'This isn't the first time he's done this. He's like a sulky child sometimes, always wanting his own way and to hell with anyone else,' I said to Sally, a friend who worked in the next department from me. I had paused there just to vent to her before I went into my department. That way I was calm before I met my manager.

'Well, personally, he sounds a handful, wants you at his convenience not yours, doesn't want you to tell anyone you're seeing him – weird Olivia, as it's been three months.'

'We're trying to be kind to Tatiana, my flatmate.'

'Typical bloke, all about them. Men just want it their way or no way.'

'How's Jon?'

'Tosser – our fifth anniversary on Friday. I'm not going to mention it just to see if he forgets, then about 8pm I'll present him with a card and a sad face and watch him squirm. Might even get a present just to rub it in. Tosser.'

I walked on to my department. Clive had his head in the books but looked up at me then pointed over to the staff cupboard which was rammed full of roses of every shade of red and pink.

I creeked open the door and the intense sweet rose scent filled my nose and down my throat. One small card poked its tiny head from one of the blooms.

'Sorry Red. I'm grumpy when I'm not around you. May I take you out tonight as you suggested?'

'Aah how sweet!' squealed Sally 'Look everyone he's bought her like a billion roses!' She shouted out to my department. Then in my ear she whispered, 'Take it from me, he's a keeper!'

'Yes, yes he is,' I smiled.

CHAPTER ELEVEN

The time leading up to my diving holiday was spent in my staff cubby hole in earnest pursuit to pay James back before we left. As the time approached it was clear this wasn't going to happen as my shopping list to fill my suitcase ate away the money I owed him.

'James, sorry, sorry, sorry. I know I still owe you £98 plus the taxi fare to the airport, whatever that maybe…'

'…and back.'

'…oh yes and back.'

'It doesn't matter, Olive, I'm not in any rush,' James said on the phone one morning.

'That's a relief as unfortunately my landlord is in a rush for the rent and so is Mr Credit Card who is insisting I also pay him back. James, everyone wants a piece of me but my bank balance is as thin as a used Rizla paper.'

'You sound like you're at work. Having fun?'

'As always. Month's-end figures need to be done and Clive said, other than himself, I'm the only other person he can count on to do them – hark me, guess this time next year I'll be ruler and chief of this store.'

'Ha ha, then we'll all be on the staff discount list!'

'Of course! Anyway, being in charge makes a change as usually all I'm in charge of is making my own coffee! Hang on, I think that's Mark?'

'Shall I book the taxi for ten? The flight isn't until two – I think.'

'It is Mark, it is!'

'That gives us about an hour to get there, plus check in.'

'Aah, how sweet, he's looking for me. I think I'll just watch him look. Ooh! Now my phone is beeping.'

'Olive, 10am?'

'"Where are you?" it says. Ten is great. Gotta go. Luv ya.'

I opened the door just as Mark was staring blankly at the counter.

'Ta da!'

'Wow, what are you doing in a cupboard?' he said.

'Stock taking.'

'You're actually sitting on a footstool.'

'Helps me count! What can I do for you?'

'Just needed to see you.' He looked tired, his eyes were dragged down his face by his frown.

'Work is crap. The project we've been working on and thought was complete isn't. I don't know, just needed to escape and see you.'

'I'm here, I'm always here for you Mark. You know that.'

In the corner of my eye I noticed my computer screen go blank; all the month's figures had vanished. I leant back in to my cupboard, 'ctrl-alt-delete, please work, please work,' I whispered.

'I need a break,' said Mark.

'Ctrl-alt-delete, why aren't you working? A completely blank screen. Please come back!'

Panic kicked my chest as I realised the whole stock figures for the entire year had disappeared into the ether above my head.

'It's fine Mark, please everything will be okay,' I said whilst randomly tapping my key board.

'Can I take you away this weekend? Paris. Just you and me. I did some research and I know you're on leave next week – you may thank the indiscretions of your assistant – it'll be the break I need and we'll have the whole weekend, just you and me.'

'Aah, I'm so sorry Mark, that sounds amazing but I'm away on holiday. I did tell you; James, diving, booked before Christmas, remember? I'm really sorry but I can't make this weekend because of it – can you see a bald-headed man behind you by any chance?'

I edged my way around both Mark and his romantic offer in search for my manager who could claw back my figures.

'Can you not cancel it? I really need you and I need a break. I think I've lost this project. I'm so stressed that I can't breathe. Please, Olivia, I'm asking nicely.'

'Erm, no, I can't cancel, I can't really. Don't look like that, you're making me feel sad too but it's all paid for, sorry but… one second… Clive!'

'Please, I'll reimburse any money you've paid out. It's been such a shit week and I really need you right now. Olivia, I can't put this any other way, I need you.'

'But it's all arranged Mark.'

'Again, I said I need you Olivia, can you not hear me? Please, I'm now begging you, just cancel it.'

His voice had risen with each sentence and his soft eyes and hardened to a glare.

'No Mark, I won't cancel. Mark please don't walk away, it's all arranged… Clive can I grab you?'

'I know it is Olivia, but as I said I need you far more than James,' he said with deliberate force, 'I admit I'd forgotten about your little trip. Please Olivia, this weekend to Paris is actually all arranged, I mean that. I wanted it to be a surprise. We are staying at Le Grand on the River Seine, we will be dining at l'Auberge and we will enjoy all the romance Paris can throw our way. I really want to show you how much you mean to me, but if you don't feel the same then well, let's just say, I get it.'

Mark leant in closer and said, 'Maybe I'm not what you're looking for but I have a feeling you're everything I want. You're beautiful, sweet and you understand me. I know you do. I suppose what I'm trying to say is: come away with me to Paris. I need you, James does not.'

Clive was at my side by the time Mark had finished his corporate speech. He walked away leaving me with questions of priorities in my head. The first of which had to be a computer that needed a slap from my manager.

Of course, I plumped for the romantic weekend away with Mark. The choice was easy, one made easier by a further phone call from Mark urging me to go away with him.

Of course, James was amazed and bemused at my decision and I was sorry the moment I uttered the words that I wasn't joining him. I resolved that I had at least fought for my holiday with him, but Mark is my partner and he had arranged this weekend just for me so why should I choose James over Mark?

'You'll receive a cheque directly from Mark, I promise, and it will be far more than you paid… look at it as spending money,' I said to James.

'It's not the money I want to go away with but you! I'm sure Chris would be made up to jump into your seat so no need for your keeper's cheque book – tell him I don't want his money.'

'Don't be like that James. I know I'm being a shit right now but it's not his fault, he just wants to treat me. He's so unhappy at the moment. No, don't huff at that, he really is. You should see him, he works so hard and any spare time he has is catching up with emails or making frantic phone calls because something has gone wrong and something about crisis meetings and… James – please look at me.'

'Come on, the man who runs an empire in the sky is at crisis point and he then decides to go to Paris? Rubbish and you know it.'

'He's put a lot of effort into this weekend for me and it'll be the first time we'll have been away. I want this so much James. I know he's the one for me and I have to invest time with him right now. He's like a little lost lamb, stop groaning, he is and he really needs me. It makes me feel special that I can help him. He's trying so hard.'

'Get away, you're telling me he organised a whole week-end conveniently on the week you're supposed to be away! Well, if he did then, of course, that phone call to his secretary must've taken ages!'

'I'm really sorry James. I can't say any more – don't look away, this isn't my fault and we can go again anytime and…'

James shook his head again and instead of his usual peck on my cheek he grabbed his duffle coat and strode out of our coffee shop without saying goodbye.

Guilt for James? Of course. Excitement for a romantic weekend to Paris smothering my guilt away into oblivion? Of course. (All answers start and end with an 'of course' – an easy deflection from responsibility.)

Each day leading to the weekend I daydreamed about our trip. As I sat at work or at home in my armchair or lying in bed I indulged in watching what my imagination drew for this city: I could see tall Parisian buildings with Parisians cycling by. They all wore berets, some had garlic hanging around their necks but most were young women cycling with flowers in their front baskets. I watched Mark laugh with me along the River Seine and I watched him stare into my eyes over coffee and croissants at a Parisian café which overlooked a medieval square. I did not know where our hotel was as I had no idea of the geography of Paris but I imagined it to look directly over the Eiffel tower, the Louvre and the River Seine. I could hear his laughter but, essentially, I could hear Mark tell me timidly that he loved me, that he would treasure me all my life and that he was finally happy now he had found me.

I packed Friday morning with all the new clothes that Mr Credit Card kindly lent to me on the understanding that one day I would pay him back.

Mark was due to pick me up at 4.30pm and I was perched at the end of the yellow corduroy armchair eagerly waiting for the doorbell to ring so that I could rush into his arms and away we go. The pick-up time came and went and by 5.30 I was calling Mark as I knew our flight was at 7.50 from Heathrow. There was no answer and by 7.05 I finally received a text message from him.

'Late due work. Paris not going to happen today. I'll pick you up early for a morning flight instead. Sorry, sorry, sorry, but the crisis happened and work calls. I guarantee I'll make it up to you. Just trust me.'

I sank back into the armchair frustrated and angry and by 9pm I was in bed waiting for my alarm at 5am in anticipation for an early pickup.

In the morning I returned to my perched position and waited for the doorbell to ring. By 7am I was texting Mark to ask what time I could expect him for our flight and indeed, what time was our flight? As the morning slipped by my story of a Parisian romance was being chiselled away. By 10am the morning stroll along the Seine followed by coffee in the square broke off. By lunch time I feared my lemon dress dinner date was going to be ripped out. I rang and texted Mark and by 12.15 I could feel tears dripping from my face taking with it the mascara I had applied so many hours ago. Finally, at 1.47 Mark answered his phone.

'Where are you?' I shouted, 'Thanks for ruining my weekend! I'd be diving at the bottom of the sea if I hadn't agreed to come on a romantic weekend away. So much for romance; so far I've seen the inside of my living room!'

'Olivia, stop shouting I can explain, I couldn't get hold of you to tell you that everything has gone tits up, literally five months of work has literally gone down the toilet. I'm sorry, Olivia, and I'm sorry to say that if you want to be with me then you need to understand that, as much as I hate it, work sometimes has to take precedence over life. I don't like it and you don't like it but that's the way it is – Yes? Now I'm still here from the day before. Our team had to put in an all-nighter – we literally haven't left the office to even shower. All I've eaten in the last twenty-four hours has been Chinese takeaway at eleven last night. I'm knackered, hungry and what's worse I stink.'

Mark paused and I could hear the background banter with his workmates over whether he stank or not.

'I know you're disappointed and really I'm sorry. I promise I'll make it up to you, I'm just stuck here,' he continued. 'Let me make it up to you. I'm almost finished but I can't make today as I really need to sleep. Please understand and let me take you to the Wolsey for breakfast?'

'Breakfast?'

'How about this: I'll sacrifice sleep for you and I'll be at yours for around ten tonight and we'll go out whenever we get up, sound good? We'll spend all day together, we'll go for walks, read the Sunday newspapers in the pub just as you enjoy doing. Good, yes? I'm sorry again. I hate the idea that I disappointed you but if you want to be with me then this is the price – hopefully in time you'll see it's just a small price... Yes? Say you agree with me...'

'Mmm, it'd better be a good spot by the window.'

It was 2.07pm when I put the phone down which was seven minutes after James and Chris took off from Luton Airport for my diving holiday.

At 4.11pm Interflora arrived with a dozen red roses and a teddy bear holding a card with a heart and the words, 'I'm sorry' written across it. I hugged the bear and decided it was indeed a small price to pay for a lifetime of cuddles.

Mark did turn up that evening but we did not go for breakfast at the Wolsey as Mark wanted a lie in until 11am. We did spend Sunday together but we didn't go for a Sunday walk or find a pub to read newspapers. Instead Mark watched TV for hours.

Conversation with Mark was kept to a basic level whilst he relaxed in my flat. In the silence of watching Sunday television I caught myself looking at the clock and wondering how James was getting on – if he'd found the dive centre yet? If the next day dive had been planned? I thought about whether he was lying on a sun lounger by the infinity pool and perhaps contemplating drinking a cool beer whilst basking in the sun. Was he happy or was he still angry that his best friend had abandoned him in favour of a man who was slouched in grey tracksuit bottoms watching *Can't Cook, Won't Cook* and who hadn't spoken a word for over an hour.

At one point I wondered how long it had been since Mark had blinked as the muscles in his face appeared to have disappeared; his forehead, eyes, cheeks and mouth were all slouched upon his face. The only part of Mark's body which moved was his chest as he breathed in and out again and again and again.

I too, hadn't spoken for an hour other than to say I liked Fern Britton. I was bored in my flat, which was made worse by torturing myself with the comparison of where I could be. By three o'clock this boredom changed to anger. After I had painted my nails 'deep azure', I started to fidget with frustration; I even attempted to clean the flat which, at any other time, was a task beyond my interest and ability – especially as my nails were freshly painted. This sparked some reaction from Mark.

'I hate your flat, always have done,' he said.

'Mark, my flat may be one up from a Beirut prison cell but I don't care – I'm bored and I need to escape its confines where, thanks to you, I've sat in squalor for the past forty-eight hours and you – you have managed less than fifteen. But hey, thanks for pointing out you hate my flat. Move your feet you're squashing Tatiana's cigarette boxes.'

Mark found life in his legs and jumped to his feet.

'You're right, once more. I'm sorry.' He grabbed my face and held it captive in his hands. 'Listen I leave in one hour. I'm meeting the guys at five and I'd love you to meet them, yes? Wear your blue jeans with that silky top of yours. And put your hair up. I like it that way.'

'Seriously?' I said. 'That's what's on offer? The pub?'

'Come on my Red, I know I've screwed up but let me take you out to meet my mates so they can be jealous at the catch I've caught.

'Don't look angry, we've discussed this – it's work. If you don't like it then you need to find someone who doesn't have such a demanding job – teacher maybe, how about a boring accountant? He'll be home by five. Can my Olivia put up with someone like that? Ah, that's better, I see a smile from my lady! Come on, get yourself dressed and I'll show you off.'

I pulled myself away and got dressed to meet his friends but I was still angry that my weekend had dribbled away to a pub drink and so I adopted a sullen pout for the final hours of Sunday as punishment to Mark.

His friends were the same type of men I had met on countless occasions at any London club; they were mainly overweight, they were all wearing jeans, a white shirt and a tweed sports jacket. Their laughter competed for supremacy in the bar with surrounding polite conversation. Other people looked at our group with annoyed sideways glances when their conversations were interrupted by raucous laughter.

Mark finally declared to his clan that he needed to get back home to prepare for a meeting in the morning. As we left the bar Mark turned to me.

'They like you, they think you're hot.'

'I'm surprised as they probably said all of two words to me. Oh, and I would have appreciated the odd acknowledgment from you.'

I was, however, slightly surprised at their approval as the sullen pout I had before entering the pub had turned into an angry grimace by the time I left.

'I'm not returning to your flat,' he said bluntly. 'As I said, the only reason you don't have a rat problem is because even they refuse to enter that hole.'

'Don't then.' I looked away from him as I didn't want him to see that I sympathised because even I didn't want to return to the nicotine-stained ashtray I reluctantly called home.

'Ah, come on, please cheer up Olivia. I know you are still angry with me and I'd be angry if I were you. I'm embarrassed by how things have gone so wrong over the last week.

I'm genuinely really worried that I might have upset you. I need you and I can't have you living where I can't see you whenever I want, I'm asking would you like to stay with me?' His left hand pulled my hand towards him,

'I don't know, I have nothing with me for the night.'

Mark smiled and drew me nearer, 'No, not the night. I want you to stay as long as you like Olivia.'

Those few words made my heart beat faster than any twinkling star shining upon a Parisian glass of champagne. The sky above me was a murky grey, cloud covered the night moon but I didn't care and I no longer cared that my diving holiday with James had been replaced by a pub drink. I was going to live with Mark.

It took me my one week's leave to pack my possessions and move from Baker Street to Embankment. Tatiana said very little and Carolanne kept reassuring me that there was always a home here should I need to return. Even before I had left, the thought of returning seemed too depressing to contemplate and I resolved that should I have to leave Mark's flat for any reason then I would find anywhere other than a flat that had been decorated by a collection of smokers' lungs.

Mark's flat was a huge modern apartment which overlooked

the River Thames. The building appeared to be predominantly made from glass and steel girders. There was a window cleaner permanently employed just to clean the building and on occasions I would see him dangling from various apartments.

The lobby of Mark's building was swathed in beech wood which had been polished to beyond its natural shine; at times I wondered whether it was indeed fake and if it was just a cheap plastic which covered everywhere from the floor to the reception desk and beyond to the lifts. Naturally, Mark's apartment was on the top floor. Its front door was the same wood as the rest of the building but inside, the wood had been replaced by an almost white marble with a grey vein running through the stone. This covered all the floors apart from the bedroom which had a cream, thick pile carpet.

The apartment had a mezzanine floor with a balcony which looked down upon the living area and onto red leather sofas. Mark's modern art collection covered the whitewashed walls and, together with his sofas, these were the only splash of colour in his home. Outside great waves of colour from the sunrise or sunset were displayed in all their magnificence by the huge windows and doors which opened up onto a huge balcony. I often felt the urge to step outside whenever the sun came up to say hello or dropped to say goodnight. I needed to step out of the flat to breathe in the sun, which set over the tranquillity of the River Thames. The water and the sun were the only touch of Mother Nature in the elegance of the man-made structures surrounding me.

Opposite Mark's apartment lay London's business district and each side was the regal splendour of Sir Christopher Wren's architectural imagination, from elegant bridges to St Paul's Cathedral. I am not sure which I admire more: the pull of a genius's structural imagination or God's architecture. Over the years both have given me great comfort.

James returned from Egypt and within hours he had

contacted me to find out how my trip to Paris went. I couldn't meet him for a further week because of the move but finally we met at our usual coffee shop. I was too excited to let him speak first or even kiss me hello. I just wanted to share with him all that had happened and for him to feel some of my happiness that was spilling out from within me.

'He didn't take me to Paris, before you ask but, more importantly, I don't care as guess what! I'm no longer living with Tatiana and I've moved in with Mark… oh, hurry up and sit down James, just throw your coat down. Now, tell me what you think?!' I exploded. James seemed laborious in his movements. As he sat down he muttered, 'Mmm, if that's what you want.'

I caught the subtle shake of his head.

'So, it's serious then?' His tone was hard and his expression was dull and uninterested.

'Of course! I don't get it, what is the problem people have with Mark? He's sweet, generous, kind and oh James, he is so romantic – I've not cooked yet as he is always taking me out to these amazing restaurants. Two nights ago he picked me up from work – complete surprise by the way – in a chauffer-driven car (albeit from his work) and took me to 'Le Brams' in Marlow… Amazing!!'

James rolled his eyes then searched for his wallet to buy coffee.

'On me,' I said. 'My rent has halved since moving in as Mark is only asking for the bills to be paid for.'

'Really? The multi-millionaire is charging you rent? Nice!'

'On my insistence.'

'You can do better, Olive.'

'Better? How? He's rich, he's successful and I now get to live in the most incredible place in London that people pass and actually stop to read the inscription above the entrance of the building then look up to stare in awe. And I now live there… me!'

'Whatever, Ol. I need to make a move. I got Chris coming round later and I don't' want him thinking I live in a pigsty cos I don't' have an inscription above my door, so best get back to clean up.'

'Now you're being childish. Snap back to being the adult, plus I know you're lying as I know Chris is in Wales at the moment so instead come to my new flat and tell me all about Taba and all I missed.'

'Do I have to? I've managed to dodge Tatiana all these years so I'd like to continue by dodging Mr Sunshine.'

I detected a hint of a smile beneath his beard.

'Don't worry about Mark. He's not there as he has a corporate golf weekend and won't be back till Tuesday.'

'Away already? Love really is a happy garden of togetherness.'

I know I could have retaliated but I didn't have a defence and I didn't want James to sully my image of Mark and his apartment. I wanted to keep them both on the top rating programme I had playing in my head.

I saw Mark every day for the first week then, for the following three months of living with Mark, I saw him only five times. When I did, he promised that when a particular project was over and various weekend commitments had been accomplished then he would take me away somewhere and he would treat me to something special. He didn't elaborate on where we would go or what my special treat was but it satisfied me for those three months; especially as, contrary to James' scepticism, at the end of these three months Mark presented me with a gift. It was still wrapped in the envelope it had arrived in. I tore open the wrapping paper to reveal my own Coutts credit card with my name engraved in tiny letters beneath Mark's bank account number. I looked up at Mark who was grinning with pride. His dark eyes squinted from the Saturday summer sunrise light that filled our bedroom. I was still in bed when he gave me my present and as soon as it was lying in my hand he gushed,

'It's yours. Go out for lunch, dinner or even breakfast on me. I thought you needed one as I know that little job of yours doesn't pay well and now maybe you can cut down your hours and shop to your heart's delight.'

Mark seemed so pleased with himself:

'You can buy clothes and whatever, in fact I have a summer ball in a few weeks' time, and it's at the Imperial War Museum so it should be a laugh seeing all the artefacts decorated. They're usually a laugh so come, and buy yourself something sexy but elegant. I like black dresses, yeah, maybe a tight black cocktail dress. Actually no, make it long with a slit to show off your legs. A bit like that blue one you've got, but black.'

'It comes in black,' I replied.

I wanted to hug him and scream, 'Thank you, this is the best present anyone could give me,' but instead I kissed his cheek.

I calculated, whilst fondling my credit card and Mark cooking his full English breakfast, that I would be the perfect girlfriend: I would listen calmly to his woes, wait on him whenever he was home, always be available for work functions and now that I had access to a perfect wardrobe then I would dress beautifully, just for my Mark, just the way he liked.

CHAPTER TWELVE

My life altered considerably after receiving my credit card. I continued working at Liberty's but on reduced hours from Monday to Wednesday. Mark conceded that I enjoyed working and so what was the necessity to leave?

I no longer went to London clubs as it meant going by myself; James hated them, my sister was never available, Carolanne had started seeing Toby, an accountant for KPMG (but who had aspirations to brew his own beer by the coast). The only person left was Tatiana but she had replaced me with Renka and they trawled the London circuit together.

I wanted to keep my spare time for Mark; I didn't want to waste a drop traipsing round London night life that no longer suited a woman in her late twenties with a boyfriend. The only time I really wanted to go was with Mark, but he told me those nights were reserved for 'the lads'.

One thing certainly remained and that was my bust sucking machine which I used whenever Mark was away. But after nearly five years of having it, I had not increased in size.

To accentuate my paranoia, the other women in my apartment block were all glamorous, elegant and well-endowed.

I avoided these women, which was easy to do as if I did pass any wife in the hallway, lift or lobby then we would merely offer a cursory nod to one another (in the years I lived there that was the only interaction I had with anyone apart from Joan or Peter, the lobby receptionists, with whom I enjoyed a vacant chat about the weather or how the seasons were changing).

'If you're that paranoid then get a boob job, Olivia,' Mark said whilst replying to a stack of emails one evening.

'Where did that come from?' I asked.

'You think I've not noticed?' He snorted. 'Don't look hurt, I'm trying to help you. You don't like something then change it. In fact, you should talk to Patrick's wife; don't know her name, blonde woman.'

'Why? Has she had a boob job?' I asked,

'No idea but she's got a great pair, so you could ask her for her size or whatever.'

'Thanks for that comment. Now I just feel even more inadequate than I did thirty seconds ago,' I said.

'Well, like I said, do something about it. You don't want to be unhappy all your life do you?' he said casually, returning to his emails.

'But that seems so fake, so artificial to have silicone plastic stuffed inside me and trust me, I've thought about it. Is it not better to keep some things natural as Mother Nature designed me?'

'Aah, Olivia,' he began, 'you do talk crap when you want to and you're wrong. Most women I know have man-made boobs; even my mum has them. In fact, she declared that it was from having me that she needed the lift,' he huffed.

This was a woman whom I'd never met and according to Mark I never would as she lives in Switzerland with her new husband. To this day, all I know about her is she likes skiing, she has a boob job and looks many years younger than her twenty-year junior husband.

'I think they look better anyway. Man-made stuff usually does,' he continued, 'after all, us humans moved from living in natural caves to houses made by bricks and mortar that kept us both dry and looked good, plus they demonstrate how far man has come by the size of our house and so distinguish us from our caveman ancestors and other animals. You understand, Olivia? It's progress; another example: we have electric lights which is better than natural light – would you want to live without light in your home? No, I thought not. Another example: we have progressed from walking on two feet to trains, aeroplanes and cars. Now, isn't life better with the Porsche in the garage or would you prefer to return to walking everywhere?'

He looked at me and squeezed his forehead so that his eyes squinted at me; this was his cue for me to answer him.

'Oh your car is better than walking of course,' I dutifully replied.

'Well then, if we can live in a man-made world, which is fake and artificial, as you say, which in fact, improves our lives immeasurably in comparison to when we lived with nothing in the desert and had to fight for survival, then what is wrong with improving the way you look courtesy of the skill of a surgeon who, incidentally, is far more knowledgeable about this matter than you, Olivia, could ever hope to be?'

His black eyes squinted at me again.

'I suppose nothing is wrong.'

'I'm right, yes?' he locked my eyes to his. 'Well, I'm right aren't I? You need surgery then have surgery – look at me, Olive, not your skirt – I'm right aren't I? Come on my lady, I just need you to be happy and for you to feel your best. If it means surgery then so be it. I can afford it and it'll be money well spent.'

I nodded my reply,

'So look into it and I'll pay. In fact, Gary at work, his wife has had them done recently so I'll ask him where she went.'

Five days later Mark came home with a scribbled piece of

paper with the name and number of Mr Bancroft, a Harley street surgeon and 'He's very good, Mary. x' beneath his name. I assumed Mary was the name of Gary's wife and I concluded that if she thinks he's good, plus he works in Harley Street, then I didn't need to look any further or do any research on who would slice open my chest and squeeze silicon into the opening – he would do.

I managed to get an appointment for the following Friday which gave me a week to ponder over whether I really wanted to undergo major surgery on a healthy body. Part of my logic screamed that it would hurt and I'd be under a general anaesthetic with all the problems associated with it, plus there are horror stories of these procedures going wrong and my bust could look worse than before. Wherever I searched I found many emotional testimonies displaying disastrous surgery across the £1 magazines, alongside 'How to Lose Weight in Just 4 Weeks' and stories of: 'My Husband is Cheating on Me with My Mother'. However, the other half of my logic calmly played its trump card that Mark thought I needed it and he has gone to all this trouble to find me a surgeon, plus he is paying for it. That logic won and by the time the appointment came my nerves had changed to excited anticipation.

Mr Bancroft's office was at the end of Harley Street, close to a garden square where I sat for forty-five minutes prior to my appointment. I was early and I thought how pleasant it is to sit on a bench overlooking a small box maze. I smiled as the beauty of mother-nature was displayed around me. The tiny hedge leaves were vibrant green and spider webs adorned them, glistening in the sunshine that had emerged after the morning rain. Squirrels scampered around hunting for nuts and small colourful winter flowers proudly huddled together in friendship groups. In contrast, the garden was guarded by tall trees that had shed their leaves and appeared skeletal with long claw fingers sprouting from a thick grey trunk. I mused they were merely sleeping and all they needed were some fairy lights hung from their branches until the trees' own beauty blossomed to life in the next season.

Eventually I walked up the five steps to the shining black imposing door of the clinic. The receptionist buzzed me in and I entered a modern whitewashed waiting room. I was given various forms to fill in whilst I waited on a firm white leather chair. I was called in for my initial meeting which, according to my pamphlet, was a counselling session and to discuss the operation. I saw the nurse who informed me that she was also there to check my medical history and to discuss my treatment. She was wearing a nursing uniform fashioned from the NHS hospital of the 1940s with a blue matron cardigan. On her chest was a nurse's fob watch and her blonde hair was tied neatly in a low bun. Just by the look of this lady I felt reassured that this must be a highly trained nurse who cared for my well-being and who was deeply concerned for the success and safety of the operation.

She began by going through the 'peripherals', as she put it, then briefly discussed the breast augmentation. The remaining twenty minutes of my thirty-minute appointment was discussing the packages they offer. She explained that as I was going in for one operation that it would be less stress on my body if I combined other treatments such as, some ladies have a tummy tuck or liposuction. I explained I was a size six and I did not think I needed a reduction in fat, to which she gave a condescending grin.

'No dear, these were examples. It is merely to highlight that were you to consider further treatments then it would be beneficial to you both physically and financially to combine treatments together.'

She recognised my confusion and launched into where I could benefit from the surgeon's knife: I hadn't realised that my bottom sagged or that my eyelids drooped or that my stomach was not taut or that my knees were not symmetrical and my cheekbones were not clearly defined. All these imperfections could be corrected on my twenty-eight year old body by the skill and expertise of Mr Bancroft.

She finished by saying 'Whatever you decide upon we can arrange a financial packet to suit you', but she kindly went on to say, 'My dear, don't decide now, we will book you in at your convenience.'

She softly lifted my hand into hers and finally she smiled.

'Your surgeon, Mr Bancroft is waiting for you upstairs in room three. I will inform him that I consider you fit and well and therefore a suitable candidate for a breast augmentation. Well done, Olivia.'

I entered Mr Bancroft's office. The décor was public school headmaster's office with a huge Edwardian writing desk covered in important-looking papers, a computer and a green banker's lamp.

Mr Bancroft was a short, middle-aged man in a full tweed suit; his waist jacket also housed a fob watch and in his left jacket pocket were half-moon steel glasses. He stood to greet me and I detected a faint smile underneath a full beard and moustache.

The meeting was clinical: I showed him my breasts, he drew all over them, squeezed them, then drew some more. I thought how ludicrous that in any other environment this could be mistaken for an awkward, embarrassing foreplay but here it was a formal preparation performed on the awkward and embarrassed client. It was done in silence other than mumblings from Mr Bancroft. I felt obliged to offer some form of conversation;

'Your nurse mentioned I needed a knee lift, I didn't even know it existed! – I'm new to all this, so not sure about it all.'

'Mmmm, do discuss any concerns with your nurse, turn to the side please. Thank you. Do up your blouse, we are finished.'
He promptly turned away from me whilst I scrabbled around for my bra and shirt buttons.

He sat behind the desk and scribbled on my forms. He then gestured to the size and shape of implant that would be suitable for me. I blindly agreed with everything he suggested and he continued to write. He then told me about the process and I nodded in the hope he would stop and leave me in ignorance. He did stop and scribbled on my form some more. He then told me that it would be performed a week Wednesday at their Farnborough clinic. Did I have someone to drop me off and pick me up? Again I nodded and again he scribbled on my form. He then looked up and offered his hand to shake with a thank you and good-bye.

And that was that – I was booked into getting a new torso in less than a fortnight. In those twelve days, I packed my hospital bag on day one. On day two, I received a call from the clinic asking if I wanted to discuss any other procedure. I saw Tatiana on day three who was visibly envious but outwardly supportive and reassuring that I was doing a necessary operation to enhance my life by enhancing who I was. She then went onto explain that she was practicing meditation and seeing the world in a calmer-coloured spectrum. On day four I saw Carolanne and we laughed at Tatiana's attempt to calm her life down but the amount of coke she snorted robbed any calming benefit. Carolanne hugged me and told me I was as ridiculous as Tatiana's new diet of mung beans and cabbage – I did not need new breasts but she supported me anyway. On day six I told everyone at work that I was going away for three weeks for a boob job. Their response was a polite, 'Oohh, good for you.' On day seven I told Janet who declared down the phone, 'You're mad but what a surprise! In fact little sis, what I am surprised at is how long it has taken you to get one. I wonder how long it will be before you get more work done? Nice job if you can get it. Don't mind me, I'm just off to work then home for more studying whilst looking after a little boy.'

On day nine, I told James. We met on Sunday at our pub

and after telling him he responded by smacking his head into his hands.

'Ah, you're kiddin' us, you're mad Ol! Why for the love of God are you doing this? There isn't one thing you should change about yourself, nothing.'

'As Tatiana says, it will enhance my life by enhancing who I am…'

'Of course she would say that. She's as fake and as insincere as that statement. How much is this costing anyway?'

'£3000 plus VAT.' My defence was weakening further and crudely I tried to bolster it by saying, 'But Mark is paying so it's okay.'

'Mark, Mark, Mark! Why did I think anything else. It's like taking a chisel to Venus and adding Playdoh to her chest. There's nothing you should change about yourself, NOTHING.'

I grabbed his strong hands and looked into his green eyes.

'You're a sentimental carpenter but I love you for it.'

'I wish you did, then you'd stay as you.'

On day ten I received a final call from the clinic confirming the details of my operation and also to confirm that I was not interested in any other operation alongside my breast augmentation. I thanked them and said I wasn't but that I would see them tomorrow for my procedure the following day.

Mark dropped me off and said he couldn't stay as he had to get back to prepare for a major presentation on Thursday but that he would be there to pick me up the following Monday.

The hospital fashioned itself as a spa hotel, with a fountain in the reception area. It was difficult to relax as I was to face surgery the next day and I knew I was giving my only body to a relative stranger to do as he pleased.

In the morning the anaesthetist visited me, followed by Mr Bancroft. They both spoke in a soft soothing tone to reassure me that everything was scheduled for 10am and when I woke up I would have the breasts I had always dreamt of. But no amount of reassuring smiles could calm me; from the hospital wardens who loaded me on to the wheeled theatre bed or the nurse who held my hand as I was wheeled down a brightly lit lime green corridor into a waiting room. The anaesthetist introduced himself again then stuck a needle into my hand and asked me to count down from ten. My heart beat rapidly as I began my counting and I tried to scream that I no longer wanted to change two cup sizes; it was not worth the odds stacked against me, which threatened anything from deformed breasts to death. By number six my brain was slipping down a black hole and the small waiting room I had been lying in disappeared above me. I had been caught by the cosmetic fishing hook and I was to be dragged down the stream I had been paddling in and had no control where it was to take me. All I had was hope; hope that the spot I would be left at would be a serene lily pad and not a fishmonger's wooden slab.

I woke in a recovery room to the chimes of chatting nurses, and shortly afterwards I was wheeled back down new, softly lit lemon corridors to my peach room. I was groggy but relieved that it was over. I smiled to myself about my hypochondria as the nurses tucked me into my bed and gave me a few pills to swallow. Once they left, I sat in my bed and waited for a visitor, anyone to congratulate my return to the conscious world. No one came that day or the next day except for Mr Bancroft who checked my wounds and told me I would be able to see them before I left in two days. He allowed me to get out of bed and to wander around the hospital patient area; So, I shuffled down the corridor in my silk kimono and slippers, ignoring my tender torso.

In the café area I met two women who were bandaged across their face in exactly the same way. I couldn't describe these women as the bandages covered their faces but one was blonde and the other a brunette. The brunette caught my eye and stopped her conversation with her friend.

'We have both been in exactly the same car crash and had exactly the same wounds afflicted upon us or at least that is what we are telling everyone when we get home.'

I smiled and shook their hands, 'Hi I'm Olive, I've just had breast augmentation.'

'I'm May and this is Sally. Both face lifts and I can't wait to peel off these bandages and see twenty-something me staring at forty-something me.'

'Wow, exciting. I think I'm looking forward to seeing my boobs but I'm nervous, Mr Bancroft is showing me either Sunday or Monday.'

'Don't be, sweet pea; Mr Bancroft is a miracle worker.'

'Miracle worker,' echoed the blonde.

'I will only use him from now on. I have used others but I think he's the best; he's done my boobs twice. He's done a tummy tuck, eyelift and he's just done our facelifts. I had a Mr Turner for my lipo and Sally, you've used Mr Turner for your eyelift and you had him for you boob job.'

'Yes, I also recommend him but Mr Bancroft just has the edge I think. They are both on my Christmas card list but Mr Bancroft will be doing my arms – I'm going ahead with my arms in a few months.' Sally lifted up her arms and squeezed the small amount of drooping fat.

'I can't live with that and I think it's getting worse as I get older.' She then turned to me.

'Is this your first op, sweetness?' Her voice was muffled by the white bandages that stroked the edges of her bruised lips.

'It is, but probably my last. I was just small and wanted to be bigger and my boyfriend paid for it,' I said.

'Nice boyfriend! Keep hold of that one!' Sally squealed.

'Trust me sweet pea, as you get older this hospital will be your retreat, the receptionists will become your friends, the nurses will become your confidantes and your surgeon, your God; and the person taking you to the altar will be your boyfriend or your husband. If you want to keep a man then keep your looks and to keep your looks will be in the hands of your surgeon not God.'

'And why not?' interjected May. 'Why should beauty be confined to just a few years in your life? And I mean a few. When we are teenagers we haven't the confidence to display what we have nor do we have the money to afford the style to show off our young self, but by our mid-twenties we have matured into our beauty as Mother Nature designed, plus we have the confidence to display it in all its wealth and by our late twenties to early thirties, we've got our man then...'

'Then it's gone! Gone by thirty-five at the latest!' continued Sally, 'Women have probably shot out a couple of kids; they have saddle bags, baggy boobs and bags under their eyes. They don't have time for the hairdresser and when they do they opt for a sensible cut to match their sensible shoes. Fine lines have spread across their face and their saggy stomach begs for stretch draw string trousers.

'And do you think the husband sees his young bride as the idol he caught all those years ago? No! Because he's no longer looking as his eyes are directed right at his twenty-five year old secretary who doesn't have a wrinkle on her smooth, tight, toned body.' Sally was triumphant in her conclusion and banged the table for dramatic effect.

'I'm twenty-eight but maybe in years to come I'll reconsider,' I said vacantly as there was little I could relate to in their berating of aging women.

'You should, sweet pea, because the stigma of thirty-five is close by and your boyfriend's secretary is coming up at the rear; she may only be at school at the moment but she's coming and she's coming for your man and she will be the one he suddenly spends all his money on.

'Plus, why not enjoy beauty? Keep it going, why confine our looks to our young life? It's what we've done. I know you can't see May underneath this white hospital mask but trust me she's stunning, as stunning as she was when I first met her back in the seventies,' Sally banged the table again.

'Ooh, thanks sweetie and you are as gorgeous as when I first met you and Jon is a lucky, lucky man to have you.' May then turned to me. 'You'll be back,' she said.

I smiled and made my excuses to go. I thought about their advice and wondered if that would be me in twenty years' time, perhaps with Carolanne to remind me that I'm beautiful and that Mark is a lucky man to love me.

On the Monday Mr Bancroft returned with a nurse and unpeeled my bandages to reveal my pert solid round breasts. There was bruising and scaring just beneath the breast and a red scar line leading to my nipple but apart from this they were huge, far larger than I expected. Mr Bancroft reassured me this was merely the swelling and they would reduce in time.

Mark picked me up at 5pm and drove me home in his new racing green TVR. I sank down into the cream leather seats, the engine clicked on and rumbled, vibrating my seat, then we roared away. The powerful engine threw two people along the road at our top speed of 113 miles per hour. We raced over the tarmac, braked forcefully into bends and just skimmed around corners. As each traffic light threatened to turn red to spoil our speed, then the accelerator pedal was pounded harder and we brushed through amber lights just as they turned red. As cars approached ahead Mark eased to the other side of the road to check it was clear then he changed gear and we screamed past the blocking car then squeezed back onto our side of the road with only a Rizla paper gap to spare from the oncoming traffic. And all too soon we were home.

Carolanne and James said very little. Those at work nodded their approval. Tatiana huffed and commented they didn't look natural as they were too round but it was Mark's reaction which reassured me I had done the right thing:

'Fantastic,' he said as I revealed them for the first time once the bandages were finally removed and the swelling had receded. 'Fantastic, Ol, really fantastic. They're just what I envisaged, just what I wanted for you. You see, I was right, right all along.'

It was two in the morning and we were both in bed, He was lying with his toned, muscular arms behind his head and I was kneeling in front of him to fully display his new piece of art. The bed side light gave an amber glow to the white silk bedroom. Mark sighed and then looked up at me. His black hair drifted over his dark eyes.

'I'm right about you aren't I, Olivia?' He paused and nodded to himself. 'Yes, I know when something is right and that's you. I need you and you need me so let's make this a permanent contract. Let's get married.'

He looked at me for my answer but a chill tickled my back. I covered myself up with the duvet as I felt exposed to the morning air and I didn't want to be naked at what I envisaged should be the pinnacle of my romantic experiences; a flash moment in my life which would lead to a memory I could relive whenever I chose. In that memory I did not want to see myself naked having just discussed the size of my breasts. A loving gesture felt crass.

'Are you asking me to marry you? Should you not tell me you love me first then ask for my hand in marriage on a summer's evening beside a babbling brook?' I smiled at him to show I was joking.

'I don't need to tell you I love you Olivia... The words "I love you" are secondary to what I feel for you, they're just a by-product of a thought of love to reassure the other. I don't need to tell you; you know I do, and I know you love and need me. But if you need to hear it then, yes, I love you Olivia. I love and adore you very deeply.'

'I do too!' I gushed out clasping my duvet firmly around my body. He looked at me still with his hands supporting his head upon the pillow. Moonlight mixed with the electric light and the cold night atmosphere whispered we were alone in this apartment and alone in this vast city; we were the only ones in this country and the only ones living on this planet. I shivered and he gave me his hand to rest my hand in.

'Well?' he whispered. 'Are you going to say yes or no?'

'I don't have a ring,' I shivered again, 'Shouldn't there be a ring?'

He squeezed my hand tightly momentarily hurting my fingers as they compressed together.

'I need you Olivia. Will you marry me?'

'I suppose so, yes,' I whispered.

I did not sleep that night. Instead I listened to the rasping snore from Mark who had fallen asleep only a few moments after receiving my, "Yes". I no longer hugged the high I had from my operation and I no longer felt the brief kiss of romance from Marks' question of marriage. Instead I was confused at the low feeling I sank into whilst lying in the bed.

The next morning I followed Mark around the apartment whilst he went through his morning ritual. I was waiting for another discussion about getting married but he seemed oblivious to my search. He was eating his cornflakes in the kitchen, standing by the coffee machine that had faithfully given him his morning Columbian espresso shot. Bizarrely, I envied the machine – it knew its role and delivered its assigned daily product. It did not need to question its being and it was content just sitting in the kitchen until such time that it would be replaced by an updated coffee machine.

Mark finally broke the silence whilst munching on his cornflakes.

'What? What do you want?' He spat his question at me and slight flakes of soggy corn landed on my chest.

'Oh nothing,' I replied.

'I'll be late tonight.' He turned to throw his half empty bowl in the sink. I winced at the gloopy mass of cereal dripping from the bowl ready for me to scrape out and throw into the bin once he had left. He strode out of the kitchen to the hallway to grab his coat.

Just before Mark left the apartment he always looked into the gothic mirror hanging next to the door to smooth his hair and readjust his tie. As he began this familiar ritual I grabbed this moment to blurt out:

'So…the wedding, er, should I start planning?' I was clenching my dressing gown waiting for a look of dismay at the effrontery of my question. I was also waiting for a snigger of 'Darling, I was only joking.' I ventured further.

'Maybe September this year I thought? September is a good month to marry as it's usually a warmer, sunnier month than August. I could have a quick look at venues.' I paused to allow him to reject my suggestions but again he did not flinch so I meekly continued:

'Or maybe Christmas, whatever you prefer. Or we can wait, maybe wait? After all it's so soon from well, last night and you asking me and so maybe just wait. Yes, just wait, okay.' My voice trailed off as he opened the front door but as he joined the outside world he turned back at me.

'No, September is good, whatever you want. I know the Crayford's had a wedding planner. Don't know the name but she organised the Tote's wedding. And Olivia, don't worry, I meant what I said, every word. I love you and you're the first woman I have ever said that to.'

He winked as he left and I remained in the hallway spinning in love. But, within minutes of Mark leaving, my mobile phone rang and it was your mother who screeched down the phone:

'He asked me, Ol, he asked me!! I'm getting married!!' Janet screamed her joy at me.

'Seriously? Ah, so am I,' I replied.

'Eh? You too? Spooky. Though you don't sound too happy?'

'No, no I'm overjoyed,' I mimicked her delight but, truthfully,

I was overwhelmed at the coincidence but also frustrated that my news had been eclipsed by Janet's.

I listened to how Colin had arranged for them to go out to some secluded spot by the River Thames in Richmond but it had rained heavily so they dived into a transport café along the A3. However, Colin was momentarily overtaken by intense love for her so that he had to ask her right there over their sausage sandwiches whilst waiting for a bowl of chips. Apparently, the owner had overheard his proposal and he gave the chips for free. They laughed that they only had the money for one bowl but if they had known it would be free they would have ordered two. But Janet didn't care as it was the most romantic day of her life and she was going to marry the man she loved.

They were getting married in August and that was all she could focus on now. I copied her happiness from the 'Oh my's to the 'I can't believe he's asked me,' that sprinkled through Janet's phone call. I evaded her questions on my sedate proposal but instead I focused on the wedding day, boasting that I already had a wedding planner.

'I would expect nothing less Olivia.'

'She has organised the Totes marriage at St Catherines – you saw that in *Hello* magazine? Well that was one of hers.'

'*Hello* magazine you say? No wedding day is complete without a social photographer to help finance the day – those romantic multi-millionaires. Unfortunately, it's just me and a WH Smith clipboard and pen.'

Within a couple of weeks I met my wedding planner. She was a tall lady in her late forties, called Kiki, she had been married and when her marriage broke down she received enough money from her ex-husband to give up work and start her own business. She had been organising wedding days for fifteen years and she rattled off a list of famous people forwhom she had created a perfect day. The fact that only a handful of these wedding days had led to a marriage was irrelevant.

'If you can cherish the first day of your marriage then you will always share one perfectly happy day together. What a great and binding gift to have with each other no matter what subsequent days give,' she said whilst leaning on my balcony overlooking London. I looked at her quizzically and she continued her rehearsed script:

'A wedding day is a perfect memory that displays to your family and friends that you are in love. At that moment no one, can question this, including the parents and close friends who are the first to voice their opinion over your life choices. Am I right?' She winked. 'They can't question anything especially if they are sipping champagne and eating oyster canapés... am I right or am I wrong here? Trust me Olivia, your wedding day will give a lifetime of happy memories and it will be talked about by others for years to come, right? And look at it this way, one beautiful memory is worth hundreds of cloudy memories, correct? Leave it to me and you will not be disappointed.'

She left and I was left feeling confused as to my role in the planning of my wedding but it soon became apparent with the subsequent emails: I was to be presented with a number of options about various aspects of the day but the one I was to choose was the one Kiki recommended.

The only input I gave was for my wedding dresses. I chose three, all designed by McQueen. But even here my involvement was limited. I had an initial fitting for each dress but as a bust was made of me they did not need to see me until they were ready for a final fitting. I had lost a bit of weight by the time my wedding day arrived but they merely made the odd adjustment; for example, they cleverly padded the bottom area to fill out the dresses and give each one the ideal silhouette. It also meant I had my own portable cushions wherever I went.

As summer approached I was reminded of Colin and Janet's wedding day when an invitation fluttered through my front door. The invitation was handmade and I confess, Mark and I were impressed by Janet's craftsmanship. It was made of translucent peach paper adorned with individually cut butterflies and tiny flowers, all made from school tissue paper. When I opened the card more paper butterflies floated over my lap and on to Mark's red leather sofa. Although it was irritating to have to get the vacuum cleaner out to clear away these stray butterflies, the invitation did give me a June day smile.

She had not included a wedding gift list and when I rang her to ask she just said she knew her friends were as broke as she was, but as I had money then she would be very grateful if I could contribute to the 'Colin and Janet wedding fund'. I asked Mark and he wrote a cheque for £500 and I sent it off to her. A few days later she rang to thank me for funding her whole wedding.

'Seriously?' I exclaimed,

'Don't start, Olive,' she paused.

'But it costs less than a cheap weekend away! Oh, find the funny side, Janet,' I interjected.

'No, I won't react, I know you, I know you think that comment is funny but I'm happy so, today I can rise above it.'

'Of-course I'm joking, but actually, in all seriousness, hopefully the fact we've paid for your wedding lightens the blow that I'm afraid Mark can't make it, he has a business trip to Singapore. Really sorry sis, but I'll be there.'

'The blow is light – thank you for letting me know; he has already been scrubbed off the wedding list.'

'Thanks for understanding I can explain…'

'No explanation needed sis. Our loss is Singapore's gain or the other way round depending on the way you look at it,' she concluded.

August 21st arrived. I wore a Prada black and white panelled, off the shoulder fitted dress. As I dressed I thought about what £500 paid for when the shoes I was wearing to her wedding cost nearly that much.

The reception office was in the white Edwardian council building in Leatherhead. The room was elegant with wood panelling all around and happily that August day was bright and warm as it had emerged from a week of torrential downpours. I took my seat amongst the other guests and I was slightly alarmed they were all carrying wellington boots. A lady with a round cheerful face came over to my row and leaned over to my chair and presented me with a green pair of boots with dried mud all over them. I must have looked shocked.

'Oh I'm sorry, I'm Claire,' her voice bubbled. 'I only have these spare in the shed and Janet said she couldn't get hold of you to bring some boots and then she said you probably don't own a pair,' she smiled. 'We did giggle at that, sorry! But please take them with my love. Ooh, she's here, I'll let you be. Lovely, to meet you!'

I forced an appreciative but confused smile then placed them by my side. I turned to see Janet walk in with you, a handsome eleven-year-old boy dressed in a suit and converse trainers. You held my beautiful sister's hand and walked her down the aisle. Your mum was discreetly shaking in a pretty pale yellow 1960s' dress with embroidered daisies around the hem, which she had found in a charity shop. Her bouquet was made up of three white gerberas and a further white gerbera clipped into her hair. Janet looked radiant and her innocent happy face was reflected in the look of the groom.

When Colin turned to see his bride for the first time I caught his look towards your mother of intense pride, happiness and love. His eyes shone with tears which threatened to fall upon his cheek and his smile was for Janet only. His gaze did not waver from her as she walked down the aisle. As the vows were read their hands clasped each other as if their fingers were twenty little people who had found each other after a long absence. My heart forgot that it was here alone and it forgot it felt lonely amongst strangers, instead, it sang for my sister.

After the ceremony, everyone piled into one another's cars. I crammed into a Ford Fiesta and I tried in vain to protect my dress from wellington boots, which were thrown onto the laps of the passengers in the back seat. It became apparent why we needed the boots when we parked at a farmer's field owned by a friend of Colin. I delicately tumbled out of the car and saved my fall by grabbing the jacket of the driver who helped me to my feet.

'Best put those on now,' he said, 'it's a muddy walk to the reception.'

I followed everyone else to a small open field which was about the size of a junior football pitch. Around the sides Janet and her friends had spent the previous day hanging Christmas fairy lights, which were lit by a generator. This generator powered a burger van and a music system. Hanging from the string of fairy lights were old camera pictures of Janet and Colin when they were children then pictures of them together on holiday, at parties and just generally in love.

Bottles of wine adorned school chairs and bottles of beer sat proudly in tubs of ice. There was cheer all around and people danced to music and drank wine and ate burgers under the stars and the bright, full moon until early hours of the morning when the sun crept above the horizon to join in on the celebrations. I no longer felt awkward in a designer dress whilst wearing borrowed wellington boots and a borrowed orange fleece jacket. I forgot how Mark would have scoffed at my family's wedding and instead I joined in and kissed my sister and my new brother and I wished them a long and happy marriage. I mostly danced with you, my sweet Jason and laughed at your attempt to teach me how to do a 'pop' or 'bop' dance.

When it was time for me to leave I rang James and told him what a wonderful wedding I had attended. It was a joyous celebration for a marriage that I believe has just celebrated its' twenty-fifth anniversary. I wish I was able to have joined you and your parents in celebrating their marriage. I wish I could have eaten burgers in your parent's garden and danced to 1990's music and reminisced over that day with their friends but alas, I spent that day looking at the sky and imagining the fun you all had.

CHAPTER THIRTEEN

JASON

My dad came around early – too early for a bank holiday Monday. I was enjoying a rare lie in when the door clicked open. My initial thought was I need to get back my temporary key I had given to Dad when I had moved in two years ago, and my second thought was I need to cancel the breakfast date with my new girlfriend, Jessica.

Jessica left through the front door and I went out the back to help Dad sow the green beans which he insisted I was to water every day (he ignored me when I told him that these baby seedlings would definitely shrivel away as their ancestors had done in previous years).

'You're a heathen, young man; these plants will give you great beans just for the payment of a few drops of water.'

'Naa Dad, trust me, the rent is way too low for the amount of effort I have to put in to house them,' I replied.

I offered a fork for my sixty-two-year old dad to turn my earth whilst I slouched into my garden chair with beer stains all over it from past BBQ parties.

'Dad, what was Aunt Olive's wedding like? I don't remember it.'

'Why would you want to know?'

'Just this letter I suppose, it's got into my head.'

Dad stood to his feet to ease his back;

'Well you don't remember because the gold invitation didn't invite you so you stayed with Hayley and her kids for the weekend.'

'Gold invitation? Was Willy Wonker guest of honour?'

'Many Wonkers were invited but strictly no children – would have ruined the look of the wedding. Anyway, the invitation was indeed gold, with diamanté studs that wrote out Mark and Olivia's name – the thing actually shone. As I recall, in a separate gold envelope were directions for the day; not how to get there but where we were to stand at various times and best of all, the colours we were allowed to wear. I say 'colours', it was either blue or white. Your Mother was furious with me as I wore my blue jeans with a white shirt. Apparently, that wasn't posh enough and she was worried it would offend the bride and groom, I'm afraid her protests were met with apathy. Ooh, pass me one of those, Jay.'

I handed Dad a mid-morning beer.

'Okay, so go on. Was it worth the wedding planner's invitation? What was it like?' I enquired.

'What you'd expect from the average £100,000 wedding.'

'A hundred grand?'

'And remember this was just over twenty-five years ago. At the time your mother and I didn't have a penny to our name and we were sitting on reception chairs that cost more than our monthly outgoings. It was iniquitous, but then my bank balance wasn't Mark's or in fact any of the guests there, so I was a lone scoffer. I actually bruised that day from the times your mother bashed my arm to tell me to shut up.

'The whole wedding was at the Fairbank stately home in

Hertfordshire. It's a grand place owned by the Fairbanks. You might remember in the papers recently, about the son who was in line to inherit from his father, Lord Fairbank? The young lad had died of a heroin overdose and his twenty-nine-year-old body was found decomposing in a ditch off the M3. His older brother had committed suicide some years earlier so, now, the estate will pass to Lord Fairbank's new child with his 'twenty-something'-year-old Scandinavian wife. Let's hope the five year old doesn't follow the same path of his poor rich brothers else the Lord will be in a bother as to what to do with the estate. I doubt he could father many more children, especially as he's already eighty-three but you never know what other illegitimate children of his are out there to claim their dead dad's fortune.

'Now, whether it was the curse of the sixteenth century building or whether the guests were all on a revenge attack against their liver, but most were absolutely inebriated by midday.

'So, for example, when Janet and I walked into the Elizabethan entrance, we were initially taken aback by how beautiful the hall was. There were priceless paintings of Fairbank ancestors staring down at the huge hallway with century old armour guarding a six-foot-tall stone fireplace. The hallway was flooded with multi-coloured light from a huge domed stained glass window. But instead of wallowing in the opulent elegance of this place and marvelling at the English craftsmen of yesteryear, your mother and I were greeted by a young woman in a blue dress unconscious at the bottom of the staircase. One breast had fallen out and it was on display for drunken men to laugh at as they passed her. No one attempted to help her and when we tried she told us to 'F-off'. I stress, she was literally the first person we saw and it was midday.

'We were ushered round to the back of the manor and offered champagne about every five steps that we took by anxious, nervous, young waiters. I was put off the champagne and canapés quite early as when I reached for my first, some bloke pushed passed me and the waitress to vomit red liquid in an indoor tree pot which was standing between us. A ficus tree as I recall.

'Outside was as beautiful as indoors but, thankfully, in comparison, there was calm. This may have been due to the magnificent view of the Chilton Downs which was displayed in all its glory from the marble balcony that led down to a topiary maze. This 200-year-old maze began the grounds for the estate and there was a gentle summer breeze that greeted us, however, I suspect the calming effect of outdoors could also be the fact that the outdoor bar was some way from the balcony, so very few people were there.

'Anyway, we had been ushered outside to wait for the arrival of the bride. The ceremony was to take place under the sycamore trees but first Janet had to walk in her heels to the helipad about half an acre away as Janet had been coaxed into walking Olivia down the aisle.

'This was the last thing your mother wanted as she was still angry over the snide remarks Aunt Olivia taunted us with down the phone over how cheap our wedding was going to be and afterwards an insincere, 'well done on being able to pull it off'.

'She didn't say that in her letter to me. She said she loved your wedding.'

'She did? Well trust me Jason, she's just mellowed in her old age. So, about three days before the wedding we were tempted to call in sick after Olivia rang to patronise Mum over whether she understood exactly how to greet her from the helicopter and how to walk her down the aisle.'

'Seriously?' I exclaimed.

'Yes. She arrived by helicopter which meant there was a chorus of 'oohs' and 'ahhs' as she flew overhead and careered her way down to the helipad. It was as if Neil Armstrong was landing on the moon all over again but this time my new wife was there standing on a black piece of cardboard to greet him as he landed. Poor Janet, nobody thought that where she was ordered to stand meant she would be blasted by the prop wash of the blades whilst your aunt landed. We all couldn't help laugh at the spectacle, me included, at your mother's expense. She was wearing this blue and white spotty dress which wrapped itself around her despite all your mother's valiant attempts to tame it back down her legs. But the funniest part was, when the blades stopped turning and the air stopped churning, the dress had settled back down but your mum's hair was still wrapped around her face and when she walked down the aisle it looked as though a wild poodle had dropped on her head. In contrast, I have to confess, your Aunt looked pretty good.'

'Go on then Dad, impress me; what was she wearing?'

'I don't know, don't ask me, the standard uniform every bride wears – a white long dress. At least your mother bucked convention and wore yellow. If you want more detail your mother will be here soon; she's popping in on the way back from the library.

'Actually, one thing I do remember well: Mark was wearing a white suit and he was also really drunk. As Olivia walked towards him he didn't look back and didn't acknowledge her until she stood adjacent to him. I suspect it was because he needed the world to stop spinning before he gave a cursory nod to his bride. When the vows were read it seemed like all he wanted to do was get back to the bar; he repeated his vows in a monotone voice and nodded when they were announced: 'Mark Mathew Hopkins and wife,' then he cheered to his work mates who were sat directly behind him and pulled Olivia forcefully towards him as if she was the UEFA cup he had just won. Ahh! The doorbell, your mother's here. No more beer for me then.'

Mum sat on the spare garden chair after brushing it down then sat on her jacket to protect her skirt.

'Really Jason, you're thirty odd, it's about time you bought some decent garden furniture; John Lewis has a sale on. You must go and see.'

'I promise Mum, it's next on my list of stuff to buy after furniture for my house, a new car, and a decent holiday.'

'Sarcasm gets you nowhere. I'm only thinking of you and I'm worried about you. You seem so down at the moment. Are you getting enough sleep?'

'Nope but no change there. Anyway, I was asking Dad about Aunt Olive's wedding. What do you remember?'

'Drunk and stoned guests rolling about at the Fairbank estate – darling, you must visit, it's stunning; the manor is open to guests during the summer.

'Don't roll your eyes. Anyway, I also remember being whipped by helicopter air and almost breaking an ankle trying to walk behind Olive who looked amazing thanks to the trickery of the designers. She did look amazing, don't you agree Colin?' Dad nodded over his gardening fork,

'She was very thin, but her dress cleverly hid this. It was a silver white dress with crystals around the bodice. The dress hugged around her bottom then flared out to about a two metre train; she looked extremely shapely thanks to the padding the designers had sewn around her bottom and hips to fill it out.

'I, on the other hand, looked like the wicked witch of Oz who had just arrived via a typhoon and because I was driving home I couldn't drink, so I also felt like the school teacher checking on a teenage school disco.

Oh my! And the engagement ring Mark had presented her with a few weeks before the wedding; I hadn't seen it until then. It was a red diamond surrounded by cluster diamonds. Apparently, a million carats of diamond are mined per year but only twenty carats are mined per year of red diamond. That is why they are so rare and expensive and the deeper the colour the greater the rarity and subsequent cost. Olivia's was blood red.'

'Where was your engagement ring? I don't remember ever seeing it.'

'My engagement ring was a new washing machine, don't laugh, that machine lasted for years and in any case, I prefer the simplicity of my simple gold band and wrapping your father around my other fingers.' Mum winked then continued.

'But Jason, oh, the guests were so rude! For example; after the wedding breakfast in the banqueting hall, there was a group of men piling wine glasses in a tripod stack. The glasses would fall and break and as I watched I could see the waiters getting angry until eventually one brave lad came over and asked a man called Edward to stop.

'"Why should I?" this fluffy blond-haired man barked back to the waiter.

'"Please sir, we don't want to spoil your fun," the waiter said, 'but we have to collectively pay for all breakages, plus it's dangerous for both you and us, who ultimately have to clear the broken glass away."

'This reasonable request was met with a nonchalant shrug from Edward and a few bursts of dismissive laughter from Edward's audience.

'"So you, a waiter," he replied, "are asking – no, demanding – I cease my engineering experiment in stacking glasses, when I'm the guest of the couple who have paid a vast fortune for the use of this place? And that very couple have not asked me to stop and if they were here they would probably be aiding my waterfall experiment. In addition, waiter, they have paid, not only for the use of this place but for everything and everyone in it so, as a guest of the beneficiary I can, by default, make full use of its contents in any way I see fit and that includes breaking glasses and watching you clear it up. As for you having to pay for the broken glasses then may I suggest you get a better job?' He paused, 'Oh no, you can't. You have an education given to you off the back of a state funded fag packet."

'Edward then deliberately smashed another glass and his audience applauded. Sadly, the waiter walked back to the kitchen. However, as a lesson Jason, the only reason I remember Edward's name was because I saw his face on the news some years later. He was Edward Tawn, the man who defrauded Merissa Bank by investing the pension pot in dodgy stock for his personal gain. All employees lost their pension when the stock plummeted and he was sent to her majesty's hotel for a number of years.

'There were some decent guests but they were mainly Olive's friends, such as her Liberty work mates or lovely Carolanne. She was there with Toby her then boyfriend (and now husband). We still see them from time to time as they don't live too far from us. Carolanne was her usual chirpy self, albeit far too pretty for me to stand too close to,' Mum giggled.

'Carolanne has always been effortlessly cute, her hair seemed to bounce in time with her chatting and no matter how well I thought I looked that day I always paled into obscurity when I stood next to her. That day she was wearing a blue tulip dress with yellow stilettoes. I coveted those shoes all day, they would have gone so well with my blue polka dot dress. But that aside, we had fun together and later that evening we all stood in awe at Olive's change of dress for the evening reception. Olive's second ensemble was a long sequined gown that hugged her tiny frame but, thanks to padding and her newly padded bust, your aunt looked like a Disney heroine.'

'She looked like a silver-fish, Janet,' Dad exclaimed.

'Oh what do you know Colin, you didn't even notice when I had my hair chopped last week.' Mum then whispered to me, 'Two inches was slashed from the end of my hair and he didn't notice! Anyway, as if two dresses weren't enough, at midnight Olive changed again for the fireworks over the lake. This time she was in a short, slinky, silk, midnight-blue dress with a velvet wrap. Your aunt looked like she had been commissioned to model the *Vogue* edition on what to wear at an extravagant wedding. I liked all her outfits but I was envious of the wrap as it was really chilly watching the fireworks and your father hadn't bought a jacket for me to steal. Did he tell you he insisted on wearing jeans? Jeans to a wedding, what was he thinking?!'

'Give up, Janet, it was twenty-five years ago!'

'Well, if you had been dressed appropriately then I could have had your jacket.'

'I kept you warm by cuddling you throughout the display and, in any case, it was a blessing as you wanted to go home, declaring you were too cold.'

Mum nodded and added.

'We were also quite bored by the end of it as there were only a few heads still on this planet and those who were still sober, like Carolanne and Toby, were waiting for the strike of one when they could slink away. Everyone else were boring drunks.

'I couldn't relax at this wedding; it was a show which had many impressive dance moves but very little passion.'

Mum sighed and put on her gardening gloves to help Dad. I half-heartedly offered to help but thankfully was met with a plea for two Earl Grey teas. This I didn't have, so instead I offered two filter coffees. Before I left for the kitchen I asked about their honeymoon.

'Where else?' Dad smirked, 'two weeks in the Maldives.'

'That was one good thing for Olive; at least she could go diving, even though she was on her own,' interjected Mum.

'And where was your honeymoon?' I asked.

'A week in Devon and it was beautiful; just you, your father and me – very special memories.'

Mum and Dad left just after lunch and I was left staring at the doomed beans. I returned to my beer-stained garden chair and started on Aunt Olive's manuscript before Jessica arrived for her replacement dinner date of Chinese takeaway.

Olive

Twenty-five years ago...

The honeymoon was strained as Mark was visibly bored and by the end of the two weeks this boredom morphed into frustration and then into anger at everything – from the way the sheer voile curtains billowed throughout the night, in tune with the lapping sea surrounding our private beach hut, to how the waiters would dare to clear away his glass and impertinently replace it with the same drink before he had completely finished the first.

I managed to escape him for two hours each morning to dive in the clear waters of the Indian Ocean. I saw turtles, sting rays, sharks and a rainbow of electric colours from the majesty of the underwater kingdom.

These dives were the greatest show I had watched underwater but I had no one to share it with other than to secretly text James of the days' sightings. He always wrote back that he was excited for me and he would joke how he wished he was there with me instead of work. Mark purposefully ignored my exuberant offerings about the world just beneath our water hut. As a protest to me, he even refused to go snorkelling declaring that it was all boring, and he had seen enough in fish tanks in restaurants and who cares about fish anyway?

'The oceans, other fish, people who survive on fish, shall I go on?' I replied.

'Missing the point as usual. What I'm trying to say is this so called paradise is costing nearly fifteen grand; you know you can buy a house in the north for the cost of this holiday...'

'Honeymoon.'

'Whatever you want to call it. They can't even get in a decent whisky, but I'm supposed to be compensated by fish?'

He flopped back on the bed blindly searching for the television remote.

'How much longer of this hell hole?' he whined.

Apathy was creeping into our marriage and it was only day four of the honeymoon. Occasionally I asked if he would like a walk. He always refused, allowing me to wander alone along the silky, smooth sand with the gentle, clear water tickling my toes and the sun following me as my companion. When I returned to Mark, he was invariably sitting on the beach hut swing chair with his feet resting on our balcony frame. If any part of his body was destined to burn then his feet were to be the victim and naturally, after just a few days, his feet resembled lobster slippers which added to his anguish over his now hatred of my paradise island.

By day five, I increased my dives to twice a day. The second dive was an hour after lunch so I would sneak away by two. He didn't notice as by now he was reacquainted with his laptop – after just a week's absence he was back replying to work emails. Each day I would return just before five; he would ignore my entrance and continue to ignore me until I had changed for dinner. At that bewitching moment Mark Matthew Hopkins shrugged off his bad mood, turned off work and stepped out with his wife to find the bar.

'Finally something to do here,' he pronounced every night.

'Other than diving, relaxing and enjoying this paradise,' I replied.

'Exactly. Boring and complete waste of money,' he scoffed.

'A full moon,' I noticed, 'it seems larger here don't you think?'

'I don't. I'm trying out their rum tonight – given up on their selection of whisky. They're an insult to my taste buds. These people don't have the faintest idea what they're doing. Bring back the UK.'

'And back to your drinks cabinet in grey England.'

'Shut up, Olivia,' he said as he sat down on the bar stool and turned from me to the bar man.

He was not interested in anything I had to say and I had little interest in his monosyllabic offerings. But my honeymoon was blissful for the diving and the beauty of the island and I often wished I could relive those two weeks, but without my husband.

It was the beginning of October when we returned. I now had far more time on my hands as I had stopped working for Liberty's as, although I had become a manager there, Mark decided it was inappropriate for me to work as it was taking a job away from someone who needed the money and adding that I had worked for nearly ten years and I had contributed enough to the government's tax pot. I agreed. As compensation Mark increased the limit on my credit card.

I avoided Liberty's and I avoided my work friends. I didn't want to hear about their working days; all the interesting customers they met or the after-work drinks they'd had without me. I wanted to abruptly move away from my memories of the store and step into my new position as Marks wife, (I did eventually venture into the store after many years had passed but by then everyone I remembered had left).

My daily routine now consisted of organising Mark's social calendar, the daily running of the apartment and luncheon dates with friends. These friends were split into two categories: those I wanted to see and those I felt obliged to see for social politics. The former consisted of James and Carolanne and the latter with everyone else in my address book – otherwise known as my lunch friends.

I became very close to friendship group one and they too, were close to one another. Carolanne now regularly joined James and me on Sunday pub walks and if I could not accompany them (because Mark was home), then they would still meet. On those occasions my mind was distracted away from Mark to wondering how their day was treating them – perhaps a morning coffee followed by a pub lunch discussing a Sunday paper article then a leisurely walk along the river? It was difficult to bring my thoughts from their day to mine as the alternative was either being berated by Mark for not foreseeing something in his social diary that could have had, but did not have, calamitous consequences to his day or watching Mark snore on the sofa whilst watching a Sunday 1950s' western movie.

I did not recognise the specific switch from willing days to disappear so that I could spend precious few hours with my husband, to then willing those shared hours to speed up so I could enjoy precious hours without him. Fortunately, the hours without him were increasing every week and I came to regard Mark's apartment as my own and him as a guest in my home, interfering with my daily plans to meet friendship group two.

My lunch friends' lives were identical to my own and I met various sub-groups of the main friend group for lunch on most days. These meetings would start with the formal ritual of expressing, 'Oh hi, you look amazing! I love your outfit/shoes/hair/handbag!'

Followed by a cursory kiss before all were seated and the luncheon meeting began. The conversations with any lunch group friends were never a cohesive, flowing, engaging chat; more, who could monopolise the table the longest before another seized their opportunity to contribute an unrelated topic about their week. The key phrases that were thrown on to the exclusive, expensive and always exquisitely elegant restaurant table were: 'upcoming black tie event', 'feeling fat so I must not eat lunch', 'hubby has tickets from work for an amazing event', or if there was a direct competition from another lunch friend then, 'We are sooo lucky to be going to the event as tickets sold out long ago but hubby has connections from work.'

After a light lunch had been picked at then the meeting would enter the wine segment; this naturally led to the final part of the meeting of 'any other business'. This was the cue for the competition to rank up a notch to who could monopolise the group with tales that began, 'I was sooooo drunk...'

It was tedium with crudités. But I always participated as it broke up my day between shopping and organising. However, although I could not remember the specific stories from anyone, I always dragged away with me the essence of their tales, which was to describe a life that I perceived to be far more fulfilling than my own.

I learnt to battle the onset of feeling inadequate by boasting about Mark's achievements, promotions and all the work events I accompanied him on. I threw in the same phrases as everyone else and I accepted they did not listen to me in the same way I did not listen to them. If they had, then they heard a growing lonely life which was disguised by a glamorous, adventurous lie.

After nearly two years of marriage Mark instructed me to accompany him to New York. A wealthy Russian was potentially investing in Mark's firm and he needed to go out to secure the legal side of the union but Mark needed to woo him first to guarantee the investment. Mark wanted to demonstrate he was trustworthy and a wife was a necessary actor for that show.

I spent over a fortnight planning my wardrobe and buying the appropriate evening gowns for the events Mark had briefed me on. I always timed these purchases just before my lunch date so that I would be a few minutes late and arrive appearing flustered declaring, 'Sorry I'm late ladies but Mark has just told me about the gallery ball and I had to have this McQueen dress to go with the red sling backs I bought last week.'

Naturally this led to an outfit being pulled from the enormous box bag so that it could be serenaded by satisfyingly jealous 'aahhs'.

New York was important as it was the first Atlantic crossing I had made for Mark. I had not been to this city and I tingled with anticipation for days before I left. I bought a guide book as I knew Mark would be working for most of the trip. This leant a certain freedom to where I could go, but by then I was institutionalised to my 'working day' of shopping, so the landmarks I filtered from the book were Bloomingdales, Tiffany's and of course Fifth Avenue.

We stayed at the Roosevelt Hotel, close to the Grand Central Station and convenient for most shops. True to Mark's word he disappeared in the early morning and I spent my days shopping and waiting for his return. On the third day I returned early and dressed in an emerald green cocktail dress and silver stilettos. I sat for over an hour waiting for his return and when he did he stormed into the hotel suite declaring we were, 'late as usual!' I waited by the door for him to shower and change which took just under twenty minutes. I didn't say anything in that time for fear of fuelling his frustration but merely waited patiently for him. After these twenty minutes, Mark emerged and raced passed me, out the door and straight for the floor lifts.

'Jeez, hurry up woman. Did you not hear me that, yet again, we are late?!'

He said this at me, not to me, as if he was biting the air around my head and as a reflex I retreated into the corner of the lift. The past two years had taught me that it was easier to smile a scowl rather than to protest – sarcasm led to arguments and arguments with Mark lasted until I gave in and agreed he was right.

We arrived at the Russian's New York, Upper West Side home which was seven stories high and an immaculately restored example of 1920s' American architecture. We were there as Mark had been invited to the unveiling of the Russian's latest purchase. It was an Aveer Karesh painting of a view of Earth from the International Space Station. The Russian had paid $3.7 million for it and it was to be hung amongst the Russian's other collections from the same artist. The picture was displayed in one of the thirty-two rooms in his home. It stood alone in the empty room whilst guests surrounded it, eating canapés and drinking champagne. The room was connected to another whitewashed room which was also bare except for a dozen pictures hanging on the walls staring back at the spectators.

I did not see or speak to Mark for the first hour. I wandered around with my cocktail, occasionally smiling at other guests and waiting to be summoned by Mark. I could feel the usual event boredom upon me but on this occasion I was saved by a man in his late thirties. He was a short, plump man with a monk's hairstyle. His forehead was covered by a sheer veil of ginger hair. This fine ginger netting had been swept back in an attempt to hide the glaring white bald circle on the top of his head. This was the only obvious sign of vanity as every other part of him was understated from the baggy grey suit to the sensible brown shoes. From the way he stood and nodded at anyone around him he clearly had not paid attention to the protocol of being politely intimidated by those of a higher social ranking than his own.

'Another red head I see!' he said as I passed him.

'Strawberry blonde,' I whispered.

'Aah my wife would be impressed by your euphemism of our hair colour. She is a lecturer at NYU on English Lit. She loves it when people curl around what I see as fact. On this occasion I concede defeat; we are strawberry blonds. My name is Henry Brown and my wife, Amy, is somewhere here. How do you do.'

'How do you do!'

I shook his hand eagerly as I realised this was the first time I had spoken to anyone in two days apart from thanking a cashier for my purchases. Amy joined our conversation briefly but she kept disappearing to check her mobile as the babysitter for their nineteen month old had been trying to contact her on her phone but the signal was poor in the gallery.

Henry explained he was an NYU physicist and had pulled many strings to be able to get an invitation to view the Karesh collection. He explained the artist was exploring our position in the universe. He showed me a painting which was a series of telescope photographs, the first a black dot in the Earth's night sky. This was then magnified to show the colossal depth of the space in that dot. It revealed millions of stars and planets belonging to many galaxies in that one innocuous, tiny piece of the night's sky. Henry explained another painting of plumes of magenta, orange and yellow, and tunnels of smoke, which showed the birth of a star. Another painting was the back of a naked man looking up at the night sky with a flint in his right hand.

'This painting is poignant as it shows that even though the human race has been in existence for less than a breath from the universe, we have intelligence, curiosity and ingenuity combined with resilience to failure. It means we have progressed from animals in the Sahara, discovering basic tools, to venturing out into space – mainly due to the evolution of our cerebral cortex, but that's another story. Nevertheless, our knowledge is pitiful to what we need to know to venture further and explore deep space. For me, I sit in this juxtaposition that we've come so far, further than any animal living or that has lived, but we are still just insignificant clusters of atoms in a very big and encompassing universe.'

'I feel so small,' I said.

'That's the universe; look at it and the stupidity of us, greed… I don't know… fast cars and so on, are irrelevant in comparison to life.'

'I was always told that art is just a display of someone else's perception on life, but great art makes you think; this has, but I still feel small!' I said.

'Thank the universe. Now where's my wife? Ah, over by the window, please excuse me.'

Just before he turned away Mark was by my side staring at the two of us.

'I'm her husband,' Mark said.

'Hello, I'm Henry Brown.'

Henry offered his hand to shake and dropped it after a few long seconds.

'I do apologise, I was monopolising your wife's time by explaining the significance of these magnificent paintings.'

Mark gave an indignant stare.

'Have you enjoyed these paintings?' Henry offered a smile of friendship. 'I particularly love the symbolism of this painting; as I was explaining to your wife, how the flint represents the beginning of Man's true ability to search for solutions to what is initially perceived as impossible.'

Henry gestured to the painting as if gesturing to Mark to join in on the discussion, but I already detected the familiar glaze in Mark's eyes.

'It makes me proud to be a physicist as in my very small and puny way I feel I'm contributing to the advancement of the human race.'

'Of course you are. An amazing job you have. I have such admiration for you.' I offered. 'I think it's scientists like you who have made the important advances in our lives possible. Though I think my sister will contribute – thank a teacher!'

My attempt to lighten the air was then marred by Mark.

'I don't know why you think you're so important: who gets spacemen into space? Who gets rockets and spaceships to fly?'

Mark pounded these questions at a startled Henry.

'I'm not sure I understand the question but it's engineers and physicists and...'

'No,' Mark interrupted. 'It's governments who pay your wages but the government is paid by the money men, aka me and crew, so it's me who gets spacemen into space.'

I slyly looked at Mark and whispered, 'What is wrong with you? Shut up!'

I looked back at Henry with a crooked smile as my attempt to telepathically say I was sorry for the ignorance of the man I chose to marry.

But before I could apologise Mark grabbed me by my arm and yanked me away from a baffled Henry. He positioned my arm at an uncomfortable angle; it felt like my arm had defected to Mark's body and it was now pulling me by my shoulder ligaments out of the room and out of the apartment at a fast pace. I looked like a naughty toddler who was being pulled out of the toy shop by her parent for being an obstreperous and disobedient little girl. I can still see the rush of people's heads turning to briefly look my way as I flitted pass them.

As we approached the apartment building doors the doorman swiftly opened them and instead of saying good evening he said, 'Madam your coat?'

Mark spat, 'Get lost, she doesn't need one'.

The doorman hailed a taxi cab and I was thrown in and as soon as I clambered to my seat I stared at my shoes in shame to avoid the pitiful disbelief from a doorman whom I would never meet again. Mark slammed the car door and told the driver to take us to the hotel and thus began his admonishment for my behaviour.

'What are you, Olive? You're pathetic.'

He pulled at my chin so I would momentarily stare at him long enough for him to remind me how pathetic I was.

'Pathetic!' he said again. 'I was so embarrassed by you. How do you think it makes me look if my wife is not by my side and doesn't even look my way or speak to me all evening? I had to constantly apologise for you, saying, 'I'm sorry my wife is somewhere, oh, er, I don't know where though'? How does that make me look? An idiot that's what!

'I needed to introduce you to various people and their wives and where were you? Nowhere, that's where. And what's worse you couldn't be bothered to even check I was okay? Did I want a drink or whatever? No, you were too interested in talking to some other bloke.'

His voice had lowered to an angry punch that pushed its way

down my ear. All I could offer to try and diffuse his anger was a foolish, 'You embarrassed by me? I've done nothing wrong. But if you want me to say sorry to make you stop, then here it is: I'm sorry. You want to hear it again? I'm sorry, I'm sorry!'

This one sentence was repeated by me throughout each wave of angry spats from Mark which continued for at least ten minutes. Finally, Mark fell back in his seat to catch breath yet he solemnly continued in a tired whisper whilst looking outside on the New York streets, which were floodlit by a cold full moon.

'Sometimes I feel so ashamed you're my wife, the way you behave towards me. And look at you, that dress looks cheap, it doesn't even fit properly. You are cheap. But what else do I expect from a woman with your background. Yet I ask why? After everything I give you, I get nothing Olive, nothing in return.'

He sighed and closed his eyes as if he was embracing the punishment from the heavens for his stupidity at marrying me. He then suddenly opened his eyes and looked at me, his voice broke away from the whisper it had been to a rising roar; starting slowly then reaching a crescendo within two blocks.

'I saw all the other women and you're nothing in comparison to them. You look a mess, you are a mess. Why can't you be like the other wives? Why can't you dress like them? I suppose you can't; you're too cheap. You need to start looking better to make up for your ignorance in how to behave – in fact start now. Stop the car,' he shouted and grabbed my arm again. 'Go on get out and don't come back until you look like a woman should look!'

He then yanked me over his knee and pushed me out of the taxi.

'What are you doing, Mark? Get off me.'

I put my hands out to stop my fall to the pavement but the weight of my body made my arms crumple so it was my head that broke my fall. I tried to scramble up to try and reassemble some dignity but Mark was pushing my legs out of the taxi so I resorted to an army shuffle to try and escape.

'You deserve this, bitch…'

I heard the car door slam and saw the taxi pull away. I started to shake with mixture of humiliation, confusion and fear. I was still sitting on the floor whimpering to myself and not daring to look up in those first few seconds in case I caught sight of a stranger's pity. I scrambled to my feet and held my throbbing head and looked around me through the smudged view of tears.

There was no one around. Initially I was relieved by this, but it soon gave way to panic and a pathetic whimper of, 'Help!' I blindly started to walk down the street I had been thrown into. I didn't know where I was, I didn't recognise any part of any street – I didn't even recognise it as New York, but how could I have done? It was a city I did not know and I had only been in for a few days.

When I was thrown out of the taxi it was just after eleven and I spent the first part shivering in bewilderment holding my throbbing head and wincing from sporadic fires of pain. However, by midnight, I was, instead, shivering from the cold and holding my bare arms in defence of the night wind and stroking the bristling hair on my skin. Any person I did see I avoided, not from shame but fear of night prowlers. I was acutely aware that I was a lone woman in the back streets of a city wearing a tight cocktail dress and stilettos. Any subsequent defence in a court of law for my attacker would surely ask why I placed my head in the lion's jaw? So, when I heard heavy footsteps behind me I instinctively started to run.

'Noooo! Stop love, honestly stop! I just want to make sure you're okay?' bellowed a Scottish male voice.

He was now beside me walking at a brisk pace to keep up with my stiletto trot.

'I'm not going to hurt you. I've just been watching you for a little while. Please stop, I'm not going to touch you, I'm gay and my boyfriend is just over there, trust me I don't fancy you petal.

And I can see you don't have any money on you, though I love the Louboutin's!'

I stopped for him even though I had no guarantee that this was not just a lie from a lazy rapist with an eye for good shoes who couldn't be bothered to run to catch his prey.

'Right, if I'm out of line I'm sorry, but we've seen you walk this street twice and firstly, if you're a prozzy then you're wasting your time here as we're all gay, but if you're not, then what are you doing out at midnight in these temperatures?'

I replied by starting to cry.

'As I suspected, come with me love, I'll get you a coffee.'

I followed this leather clad man to an all-night café bar. I was now calm enough to notice how all the buildings around me were almost blue from the intense shine from the moon. I sat with him and his partner and I lied to this kind couple that I had drunk too much and I had left my loving husband at a party and I foolishly got lost. I said that at one point I tripped and hit my head but I was fine and I just wanted to return to my hotel and return to my husband who was clearly very worried about his exceptionally foolish wife.

I don't remember their names, I only remember how safe I felt walking next to them. They made sure that I could enter my hotel at this time and when they parted one of them hugged me and told me I was too beautiful to be so silly but if I ever was again then I should wear a coat and easy walking shoes.

As I approached my door my heart quickened but it was for nothing as the room was in darkness and when I crept in to the bedroom Mark sleepily muttered, 'You're back then.' I slid into bed and silently cried myself to sleep.

The next evening Mark returned with emerald drop earrings.

'To match your eyes my lady. And he signed. At last he signed the contract this afternoon,' he said sweetly.

I chose to take it as an apology and so I decided to stop crying and be grateful for this gift.

I've never worn those earrings and they still reside in their black leather box, inside a black leather jewellery box, inside a steel safe.

When I returned to England I saw my luncheon friends and I duly boasted about the wonders of New York.

'Such an incredible time… Mark spoiled me when I saw him but thankfully it was mainly a business trip for him, which allowed me time to explore New York to my heart's content.' I said.

'Amazing!' they all replied.

I didn't mention about being abandoned in an unknown city wearing the Louboutin shoes I had shown them before I left for this enviable trip…

CHAPTER FOURTEEN

OLIVIA

About twenty-two years ago

Three years into our marriage we moved to Surrey. The house had seven bedrooms plus the obligatory swimming pool. I had not seen the house before I moved in as Mark had found and bought it without telling me. The first I understood that the London apartment was no longer my residence was over breakfast on Easter Friday.

'It's on Cavendish Avenue; seven bedrooms, swimming pool, summer house with sauna. I'll be installing a gym above the triple garage but other than that everything is ready for you to move in – you'll like it. A big white building, newly refurbed, plus London Interiors in Holborn are choosing the furniture for you – though I'm sure you can choose the odd cushion if you want.'

All this Mark said whilst reading a newspaper article about the slump in oil prices. Eventually he looked up as I had not replied.

'You'll like it. It's on Cavendish Avenue which is the road to be on, the best; even getting a house on this street is difficult let alone affording one. It's definitely the type of place that ordinary people just look at and dream about having.'

Mark looked directly at me.

'But the little people could never achieve in reality,' he continued with a wry smile. I was distracted by a small dab of marmalade that had escaped from his toast and settled on his stubble chin.

'Seriously, the kudos you'll have from me buying this place means you'll be thanking your generous husband for the rest of your life. You don't understand now but you will. Matt and Steve play golf literally in that road – golf course – best in the country – on that road. They can't believe I've bought a place there.'

Mark paused and with a quizzical expression continued.

'Well? Are you going to say anything or just stare at your coffee mug? Anyone would think I'm sending you off to sea not sending you to a seven-bedroom house with a swimming pool on Cavendish Avenue – I'll say again, Cavendish Avenue, as you're obviously deaf to what I'm saying to you.'

His left eye lifted up pulling that side of his face to a crunch just beneath his dark hairline.

Mark was still wearing his plaid pyjamas at noon as his tribute to a religious holiday was to return home late then take church service in bed watching the TV.

These long weekends or holidays crunched my stomach until it ached as my apartment returned to him for these days. I avoided the rooms he was in or if I was trapped by him, such as now over breakfast, then silence with a smile was my guard tactic.

'Sounds nice,' I smiled. This released his face back to the stern expression it usually carried. He brushed away the marmalade which then smeared across his right index finger.

'Don't you want to look at it?'

His voice softened and became slightly childish.

'I tell you what, Ol, I know last Tuesday we argued and I know you're sorry.'

He leant in and pulled my hand towards his and gently stroked each finger in turn transferring the sticky marmalade onto my hands. His dark eyes sought mine and, when they were locked with his, he stroked my face transferring any residual mess onto my cheek.

'You know I'll always look out for you and make sure my girl has the best. You'll love it there and we can start fresh, just you and me in the country.'

His voice was as soft as a lullaby.

'How about I get you a new car? You'll need one and I want to buy my lady a new car. I think a Porsche will suit you.'

He lent in further to hold my face in his strong hands. It was a tender moment which I grasped and snuggled into, a moment which diffused the memory of his angry screams. At that moment I wanted to believe that it was Mark who held me and stroked my hair but the pressures of his job turned him away from himself to Mr Hyde. There could not be another explanation as how a man could be tender on a Friday but a spectre on the Tuesday – just four days before:

He had returned to the apartment on Tuesday night just before 10pm. I knew he was angry the moment he opened the front door as he threw his case to the right instead of taking it to his study. He didn't look my way but instead walked pass me as if I was a ghost he had not yet sensed in the room. I stood up as soon as he entered and patiently waited for him to speak to me.

Whilst he poured himself his Hennessey cognac, I secretly cancelled the call with Carolanne who had been telling me about James' new girlfriend. I silently closed the phone cover then stealthily placed it in my jean pocket.

'Who were you on the phone to?' He said in a monotone solemn manner.

'Oh, erm, no one.'

His face snarled in reply.

'Well just Carolanne,' I said, 'nothing special.'

There was silence which I foolishly tried to mask.

'James has a new girlfriend. I don't think I've ever known him to have a girlfriend, so…well, that's all it was, nothing special, really Mark, nothing.'

Time had slowed to a heartbeat straining to recover from a heart attack but, with the jolt of a defribrillator, time sped up to race ahead as Mark swirled around on his feet and grabbed my hair and yanked me towards the bedroom. I pulled on his firm grip to alleviate the sting from my hair follicles popping out of my head. When close to a wall he pushed me against the hard brick and held me there by propping me up, his left hand wrapped around my neck. I was conscious of the pain from the loss of hair but my main focus was on the pain I was inflicting on myself by involuntarily crying when I should have been breathing. By whimpering I couldn't breathe and so I would panic and splutter, gasping for air like a seaman overboard in a storm. Mark was hollering down my ear making my eardrum vibrate.

'You're a selfish woman only thinking about yourself.' He began, 'You're an ugly disappointment' was another sentence I caught between valued breaths. 'You're always here in my apartment lounging around calling your pathetic little friends… ugly… stupid… pathetic.'

I could only make out words from Mark's rant about my pitiful existence as my eyes began to pulse in time with my throbbing veins in the side of my head.

Without warning Mark threw me to the ground in the bedroom and my lungs pulled on the air for blessed oxygen. I wrapped my hands around my throat to comfort it and reassure it that once more, it could swallow air. Mark then left me in the bedroom to go back to his cognac.

He didn't speak to me for the rest of the evening and I did not dare to speak to him. Instead, I indulged in self-pity, berating myself that I was indeed pathetic and useless. I remained on the bedroom floor for over an hour before I crawled to the bed and hauled myself up. There on the bed I tried to ease the pain in my throat by stroking it, but my sobs caused my throat to vibrate and my head to spin, yet I could not stop my eyes from crying for a further hour.

As night crawled on I reflected on how this had happened again. I concluded that in some ways it was my fault; a year had passed since New York and in that time, I had learnt to slither into the background to avoid Mark's rants; sometimes I won and sometimes, like that night, I lost. Still, I admonished myself for not escaping sooner when I recognised the change in his eyes when he walked through the door; I could easily have escaped before he turned his attention on me.

My tears immediately stopped flowing when Mark entered the room and prepared himself for bed. I was scared and apprehensive so I quietly got dressed and slid in beside him but only when he was sprawled across the super king-size bed and his low heavy breathing indicated that he was in his slumber. I lay awake at the edge of the bed for six hours watching the blue night light from the city dance across my room. I wallowed in hatred of myself and reasoned that if I was not such a useless woman then I too would be sleeping as soundly as the man lying beside me.

As soon as daybreak knocked on my window I was up and racing to get dressed before Mark's 6.15 alarm went. When I looked in the mirror I could see the distinct reminder of Mark's left hand around my neck; the colour matched the red rim around my eyes.

I avoided Mark until he left for work forty-five minutes later and as soon as I heard the door slam I resumed the crying of the previous night until boredom of self-pity allowed me to drift off to sleep at midday. When I woke my heart was racing again as it was a text from Mark: 'Hi Hun, not home tonight. Should be back late Thursday x.' It read.

'Thank you,' I whispered.

My thumping heartbeat softened to its usual tone. I wandered around the apartment trying to ignore the pounding in my throat and head. I had taken tablets but nothing worked and even by Friday the pain was still tapping in my head stopping me from concentrating on anything else. Even when Mark was waiting for a reply from me over breakfast and wondering why I was so ignorant as to not be excited about moving to Cavendish Avenue, my head and neck throbbed in my thoughts, stopping me from processing what I was hearing.

The pain momentarily stopped nagging me when I was being held in Mark's arms over Good Friday breakfast. When Mark let me go he stroked my hair and stroked my face then held my hands.

'A new start my lovely lady, a new car and a new home. I'll give you all of this as you're my wonderful girl. Yes?'

His eyes were imploring mine to answer and I sensed desperation in them to know that I was happy and excited about what he had given me.

'Cavendish Avenue, Wow lucky me!' I duly gave to my husband.

I had rehearsed 'the loving wife' play many times and once more I held the script in my hand and performed for my husband. He in return was an attentive and cheerful audience. I reasoned that something on Tuesday merely upset him and when he arrived home he was upset so took vengeance on the one he loved; that was me. For that, I should be grateful. I also reasoned that I had cried for an hour on the bedroom floor then an hour on the bed. I had lain awake for six hours and I bore the pain of his anger for a further six days. I subsequently lived with a red neck for nine days but his anger had lasted until 10.23pm that evening, just eleven minutes. It was not in proportion; a snippet of anger for six days of anguish. I concluded I was being irrational especially as my happy husband had bought me a huge house on Cavendish Avenue with a new white convertible sports car. This car, with the number plate 'OL1 V1A' was waiting for me in the driveway when we arrived just three weeks later.

Cavendish Avenue was a long road; it needed to be to accommodate the enormous houses that resided in its coveted address. Although each house was the size of a country hotel they were difficult to see as they were all flanked by tall imposing gates and long high hedgerows protecting the residents from prying eyes. These inquisitive tourists, however, were few in number as both ends of this road were guarded by a security hut with a security man in a blue security uniform who was there to operate the security barrier owned by the company 'Security 4 U'. This name was branded across every lamppost, gate and even across the pavement in front of each house. It is the only company name which, over the years of living there, irritated me to the point of wishing to become a graffiti artist just to spray red paint over each banner with the tag 'bog off security'. Of course, this never happened as my red splodges would have ruined the immaculate look of the avenue. Red did not match the emerald green grass verge with each grass strand standing to attention. Nor would red have complimented the racing green hedges guarding the houses and red certainly did not fit in with the shimmering black gates closing off each house.

There were no pot holes or cracks in the pavement. If any work was needed on the road then the contractor was obliged to resurface that entire section to ensure the road remained an even, dark colour without vulgar markings which could make the road look like an old, withered patchwork quilt like all other roads in England.

There were no stray cats or foxes darting between hedgerows, no dog poo littering the street because no dogs were walked as there were no people along the road. If any resident had a dog then some employee would walk the dog in the acres of garden surrounding their house. Occasionally, a horse and rider trotted by or the odd tourist hiker cyclist tiptoed along but other than these people the avenue was empty, save for the residents who were comfortably ensconced in the comfort of their sprawling mansions.

I was now one of these residents; 'the wife in the country', and it was not long before loneliness came to live with me. Mark had deposited me at the house and the very next day he left for London and my old apartment and only returned to the house at the weekend.

I was left with my clothes in my wardrobe and my possessions scattered across the house by Anne, the interior decorator who had clearly struggled to find an appropriate hiding place for my mementos of Australia or the framed photographs of my life as these memories did not fit into the vision of each room. Most of my pictures and artefacts were placed on a shelf in my purple velvet dressing room. Even there, they were tucked in between my hanging evening wear and my 'autumnal colour' day wear. Others were conveniently lodged in hidden corners of the newly decorated rooms. These rooms were sumptuously filled with colourful accessories and vibrant furnishings. The hallway had a chequered marble floor with speckled gold leaf wallpaper framed by ornate cornices and coving. The modern staircase was made from mahogany and glass with swirling black metal separating each panel from the foot of the stairway and continuing to the first-floor balcony. It overlooked the entire entrance hallway and allowed any guest a peak upstairs, as the glass panelling showed off the white walls with large black and white framed photographs of Mark and me separated by each black bedroom door.

The kitchen was the largest room in the house, with a central island as its focal point. I had every modern amenity, which allowed me to cook for restaurant numbers to the highest Michelin star standard, from a proving cupboard to a champagne cabinet. It was sadly a waste as the most I ever made in there was a sandwich, but caterers were grateful when they were required to cook for Mark's business guests.

The house was redecorated every two years but our interior decorator would begin her research for our house nearly two months before any work began – although, the house largely remained silky white as the only alterations seemed to me, to be the furnishings. The brief from Anne after the work was completed was mainly written for my florist as the subsequent weekly order of household flowers had to compliment the new cushions and rugs. There was one consistent flower that was ordered amongst the others each week and each year and they were white lilies.

My days were spent doing exactly the same as I had done in London. I met new country friends via my London friends who had followed me to the country.

At the beginning, Mark was there most weekends and he preferred me to be home for the whole duration so I could not plan to see any friends over Saturday or Sundays. When he chose not to come home then these days were a laborious trudge to Monday. Mark often omitted to tell me that he was not returning Friday evening and left it to me to figure this out by Saturday afternoon. Prior to this realisation, Saturday was spent in a frantic, fractious and anxious state awaiting his return. Thereafter, I plummeted to an apathetic state watching television on my own for the remaining part of the weekend.

A solution to my boredom came to me over such a weekend. It started as a frivolous thought, one which ordinarily I would smirk at then toss it out of my head, but this pecked away at my brain nagging me to pay attention to it. The idea initially started as a solution but then grew to an excited Eureka moment which sat me up from the sofa and actually encouraged me to turn down the television so that I could concentrate on the developing plan. It was ideal, I had been married for a few years, and I had a beautiful house and time to spare. A baby, a cooing baby of my own, would mean I would have other mums to be friends with and parks to explore together. But greater still was the idea of having a tiny child to love and to love me back. At that stage the only barrier was Mark, but if I slowly suggested to him the prospect of a child at the right moment when he was home and in a happy mood then it would be just a matter of time before he agreed. In the meantime, I needed to wait for this moment to arise, until then I sat back and turned up the television once more to watch the end of my Saturday afternoon film.

Spikes of joy in the tedium of my week were the days I loved above any other day and this was when either Carolanne or James was free to see me. Carolanne had moved to Windsor with Toby, to a small cottage overlooking the Great Park. She no longer wore makeup and preferred to pull her hair into a pony tail above her head, don her wellington boots and walk her black Labradors, called Susie and Trixie, with her husband. I was always welcome there and we chatted about everything, except one topic which was Mark – I was happy to oblige. Similarly, when I was with James I also didn't mention my husband but this I preferred as I wanted to hear about him and his life and I wanted to just listen to his thoughts and listen to his sweet kind words to counteract the bitterness of Mark's daily acerbic remarks.

Seeing James was getting harder as his stage business was growing and we led lives that were as different as two cultures in two different countries. I was aware that I needed him more than he needed to see me but he never refused to meet and, when we did see each other, we spoke of walking in the hills, of diving, what was happening in the news – anything other than my life though sometimes I lapsed and wandered away from idle thoughts.

'So good to see you, James.'

'I'm sorry I've been a crap mate recently,' he said. 'Work is manic and nobody seems to give a toss that I love my weekends and meetings seem to be organised for then. But today – well, till three at least, I'm all yours, Ol.'

He grabbed me and placed an arm over my shoulder like a warm blanket as we walked.

'You don't seem yourself these days Ol,' he continued. 'Carolanne mentioned it as well. You okay mate?'

'You ever wonder, James, when sadness stops and depression begins?'

'You depressed, Ol?' James stopped our walk to look at me. He was framed by the sun and I could barely make out his face. The hum of the A241 distracted me from my thoughts and I said, 'Of course not, how could I be?'

A skateboarder whizzed past us forcing James' arms to drop from my shoulders.

'I suppose I'm just a bit overwhelmed by the move. Maybe I'm missing London and seeing you whenever I want. It's great there though, the house is amazing. I wish you'd come and visit?'

'Yeah I will I promise, it's just life is mad at the mo, work is crazy. Sorry,' James said.

'Of course, I completely understand. I'm crazy busy myself. But seriously, anytime you're free. You know – anytime. Erm, are you around this way much?'

I grabbed his hand to hold as we continued our riverbank walk.

'Are you depressed Ol?'

'No, no, of course not. Mark is taking me to Barcelona at the weekend. It will be amazing. He's so sweet to me.'

James dropped my hand and placed his in his pocket.

'I'm not depressed or sad,' I said. 'I was just curious – for a friend of mine, she's always crying and moaning and...'

'Coffee shop ahead. Coffee? I dunno, if you're still down

after two weeks then, yeah, I'd say she's depressed. I'd also say be a good friend to her and always be there when she needs you. You know I'm always here for you, Ol. I promise.'

It had been months since the last time I had smiled voluntarily. Mark's comments now resided in my head and refused to leave me so that at any opportune moment, from shopping to sitting quietly reading a book, I could hear Mark telling me how boring I was, how I was an embarrassment, how ugly and inferior I was to other women he knew.

Mark's rages were sporadic but always expected, the violence was mainly his words beating me to submission and I duly kowtowed to him as I knew his rant would ease to a simmer if I did not retaliate and turn up the gas beneath his tongue. I had dwindled to a small child around him and my ears were able to close up to most, but not all, of the battering I received when he was home. Yet strangely, my heart would leap when I saw his car driving up as this meant I had his companionship to alleviate the boredom. It also meant the possibility of me receiving a kind warm loving husband who said 'maybe' to my baby plan.

I was able to assess his mood from the way he got out of the car: if he closed his Jaguar whilst looking towards the front door searching for me then I knew my weekend would be magical and full of baby talk. But if he slammed the door, abandoning his car somewhere in the driveway, and then barged pass me as if I was part of the opened front door, such as the knocker or the letterbox, then I wished for the tedium of a weekend on my own watching repeats of Hollyoaks.

A weekend like this was in the middle of March, nearly a year after leaving London. On this occasion I could tell Mark's dark mood from the way he raced into the driveway tossing the small stones behind him. He screeched to a halt displacing all the stones to one side in the car's wake. Before he even got out of the Jaguar, I wanted to slam the front door closed and barricade myself in with the television remote and earplugs in against the banging front door. Alas, he pushed passed me.

'I want to sue the government for my loss of earnings from being held hostage by the M25 for three hours!'

Thoughtlessly, I giggled which was met with a snarl from Mark. Friday evening was held in silence, as was Saturday morning. Every so often I tried to start a conversation but the flow went one way. I mentioned the prospect of going for a walk together but this was met with a stare and another snarl.

A week of praying that my husband would be civil to me when I next saw him allowed my brain to lapse into ideas to solve his temper. I offered an alternative to his dark outlook by reminding him about last week when he was happily talking about the top private schools where his boy would attend or the large wardrobe he would have built for his daughter's shoes and dresses (I didn't want to rile Mark that perhaps our unborn and as yet to be conceived daughter, could also attend the same top school; instead, I just encouraged his daydreaming with agreeing to everything he said). Stupidly, I tried to encourage him to relive those dreams of last Sunday or relive the night time 'baby' telephone call only two days ago, but this time Mark grabbed the back of my head and pulled me to my feet.

'A baby? A baby with you? Why would I want a baby with you. Why would any man want a baby with you? And in any case, you pregnant yet? No, you can't even get that right you're probably barren – useless woman, just as well as I don't want anything from you.'

'I thought that's what you wanted as well?' I pleaded.

My head was now firmly in his grasp and I was pulled by my hair to the hallway mirror where my head was pushed against my reflection so that the left side of my face was merged with the left side of my reflection and my eyes had to strain to the right to avoid my distorted image. In their path my eyes were met with Mark's face – it was puce with anger. His teeth were so close to my eyes that I had to close them to avoid any scrapes on my eyeball whist he hollered at me. His breath reeked of cognac and cigars which stung my nostrils.

Eventually, he pulled my head away so that I could look at my reflection which was red on one side and wet from tears around my eyes.

'Look at you!' he continued, with my head still in his left hand, 'Look at you!' This time he shook my head as if I was a rag doll.

'You're an ugly woman; your red hair makes me sick, your pale skin makes you look like a freak – because you are a freak. Why would I want my child to look anything like you? I have a responsibility to this world and if I am going to send half of me out into it then it will be matched with the right stuff and that doesn't come from you.'

Mark continued but my mind had started to shut him out and, unfortunately, my thoughts were no kinder. Instead of Mark's bitter words I stared at my reflection and felt ashamed of what I saw. My eyes stared at how my ears stuck out and my teeth were askew, that my eyes were small and hooded, and my skin was indeed pale with freckles. I was being held around the neck by my husband who deemed me unfit to have children and just at that moment I agreed with him.

'Are you listening to me, Olive?'

Mark didn't wait for an answer but instead yanked me away from the hallway and pushed me outside smashing my head against the back door frame as he did so. My head squealed in pain and I grabbed it feeling the warm trickle of blood oozing between my fingers. Mark slammed the door on me and left me crying in my dressing gown in the rain. As my body became soaked I grabbed for my cell phone and called the last person I had spoken to on it. I called Carolanne and begged her for help. I do not remember her reply but I remember lying in the rain until I stopped crying and then I remember her banging on the front door and hearing her shout at Mark, softly at first then louder as I heard her get closer to the back door searching for me, screaming, 'Where is she? Where is she?'

I sprang to my feet and almost toppled with dizziness. My panic about Mark had given way to my panic about how to explain why I was outside in the rain and how to explain to Carolanne why I had called her – but especially how to explain to Mark why I had called her – a thoughtless momentary lapse and, as soon as my hysteria had subsided in the cold rain, I wished I had shown control over my feelings and not pulled out my phone from my pocket.

Carolanne opened the back door and ran towards me. For a brief moment I allowed her to hold me up and support me whilst I staggered to the house and away from the rain.

'Oh my poor, poor dear Olivia, what has he done to you?'

Carolanne took off her Parka jacket and wrapped me in it then started to gently clean my cut with wet kitchen towel.

'I knew he was treating you badly. I knew he was wrong for you. Stay still sweetie whilst I look at your head'

'It's nothing, we just had a small disagreement,' I said through tears.

'How dare he touch you! How dare he do this to you? He's a monster.'

Carolanne then turned her head away from me and screamed, 'Yes you, you're a pathetic monster Mark, don't cower in the hallway I can see you – you coward!'

'He didn't mean it, it was me, I was nagging him honestly Carol, I shouldn't have called you...'

'You think this is funny? You're a vampire Mark, look at her – you've sucked the life out of her... Go on, Mark walk away – pathetic!'

'Please don't Carol, you'll make it worse,' I pleaded.

My voice was muffled by Carolanne's huffing. As she breathed out over me I could smell her humbug sweets she often sucked in her car and when she breathed in I could smell the scent of rosewater that she bathed in, made from the roses she lovingly tended to in her garden.

'You'll come and live with me,' she said softly, 'In a moment I'll call Toby and tell him to make up the spare bed after he's cleared out the spare bedroom of all his fishing paraphernalia. In fact you'll be doing me a favour Ol, as he can eventually throw out the rubbish he never uses.'

'You can't make him do that? He'll just tell you to get lost especially for a hysterical friend who is just wasting your time.'

'I can and I will! Stay still, sweetie, as I need to look at this cut. It's not too bad, I think it's just superficial. Stay calm, sweetie, I'll get you out of this I promise.'

Carolanne's head then swivelled round to greet Mark hovering in the background.

'She has a deep, deep wound thanks to you Mark, you evil vampire.'

Mark looked childlike and genuinely worried. Whether that was about my welfare or that he had been discovered throwing me out in the rain I do not know.

'I didn't do anything to her – Olive, tell her this is all rubbish on your part,' he shyly offered.

'Shut up, I don't want to hear you. Come on, Ol, come back with me.'

'I'm fine, honestly, nothing happened, nothing. Please forget it!' I pleaded.

'See. You heard her, nothing happened, I don't know why you're here,' squawked my husband.

'If you were half a man then you'd leave, just go, leave her here with me and you disappear.'

Mark attempted to defend himself but, after further futile exchanges of trying to reclaim his position of innocence in the hands of a nagging, cruel wife, he conceded defeat and grabbed his work case and left.

I knew he was returning to London and I knew he wouldn't return until time had eased the memory of this day to a mere embarrassing sticky moment that he could justify as, 'him overreacting to my annoying behaviour'.

He would return with a gift and a kind word of how he had missed me and that, 'You know it won't happen again but, please Olive, don't push me to get so frustrated with you. Let's just forget it.'

And I will respond with a, 'Thank you for my gift.'

However, on this occasion it took until the end of April before he returned home-armed with a pair of pearl drop earrings.

In the following two months Carolanne called me daily and visited me at least twice a week. I had convinced her that this was an unusual occurrence and we were trying for a baby and the frustration of this not happening had got to the both of us. I explained that I had screamed and shouted at him and that it was me threatening to leave, but as I ran out of the house I hit my head on the door. Mark had not noticed this and in his frustration he closed the door and didn't appreciate that it had locked until my dear friend arrived to relieve my silly whim.

I discovered many years later that Carolanne had not believed any of my explanation but instead spoke to James, Colin and Toby. The three went to see my husband. I am not privy to the conversation they had as Mark never spoke to me about it but Mark did not physically harm me again until the day we parted.

When Mark returned in April, there was a difference in him; he was calmer and at times sanguine about his stressful life. He was kind, gentle and once more I was pleased he was my husband. By the summer we were celebrating that, after an eternity of trying, we were finally pregnant.

It was a burning hot August day, the type of day that was uncomfortable just sitting; my hair clung to my sweaty forehead and my white cotton summer dress felt like a polar bear skin hindering any coveted cool air that might float my way. Ordinarily I would have swum in the pool then hidden from the sun on the patio bed but this day I was happier than I could have been, as I held a pregnancy test that told me that finally I was to be a mother.

Mark joined me for my twelve week scan in the September and I knew he was as excited as I was as he held my hand in the waiting room and didn't let it go until I was lying on the scanner's chair with jelly on my stomach.

Up until this point the pregnancy had been easy: I didn't have morning sickness or any aversion to food, I didn't have tender breasts and any mood swings were merely oscillations of happiness from calm satisfaction of life to overwhelming excitement. Mark seemed to share these moods with me. He would hug me at his whim and tell me how proud he was of his beautiful lady in waiting.

Mark's hand dropped away from mine as the image on the screen was explained to us: There was no baby as it was an empty sac. There was no heartbeat as the embryo had not developed, most likely, due to a chromosome defect. The sonographer was very sorry but I would most likely miscarry very soon.

Alternatively, I could have a 'D&C', to have it removed from my body. This I had the next day at the Victoria hospital. I know Mark was with me when they wheeled me away from the hospital suite to the theatre but he was not there when I returned, instead his driver greeted me with a bunch of pink roses for when I was ready to go home.

I didn't ask where Mark was but instead I stared at the walls of my room and occasionally I looked out at the grey autumnal day and the damp cars in the car park which my room overlooked. The paisley pink walls of my hospital room had yellow daisy pictures hung all around. It was designed to cheer the patient up but I found them condescending and almost disrespectful to the mourning I felt of losing the wonderful joyride I had ridden since the beginning of August. Now everything was as grey and as pointless as that October day.

I was deposited back at home and as I got out of the car I cried at the prospect of returning to the mundane drudge of my life without the excitement of a child to share it with me. I would return to the weekly shopping and facials and hair appointments. I would return to the weekly luncheons with friends who did not know I was pregnant and who would never know I had a miscarriage. Instead, they would hear of the forthcoming extension to the swimming pool to incorporate a larger gym and the upcoming Halloween ball in aid of some charity.

I walked through the door still sobbing. Mark was in the kitchen reading the newspaper.

'You're tired; go to bed. I'll wake you if I need you,' he said without looking up. I duly agreed and went upstairs.

I was woken just as dusk turned the grey day to a murky evening. The street lamps in the distance had not yet turned on and I felt as groggy as the soggy, muddy puddles scattered across our driveway. I could hear Mark on the phone and I went to the landing to make my way down to be with him, but I stopped short of the stairs and looked over the railings into the green, dark library. Mark was negotiating a price on something but it was hard to distinguish between each word. A prickling down my back hinted this was a conversation I needed to hear.

I crept down and hid in earshot of my husband's conversation. Mark was wearing gaudy, Bermuda shorts and an old white T-shirt that was misshapen and baggy around the neck. He was hunched over the desk and holding the phone close to his ear. His voice was a low whisper but still audible from where I was standing.

'...agreed no more than a thousand... the same as before...'

Mark wiped his mouth then brushed his hands through his hair. Around his side-burns grey strands had invaded his face and the odd grey friend had sprung up in places across his head. The hair was still full and swept away from his face, which was just beginning to fill out from the excesses of good cognac. Beneath his eyes, purple cushions were taking form and his forehead was starting to show the indentations of deep lines.

'I need assurance she'll be discreet… No don't tell me 'of course', this is a different place than your girls are used to…' He paused and stood up to look out of the window.

'Okay, call when she's five minutes away and I'll direct her round to the back door. As I said to you at the beginning, my wife is asleep upstairs as she had a miscarriage earlier today so she can't be disturbed… Yeah, yeah, funny, I'll send her your condolences. Just make sure this Mandy woman is quiet.'

Mark put the phone down and I quietly scampered upstairs. My suspicions were growling in my stomach that this was another woman, but not today? Surely, this was just an overly concerned husband who had ordered a pizza or maybe an Indian take-away. Maybe he just wanted to make sure the delivery lady was quiet and discreet so that I was not concerned about how much salt and fat he was eating?

I went back to my bedroom and sat in front of my window. I could taste bile in my stomach as my body shivered and became taut every time I contemplated the notion this was not an Indian take-away. I couldn't keep my head from resting upon the window pane; my tears dripped from my face onto the glass and marked their way down through the condensation from my breath. Eventually I spied a tall blonde woman walk from the far gates. She was dressed in a navy suit, with white high heels. From afar I allowed myself to presume that she could be a business woman and had an appointment with Mark, but as she got closer the shine on her Viscose suit suggested she was not here to sign a deal.

I heard the muffled voices of Mark and this woman. I felt strong enough, on this occasion, to go down and confront whatever I was to be greeted with. The library door was now closed and as I reached for the handle I closed my eyes and begged to be confronted with Mark eating a pizza. When I opened them, my eyes confirmed he hadn't ordered his dinner but he had ordered a woman. Her hair was bright yellow, coiffured and sprayed to the size of an eagle's nest on top of her head. She wore a red lace, loose teddy which matched her red mouth. She was kneeling on the floor and Mark was standing in front of her slightly to the side still wearing his old T-shirt.

I regret so many things about the exchange which then took place.

There are many exchanges I have had in my life which, if I was allowed to re-enact them then I would be the victor from my eloquent and commanding speech (which in reality, I subsequently had in the privacy of my head). As the prosecutor I would be able to shrivel their defence to a jibbering mass of apologies and the woman would be grabbing for her clothes and running for her car, cowardly leaving a pathetic, crying man in her the wake. Unfortunately, the actual exchange was Mark turning around and yelling.

'Get out!!'

And the woman's mouth creaked open to smile like a snake on a tree about to pounce on a helpless rat for its dinner.

This was my first regret. The second was allowing myself to be ordered away like a waiter and saying nothing, not even a whimper in protest.

In my shock I closed the door and ran back to my room. When I got there, I paced the floor until I felt the residual blood from my miscarriage drip down my legs. All that had happened had distracted me from me, and I had not attended to myself in many hours. This blood reminded me that my stomach still ached from the procedure and the blood needed to be cleared away.

My final regret was sitting on the bathroom floor waiting for her to leave and in my low, depressed state, one of my thoughts was actually feeling embarrassed for my husband that he had been seen by someone, anyone, still wearing that old grey tatty cheap T-shirt. As soon as this thought entered my head I slapped my cheek and berated myself for my worrying more what a prostitute would think of my husband's dress sense than the humiliation and betrayal of his wife.

Finally, I heard her leave and after a long while I heard another bedroom door close. I knew Mark had gone to bed in another room. I eventually fell asleep upon the cold tiles with my head resting upon my bloody towels in the en suite bathroom.

Mark was not there in the morning and I didn't see him for a further month. I wandered the house like a zombie, sleeping for hours during the day and lying awake at night, I cancelled every lunch date and beauty appointment. The only time I left the house was for a doctor's appointment three weeks later to check there was no infection from the miscarriage.

'All is well, Olivia, I know this is a hard time for you but you will get pregnant again; you're still a young thirty-four year old woman. Give it another month and try again but, in the meantime, just enjoy the time with your husband as I'm sure this time next year you will have a little one to occupy your time.'

'Definitely,' I said, 'my husband is keen to start again, he's even bought me a new-born romper suit to cheer me up! He's been so supportive and we are looking forward to adding to our happy home in Cavendish Avenue.'

I knew it was a cheap lie but it was a tiny, momentary boost to my ego by scoring points from an unmarried, frumpy, but kind and concerned doctor. I doubt she even noticed the name drop of Cavendish Avenue or even cared, but to me, at that moment, I wanted to feel superior. It didn't last long, like most ego statements I just felt foolish as soon as I'd said it.

There would never be a baby for me as Mark didn't get close

to me or chose to love me again. He isolated me more over the coming years and although he never physically hurt me again, he hurt me in so many other ways; but none so great than how fate chose that I would never get to love my own child.

I still see the baby I should have had wrapped warmly and safely in my arms. I often see him as a two year old giggling around my feet then asking to be picked up with outstretched arms. I see his blond curls and his rosy cheeks and I hear his laughter as he explores life with me by his side. Even today, as I sit in my chair, I can see the triumph in his eyes as he wins medals for his sporting abilities or for his school achievements and I can feel the swell of pride as I watch my baby grow to a man.

Over the years I found myself taking peeks in strangers' prams just to glimpse their sleeping baby or I would be transfixed by young mothers playing with their children in the park. But when they moved on then I fell out of my trance and continued to live the days fate had given me of shopping, lunching and pampering.

CHAPTER FIFTEEN

About eighteen years ago

Tatiana came to visit me one December. I was grateful to see the woman who had all but disappeared from my life for over two years. Her secret jealousy of me meant she was running a personal social race against me and many of her equally affluent friends. Only when she felt she was gathering a competitive speed to overtake me would she then knock on my door. The race she was running was turning into a sprint for the social gold medal and today she felt confident in her pace to knock on my door.

'He's a futures banker in oil and energy and stuff like that,' she enthused.

'He reckons he will hit the big one when he gets the promotion as he'll head a team of five and, therefore, get a share of the profit they make per year as his bonus. His bonus last year was around three million but he definitely thinks it'll be more like seven this year – courtesy of his underlings. He is soooo sweet to me and he has bought me a gorgeous new mini car. Oh, Ol, look at these diamond earrings he bought me when we were out in Stratford-upon-Avon last weekend.'

Tatiana leant across into my chair space and thrust her earlobes into my face. She was still as slim as the day I met her, though I suspect her efforts to remain slender extended to a chemical buzz to extinguish the nuisance hunger pangs. Her hair was now cropped into a neat bob that framed her face. The lines of age were creeping across her forehead and the once youthful glow had faded beneath dark foundation. Her lips were pursed as she waited for my comment about her earrings. I smelt the distinct smell of Tatiana that swept me back to our London flat we once shared: a vile mixture of perfume and nicotine, enhanced with a few drops of sugar-free mint gum.

'Wow they're stunning Tats, really clear and a great cut and size,' I dutifully said.

'Yeah, all of that and they were so expensive, but I don't think it matters when you're in love; and I think he's going to pop the question as we were also looking at rings but I didn't like any of them and he said I deserved something really special and...'

I started to fade out of the conversation. I could feel the warmth of my usual tired eyes dragging me away from the room I was in to a buzzed, fuzzy space – a recent standard 'state of being' where I perched on the cusp of consciousness and unconsciousness. If I gave in then I would fall into a deep sleep but if I fought, then I would stay awake. That day my fight was weak and all I could muster was an unenthusiastic grasp on reality. My head was supported by my right hand, my eyes were heavy and my blinking was slow so that at times a blink would last long enough for a glimpse of restful sleep to invade my consciousness.

'...He is always taking me out, Ol, aah and to the most incredible places; for example, just off Soho there is a roof top terrace restaurant. No one and I mean no one but the select few know about it... But the way he tells me he loves me, Ol, he's so tender and genuine... I know he's planning to ask me really soon...'

A secret slumber was taking hold of me and my last fight was to move around in my chair, but all I wanted was to curl up again in my bed and close my bedroom door to the world behind me and sleep. Instead I was kept from my bed by Tatiana droning on about Clive or Cliff or perhaps she said John? Yes, it was more like John.

Look at her, so animated in her gusto about some bloke who takes her out and buys her jewellery just so he can sleep with her, I thought.

'We'll probably be going skiing to Canada this year,' she continued, 'he has some works do there and wants to show me off to his work friends...'

Only so they can judge you and give you a rating out of ten; if you score more than eight then he will keep you for another season until either a nine comes along with a red smile to suck his money from him or you drop down the ranking to a seven then six then a nothing and you will be gone.

'...I've met his sister and we are now the closest of friends – she soooo gets me and where I'm coming from; she absolutely loves me...'

That's one good sign as these men keep their families apart from their women unless they deem them suitable to meet the parents and siblings.

'He's away now until the end of the month, on business...'

Not a good sign...

'It means I have all this time to catch up on my dearest friends.'

Thanks for squeezing me in every two years...

'He's in the States so it's hard to talk, as if he's not in a meeting then he's in bed or I'm in bed because of the time difference and I can't call him in case I disturb him, but he texts all the time...'

And there it was! John, Cliff or whoever, was in fact Dick, the usual prick with money – away when he pleases and his women are where he wants them: at home deluding themselves they were in love and this love was shared by the two of them.

Tatiana's voice now hummed through my head and I wavered in my chair. I moved to wake myself up then inadvertently blurted out, 'He sounds like a typical prick. Give up, it won't last.'

The sound of my own voice jolted me back to my pale blue living room. I looked at my silver rug, confused as to whether I had actually said these words or merely thought them. I looked up to Tatiana and her stunned gasp confirmed that my thoughts had escaped from my mouth.

'Excuse me, Ol? Tony is not a prick, I love him and he loves me!' Her mouth was still a surprised O which gave me just enough time to squeeze in, 'I'm sorry, I'm sorry, of course he's not, and he sounds amazing, really sorry,' before Tatiana launched into an attack.

'I don't know what's wrong with you. I don't hear from you in ages, I try calling and calling. Everyone is worried as you are never around and, seriously, Ol, you look a mess. And you think you can judge me?' She paused: 'I don't know where you've gone but what I'm looking at isn't my Ol. Tell me one thing: when was the last time you washed your hair?'

This attack was in fact gentle but my defence barrier was weak and my mouth began to quiver.

'Ol?! Please what is wrong?' her voice had softened and her tenderness cuddled me. I was surprised by her sweet retreat.

'What is the matter? Please I want to help. As I said, everyone is concerned by you but no one can get in. Quite frankly Ol, I'm amazed you said yes to me visiting today. You've put me and others off for ages.'

The quiver on my mouth gave way to a yell, then a yelp and the tension on my chest burst in front of the one friend who in hindsight, I should never have allowed to see the cracks in my head.

'Mark is seeing other women and doesn't care. There are many other women who sometimes come back here – here, to my home Tats, my home and I can't say anything. I mean, I literally can't say or do anything about it but dutifully hide away in my room. I never see him and if I do then I'm a nuisance to him. His friends come back here and treat me like I'm their personal butler but I say nothing – nothing! And it's because serving his friends gives me an involvement in Mark's life. Except, he doesn't see me as his servant instead I think he sees me as his dog at home in the country; an animal that has its kennel on the first floor, covered in as many designer cushions as it likes.

Do you hear me, Tats? I'm an animal to him that he bought for Christmas and regrets buying. I sit on my cushion waiting to be petted but instead I watch my master bring woman and drunk friends back to kick me about and, Tats, I say and I do nothing… Nothing!!'

The pressure had been released from my chest and for a short while I could breathe long restful breaths.

'Does he hurt you? Physically I mean?' Tatiana's voice was still soft.

'No, he doesn't hurt me; it was a figure of speech.' I slung my head low and cried.

'He just doesn't love you the way you would like?'

Tatiana paused and I could hear her draw a deep breath.

'He doesn't hurt you but he doesn't love you the way you would like.' Tatiana straightened her skirt, 'Sweetie, get over it.'

Tatiana then looked at me and cupped my head in her hand.

'You have so much here. So what if he doesn't whisper sweet nothings, after a while no man does. All women, and men for that matter, need to understand that love is lust; it's no deeper than a mattress and lasts no longer than the time spent on it.

But we kid ourselves that any subsequent feeling is a gift given to us by fate. It is not. It's an arrangement for two people to coexist and these two people continue together because one receives what they want and so stays and vice versa. For you, Olive, it's his bank account, it is the ability to buy whatever you want; you can go wherever you want and do whatever you want. You don't live in a kennel, you live in an enormous house with a pool and a gardener. You have a choice of sports cars and a top Range Rover.

Sweetie, take hold of your life, look at it, smell it and tell me you don't have everything you desire. The only payment you need to make is to accept Mark and his occasional visits, and if you're looking for love then you have lost sight of what your relationship is made of.'

Tatiana lent back in her chair and when she resumed, her voice was lowered by an octave;

'Now sweetie, if you want to keep that credit card then you have to deliver what Mark wants from you. That is, his wife in the country that his friends secretly desire, which gives Mark the cache of a sexy wife at his country estate. You're there to show off and shut up. So use your plastic and sort your look out. You look tired and things have started to sag. For example, I'm thinking about Botox as I know these lines, the ones just here…' she pointed to around her mouth then onto between her eyes, (I didn't want to add that she should also be pointing to her forehead).

'I'm also thinking about fillers for my mouth as I can already see the fine lines being drawn around my lips. Olive, it is for me, to give me the confidence to keep Tony, the man in my life whom I claim to love. You need to do the same sweetie, you need to take on the women Mark is choosing and make sure he looks at you once more.'

I could have argued for love, that it's not just a hormone thrown to us by our manipulating, controlling brains but it is a heavenly present to reward us for taking on the challenge of living. It is there to colour the spring with blossom and to warm our hearts in the winter. It is there to make us feel the majesty of our bodies and rejoice that we were chosen by God to be on this Earth and to create another being as blessed payment for finding the one given to us by the angels to love and cherish.

I didn't even try as I no longer believed the ideal dreams written by a cheap teenage girl magazine. And even if I believed in a celestial feeling of awe for another person then, instead, I was angry that this love had evaded me. The heavens had not deemed me adequate to be bolstered by love from another person and God didn't see that I should be rewarded with a child.

So, as I slouched in my yoga pants in front of Tatiana my head nodded in agreement. She was right; love was a business agreement between two people, each member signed a contract to provide for the other. It was an equation of balance and this relationship could falter if either of the business partners found the balance had tipped and one was putting in less than the other. The contract was then broken and the partnership would dissolve.

My contract with Mark was cracking because, although Mark continued to invest in our relationship, I was not providing the image of dutiful beautiful wife at home. It was no wonder that he was looking elsewhere and, therefore, if I wanted to keep my business with Mark then I needed to reinvest in our relationship.

I looked at Tatiana and studied her glossy hair and I ran my fingers through my frizzy bomb. I had not washed my hair in five days and my pillow had matted my hair together. I had not been out of the house in over month as I was deliberately avoiding my usual mundane life and Mark had not been home in five weeks and, therefore, grooming seemed an unnecessary waste of my time.

Tatiana was an old friend and I hoped she wouldn't notice my sullen face without makeup or the clothes I had put on because they were either lying on the floor in front of my bed or, as in the case of my underwear and sleeveless vest top, I was already wearing them from the night before.

205

It was a hope which was a cover for the rude fact that I had lost caring and having hope about anything, including what Tatiana thought of my attire. It all seemed a drain on my energy. But Tatiana had noticed how I appeared and so would Mark if he was here, so why wouldn't he leave me? Why wouldn't he look at others for his entertainment? I had no child to divert my attention and all I had was this house and my wardrobe and I needed to protect them.

Tatiana touched my face.

'We are in our mid-thirties and our membership to the young beauty club is getting close to its expiration date. Unless you do something about it, sweet-pea, then you'll be kicked out without the prospect of getting back in.'

She then grabbed my hand.

'Don't let time spoil what fate gave you. You were given beauty, which Mark bought. Yes he has a wandering eye but it won't be long before he throws you away for another.

I'm going to see a guy who was recommended to me by Alice, you know her, 'wife of a senior judge Alice'. She sees a guy in Merchant Street who she swears by. Now Ol, be honest, how old do you think she is?'

'I don't know.'

Alice was a striking woman with a stern face; it matched her coiffured brunette hair and tailored suits. She always looked as though there should be a black stallion trotting beside her; a horse available for her to ride through nuisance crowds when her riding whip was not sharp enough to push the little people out of her way. I don't recall her claret red lips ever smiling but those lips were painted on a smooth clear face. Perhaps this soft skin belonged to a woman nearing her fifties.

'Late forties maybe early fifties?' I said.

'Don't be daft, she's got a daughter older than us – does Alice look the type to have been a teenage mum? No! In fact, you know her daughter Francesca – dumpy frumpy Fran? Fran who now looks older than her mum?'

'I've no idea then as I thought she was fifty.'

'Sixty-four!' Tatiana jumped in, 'Sixty-four years of age and she looks A – May – Zing. Botox, fillers and a lot of work. Trust me sweetie, Mark will turn his head back to you and decorate you with diamonds. Come with me next week and it will be the beginning of a journey to the Wizard of Oz's secret yellow brick road to the fountain of youth.'

After coffee Tatiana left but before she went she concluded by saying, 'You know Ol, life is not controlled by the Wizard of Oz but by ourselves. We are in control, no one else. Those who believe they can do nothing about what God has thrown at them are those who are inherently lazy. All God has given anyone is choice. Olivia, your choice is Mark or no Mark. The latter should only be embraced if you're truly unhappy.'

Tatiana stepped out of the door and looked at me again.

'But if you are truly unhappy then leave, go, leave it all behind – perhaps I'm a good enough friend to say that to you now?'

I closed the door and I retreated to my room but, instead of falling on my bed into the indentation my body had left since my cleaner had been, I walked over to my mirror. I felt bolstered by Tatiana and 'hope' rested on my shoulder and nudged me away from my depressive state.

I sat and stared at my reflection. The image that glared back at me, my dear Jason, I am ashamed to say, made my sadness lift to anger. It was not a slow process but sublimation from depression to rage. I pulled at my matted hair, slapped my dry, lined face and tugged at my hooded eyes. My nose was hooked and the tip was too pointed. My teeth were crooked and my lips were full but the cupid's bow was too pronounced. My chin had started to sag to meet my lined neck and, although my breasts were large and full, they too had begun to droop as they were nearing their replacement date. My stomach had a small pouch which mirrored the pouch under my arms and on my bra line.

Yet in amongst my angry rant there was a whisper from hope; I knew enough people to tell me which magicians were the best to reinvent Olivia to exactly what I wanted to be and so, the energy that eluded me for so long returned with gusto and I ran downstairs and sent off a flurry of emails to friends for names.

I began gently with my first doctor, a Dr. Dean Gregory. He was a facial and body architect and came highly recommended by my beautician as the best general cosmetic surgeon. He explained in dispassionate terms the recovery for each procedure but he spared me the details on the operation itself and, instead, began quoting the cost;

'For the breast lift, £3000 or thereabouts; for the tummy tuck, £4500 or thereabouts; for both at once, a discounted £6500 or thereabouts.'

I must have looked shocked as he then said, 'I don't do bargain surgery. For that price you get the best of everything. You'll be well medicated.'

For this money I get expensive drugs. However, it was not the shock of the cost but rather his blunt manner of describing major surgery.

'Maybe, Ms Olivia, a little at a time, instead of jumping in at the deep end? Perhaps this will give you more time to think. Instead, perhaps we will start here?' And with the aid of the end of his ball point pen Dr Gregory drew virtual lines across my face.

'Botox across here and down through the eyes perhaps around the mouth here and here... again, Ms Olivia, you look shocked?'

He looked at me and I smiled and I shook my head. He was a tanned man in his fifties. His skin suggested a touch of Iranian in his blood. His hair was black and curly which was cut to a coiffured, neat style swept away from his face. His suit was a navy pin stripe which, as I was to learn later, was the standard uniform for most plastic surgeons. His white shirt was rolled at the sleeve revealing muscular forearms and a gold Rolex watch. When his hands swept across my face as he continued to draw lines across my imperfections I could smell sweet, spiced soap.

'It's perfectly safe, Ms Olivia,' he continued. 'Botox has actually been around for some years and believe it or not, although it has had bad press claiming it is the Earth's most toxic protein, Botox is the nickname for botulinum type A. Its name, botulism, comes from the Latin butulus, which means sausage. I'll be injecting a bacteria by-product that grows on decaying sausage, but only a minute percentage of the actual toxin goes into the syringe. It is just enough to paralyse the muscles that cause wrinkles. And voilà! No lines. Now has that reassured you?'

His mouth cracked to a slight smile. Obviously, I was not reassured but he had come recommended so I said, 'Of course, decaying sausage, so interesting!'

'Now, around the eyes I would suggest filler but not just yet, maybe within the next five years or so, but those lips could do with some plumping. There are many to choose from lip implants to fat transfer. They have different lasting qualities. Perhaps for now you could consider just filler for the lips; it will last about six months and you can re-inject each time you return for Botox. I suggest for you, hyaluronic acid filler. Hyaluronic acid is naturally produced by the body but as we age we produce less. It is a molecule, which is a sponge like carbohydrate, that naturally binds to water so when I inject the acid filler under your skin the area inflates with fluid and voilà: a defined cupid's bow and kissable lips.'

I touched my lips and I felt disappointed as I was not aware that my lips were inadequately thin and unkissable, so again I nodded and agreed to having the procedure.

The receptionist booked me in for the following Wednesday and suggested that I pre-book the following appointments just in case Dr Gregory was booked when I needed him. She reassured me that all his patients did this and indeed I was very fortunate that I was able to get a cancellation for the 21st, next week. I nodded and left the clinic.

Botox is an easy procedure: the dermatologist or plastic surgeon asks me to screw my face and then he injects the liquid into the muscles which have caused the wrinkles. The number of shots depends upon the size of the area, so my forehead receives four or five shots whereas around my neck he would do two or three rows of five injections to relax the platysma muscles. The injections do hurt but it is only every six months so I can bear the discomfort for the gold allure of smooth skin.

The first time I had filler in my lips caused a little more pain than in subsequent appointments especially as the numbing cream that was applied prior to the procedure was as effective as just licking my lips, but I bore the pain for kissable lips.

During the early days Tatiana was my ally and between us we were each other's mirror.

'Ol, you look incredible, it's really changed you… at least ten years younger… so much prettier than you've ever been… so much prettier than the twenty somethings that rely on their youth as you have something they don't: money and Botox!'

I returned the compliments to her in direct proportion to the compliments flowing my way.

After the first time of receiving this procedure my confidence returned, slowly at first but as time went on it was drip fed into my veins until I searched for my reflection once more wherever I went.

Finally, I got to the point that I wanted to see my friends again. So, when James asked if I would like to meet his new girlfriend and to take a look around his new house just outside Pulborough in West Sussex, I said yes. His stage company had expanded and now he needed a large warehouse to work on the set designs with his team of five other carpenters and this he found just off the South Downs.

I hadn't seen very much of James but every so often I would

text, 'I miss you' and 'How are you doing?' or 'You don't call me anymore.' These nudges always rewarded me with a phone call from him.

In this way James continued to be my medicine. He kept me from returning to the sickening depression which lurked around me; whenever this devil desolation crept beside me I would seek an excuse to nudge James to call. However, I was not expecting to hear about another woman.

'Jane, I've been seeing her for a while now but we weren't sure how we felt and well, now we are,' he said on the phone.

'Ahh, mmm, she sounds lovely,' I said despondently.

I wondered what she looked like – I knew she had an eight-year-old child, so most likely quite old and probably plump. He told me that she worked with horses so she probably wore the same yard clothes from morning to dusk.

'She really is lovely and she'd love you.'

'Mmm, yeah, I'm sure I'd love her too.' I said.

There was a prolonged silence on the phone.

'You know Olive, I'm always here. It changes nothing, I'm always here. I know I keep using the same excuse that it's crazy busy at work, but it really is.'

There was another pause on the phone then:

'Jane says I need to get you over so she can meet you. She's sweet like that. I just wanted you to know that and she wants you to know that I'm always here; we're always here for you.'

'I know, of course of course. But you don't need to worry about me. How strange you should say this but how sweet of Jen, sorry, Jane.'

'I know I've not been around that much lately, but you can always call us. Like I keep telling you, day or night just call when you need us. You know that right?'

'Of course, and like I said, I'm so pleased for you but everything is perfect my end. I know I've not been round much either but the new pool is almost finished – the heating wasn't connecting or something like that, but I'll have more time on my hands once the workmen are finished.'

There was another silence on the phone.

'I couldn't make my mind up over the tile colour and so… well a light, goldy green was chosen so…'

'I saw Carolanne with Jane the other week… shame you weren't around. Carolanne is concerned,' he interrupted.

'Oh, Carolanne! Why the concern? Now last Sunday where was I? Oh yes, last Sunday, I was out with friends for lunch. I can't remember where but it was fantastic.'

'Listen, it's me… You know what, it doesn't matter. Anyway, Jane will be annoyed with me unless I get a yes from you to come over, please come. As I said, she's great, right amazing and an amazing cook.'

There was that word again, amazing – who is amazing? What does that description even mean? Was it the pool workmen who left the job early because they had overrun but, 'don't worry love, we'll be back sometime', leaving a hole in my garden ready for the summer frogs? Or was it Cynthia from my lunch friends who had not invited me to the NSPCA charity lunch for the second year running? Or was it Jane? The woman who is dating my James?

No, Jane could not be amazing; I decided she was an old, fat, horsey woman who ate too much carbohydrate and was using my friend as a convenient second father.

'Well Mark is in the States, so of course I'm free and I can't wait to meet the woman who has stolen your heart.' I cheerfully screeched.

As I put the phone down I reasoned that this relationship could not work and it was important for James to have me, his friend, on hand when he realised there is more to life than eating lardy scones.

That Saturday I wore my red Dior chiffon dress with heeled espadrilles. My hair had been done the day before and I had introduced the odd blonde highlight amongst my red hair which according to Ivan, my hairdresser, gave me a youthful glow.

I parked my Mercedes at the end of their driveway – I instantly regretted my parking choice but the alternative was to continue up the pathway to their front door but I wasn't confident that I would be able to reverse the car back at the end of the day as the driveway was so narrow. But parking this far away from the front door meant I had to meander my way along a dusty path trying to avoid the small mud puddles that were strewn across it by the recent rain.

The cottage was old and well worn. Its appearance was of a little, gentle old lady sitting on a porch surveying her land from where she sat all day. The roof sagged in the middle and the small windows twinkled from the thick 17th-century window panes. All around the house were forget-me-nots and other meadow weeds which brightened the aged house in late spring.

I knocked on the green door. I needed to duck as I walked into a dark but welcoming living room. The main feature of this room was the inglenook fireplace, it was huge and it exposed the vast thickness of the cottage walls. From this pink room I was shown to the second and last room which was a dated pine kitchen with flowery curtains instead of cupboard doors. The oven stood alone in the corner, it was old but from it there wafted a delicious smell of our lunch. Next to the oven was a bunch of yellow daffodils which had recently sprung open to enjoy the gentle breeze that flowed from the open kitchen window. Next to this vase of daffodils there stood a tall slim lady. She was in her late twenties, she beamed a smile at me and Jane moved forward to greet me.

'And this is Jane. Jane, this is my mate, Olivia.'

You're so young, I thought.

'I've heard so much about you; I'm so pleased to meet you,' I said politely. Jane moved towards me and grabbed me with both arms. Her hug was generous but unexpected, so I instinctively flinched.

'I'm so sorry,' she said as she released me, 'but I'm so happy to meet you and, wow, you're as beautiful as James said you were. Just beautiful. What a pretty dress!'

'Dior,' I replied.

'Ahh M&S for me, given by my mum. I know it's not flattering but I love it as it's so comfy.'

I couldn't return the compliment about her dress as the cream wool thing was clearly not given by her mother with love but abandoned to a new charitable home. She had teamed this shapeless dress with a flowery pinafore which smoothed her dress over her stomach to reveal a bump on her skinny frame. *Ha! You maybe skinny but without a gym membership then that stomach is going to continue to grow.*

'Please come and sit. Camomile tea? I'm sorry but I don't have ordinary tea as we're trying to give up caffeine. I do have fresh orange juice if you'd prefer?'

How patronising! To assume your guest would not sympathise in your quest to detoxify.

'Camomile is fine, though I normally drink linden-flower tea, it has a greater detoxifying quality to it. Do you have any?'

'Oh, I'm sorry I don't, er. I have water?' she stammered.

I could tell she was nervous and perhaps she didn't deserve the comment I had made, but James was my friend and I needed to know exactly who she was. So far she was a skinny woman who didn't work out but relied on health food to keep her slim; but this technique was clearly failing and so, when compared to a naturally slim woman such as myself, then she had to resort to undermining them. How rude!

We sat down for lunch and I watched Jane flurry around this small kitchen to serve us. The smell was intoxicating, I could already taste herbs with red wine. I pinched my hand to distract me from my stomach craning its way out of my body, screaming at me to take a huge portion of whatever was about to be served from the steaming pots.

Jane was attentive but remained jittery. I did little to sooth her as I was preoccupied with talking to James but his attention was fixed on her and trying to ease her work load and he prefixed every sentence with 'Janey'. But how could he call her Janey? He hardly knows this woman? She was awkward, with a straight blonde bob which enhanced her razor nose. The straight edge of her fringe complimented her slightly buck teeth which forced a permanent smile. It was, at least, a comely solution to a peculiar facial feature.

'I hope you like this – it's chicken and tarragon hotpot. It's my mum's recipe. The chicken is from the farm shop down the road and they're reared on corn, hence the yellow colour. All the vegetables are from either my mum's garden or ours,' she said as she sat down to eat with us.

'Ours?' She's far too familiar with James having only known him for a short while.

'The peas are last year's; obviously kept in the freezer but it's a bit too early for fresh peas,' she added.

'Last years? I didn't know you have been living here that long?' I quizzed.

'We haven't but I have,' she said. 'James moved in not long ago but he helped me pick the peas last year. Please tuck in and I hope you like it.'

A year? James has only just mentioned you...

'It looks delicious, Jane.'

'Have you come far?' she enquired.

'Not too far, no. It was an easy drive,' I replied.

I hope you noticed my Mercedes SLK in your driveway next to your shopping bicycle.

Small talk dominated the conversation and after a while I wanted to just ask her to leave me and James alone to catch up (after-all, I had not seen James in... was it over a year?) Unfortunately, she was too genteel to sit quietly and instead talked about the local school her son went to or the gardening, which she enjoyed. Eventually I resorted to turning my shoulder away from her and towards James. I asked him direct questions about his latest work project and how was Carolanne when he saw her? Anything that excluded Jane from the conversation. Yet she persevered and interrupted.

'We saw Carolanne again yesterday; Toby needed to borrow our hedge trimmer. They were passing but ended up staying for dinner, which was wonderful, wasn't it James? Twice in one week. I do love Carolanne and Toby is so funny; he joked about their neighbour's dog. Oh, he did make us laugh! Ah and we got some of his newly brewed beer – what has he called this batch? Dogs' breath beer? How funny! Oh, and Carolanne is lovely, and she's looking so well, I always wonder whether...'

'Anything else going on with you James?' I interrupted. James looked over to Jane and answered, 'Actually we do, have some news,' he began.

'We've known for a little while but we wanted to be sure.'

James leant over to hold the hand from a beaming, gleaming Jane.

'We've just had our first 'little un' picture and so far all's good.'

My stomach lurched when I realised his riddle.

'We're due mid-October and you're one of the first to know,' she added.

My breath was short and I managed a smile to disguise my jealousy, my deep, instantaneous, crippling jealousy.

'Congratulations, I, er, didn't know you were trying.' I mustered, but I actually did not want to know the answer. Instead I wanted to sit at their table and hold onto my chair. I wanted them to both quietly get up and go away and leave my head to swim around the fact that this petite young girl was to have my James' child.

'We hadn't really been trying to be honest. I suppose you would call this little one a happy surprise,' she said. 'It didn't seem real until the scan and we heard the heartbeat of our child.'

A sound I will never hear.

James then looked at me and beneath the table he grabbed my hand and gave it a small squeeze with an accompanying wink.

It wasn't enough. I continued to listen to her excited talk for their future as I writhed in secret agony over the lack of mine. Finally, the tortuous lunch came to an end and I hurriedly made my excuses to leave as soon as I could.

I walked to the front door and I looked around once more at their home. This pretty cottage had housed many families; it kept each one safe and warm and nurtured each child that came under its roof. It was now the turn of James and Jane and for the next phase in their lives they got to live in the loving embrace of this old lady. I turned to Jane and I was suddenly struck by her sweetness. But worse than this, I knew from her smile and unassuming manner that she was an honest and loving woman who would be a giving mother. In contrast, I had shown myself to be the bitter house guest who did not deserve the sweet hospitality from this lady. She hugged me and I left.

In my car I could feel the clutch of depression around my throat. Tears began deep in my stomach and they rose steadily towards my eyes. I tried to stem their flow by staring at the car in front of me or turning my music up. As they eased their way into my tear ducts I shouted at myself to stop being pathetic.

I was now on the M25 and I had a further four junctions to contend with in this enclosed box. The traffic was beginning to slow and a red sign ahead warned me there was 'Queuing traffic' after the next junction. My breathing quickened as I felt claustrophobic, surrounded by other cars who were slowing down in their lane or weaving in front of me to take advantage of the slightly greater speed my lane had over the next. I became intensely irritated by old cars assuming they could overtake my Mercedes. The presumption of these cars fuelled my anger and I began to hit my useless steering wheel for leading me onto this motorway which no longer served its purpose as a road. There were back roads I could have taken which would have avoided this pileup, yet I was trapped by old cheap vehicles laughing at me for having a sports car on a road with a top speed of 5 mph.

'Where do you think you can go?' I screamed at a green 1982 Fiat Panda; 'cutting me up only gets you two metres closer to the inevitable standstill!'

It had squeezed in front of me and now my view was of a 'Caution: child on board' sticker.

'You think you're so clever? Who are you? No one. Nothing! That's who!!'

My car slowed to a stop and I was able to press my hands into my soggy eyes,

'What's so special about her? Nothing, nothing, she's nothing!'

'She is pathetic,' I reasoned. 'Nothing better than me, nothing! I bet she purposefully got pregnant just to catch James. Yes, that's what happened, she knew she would never have him otherwise.'

I concentrated on slowing my breathing down as I changed from first gear to second.

'...don't be stupid, there is no room for you in front of me!'

I sped up a little to close the gap between my Mercedes and the Fiat to stop a Blue Vauxhall nudging its way to my lane. I watched it as it surrendered its claim and I felt a small surge of satisfaction as it pushed its way in behind me.

This lull in anger gave way to a familiar hatred of Olivia and once more the devil depression chatted in my ear.

'How sweet Jane was. How kind and gentle she was. It was fate that James should meet her and the gods have given them their child. Whereas you, Olivia, you have nothing but this traffic jam,' he said.

I had heard his voice many times but this time I was angry enough to chat back.

'She is ugly with her straight hair, sharp face and buck teeth. What could James see in her?' I seethed.

'He saw a spirited, contented woman with a love of her life, something you have lacked for many years, and as for sharp features: her hair maybe straight and her nose too long but her smile welcomes any stranger. You cannot compare yourself to her. And what about your imperfect face? Your eyes are too small, your nose is too bulbous and your smile is distorted by your discoloured crooked teeth.'

I heard him laugh then I heard a car horn as I was jolted to move away from staring at my teeth in my wing mirror to place my hand back on the steering wheel and catch up with the queue of traffic that had moved way ahead of me.

'You are correct,' I replied; 'my teeth are crooked and they are not perfectly white, who am I to laugh at another when I need to perfect myself?'

This realisation that life could be sorted so easily silenced the drone of criticism from my depressive companion. He clearly agreed and backed away and my tears dried up for the final part of my journey.

Within days I was checked into Mr Sherpova's dental practice and I had him peer into my mouth and reassure me that I would very soon have a beautiful smile as I deserved.

'After all,' he said, 'You are a pretty little thing and it would be a shame to spoil your face due to the odd wonky tooth.'

It took less than fifteen minutes for Mr Sherpova to convince me that porcelain veneers were the ideal option to ensure a brighter smile. He added that the price was relative to the result; I could choose an over the counter tooth whitener for as little as £30 but, 'Really, will that give you the smile you deserve?'

Mr Sherpova was an elderly Egyptian-looking man. His brown skin had a greyish tinge and he seemed to quiver each time I nodded to any of his supporting argument for veneers.

'Your smile could last up to fifteen years and after that you simply return and we redo the procedure which is a great result for me as I get to see your pretty face once more.'

He offered me an insincere smile to round off his insincere compliment.

'Fifteen years you say, that's certainly better than I expected.'

'So veneers it is then, Ms Olivia?'

'Sure, yeah sure.'

'Good girl, a better choice. Beauty and brains what a wonderful combination. You listened well and understood it all; not many pretty women can do that.' He smiled and his assistant squirmed.

I was not entirely convinced by all of his points but my mind was distracted by the uncomfortable position I was in. The consultation took place entirely on a typical dentist's chair with Mr Sherpova leaning over me and his dental assistant hovering behind. I was intimidated by my ignorance of all the different procedures. His rehearsed speech was my research so I based my decision to spend £1200 per tooth on whatever he advised.

Within weeks I was checked into his Kensington High Street dental surgery to have each tooth filed down to a stump. He then made a mould of my teeth to get an impression of each one to have made into an individual veneer.

I had temporary caps fitted and I returned a couple of weeks later to have the permanent veneers fitted. It took a couple of hours to bind each tooth and I had to listen to the dentists hollow observations about my beautiful face, but afterwards I didn't care as I left with a Disney Cinderella smile that brightened any cloudy day.

As I displayed my teeth to my 'luncheon to late afternoon wine and evening champagne club', I paused over the thought, how easy it was to change my life by my looks. But why stop with a smile? My nose, my slouching eyes, my unshapely bottom; it was all easy to alter to the style I wanted. And why should I not contemplate a change? My forties were approaching and society does not think twice about changing hair colour to deceive others? So why would it be so difficult to tweak the area beneath the hairline?

My dear Jason, the summer my forties arrived, you were finishing university and I know you had invited me to your graduation. I am sorry that I did not attend but hopefully, now you understand that I felt I could not come because on that day in July, my nose was recovering from being broken in three places. I did explain to your mother the problem, but back then I could not be photographed with the front of my face covered by bandages.

However, your graduation picture resides in my room on my table and each time I apply my makeup I look at the picture of you in your gown in front of your university fountain. You are surrounded by love from your mother, dressed in green with a proud smile, and Colin hugging both you and Janet. There was no space for me wearing a white mask on your happy day.

That said, I regret many things but not sharing your life and hailing your great achievements has marred mine. I wish I could relive that July and, if I could, then I promise that, regardless of my face, I would have been there to watch you claim your master's degree and I would have hugged you until you felt the pride I have for you, my darling Jason.

CHAPTER SIXTEEN

JASON

I put my aunt's manuscript down and nudged Jessica awake. I'd been seeing Jess for two months but I'd known her from university. We were friends for years before she agreed to go out with me.

'Jess, do you remember my graduation?' I asked,

She sleepily looked up at me and reluctantly replied, 'Yes, why?'

'We were only given two tickets weren't we? Two tickets and if we wanted more then we had to go through a faff of getting them via the admin department and everyone complained as they wanted their brothers and sisters there – remember?'

'Yes, I suppose so. It was a pain to get my brother in as well as my parents when I graduated, but they explained it was to keep the numbers down in the ceremony hall.' Jessica still had her eyes shut,

'Aah right,' I said, 'I didn't know the reason for it but then I never needed to go through the crap of trying to get more tickets as I only needed two for my mum and dad, yet my Aunt Olive said she'd been invited?'

'So?'

'I never invited her. I didn't even know whether she could or couldn't come as I didn't invite her. Not important, in the great scheme of things, but she had one of her nose jobs at the time of my graduation and she has my graduation picture on her dressing table – didn't even know she had one. I remember that day though, not so much for the ceremony but for the hangover I nursed all day.'

Jess went back to sleep but that night I lay awake thinking about my aunt, but also getting wound up by the last-minute breakfast meeting that was organised at 7 am. I needed to catch the 5.18 train which meant I needed to be out of bed by 4.15 am.

This is an hour our body is at its lowest temperature as it's following its natural circadian rhythm under the premise that we are in a deep sleep. Therefore, to have an alarm shake our brain back to consciousness and our cold body back to life is a painful experience – far more painful than if this siren sounded just one hour later. To avoid this piercing pain my brain decided it would be better to just remain awake and periodically look at the clock and calculate how many hours remained of achievable sleep. As these hours decreased my anger and stress increased over my denied sleep. This anger continued as I shaved, showered, dressed and boarded the train.

The street lamps were still on and bedroom curtains were still shut but I was dragging myself to work to accommodate the senior director as he wanted the Stockley project account figures in early.

One benefit of getting an early train is having a seat. Usually, my fellow commuters are standing on my foot, pushing me into the back of others, flicking their hair in my face or farting on my leg and it wafting up my nostril. For many years I have spent the first hour of my days this way.

When I arrived at work there was a scattering of work

223

colleagues already at their desk. I sat down and opened the presentation file I had been working on all weekend.

'Have you heard, buddy?' called Neil from the desk adjacent to mine. He was a twenty-seven-year-old with love for pin stripe suits. His hair was cut short and gelled until it shone like a swimmer emerging form his chlorine pool.

'Obviously not Neil. I've just arrived.'

'Been here since six, usually am; get a lot of work done that way.'

'Good for you. Spit it out then, what am I supposed to have heard?'

'Yeah bud, meeting cancelled.' Neil was now standing to emphasise the word cancelled. My jaw bit into my polystyrene coffee cup.

'Why?' I screeched.

'Who knows bud, but probably be rescheduled either late eve or another dawn meet tomorrow. What I'll say to you bud, is don't plan anything.'

Neil sat down triumphant in his delivery of this irritating news. I sat at my desk staring at my computer screen, reluctant to turn it on to start my day.

'I need a new job. I need a new life,' I chanted to myself.

I looked at my phone as a distraction to the angry mood that was bubbling in my stomach. I decided to try my luck and see if my mum was up yet. She usually woke early and enjoyed tidying the house before Dad joined her for breakfast.

'Well I was actually just reading the paper before your father trudged down but I'd rather be speaking to you darling,' she said after I had spat out my frustration.

'Darling, your father and I have said time and time again you need to look elsewhere. Show them you mean business with your feet.'

'Nice idea Mum, but my bank manager might have something to say about that idea,' I sighed.

224

'Well if you can't then you can't, but please find more time for yourself my darling. You've been wanting to join an amateur dramatics for years, well now's your chance. See if Jessica would like to do it with you?'

'Again, nice idea, but I literally have no spare time to get a paper let alone join an amateur dramatics. Ah, it doesn't matter.'

'Well it should. Life's too short my little thespian. You weren't born to be boring. Ask your aunt if you need advice on that score.'

'Talking of which,' I said, 'was I supposed to have had Aunt Olive to my graduation? What do you remember?'

'Er, as I recall she was having one of her alterations, so to speak. We did invite her but, as with many events she was invited to, it was only half-hearted as she was never around; either an important black tie function she was going to or she was too bandaged or bruised, or whatever it was from her many procedures, to come to anything.

Jason, that woman was under the knife more times than a butcher's table but, lucky me, the sister who couldn't afford to go to the dentist, let alone alter my lumps and bumps, I was privileged, as her sister, to be privy to all the intricacies of her procedures, every gory detail.

She had her lips plumped with various products over the years from Gore-Tex (literally the stuff skiing jackets are made of, which apparently doesn't last) to fat transfer from another part of her body and then injected into her lips; this one she was very pleased with.

She had wrinkle-fillers around her eyes, forehead, mouth, neck and even hands. I confess I was envious of that one as the canyons around my eyes are getting so large that each time I look in the mirror I'm half expecting mountain climbers getting ready to descend down into the facial valleys. So, Olivia's skin remained smooth whilst mine resembles the London bus route map.'

'It doesn't Mum.'

'Thank you, darling, that said, I was never convinced to smooth away my wrinkles as Olivia was trying to convince me to do as, apart from the cost, I was put off by the idea of injecting a synthetic acid, which was originally used to treat lip atrophy (facial fat loss) for HIV patients and now it's used to plump the faces of perfectly healthy people to push out their wrinkles. Did you know, it's made of millions of microspheres which is also used to dissolve surgical sutures? Yes, your father really would not have appreciated the conversation with the bank manager: "Yes sir, my wife used the mortgage money to fill her face with acid used to dissolve surgical sutures."

'It didn't stop there as she had boob jobs, nose jobs, a knee lift I think, er, ooh, she had her eyes lifted, brow lifted. Oh Jason, the list was endless. Monstrous list. I'll say one thing,' my mum continued, 'she doesn't look her age. She has supped at the fountain of youth, but she certainly paid a hefty sum to dine there, or at least Mark did.'

I heard Mum sigh then she broke off to talk to Dad whilst I was still on the phone.

'No, I'm talking to Jason. He's not happy Colin. They've cancelled a presentation or some such.'

I heard Dad reply that I should get another job and that my boss doesn't deserve me.

'I can still hear you Mum… Mum stop talking to Dad, I'm still here. I'm hanging up Mum!' I shouted.

'Oh yes, darling, now remember, tell your boss that this isn't good enough and he needs to buck up his ideas.'

I put the phone down and I smiled at the innocent idea of telling a man who dictated my working life to buck up his ideas. I decided to continue reading my aunt's letter instead of doing any work, at least for another hour.

CHAPTER SEVENTEEN

OLIVIA

Taking control of my appearance almost became a full-time job and why not? Why should I not scrub away the niggling nuances of an imperfect body and face? I was certainly not the only one; many of my lunchtime friends had their surgeon on speed dial and, bizarrely, our comparisons of supposedly secret procedures bought us a tiny bit closer.

These friends were a blessed distraction to thinking about the progress of Jane's pregnancy. However, Rae Summer Tanner was born in the October and, reluctantly, I went to see her when she was nearly a month old. She was bundled into a lemon blanket and snuggled in her cot. I could feel the pride oozing from her parents. I felt an imposter standing in their living room; I didn't want to look at her or coo over her the way any other guest did, I just wanted to throw the romper suit gift at her parents and run. Fortunately, it was easy to slip away as conversation with either Jane or James dwindled to the odd stagnated sentence as their preoccupation was on the squeaks, snuffles and shuffles from Rae.

I left after less than an hour and drove back to Mark. When I saw him at home he was huddled behind his desk concentrating on his computer screen. I yearned to run up to him, hug him and to feel the same tender kisses on my forehead that Jane had from James. But I didn't dare to step into his office, instead I waited at the doorway watching him work.

'What?' he said with his eyes still locked onto his screen.

'Oh nothing, really,' I said timidly.

'Then get lost, I'm working.'

I retreated to the kitchen and sat on a stool for over an hour watching the light dim to a blackish grey. My mind was numb with the odd niggling criticisms of the familiar whispers from my devil's voice reminding me how pathetic I was. Eventually Mark walked into a dark kitchen and put the light on.

'What are you doing in the dark you weird woman?' Mark chuckled to himself as he reached for a beer in the fridge. 'I have some friends over tonight and a few will be staying,' he said. I nodded a heavy head and said nothing.

I knew these friends, they were loathsome, leaching, lecherous men who used my home as a drink and drug den. I would serve them, clear up after them, listen to their crude jokes and accept their cruel jibes about me. Mark said very little to defend his wife as he was often too drunk to care about his guests' crass conduct.

'I really don't want them here,' I meekly muttered, 'just not today, not this weekend. It's just that I'm feeling quite down and...'

'Ahh here we go again. What is it this time? You feel lonely? You feel worthless? You saw someone with a baby and now you're depressed? Heard it all before, Olive, get over it.'

'Please Mark...' Mark tutted and left me sitting in the kitchen.

Within the following hour, the first of his friends bombarded my living room. I had changed to greet them from grey tracksuit bottoms and vest, the perfect outfit for a whimpering, feeble woman sitting in her kitchen, to a vibrant lady dressed entirely in Chanel, complete with a painted smile etched across her face.

As the evening progressed they started their familiar questions. These were designed to humiliate me, in particular my sexual preferences. I slipped past their bullying and forced my smile to remain on to hide my desire to scream.

Just before midnight I was sitting in the kitchen when I heard female laughter. I shuddered as I knew this evening my living room had taken another step towards a depraved dirty cellar. In this hour, money was used to deceive my old guests that they were virile, desired, young handsome men whom beautiful women yearned for. It is the same deception women have played since we were created and decided to take revenge on men who have tried to deceive us, since time began, that we are lesser human beings because of our gender.

These women were in control and raped my husband and his friends' wallet under the guise of desire. This fact would always make me smile but instead, tonight, I felt more alone than I ever had as all I could think about was the sweet innocence of James' and Jane's household. Within their warm cottage was held an abundance of love and within mine was held sordid, sad and putrid old men. The contrast accentuated my loneliness as I knew I did not belong where I lived.

I decided it was better for me to silently slip away to my bed, but before I could stagger up the stairs I heard my name being called. I forced my smile back on my face and stood in the doorway of the cellar. There in front of me was a typical sight of about five women teasing ridiculous men out of their clothes and ultimately their money.

Jason, I won't elaborate on this scene as although I am sure you are wise enough to guess at what I saw (and it was a scene I had witnessed many times), but that night the cellar was full and my eyes drifted around the room and my mouth curled in revolt. Usually on a night like this my mind would focus on the need to get my cleaners in as soon as practical, but that night I wanted to abandon my house and move away.

In the corner by my marble fireplace sat my husband in a wingback chair. He was staring at me across the room and his eyes had an evil smirk about them. Beside him on the floor was a twenty something girl, she had her back to me so all I could see was her flowing red hair draped around her shoulders with a few static strands attached to Mark's leg.

'Olivia, join us,' he said across the room.

My disgust made my body twist. I focused on Mark who was the only one dressed and I shook my head. I knew he could see my revulsion but instead he laughed at me.

'You are my wife and I would like you by my side, so come.'

'No!' I said.

He then got up and walked over his friends to the opposite corner of the room, to where I was standing. I flinched as I was waiting for a barrage of abuse but instead he grabbed my arm and pulled me into the room.

'Please, I don't want to be here Mark, please let me go.'

Mark said nothing so I began to pull on my arm which caused me to stumble over a pale, fat, investment banker called Andrew. His stomach bellowed in and out like a Scottish bagpipe as he shuffled his 115 kilo body away from me. Thankfully I avoided falling upon him entirely as Mark yanked me away and dragged me to his corner.

'Please Mark!' I pleaded and I began to cry. Only then did he stop and look at me. We stood for only moments but these sordid seconds shifted time to feel like hours. Around us lay sweaty men entangled around faceless women, their sodden bodies slipping off one another as they slid to their next prey.

'Then go my love, my wife. Then go.'

Mark continued to stare at me and I could see his huge pupils absorbing the colour of his iris to make his eyes entirely black.

'I said go,' he calmly repeated. 'Go!' His voice rose an octave to a shout: 'Go!'

This one word was deliberate and strong and still I stood in fear, unable to move. Mark resolved my paralysis by grabbing on my arm once more and yanking me back across the room. This time, when I again fell over Andrew, Mark did not try to pick me up but instead dragged me across the floor with my feet dragging behind me.

He continued up the stairs and into my bedroom and there he pushed me onto my bed. The room was dark except for the moonlight peering into my room. It bathed Mark's face in silver and white moon beams making him look as though he was a 1930s' film star. For the briefest of time I sensed reluctance in him to move and for that moment I thought he might melt in the moonlight and move to my bed and hold me within these silver beams. Instead this film star flinched when this scene whispered 'cut' and he ran off the set closing my door behind him.

This one scene together stopped my tears and I sat on my bed tired with a thumping headache. I felt confused but my exhaustion forced me to flop on my bed and stare into a hollow space in my bedroom. I covered my ears and I allowed myself to sleep.

In the morning I pulled myself from the position I had fallen asleep in and I grabbed my aching head. My headache had not left me from the previous evening so I decided to stagger downstairs in search of water and some tablets. When I got to my bedroom door I found it to be locked. I tugged at the door handle but it was firmly shut. I called out to Mark to open it but I heard nothing except for my crackling voice and the rattling door. I banged on the door for most of the remaining part of the morning and I only stopped when I finally heard Mark.

He was not in the house but outside. I rushed to the window to see my husband get into his car with the red-head from yesterday. I didn't see anything more than her hair as she slipped into his sports car and they drove away. In vain I banged on the window. He wasn't going to hear me as his Ferrari sped down the drive way but I had nothing else to offer. I didn't have my phone with me nor was there a phone in my room to call for help.

I was helpless and I was angry. I was angry at Mark for locking me in my room with nothing to eat and I was angry at myself for being here; for being a feeble, pathetic woman that allowed my husband to drag me from my living room and lock me in my bedroom. In that room on that day I lambasted myself for being married to Mark.

I had been angry many times before but, as always, this strength did not last as by mid-afternoon, as the sun hid behind greying threatening clouds, the devil whispered in my ear once more to remind me that I was worthless and I deserved little more than to lie on the carpet and feel nothing but hunger and loneliness. His voice was far stronger than mine, and so by early evening I had set up home under my duvet on the floor and sobbed myself to sleep.

Throughout the night I wallowed in self-pity, drifting from sleep to panic that no one would come and help me and that here I would die from starvation. I calculated that I could last possibly two weeks in my room before death arrived. I imagined my lifeless body being discovered by Mark and I fantasised about the guilt he would feel at allowing his wife to die in her bedroom.

It was an indulgent thought as I knew that in the morning my cleaner would arrive and it would be a matter of waiting for her to get to my room to clean it. This occurred at around 10.15. When she opened the door she was startled to find me. She stopped listening to her iPod, pulled her earphones out and said, 'I'm sorry, ma'am, I didn't know you were here!'

'That's fine Debbie, I was just having a mid-morning snooze

with the door shut,' I replied, whilst straightening the bedclothes to distract my cleaner away from the musty smell of the room and the fact the door had been locked from the outside.

I had listened to her sing George Michael for over an hour before she came to my bedroom, which had spurred me to shower and change out of the evening clothes I had been wearing for thirty-six hours before she unlocked my bedroom door. As I watched Debbie dust the room and strip my bed I knew she was feeling embarrassed at invading my privacy. I do not normally stay in the room she is cleaning but I wanted to tell her that she had saved me and if she had not come then I would either have to wait for Mark to release me or wait for her to come again three days later. It was lunacy that I was unable to say thank you and instead I had to pretend that I had an indulgent, privileged snooze. It occurred to me that she was probably envious of the idea that she was cleaning for a woman who had leisure time to take random naps.

I left Debbie to vacuum where I had been sleeping most of the previous day and night. I went downstairs feeling envious of her working all day then returning home to her tiny house to then prepare dinner for her husband and two teenage boys. This envy led me to pick up the phone and call Carolanne instead of taking any headache tablets.

When I heard my friend say, 'Hello,' I began to sob. However, I was now so bored of crying or sobbing or whimpering that I hit my head with the receiver to try and make myself stop. I had spent so many days, weeks and months in this state of self-pity that I had begun to not notice that my eyes were often sodden with tears. I would no longer stop whatever I was doing to cry over something, but instead, I continued to cry and I got on with reading a magazine or preparing lunch or reapplying my makeup whilst crying so, when I heard Carolanne and again the tears started to flow, I heard the devil voice say, 'Not again! Olive, shut up.'

When I hit my head in anger, I thought I heard a clacker sound, like the sound of a director's clacker board indicating 'cut' to end a scene. This sound shook me and I was able to say to Carolanne with icy clarity. 'I need your help, I need to get out. I think I'm going mad.'

'Olive?' she questioned. I had not replied to her 'hello' and so her confusion was understandable but I felt a 'hi, it's me' to begin the conversation was superfluous to this telephone call.

'Mark is killing me and I have got to get out. Help me, I need to go.'

I did not wait for her reply as this was the first time since I had met Mark that I had decided I must go and my desire to leave had made me impatient, which swept away any niceties of a conversation with my friend whom I had not spoken to in over three months.

'Er, of course, I'm in the supermarket at the moment but I can leave Toby to get the rest after work and I'll leave now. It will take me at least forty-five minutes to get to you but I'll be there my sweet, as soon as I can.'

'Thank you.'

'Sweetie, has he hurt you again?'

'No, but I have to go, I've got to go. I'm going mad.'

It took my friend fifty minutes to get to me in her Vauxhall Astra. I could see through her back window, her shopping poking out of the boot space. Carolanne had put on weight over the last few years and her hair was now cut to her shoulders, which she wore in a ponytail. Her jeans were worn and her cardigan old. She no longer wore heels but comfortable trainers. She had aged but her blue eyes and warm smile was still as intoxicating as the day I met her nearly twenty years ago.

I had packed a small suitcase and I was waiting by the front door. In the time I spent waiting for her it occurred to me that Mark was not due to return home until the following weekend, nearly five days later. It also occurred to me that he did not know when Debbie came to clean my house or even if we had a cleaner. These facts helped me to dry my eyes, pick up my suitcase, hug my beloved friend and get into her car to drive away from my prestigious address.

CHAPTER EIGHTEEN

I stayed in Carolanne's spare room which was filled with boxes that hadn't been opened since the day she moved in. The room had not been decorated and it still had the mirrored fitted wardrobe from the previous owner. The house was strewn with cat hairs, dog hairs and any other animal that freely wandered the house. After a few days I was searching for the vacuum cleaner and I even considered calling Debbie to spritz their house in exchange for not cleaning mine for one week.

The other occupants were ornamental angels. They were scattered across the house on every windowsill, stair, fireplace mantel – I even found a green fairy poking its head out between the outflow pipe of the downstairs toilet and the toilet bleach.

To my orderly view, Carolanne and Toby led a chaotic life, flitting from one spontaneous idea to the next. Toby worked part time as an accountant but he was dedicated to brewing his own beer and had aspirations of setting up his own beer company with Dan, his neighbour. Carolanne spent her days tending her vegetable patch and meeting friends at either her gardening club or dog walking club and had aspirations of starting her own dog grooming company with Kate, another neighbour.

I was welcome in their house but I felt anxious that I was an inconvenience. I mitigated this by offering to help with cooking or shopping for them, but it was always politely refused.

'You're our guest, please just relax; treat this home as your own and let your spirit grow and your soul to find new peace.'

It was not long before I began to regret my choice of packed clothes. I had packed as an angry woman preoccupied with how unfair my life was. I had robotically stuffed the usual items in my bag such as a teal cocktail dress, silver sling back stilettoes, teamed with a silver pashmina. It was only after a week of living with Carolanne and Toby in their little cottage that I realised the grey tracksuit bottoms, which were taken out of the bag to make room for the red patent evening shoes that matched another red cocktail dress was, in hindsight, a foolish option.

After a fortnight Carolanne organised an intervention. I knew something was going to happen as she had returned home with strawberries, cream and some scones.

At midday your mother arrived clutching a tin of homemade shortbread. Shortly after, Tatiana knocked on the door with a bottle of pink champagne. We were ushered into the drawing room and we all sat around the coffee table prepared for afternoon tea.

'I didn't know any of you were coming,' I said. 'I would have changed, I'm sorry these trousers are…'

'Olive, you look fine and even if you didn't, none of us would care. Sit down,' declared your mother.

'Now,' began Carolanne, who had evidently assumed the position of chairwoman for this meeting. 'Sadly, James can't make it today but he has assured me that everything we decide he will support. Also, I have lavender oil diffusing and if it's too much then let me know but try and relax, sweetie.'

'Too much, turn it off.'

'The diffuser isn't for you, Tatiana, so shut-up and put up,' said my sister. 'Lovely as always, by the way Carol; bumper harvest of lavender like last year? Colin's sock drawer sachet still smells of your garden. Anyway, enough of me, decisions to be made, decisions to be made.'

'On what?' I tentatively offered.

'On sorting you out. And about time, dear sister.'

'Okay, okay, Janet! Now sweetie, it's not a case of sorting you out but, instead, offering you a way to find your path. We need you to find inner guidance which will take you towards the right light at this crossroads in your life,' said Carolanne in a gentle meditative tone.

I flinched at the prospect that I was about to be lectured at, especially from Carolanne. She had recently qualified as a holistic teacher and together with her dog-walking, she also wanted to begin her own company as a life coach, called, 'Peace Within'. Alongside all her angels were various crystals and stones. She even placed rose quartz in her water to absorb its healing energy, known as 'spirit water'.

'Find inner strength from your guardian angels. I've connected with mine and I truly feel at one,' she had said on a few occasions, though I suspected if I had tried to connect with my guardian angel, I would merely have received their name card with the slogan, 'Whatever, I'm out shopping.'

'I know all of this, I just need to get myself sorted; my head is still spinning but as soon as it slows down then I can get myself, you know, in the zone and in search of inner peace, just as you've already advised me to do Carol,' I promised.

'We know you will but we want to offer you our support and love to make this bumpy road a little smoother.'

'What Carolanne is trying to say,' interrupted Janet, 'is we've found you a house. It's only temporary but it's pretty and until the divorce comes through, it's affordable. I've discussed it with Colin and we can just about cover the rent for you.'

'I second that,' said Carolanne.

Janet then nodded to me and then Carolanne nodded and

then they both nodded and smiled in unison. Tatiana winked at me and sipped on her champagne.

'That's really sweet but I'm sure Mark will find me a place. I doubt he wants me around anymore anyway…'

Once more I began to sob as the prospect of divorce trickled into my head. I had contemplated it on many occasions but to hear it from friends stung my brain and the only way I could sooth the pain was to cry.

'He won't pay for a penny, sweetie.'

This was the first time Tatiana had uttered a word. Her spindly body was slouched back in the arm chair and her hand clasped her glass as a gesture of defiance to sober people across the land.

'After all,' she continued, 'has he even contacted you?' All three ladies stared at me waiting for my response and reluctantly I shook my head, no.

'I didn't think he had. Then you have to ask yourself, Ol, why? Could it be that he is too angry to respond to your disappearance?' she said.

'Or maybe he's too embarrassed by his behaviour and he's mustering up the confidence to call me?' I replied, to which they all scoffed.

'Or maybe, sweetie, he hasn't noticed you have gone.'

Tatiana's synopsis of Mark's lack of response made the bee sting in my head burrow deeper and again I flinched and quietly sobbed a little more.

'Either way, darling, we all know the type of man he is and his money lives with him. He has sewn every penny he owns to the veins in his body. He will not rip off one coin to voluntarily give to you and his lawyers are there to ensure he doesn't have to – even if it means whipping you in the courts until you are the one who bleeds like a pathetic school child at the mercy of the school bully. You will hurt trying.'

'A bit harsh, Tatiana!' declared Carolanne, 'Let us not focus on that as it is a bridge…'

'Or tidal wave,' interrupted Tatiana.

'No, let us just concentrate on the now. Let us focus on you and bring your new life to you. The house is perfect and I heard only this morning that Dave, the baker in the village, is in need of a full time assistant or I know that Jean at the National Trust shop needs a hand, so there are jobs out there to set you up,' soothed Carolanne.

'A job?!' I screeched. 'Sorry I didn't mean it to come out that way, but I don't know about a job. It's just that I haven't worked in nearly fifteen years, since we were first married. I wouldn't know where to start!'

'You start by turning up,' said Janet. 'And if you can't do that then you sell the emblems of your marriage – those diamond earrings can go for a start. That'll pay for a couple of months' rent.'

'Noo!' I said instinctively as I grabbed my earlobes. 'I'd rather just wait to see if Mark will give me something. I know you think he wouldn't but he's not that heartless, he wouldn't leave me destitute,' I prayed.

It was a pointless plea to my friends as if I was pleading to the jury after the verdict had been passed.

'Ahh, Olivia, listen to yourself!' Janet's tone was dismissive 'Always the same! You've always wanted to take the easy way out. "I know," you think, "I'll see what everyone else will give me," – well not now. In your middle age you can start to mother yourself not let others parent you.'

'You can do it, sweetie,' Carolanne said as sweetly as Janet's words were bitter.

I tried to dodge further awkward questions from my hostess and eventually she turned to my sister and said that I need time to contemplate my new beginning. Janet agreed and helped clear the coffee table declaring that the strawberries were delicious for this time of year and that it was surprising how sweet they were considering it was out of season for this fruit.

They left the room chatting about the state of the vines in their garden whilst balancing tea cups, plates of scones and cake in their hands.

Tatiana slipped the last of her champagne down her throat.

'You know they have found a cottage and they have, indeed, already found a job for you within walking distance of the house. The eighteenth century terraced cottage is nestled down an alleyway with a willow tree in the front garden. In the village, you can buy your eggs and milk from the farm shop by the church. Your evenings will be gentle, maybe watching television or simply watching the sunset over the corn fields behind your house. Occasionally you'll venture out after dark for a church social event, but don't worry, they will never be a raucous event as there are too few people in the village to fill the church hall. Your hobbies will dwindle to baking and walking but when you feel the loss of your past you can smile, just a little, that at least you wouldn't have to endure the occasional visits from Mark.'

Tatiana looked at me and leaned in so that I would catch her whisper.

'Are you looking forward to that life, my friend?'

I shrugged and looked towards the door that muffled the laughter from Carolanne and my sister about how difficult it is to get scones to break in the middle.

'Don't shrug. I know you, my sweet, you wouldn't last in that life. You would shrivel away and 'Olivia the Spinster' would rise triumphant. You wouldn't be recognisable shrouded in a brown oversized cardigan and sensible shoes. Your electric blanket would be your prized possession as it will be the only thing left to keep you warm at night. Your hair would frizz to a grey wool hat with a bun for its bobble. Lines would quickly etch their way across your face and you would stoop under the growing weight of boredom upon your tiny frame.

'Tell me, Olivia, is this what you crave instead of the exciting beautiful world Mark gave you?'

'I'm nothing to Mark and it's driving me insane. He left me in my room.'

'So? You escaped. He's not stupid, he knows you're resourceful and you'd be free soon enough – as you were! He didn't murder you did he? He didn't hold your throat in his hands and squeeze? He didn't beat you until you bled? He didn't shake you until your head burst? No? Instead once more, my friend, you have everything you could possibly wish for the payment of supporting a selfish man. Is it worth leaving him for that little personality trait?

I knew Carolanne and Janet would try and convince you to trial their life without any consideration that to do so, you would have to abandon your life. And pay attention, Ol, this is your life and if you choose to snuff it out then there'll be no chance to resurrect it. Mark won't take you back and instead he will stamp on your grave in revenge for leaving him.'

Before I could answer, Carolanne and Janet walked back in.

'One thing's for sure, Ol, at least you have left that monster,' declared my sister. 'I was just saying to Carolanne whilst loading the dishwasher, at least you are free from the man I wish you'd never met – let alone married. I say it to Colin regularly, why couldn't you have met someone like my Colin? Colin is wonderful and I couldn't care less that he has less money than a bankrupt banker caught by the taxman.'

'He's not that bad,' I retaliated, 'Mark I mean, he's not that bad. He may not hold me the way Colin does you but I know Mark cares for me.'

'Rubbish, rubbish! Am I really hearing this?' Janet clasped her head then shook her hands at me. 'How can you say that? You maybe my sister but the years of being married to that man has made you blind. The man doesn't love or even respect you and finally – FINALLY, you have left him and the people who do love you are here for you.'

'Stop it,' I shouted, 'I'm not a child you can bully anymore, Janet.'

'Oh, stop crying, Ol! As usual it's world of Olivia with her glossy glasses on. Well take them off and see what's really around you.'

Carolanne came to my side.

'Please don't think we're ganging up on you, sweetie,' she soothed.

'I'm sorry but I'm here,' I whimpered, 'because I had a disagreement with my husband.'

'A disagreement! A disagreement? Listen to yourself, sis, this was not a disagreement over who puts the washing away or who puts the rubbish out. The man locked you in your room after bringing prostitutes back to your house for the enjoyment of his perverted business friends and you were there to serve them. This is not a marriage; it's a man and his brothel bitch!'

'You've got it wrong, it's not that bad.' I meekly offered as a counter offer to her appraisal of my marriage. It was all I had for a defence, however, I didn't expect this to reduce my big sister to tears.

'You can't believe that!' she screamed. She didn't wait for an answer but instead stormed out of the room and out of the house.

The next few days were spent mulling over their offer of a new life for me and whether this would be a sensible turn. I felt discombobulated as for the last fifteen years I had been sailing down life's river on a yacht in comparison to everyone else's rowing boat. If I was to change course then it could only mean jumping off onto a dinghy with one oar. This hand brake turn could mean returning to the sandbank of yesteryear if my dinghy crashed into the side. I didn't want to return to watching others sail by as I sat in the mud unable to move.

Was Mark a cruel husband or was it just his personality to have rages against people he loves?

'Maybe I should be grateful that this is just the way he shows his love for me. He has no one else to vent his frustrations on,' I said to Carolanne over breakfast on the following Sunday.

'You don't really believe that do you, sweetie? '

'I know it sounds ridiculous… '

'Yes very!'

I pressed on over dinner on Tuesday.

'…Yes but, you don't see how tired he gets and we all need someone to release our frustrations on. Isn't love understanding how a person displays their worries of life as well as tenderness when calm?'

'We all need support but respect should never be absent – which it is with Mark,' replied my friend.

By Wednesday morning Carolanne was already shaking her head, 'no' before I had uttered one word in Mark's defence, but I persevered.

'We all behave differently to events in our life and our partners are there to recognise this and understand our reactions. I understand him and although I don't like how he behaves, surely I should respect that this is just his personality… he's under so much pressure at work Carol. Really it's how everyone behaves.'

'Then I pity all the other partners. Olivia, you can't disguise his venomous ways under the pretence that it's just his personality. He lives in a society with a plethora of rules on how we treat each other but he chooses to ignore all of them. We don't hide behind a personality trait to justify our actions. He chose to lock you in your bedroom. He chose to bring back women in front of you and he chooses every day to ignore the main rule, which is to respect one another, to respect you, his wife. Life is not a trial with a right action and a wrong action, my sweet; instead it should be an easy choice to love.'

The jury had left a note on the side of the bench before they left and it simply read, 'guilty'. I was defending a man and a life that had already been taken down to the gallows. My breath was wasted arguing in an empty room, so I shut up and helped Carolanne hull winter peas picked from her allotment.

The following week I watched Carolanne and Toby work together in the garden. I noticed how my elegant beautiful friend would catch a wink from her husband. I saw Toby, a cheerful, stocky, balding man, offer gentle hugs and sweet kisses whenever he could give his lips to her rosy cheeks. And I observed how she would smile to herself long after he had left her side.

I watched with envy at their love for one another but I also observed how everyday they struggled to pay their bills. Their cottage needed repairs and Carolanne needed new clothes as well as a hair appointment to cover her invasion of grey. She seemed oblivious to these worries and I assumed it was because she loved the man who shared her life.

If I was to leave my house with my swimming pool and my new Porsche Cayenne then I too would be submerged into a similar life to Carolanne, but with the difference that I would not have a man's love to disguise my crumbling house or my greying hair. I would forfeit my hairdresser, my stylist, my beautician, my surgeon, my luncheon friends with the restaurants I frequent and I would lose the man I had been married to for over fifteen years. He had rewarded me with a lavish life of cars, clothes and credit cards for the price of an absent husband or a snarling companion. In comparison to poverty and worry then was it not a small price to pay?

That Sunday was a crisp, cold, bright sunny day. In celebration of the end of autumn Toby and Carolanne decided to host a British winter barbecue. The brioche buns were bought and the hand-made chili and sundried tomato beef burgers were made the night before. By 11am the pasta, green and three bean salads were made in anticipation for the sun pushing its way through the white sky.

As the coals were lit and guests arrived, it became apparent the sun was remaining firmly behind locked clouds. Cardigans and jumpers under thick coats were thrown on as Pimms were poured and a keg of Toby's beer was opened. Janet and Colin were part of the party of twenty or so and when she saw me Janet hugged me in place of a 'hello'.

Carolanne's friends from her allotment, badminton club and various other clubs and wives of Toby's beer club all gathered around the new face at the party. I didn't feel threatened at their questions as they were all lovely genuine ladies who preferred digging the earth than judging others. Tina, one of the badminton ladies, who also worked at the Fairmont National Trust shop, commented on my cardigan and whether it was from M&S. I smiled at this short round lady with small round-rimmed glasses perched on her button nose;

'It isn't actually mine, I needed to borrow it from Carolanne as I hadn't brought a jumper with me, but yes I think it's M&S.'

I was grateful for the blue cardigan even though it clashed with my red Burberry jeans as I snuggled under a wool blanket.

Just before the strawberries and cream were brought out as dessert I could hear a commotion from within the house. Ruffled voices made us all turn towards the kitchen window. These voices became clearer and I could distinguish the angry shouts from Janet and Colin, the diplomatic intermediary voices of Toby and his beer friends and the defiant monotone, 'Get lost!' sentences from my husband.

Mark pushed passed people in the kitchen doorway and marched towards me, surrounded by my new friends. I was instantly hot and anxious. My mouth was dry and my heart was beating against my chest trying to escape the captivity of my rib cage.

'It has taken me ages to figure out where you'd be and look where I find you – in a mother's meeting with pathetic, old women. Look at you – you sad old woman.'

Mark's face was puce and an artery in his neck was swollen with blood and throbbing in time to his barrage of anger. I pushed the blanket off my legs but apart from my arms no other part of my body worked; my legs had sunk into the deckchair and my mouth refused to operate. I was unable to say anything to rebuke my husband to curb his language and lower his voice. I spied the look of horror from Tina who had been sitting next to me and I wanted to apologise but still my jaw refused to open.

Janet had finally freed herself from the clutches of her husband and came running down the garden towards Mark.

'Get out, get out! Just get out you revolting man,' she hollered, then lurched towards him. Mark instinctively ducked away from Janet's fist. When she missed she pulled her fist back to take another attempt but she was blocked by Colin who pulled her away. Colin and three others turned to my husband and demanded he leave.

'I'm going don't worry. I have no intention of staying at your pathetic BBQ. It's November if you haven't noticed, freaks!' He straightened his collar then turned once more to me, 'I'll be outside waiting, if you don't come then don't ever come home.'

Mark then turned and pushed his way through his shocked audience and I was left mortified at his behaviour. All the ladies around me asked if I was okay to which I nodded and I apologised to everyone just to ease their stunned faces and to indicate that it was alright to begin their babble of, 'I can't believe that!' or 'What a nasty man', 'Every other word was a swear word – how rude, he didn't stop!!'. Once this was over then it gave way to each one recounting the series of events when a big mean man came to Carolanne and Toby's barbecue. I knew these stories would replay over the years but I did not want to stay to hear them. I apologised once more and I went to find Janet and Carolanne. Janet knew instantly that I was going to find Mark. I looked at her sad eyes and I said, 'Honestly, Janet, I'm fine. Really, it's fine, you know I can't stay.'

I hugged her and Carolanne and then I left the party for Mark who had come to claim me back.

Jason

I put down my aunt's script, amazed that my mum would fight Uncle Mark yet she would happily watch Aunt Olive leave.

'That's because it didn't happen that way!' protested Mum.

Mum had popped round one Saturday afternoon in the hope of catching Jessica, who had gone to visit her brother.

'Firstly, we had got your aunt to the point of actually leaving that man. Bearing in mind this was a few years back when she was still strong enough to go. Regardless of what she says to you, she was excited to be going. She was open to the idea of working in the National Trust shop and okay, it's not glamorous, but she would have loved it.

I do remember the afternoon tea very well. It was organised to merely introduce her to the idea of starting fresh. I did not shout or bully her into accepting anything (which is what she has written in my letter) and Jason, Tatiana was not there; I promise you, she was not there. We knew that woman wouldn't have supported the idea of us freeing Olivia from Mark so we did NOT invite her; it was just Carolanne and me, and that was all.

A little later (after Olivia had said she wanted to go to the cottage we had found), it was indeed the barbecue at Carolanne's. Olivia was happy, excited and confident for the first time in a long time. Then, as she describes, Mark turns up. I confess I tried to block the front door to try and stop him getting in but that was all. I didn't take a swing at him, honestly Jason, how could I have done? The man was twice my size.

Anyway, another thing your aunt has omitted from her description was just how rude Mark was. The air was blue, literally Jason, the air was blue. I'm not going to repeat what he said as you're my son, but the F word was used after every word. The lovely ladies, who had spent the afternoon bolstering Olive's spirits, weren't just called pathetic as she recalls but (and please excuse my language), they were the ugly effing C word.

As for how he spoke to Olivia, well Jason, she was an 'effing this, effing that, effing c word as well, and she took it all in as if he was gently admonishing her for not doing the washing-up. Looking back, I can still see her glazed expression as he was abusing her in front of everyone. She could, of course, have been as shocked as his audience who were all rooted to their seats in stunned silence. However, I doubt that excuse, as everyone around her had their mouths wide open, whereas Olivia was just casually taking it all in without hearing anything her husband was saying and even had a small childish smile to greet his vile words.

It was Colin who demanded he left and it was Toby and others who pulled him away from his rant and pushed him out of the house. I find it very telling that she remembers it to be me – the interfering, judgemental, big sister for trying to beat up Mark. But what she also doesn't recall was how we all comforted her after Mark left and how we all tried to ease her nerves in the hope she would stay.

And she did not leave with Mark as he left in a toddler tantrum haze and drove off leaving his prize toy behind. It was the next morning that she got in her car, after texting Mark all night and without warning to Carolanne and Toby, she left for that man.'

'She didn't say you pushed her back to him, Mum,' I said.

'Well it does in my version: she said that at the time she was scared of me, that she felt I bullied her into taking the cottage and that when she left for Mark I, apparently, shouted out "typical weak, ungrateful sister!" Ah Jason, when I read that I burst into tears; how could she accuse me of that after everything we had done for her?' Mum slung her head low. 'She returned to him and even though we tried again to get her to leave him, we never succeeded and she stayed with him. She became mistrustful of everyone, even accusing me of destroying her marriage! I'm sure she blames me for all of this.'

'She doesn't mum, she's probably just telling you it was the way she felt then – not now. Did you see much of Mark after the barbecue?' I asked,

'As little as possible, thankfully. I found it very difficult to speak to Olivia and almost impossible to be civil to Mark, so I drifted away from Olivia; but my fear for my little sister kept me holding on to her like a buoy rope and I worried every day how she was coping, living in that luxurious coffin of hers.'

Mum's voice had begun to crackle so she shook herself.

'Now darling, I must make a move. Remember, talk to Jessica about coming over on Sunday for a roast. I'm most likely going to do lamb followed by treacle pudding. Jessica does like treacle pudding doesn't she?'

I nodded and shortly afterwards Mum left, feeling a little sadder than when she'd arrived.

CHAPTER NINETEEN

OLIVIA

About twelve years ago to now

After I had returned to my house, I drifted back to being Mrs Mark Mathew Hopkins. My husband had found me and as punishment for my crime placed me on a ducking stool over the edge of my luxury yacht, but, to others, I appeared to be bathing under the sun on the deck.

Mark continued to take me to lavish work parties but now he would drop snide remarks about how I was dressed or how I behaved. He performed these insults for the benefit of his audience and for the metaphorical whipping he felt I deserved. Away from his audience, Mark would bear down on me about how embarrassing it was to listen to me speak to his friends when I knew nothing about anything, so I quickly learnt to stay quiet and smile at appropriate pauses.

Away from him, meant I could get off my ducking stool and breath a triumphant breath that I had survived a possible social drowning. This sigh of relief only lasted for the day he drove away down my driveway as the subsequent days were spent waiting for his return. On these days I would listen for his sports car on my driveway and fear would invade my chest causing my heart to race, my breath to quicken, my mind to freeze and nausea to fill my stomach. There was nothing I could do to shift this choking phlegm except anxiously wait for the screech of his returning brakes.

I tried to continue to see Carolanne and Janet but I was so tired of trying to explain my choice and I didn't want to justify my life to them, consequently, the visits trickled away until they were replaced with the odd text once a month to check if I was still alive.

James was different. I didn't see very much of him as his life was fully ensconced in children (second girl came two years later), Jane, house and work. Nevertheless, I rang him when I needed him.

'Always here for you, Ol, always here for you,' he would say.

James didn't judge me nor did he offer advice; he merely listened to my tales of suited old men getting drunk at Mark's firm parties and he would hold my hand when he saw me.

'Always here for you, Ol, always here for you. Jane tells us you need to come round more. You know she's a good listener is my Jane.'

'Oh James I'd bore her I know I would. You're enough for me. I know you need to get back soon to your lovely family. Thanks again for the flowers. Please tell Jane she's very sweet to pick them.'

'Just to make you smile, Ol.'

Then he would hug me good-bye.

'Don't leave it so long next time. There was blossom on the trees the last I saw you. Now the trees are bare and I can't believe your youngest is four and starting school already.'

'They're growing fast that's for sure. I've got to go but just ring anytime. I'm always here for you, always here.'

As the years passed, little changed other than the seasons; the majority of my time was spent shopping and meeting lunch friends or with my beautician for facials and massages once a week. Occasionally I met my cosmetic consultant to discuss a procedure I was considering. Indeed, one friend I did make was Alison, the receptionist at the clinic in the Harley Street branch. She was a plump young girl who seemed genuinely interested in how I had been since the last time she had seen me. She was enthralled about my tales of parties and first-class flights to New York or Brazil (or anywhere) to accompany my loving husband on his business trips. I was able to feed her with my stories and like a good chef I got great pleasure from her enjoyment of listening to my tales.

There was one slight difference in my life and that was the time I spent with Tatiana who was single and bored. I would accompany her to Stoning Town close to where I lived. We drank in the local wine bars or fashionable bistro pubs that had emerged thanks to the stock brokers who flooded Stoning Town in the late eighties to take advantage of the cheaper house prices in comparison to central London. Their presence forced local residents further afield as they, in turn, had taken advantage of the rising prices of their quintessentially British thatched cottages. As they moved out they and their estate agents were heard muttering, 'I can't believe how much I got for that house!'

All farming land had been sold to developers and the cornfields were forfeited to make way for exclusive estates of five bedroom with en-suite, mock Georgian houses. Consequently, Stoning was now a vibrant fashionable town with house prices rivalling the most expensive areas in London.

The town centre was stuffed with fashionable cocktail bars, Michelin starred restaurants, designer clothes shops, beauticians and art galleries. So, each Friday, I stepped back to my twenties with Tatiana, but this time as a manicured mannequin modelling designer clothes. For one night a week I felt a glimmer of power over other women, whose eyes surveyed me with envy. I, once more, commanded a power over the men who were out in these bars; they were men in their fifties looking for an escape from their third divorce and lavishing champagne upon women who were looking to be wife number four. These were men I had met twenty years ago, but they now sported a pregnant belly over their red jeans or hidden by a navy blue sporting jacket. Their hair was now thin and grey and their face was lined, but their ability to woo a woman with their wallet had not changed since the first day they discovered any seedy chat up line was effective with champagne.

I wasn't looking for another husband but I was searching for a forgotten kick. This search was often a jungle hunt when I was surrounded by young girls making me disappear in the eyes of my prey. But with the help of Tatiana we always found a group of men to take the bait and feed us with compliments and cocktails. However, by the end of the evening I needed my escape from Tatiana who, by then, was encouraging someone to come back to her newly built, luxury five-bedroom house with en-suites. It was not hard for her, as Tatiana was focused on her prey; so they got in one taxi and I slipped into another.

I confess, Jason, that my head was turned on a few occasions by particularly charming men who insisted on taking my mobile phone number. The subsequent week was always exciting when I would receive flirtatious texts from them. However, I only met two men outside of the Friday night ritual because I couldn't bring myself to abandon my wedding ring, as I always felt I was being watched and, if discovered, I would be publicly denounced by society.

So, I was the only faithful member in my marriage. Mark was oblivious to society's scorn and scoffed at any suggestion that he was immoral, crass and irreverent to any social etiquette. Women flowed through him like beer through an Englishman watching cricket on a lazy Sunday afternoon, but he escaped being reprimanded because he was envied by other men, flattered by many women and his wife was too irrelevant for him to take notice of her unhappiness.

It was early one autumn day when it changed. The house had been recently redecorated and, finally, I no longer had workman in my house from 7am until 5pm. I was able to enjoy the new look of my house, and this year it followed the trend of tartan accessories with dark walnut wood furniture accompanied with varying shades of cream silk walls throughout the house. My interior decorator had excelled herself, especially in the morning room. This room was a large orangery with a high ceiling and an elegant roof lantern. She had chosen a renaissance, sky blue wall paper with small, white, felt songbirds and butterflies upon it. The seven rolls needed to cover this room cost more than the long glass breakfast table that had been specially designed and made for me by a small French firm just outside Bordeaux.

It was worth the money and effort as this tranquil room had a calming effect on me, and I would start the day by running my hands across my silky walls or the polished glass of my table and look up to the bright sky peering in on me before I went to the kitchen and made myself a hot water with lemon.

Just after 11am I heard the wheels of Mark's Porsche outside my house and my body creased at the waist in reaction to the sound of his door slamming shut. It creased further when I heard another set of wheels and a door slam. My chest tightened when I heard the collective laughter of Mark and his prodigy, Grant.

I scuttled to the garden then ran to the front of the house as I saw them come into the kitchen, then into the music room. I scurried around my house like a burglar avoiding the house tenants. Eventually I had to face them, but only after I had changed from my pyjamas to a white, long Chanel spring/ summer dress. I wore my smile and greeted these men who were already drunk or stoned.

I dutifully went to the kitchen to make a sandwich for Grant
– a burly fat man with an odour problem. It was an excuse for me
to be away from them, so I took my time and made a platter of
bacon and egg sandwiches – being subservient gave me a purpose
and a reason to be anywhere other than wherever they were.

When I returned for the second time, Grant and Mark's
demands mimicked a bored child wanting anything other
than what they had. In particular, Grant had a penchant for
watermelon and badgered me to slice the watermelon he had
seen in the kitchen. I was reluctant to do this as I was saving it to
eat throughout the day on my detox Tuesday.

I tried to distract Grant with the sandwiches on the table or
the sliced kiwi on the fruit platter but he became more insistent
and I could sense a defiant tantrum welling up ready to pop any
moment.

'Just get the melon you stupid, useless woman,' shouted
Mark.

I was not going to win with my pleas, so reluctantly I
turned towards the kitchen but I was shoved aside by Grant
who stumbled passed me to steal the prized watermelon. He
staggered back and dumped the particularly huge, green fruit on
my glass table. I rushed to protect my table and both Mark and
Grant laughed at how I checked over for any possible damage.
I looked on helplessly as they discussed how to open my detox
watermelon.

'Just thump it open Grant. Ha, you missed – you're useless!'
laughed Mark.

They then both had a go at thumping my watermelon
and each time they did, I winced in anticipation for my table
shattering. Fists gave way to kicks around the room and after that
didn't work they both laughed at the green ball and took turns in
shouting at it, as if it was one of their work underlings who had
failed to perform. After a while Grant drunkenly disappeared
and re-emerged with his weekend shooting gun.

'Ha, Grant, you prick, what are you going to do? Shoot it open?'

In their stoned, drunk stupor they both paused for a while to laugh, a full belly laugh, at the idea of shooting a watermelon open.

'It'll teach the bitch to do what it's told – this is a 308 rifle!' quaffed Grant. 'Good enough to obliterate deer, so good enough to smash open this mother of a melon.'

They both laughed again and I shuddered at the idea of this seventeen-stone sweating sack of blubber aiming at my melon with blurred vision and hitting my beautiful new table instead.

Fortuitously, Grant dropped the gun and I sneaked behind him to grab it and place it back in the hallway with Mark's gun (there in preparation to shoot game at the 150 acre farm less than a mile away from my house).

I returned to my French renaissance style morning room and, to my horror, both Grant and Mark had taken it in turns to stamp on my Tuesday melon. It was not the loss of my detox fruit that I silently screamed out at, but the mess of red flesh across my walls, floors and furniture. They had clearly been kicking and stamping on the fruit with such ferocity and venom that the melon had burst open like a bomb and spread its flesh across my white silk rugs and upon my white marble floor, it was also dripping from the glass table and had smothered itself over two of my white silk dining chairs. As I looked up my head raged at the physics needed to transfer so much energy to a juicy fruit that it could now hang suspended from my delicate wallpaper. In particular, there was a blob of black seeds and red mushy flesh sliding its way down the white velvet butterflies and songbirds; in its wake there was left a red streak which I knew would leave a lasting stain.

My only consolation to this scene was that, to their annoyance, Mark's and Grant's feet and legs were also covered and happily my table had not shattered in the wake of their pummelling my watermelon. After the total destruction of this fruit, both Grant and Mark seemed relieved and exhausted. They left the room as if they were leaving the gym after a long hard work out. They were oblivious to the subsequent footprints their feet were making on my floor imbedding the remnant flesh into the fibres of the rugs.

They disappeared soon after to go shooting, and I was left to contact Debbie to come in a day early to clean up my morning room for double rate. She arrived an hour after my call and I oversaw the cleaning of the room. As I watched her work I was amazed at how much flesh had been encased in its green skull. It had spread from ceiling to floor and went as far as the kitchen doorway.

Grant left the next day, and I was left with Mark who had collapsed upon my new plaid sofas. The television was on in the background and he had a crystal whisky glass resting against his throbbing head. He did not look up when I approached him to ask if he needed anything, but instead he kept his eyes shut. I remained standing looking down on Mark lazing across my new cushions.

'I need to talk to you, Olive.' His voice was close to a rasping whisper but the surprise of him actually talking to me took me aback as much as a balloon bursting in front of me.

Our conversations were non-existent in the past few years; last Christmas Eve, Mark slept in the second reception room and when I walked in early Christmas day I was greeted with an explosion of red vomit splattered across the furniture and white carpet. Mark was slowly waking and spied my look of horror to which he responded with a kick to my legs and a, 'Clear it up, bitch.'

By lunch I had finally mopped away the foul vinegar smell of last night's Chateau Neuf du Pape. When he came in to check my cleaning he graced me with a hung-over apology.

'Sorry. It keeps happening but alcohol doesn't mix with my anti-depressants, but what can I do? Nothing! Merry Christmas!'

That was the last conversation I had with Mark until now, a rainy day in October.

'Yeah, sit down Olive, I need to explain a few things.'

'Yes?' I replied.

'I need to talk to you as there are going to be a few changes.' He sipped his whisky and continued, still with his eyes closed.

'You won't understand but the business hasn't been doing as well as it should. I need to release some assets and I'm toying with the idea of selling this place.'

I froze as he uttered the word 'selling'.

'You can't,' I appealed. 'Please you can't.'

'I can do what I like, this is my place – I bought it and I own it. That said, there is another option, I have another place I can sell that will release some funds… Oh stop squealing Olivia. Seriously shut up!'

He finally looked up at me to indicate that I was to stop crying at once.

'As I said I have another place in Putney – don't look like that woman; you don't know about it as I never told you. Anyway, I can sell that, but it would mean that you will have a roommate. I'll be here more often, but I'm keeping my flat in London so you won't have me here all the time… ah jeez, Olive, stop crying! I'm trying to sort this mess out and, believe it or not, your crying is putting me off.'

Mark then sat up and gestured that I sat down. His tone became solemn.

'Her name is Monika and I've known her for about three years. She'll be living here until I can figure out a better solution.'

My tears gave way to bewilderment.

'Eh?' I said.

'I'm not explaining myself any more to you; go figure this out yourself.'

He looked at me waiting for me to drop my surprised look and adopt an acceptance look.

'You're a woman of the world Olivia, I know it's not ideal but hey, I could have just divorced you and where would you be then? At your sisters? I don't think so! Personally, just understand that these things happen. Divorce would bankrupt you as there's no way you could afford to fight me, you can't go anywhere, so actually I'm doing the decent thing and owning up to the situation. Think about it: I could have been a complete wanker and thrown you out of the house with nowhere to go.'

Questions raced through my head trying to reach the finish line at my mouth and be the first question released onto a stunned silence. But there were so many of these questions that they tumbled over each other and lay on my tongue helpless until I could forcibly coax one of them out.

The first question I pulled out was, 'Who is this woman?'

'She's someone I've been seeing and I'm tied to her and I can't let go.'

'You can't let go? What about me? Why my house? Where would she stay?' fell out the rest.

'Look, I can't answer these. Be grateful that I'm probably not selling the house. It's Sunday today and I'll be bringing her here on Tuesday. She's not moving in just yet, nothing is finalised. In fact, the Putney house isn't even on the market but she knows about you and wants to meet you. I have a function that evening – some Halloween thing, which you can both come to. She'll be discreet and so will I – I trust, by then, you'll be a woman and stop your incessant whimpering, and be discreet as well; otherwise I will have to forbid you to come.'

'Here? She's coming to visit me on Tuesday?'

They were feeble questions but the stronger ones were still lying injured on my tongue and these were just spontaneous thoughts that popped out of my head. Mark appeared blasé about the questions given to him in a high-pitched tone, as he merely answered with a nod.

'Not here on Tuesday. It's detox day on Tuesday!' I garbled;

that was the lowest and weakest of all my defence, but it was all my paralyzed mind would offer and understandably Mark just looked at me with disgust.

'Tuesday Olive.' And out he went.

The next couple of days were spent in a heightened state of worry. I was unable to concentrate, especially with my devil heckling me from inside my head.

'You really are pathetic,' it would shout to me. 'You have nowhere to run to, you have no other house to live in and of course he's right when he said that a divorce would leave you penniless after your lawyers extracted their fee for losing in court. This means you are trapped in your own home and so you need to pray Mark doesn't sell this house. Ha! You actually need his mistress to come here. I bet she is prettier than you, of course she is; she'll certainly be younger.'

I rebuked my devil by saying, 'I don't care about this woman, who is she anyway? Nothing, she's no one.'

But my chest would seize when my devil replied that my house, my home, my possessions would all be lost if Mark should decide he preferred her and, subsequently, I would become obsolete in his life; so this time she was someone.

I couldn't talk to anyone as I could barely breathe, and the thought of anyone's pity further crippled my lungs. The only one I could speak to was my devil and he successfully whirled my world down to the depraved base pit it belonged.

My devil took pleasure in ensuring I didn't sleep or eat as he plagued me with scenarios of what might happen if Mark threw me out of my house, such that, by 2am on Tuesday morning I pictured myself living in a ditch under the A3 gyratory with only rats for company.

On Tuesday morning I received a text to tell me I would be picked up at seven and driven to the Imperial War Museum for the function held there. Mark added that I was to make sure there was a room made up for Monika, that I was prompt for the driver and I was to be dressed appropriately for the black-tie event; 'maybe the midnight blue gown?' He wrote.

I knew the blue Dior dress he was referring to; it was nearly ten years old. I had bought it for a trip to Barbados. I was curious as to why he would want me in this dress, as on the evening I wore it last, under the Caribbean moonlight, he barely noticed me or my dress. Nevertheless, I did as I was told.

At 7pm Mark's driver picked me up and deposited me outside the entrance to the Imperial War Museum. As soon as I walked in I was summoned by Mark who had been waiting for me in the entrance. It was the typical grand affair in an imposing building. The exception to this evening was the majesty of the Spitfire hanging above the heads of three hundred guests in dinner suits and gowns. In amongst these people stood theatrical statues of ghouls and monsters and all the waiters wore Halloween costumes.

'At last you're here, stay by my side and shut up. If any of my colleagues mention Monika just change the subject to your usual inane drivel,' barked Mark in hushed tones.

'Is she here then?' I said, whilst my eyes swept across the room for a young woman possibly looking my way.

'Somewhere, I don't know. She wanted to come so I've brought her, but I told her to keep out of my way. She's here with Pete who owes me a favour.'

Mark then pulled my arm towards a group of black dinner jackets surrounding a bloody, monster mannequin. Mark clicked his fingers to usher me to his side which signalled the beginning of my evening.

Eventually, a six-course dinner was served in one of the museum's banquet rooms. The banquet room walls were covered in plush red velvet and adorned with gold cornices. Upon the table were giant candelabras, which shielded each guest from viewing anything more than the people sitting next to them. The view to my right was of Mark's back. The view to my left was of an elderly man with half-moon glasses perched on the end of his nose. I was not interested in either eating or talking to anyone around me as I was preoccupied with searching for a woman I didn't know.

When Mark released me from my duties, I escaped to the dressing room to check my lipstick and my hair. The light in the toilet was too dim to see anything with much clarity. I peered into the mirror to adjust my makeup but I needed to squint to make out the line of my lips. I ruffled my newly dyed blonde hair to plump it up, then looked around the room.

The style was Victorian vintage with a blood red, velvet love chair in the middle. The walls were covered in floor to ceiling cracked yellow mirrors that reminded me of an old-fashioned fun fair hall of mirrors. When I stepped back to look at myself in the dim light I accidentally kicked over a tall vase with fluffy pampas grass. I bent down to pick it up and as I did another woman entered. I watched a pair of silver diamanté stilettoes walk pass me as she stepped to adjust her dress in one of the wall mirrors. After replacing the vase I returned to look in the mirror next to this young lady of no more than twenty-five. She was plump with a voluptuous bosom trying to escape the confines of a red corset bodice dress which looked like it once swung upon a hanger in the wind of her local market stall. Her face was sweet with bright blue eyes resting upon chubby rosy cheeks. Her strawberry blonde hair was long and fully coiffed to a bouffant above and around her face; she reminded me of a toddler in a deep southern American beauty pageant.

Standing next to her I could make out another woman who was much older. The age gap was at least thirty years and was discernible by subtle differences in appearance. The girl's arms were white and podgy with dimples in the elbow. In comparison, the older woman's arms were so thin that her blue veins protruded from along her hands and forearms. The young girl resembled a childish Marilyn Monroe with a tiny waist, a billowing bosom and huge hips. Lumps and rolls of fat misshaped her red evening gown, but the overall shape was sexy and tantalising. The older woman looked like a starved Disney character next to her. The only thing that protruded from this woman were hip bones and two round balls stuck to her chest. Their faces were similar, but the older lady had ludicrously large lips that looked like they came from a Christmas cracker; they floated slightly away from the pale white face as though they were two dinghies floating on smooth layer of royal icing.

As I stared at the startling difference in the shape and look between a woman at the beginning of her adult life; youthful, plump and innocent, and a woman in her later years; manipulated, thin and fake, I realised that this was me and my replacement.

CHAPTER TWENTY

JASON

And that's how I remember my Aunt Olivia. She was the Aunt who bought great toys with her when I was a boy. She was the Aunt I boasted about to my school friends as she always had the latest sports car. She had a massive house, a huge swimming pool with slides, she even had a full-size gym with a climbing wall at the back.

But she was also the aunt my dad and I laughed at as she totted up our driveway in her stilettoes and tight skirts. She was the aunt my mum would leave in the living room whilst she made excuses to check on the lunch just so she could silently scream 'bloody woman!' Then rant to Dad, 'Did you just hear what she has just said to me?'; Mum would quickly reel off a synopsis of the conversation with her sister about how much bigger, better, brighter her life is compared to ours. Then Mum would straighten her dress, humph and walk back in.

As I grew older these conversations became a power struggle between Aunt Olivia's boasts about her life and Mum's boasts about my school achievements mixed with sarcasm.

'Indeed Olive, what's the point of New York without a new pair of Jimmy Choo shoes to enjoy them in? It's a good thing I'll never go as all my shoes are from M&S.'

So, I remember the toys, I remember her cars, I even remember the clothes she wore but I don't remember her face, right up to the point my aunt no longer resembled my Aunt Olive.

The face and body I remember today is the one Aunt Olive saw in the cracked mirror on that Halloween evening: there were no red curls as they'd been replaced with huge blonde hair that barely moved. She had a two-tone tan; her body looked as if it had been dipped in creosote which became weaker as it approached her face, a face that varied between ale brown to white emulsion paint depending on her outfit and style at that time.

Her body, so thin I'm amazed it could support a woman in her fifties. Her legs and arms, spindly bones covered in skin and blue veins. Her chest was a point of fascination when I was growing up as it seemed to grow each time I saw her, but her sternum still managed to protrude between her cleavage; as though it was fighting for recognition between two alien domes.

But it was her face that held the most fascination. I don't remember the original one, only the one in recent years. By the end, it was a face I couldn't relate to as living. My brain couldn't process how it moved or how it sat upon the front of her head like a mask, smoother than the dashboard plastic of my car.

Her face looked swollen as though she had an allergic reaction to the air she breathed. Her mouth and surrounding area, in particular, sat away from her face in the same way Fred Flintstone's mouth bellowed out. Her nose was reduced to a size where I wondered whether it was fit for purpose as it was so tiny she couldn't have breathed in without becoming light-headed. Her eyes were large almonds with heavy makeup, making her blue eyes the only natural human part of her face.

'Jason, she wanted youth and beauty and Mark paid to rip away the glory God had given her with love, and replaced it with a plastic mould designed by a surgeon,' Mum said, when she came around to discuss Dad's sixty-third birthday surprise.

'A bit harsh mum, don't you think?'

'Why do you think she chased youth? Why do you think she starved herself for the whole of her marriage? Why do you think she smiled more than she spoke?'

Mum had become agitated and shuffled in her seat.

'Dad's always wanted a balloon ride, how about that as his main present?' I pointed to the online brochure.

'Mark wanted an ideal woman; he wanted a doll he could paint and dress then put away in a box when he was finished. He didn't want a woman, a living breathing, thinking and feeling woman. He didn't want his wife to challenge him or ever disagree with what he was doing or saying, or reprimand him and demand respect. He wanted a nodding, smiling doll.'

'So, no to the balloon ride then?'

'He treated her disgracefully and all we could do was watch from the side lines as he destroyed the woman she could have been,' Mum spat.

'How about a driving experience, I'd do it with Dad. Look, this one offers the Audi R8.'

It was a pointless suggestion as Mum was lost, so I reluctantly entered into another discussion over Aunt Olive.

'You know, Mum, maybe you're being unfair? We're all masters of our own destiny and she chose her path; she wanted to be rich and be spoilt and she reaped the rewards from his credit card.'

'Rubbish! Yes, she was a naïve girl who wanted the easy way in life and wanted to marry rather than work, but he took full advantage of that. He squashed my plump, flame-haired twenty-five-year-old sister and pulled out a manufactured plastic doll in her place. As Olive says in her letter, I agree we can sail our life boat in the direction we want to go and hope the storms don't hit us but sometimes fate grabs hold of the steering wheel and steers us straight for the hurricane and there is nothing we can do about it. In the case of Olive, she allowed Mark to hop on her sweet little ferry; she allowed him to remould that boat to a cruise liner but with the understanding that he was the captain and he steered her life where he wanted to take it. Olive had no say in her life from the moment she agreed to marry him.

He was a cruel man who flitted between screaming at her or ignoring her. Even if we were around visiting, he spoke to her like she was a servant when he was calm or, more often, yelling the most obscene of obscenities at her as though she was a dirty slave. He didn't care that we were witness to his behaviour as he thought very little for the opinion of others. Colin once tried to intervene and point out that this was not how you speak to your wife, but all Mark did was to laugh and point out that his wife was 'a useless waste of space' and he could say what he likes.

We tried to encourage Olive to leave on so many occasions but your aunt reacted by shutting us out of her life.' Mum began to cry and once again I went over to comfort her.

'She wrote she was angry at me for shutting her out of my and your life.'

'She didn't mean it Mum.'

'But it's not true Jay. In the beginning we stopped bringing you to see her because we didn't want you to hear and witness his vile ways, and eventually we stopped going altogether as we dreaded him being there. If he was, which wasn't often to be fair, we hoped he'd be in a bad mood and merely ignore us. But if he was in a good mood then he'd make conversation with us by laughing at our pathetic, penniless and puerile existence. If we retaliated then he'd storm out, screaming to Olive that her family were pathetic and who were we to criticise him? We were, "… nothing. Useless little people." At that point we toyed between leaving in protest or snorting 'freak' and sitting back in relief, knowing that he wouldn't return. Nevertheless, eventually, our visits dribbled away to nothing because of that man.'

Mum's voice softened. She stroked her hands.

'She was always welcome at ours, and although she denies it, I rang her time and again asking to meet up or for her to come and stay at ours, but in recent years she refused us. She shut everyone out of her life, she rejected all our pleas to help her and instead she became angry at any offer of help.'

Mum closed her eyes and shook her head at her memories.

'Jay, from afar she remained a beautiful woman, the type people turned their heads to stare at but with every step closer she took, she looked more bizarre and dare I say, unhuman; a lifelike doll brought to life by her maker. Mark on the other hand, was an unattractive man from afar and an equally unattractive man up close. I confess he was once very handsome, but by his fifties he was grossly over-weight with slicked back greasy black hair. Do you remember? It was thinning on his shiny forehead and pulled back to a tumble of black tight curls which rested on his shoulders like slimy garden worms. He also paid homage to the church of the sunbed as he was toffee coloured even in the depths of winter.'

Mum's voice rose again. She squeezed her hands.

'Yet, thanks to his attractive bank balance he had no shortage of girlfriends. They were all as devious as the next, just to get their hands on his money. Such beautiful women who wasted their precious youth believing they could ensnare a rich man, but he never left your aunt, well, not until the last one. I've seen Monika and I've briefly spoken to her. I grant you, she is no different to any of the others. She had no love for him and she clearly preyed on Mark's perversions to entrap him, but she is the one who changed everything for Olive. She changed everything.'

Mum trailed off in deep thought then re-emerged and composed herself.

'Balloon ride it is as I don't want your Father driving anything faster than the Mondeo – not with his back.'

After she left, instead of picking up my laptop to prepare for the presentation I had on Monday morning, I picked up the final section of my aunt's manuscript.

OLIVIA

About eighteen months ago

Monika came home with us that evening. It was unusual as Mark kept his women separate from me, but that evening she shared our car, she shared the whiskey Mark poured for himself and she shared his bed.

I was a bystander, watching this pretty young girl re-enacting the first years of our marriage. I was numb to the pain this caused me as I had accepted long ago that I was only a member of the audience in Mark's life. I knew my chest was struggling to contain my tired heart from popping out of my mouth and scampering off in protest at being abused and wasted on a man who ignored his servant. And still my devil whispered in my ear:

'Oh, Olivia, if you want to keep your life then just disappear back to the shadows.'

So, I retreated to my room, but my eyelids refused to shut and my brain refused to close. Instead, I listened to the new fear which had crept into my brain that on top of all this I could lose my house. I would have to surrender my clothes, my jewellery, my cars, my holidays. And once all this was taken, then I had nothing and the life I knew would close the door on me after laughing at my misfortune. All my friends would join in on the revelry of gossiping about my demise from one of them to a sad, old, lonely woman. I lay awake watching their lunch meetings and how each friend would excitedly join in on the gossip ring. There would be a spike in lunch attendance not seen since Amanda Wakefield ran off with her kitchen fitter and was caught at the Alzheimer's charity lunch wearing an old plum dress and looking at least 10lbs heavier.

Early in the morning I heard a car door slam. I went to the window to see Monika get into Mark's car and drive away. I saw Mark stand to watch her go and then, as she turned left onto the road, he turned and looked up at my bedroom. He caught my eye and then walked into the house still wearing her burgundy silk dressing gown.

I dressed without looking in the mirror. The long white Chanel maxi-dress flowed around my ankles as I walked barefoot down stairs to my breakfast room where my husband was sat eating and reading the newspaper.

Mark didn't look up as I eased myself into the room. I remember flinching at the thought of his unwashed naked bottom on my white dining chairs. I pushed this thought out of my head whilst I waited for Mark to acknowledge me and tell me my fate.

I took a breath in when my husband looked up, put his paper down and summoned me in a little closer. I was only able to take a few steps as my legs shook with every pigeon step I took.

'Yeah, er, things aren't doing too well in the city,' he began. 'There's no point me trying to explain it to you as there's no way you'd understand but basically bell-ends are disrupting the market to the point that I'm not making the returns from my investments. I need to sit on my stock until everything is sorted, so I'll be making changes to mitigate the damage others have done to me,' he said.

His demeanour had altered subtly; when he spoke his eyes darted from me, to the floor, to his hands. These hands were as active as his eyes. They were pacing between wiping his mouth to squeezing one another.

'Olivia, you just need to understand that this is the best

solution for all of us. Don't blame me, it's not my fault; as I said, others have screwed up. Not me.'

Dearest Jason, what Mark had omitted to tell me in his abbreviated version of events, was that one of his companies had been embezzling money to another of his companies (namely an off-shore bank account under a false name). Mark had been covering his tracks by siphoning off money from the firm's pension fund. This had been spotted due to an anomaly in his tax contribution, which led to the unravelling of all his immoral dealings. The taxman suspended his ability to trade until the investigation was concluded. This meant that, at best, Mark was potentially bankrupt in a matter of months unless he could pay a hefty fine from our British government or, at worst, bankrupt and staying in one of Her Majesty's hostels. Of course, I was not privy to any of this information at that time.

'Anyway, Olivia,' Mark continued, 'these changes involve this house and you. Both need to go. Like I said to you before, I've met Monika and I need to think about her needs now. I know I wasn't keen, but she told me last night that she's pregnant.'

Mark looked down at his fidgeting hands.

'I'm genuinely sorry, Olivia.'

His tone was gentle but it was only a flash moment as he then picked up his paper and held it in front of his face. I had been dismissed.

My mind fused to my skull and my teeth seized together. My chest clamped to my heart and lungs and my legs involuntarily buckled.

'She's lying to you, Mark, I promise,' I warbled. 'She is lying. I know these women and they say whatever there is to get you to keep them. There is no baby, there is no child.'

This was met with defiant silence from Mark as he continued to read the paper.

'Please Mark,' I begged as I fell to my knees. 'All the years I have given you, I have dedicated my life to you. I have never questioned you or asked you to change for me. I have merely been by your side supporting you. Can this Monika girl say the same? No! Can you guarantee that she will offer the same freedom I have given you? Surely you are gambling on another woman based on a lie she has spun you?'

Mark lowered The Times.

'Olivia, she is pregnant and, by the way, don't assume that the life I have spent with you is one I have enjoyed. I may have married you but there was never a marriage. You are an ugly woman who's getting uglier with each year that passes; Monika on the other hand, is still young and fresh. I remember you at that age; a sweet red-head with fire inside you but you let that slip away. Maybe Monika will suffer the same fate that age brings to their face and body but at least she's able to give me children – you couldn't even do that!'

'I know I couldn't. I'm sorry, I'm sorry but, Mark, she's lying, I know she is,' I cried.

'She's pregnant, can't you get that? And she has been before. Look, I'm sorry but you also need to know, we have a little boy called Zac; at the moment he lives with his grand-parents but I'm willing to take him on now she's pregnant again. So, as you can see, I need to think about him as well. Now get up and leave. This house is being sold together with its contents, I never liked this place anyway.

'You're to leave me alone, go to your pathetic family, if they'll have you. Become a burden on them instead; I don't care… Leave!' he bellowed.

I scuttled away, but I stopped just outside the room only because my long white dress had caught my foot and forced me to fall to the floor hitting my forehead as I fell.

I raised my shaking body to my feet and raced from the kitchen to the hallway where I stopped at the front entrance. I grabbed the huge brass handle upon the ornate wooden door. And Jason, my dearest Jason, I truly believe it was with the intention of running away into the stratosphere above me. But my screaming body shook too much causing me to pause long enough to stop – My mind relaxed, my arms fell to my side and my breathing returned. My devil was standing beside me. He was holding my hand and for the first time since I had made his acquaintance many years before, he was smiling.

'Are you really going to accept that Olivia?' he began. 'You forfeited your life for him. Instead of you meeting your soulmate he grabbed you and stopped you from your chance of discovering your husband and creating your family. You never got the opportunity to meet your love and you never had the chance to bring your children into this world to cherish and cradle in your arms. And after all this, he wants to take away your home. This is all he ever gave you and he is to whip it away, for you to live a beggar life whilst he gets to know the pleasures of a family.

'And he will be laughing at you Olivia – the foolish woman whom he once mocked and ruined, so that you, as he promised, will indeed become a worthless dead soul, years before your death.'

Beside him, by my devil's feet, lay Mark's shotgun. It was still loaded from the hunt he was meant to go on a little while ago. The bullets were never used as Mark had been too drunk to fire them. My devil stared at it with me then pointed at it indicating that I should pick it up. I had never felt it before and I was surprised that it was so heavy, but I liked the weight and I liked the feel of the cold metal of the barrel in my hands. My hands were no longer numb and each molecule that awoke in my body helped me to stand tall.

My devil started to walk away and as he did so he said, 'So easy to do my sweet friend, so easy to do, my lady, my love.'

There are many regrets in my life which will make my deathbed a sombre place. I mostly regret losing James; I regret ever being rude to him in Australia and I regret telling him I could no longer dive with him or walk with him and I regret not being the woman in the crumbling cottage with him by my side. But Jason, I do not regret walking back into the breakfast room with the gun in my arms pointing the loaded barrel at my husband.

Mark looked up at me and his look was initially surprise but it gave way to a dismissive snort.

'Don't be ridiculous, you pathetic woman, put the gun down.' He then just shook his head and resumed reading his article.

For the first time I saw my husband: his chin merged into his bulbous neck, his kimono had slipped, revealing his sweaty, greying body. His paper sat upon his huge stomach which was pushed against the edge of the glass table giving a red indentation into his fat.

He was a filthy man, but it only occurred to me at that point that he had changed from the powerful strong man I married, to this sloth with a red lined face from drinking too much and who snorted instead of breathed. He had aged badly so that his only worthy credential to note was his wealth, but it was enough to attract a young woman to replace me.

'Olivia, I said put the gun down.'

I ignored his request.

'I told you I gave you my life and I deserve more than being thrown out,' I began. 'I did not have children or a husband because of you. Why should I leave? Would another woman who had her children taken from her leave? Would she not fight and shout at the person who took her children?'

My voice was calm and forceful – it did not quiver or tremble in front of her husband. It spoke directly at him commanding Mark's attention, so that he put down his paper and stared back at his wife.

'Come on then Olivia. Get what is bothering you out, but remember it will make no difference as you will not leave this house with anything more than what you are wearing,' he spat.

'I gave you everything Mark. Years, I stood by you as your wife. I realise now it was not a position that I should have taken, but it is one I have suffered for you for many years whilst I watched others enjoy wonderful marriages that boost their journey in life.'

'You were happy enough,' he retorted. 'You had all that good society had to offer. This marriage gave you a status in life you craved; what else did you want and, for that matter, what else does any stupid woman who does not have the brain to make her own way in the world ever want from a marriage? My mother left me, her only son, in pursuit of this happiness, the very happiness I betrothed upon you. So why complain about your lot when most women would abandon their only child for what you have?'

The chest swelled and the fist clenched in reaction to Mark's ignorance.

'Mark,' I continued, 'I realise that a couple marry for lust and stay for love, but I married for excitement and stayed for money. It has taken me too many years to know that happiness is found in love. I have not been loved by my husband and I stand as a stupid, foolish woman who realises too late that she threw happiness away for a house on Cavendish Avenue.'

'Put the gun down, Olivia, and go. Okay, okay, I'll make sure you have enough money to buy a house close to your sister, will that do?'

Mark leaned in a little further.

'Olivia, come on this is ridiculous, just put the gun down. We can talk about what you want, but first put the gun down. I don't like what I see in your eyes, Olivia; a woman of your tiny stature doesn't suit this great gun, so just put it down. Olivia, don't step any closer. Think about what you're doing. Don't raise the gun any higher. Olivia this is stupid, just put the gun down. Okay, okay, tell me what you want? An allowance? Take the car, take anything you want, just put the gun down. This isn't what you want.'

The fingers around the trigger began to squeeze and the heart began to thud against the chest. The hairs on the nape crystalized and the voice spoke calmly.

'You never loved me. You made me what I am.'

'You think I was happy? Do you think I am happy now? You may not believe it, Olivia, but I loved you. I loved you deeply. Maybe I didn't know how to show it, but can you say the same thing? Did you love me? I doubt it. You've never shown me love; you just spent my money. If anyone ruined your life then it was you; you chose to devote your years to a man whom you refused to love. Admit it, all you wanted was to steal my money, but then how can I blame you? You're just a typical woman... Ah come on, Olivia, tell me what you want to hear... Please Ol, put the gun down. ...please, I'm sorry. I'm sorry!'

The fingers squeezed and the bullet was fired.

I looked to the end of the barrel and at its head I saw a slight whisp of smoke. There was a pain in my shoulder from where the gun had jolted back when the trigger was pulled. I still had the gun at my eyeline and I was focused upon the wisps of gun smoke. My ears were ringing from the fire but I could still hear the silence, and from this I knew that my husband would be dead and his soul was leaving his body like the smoke dancing out of the barrel. I reached towards the barrel opening to try and stop the smoke in an attempt to put it back into the gun. Instead the gun slipped to the floor beside my bare feet.

I looked at my painted red toes and then to the floor; from there my eyes darted to the chair that stood beside me then to the table top and then to the first splatter of blood upon the glass. My eyes transfixed upon this small droplet and I waited in vain for the sound of Mark's angry voice asking me what I had done, but it did not come. I inched my head further up the table to see the red belly of a once breathing man. It had slipped beneath the table and through the glass table top I could see the naked body of my husband, slouched in a sleeping pose. I forced myself to look up and as soon as I took full view, my body buckled in shock. His lower jaw and his left eye remained of his face, but everything else was sprayed across my breakfast room. His head resembled the smashed watermelon Mark had bludgeoned with Grant only weeks prior. The blood clung to the room and dripped down my delicate butterfly walls, but this time there were no seeds from the melon, just globules of flesh which stuck to the windows and walls.

I looked up to the ceiling where I could see the sky through the window and uttered, 'No' when I saw a clump of flesh sitting beside two seeds that the cleaner had missed when mopping up the melon.

My body weakened and I slumped to the floor in silent screams which came from deep inside my stomach but were too frightened to make a sound. I sat on the floor clinging to my legs, waiting for the police to arrive. I do not remember the sound of the gun shot but I was certain that it must have been heard from all around. It was a Wednesday morning around 10am. My gardener did not prune the roses midweek nor did my cleaner tend to my dust on this day. But I was sure there must be many others who would have heard the shot and seen the spray of glass as the bullet left the building behind Mark's head. So, I sat and waited for my fate to arrive in flashing blue sirens and pull me away in hand cuffs.

By 4pm I had woken in the foetal position on my marble floor. I do not know how long I slept but it was a deep sleep which was whipped away from me when I saw the dried blood on my toes where I had stretched out and slid my foot through Mark's blood. Instantly I grabbed my legs in towards me and I started to shake; just a gentle pulse throughout my body which matched my slight rhythmic rocking back and forth on the floor.

Where were the police? Why had they not already arrived? Don't they have a sixth sense about a gun killing? Or maybe they hadn't been called yet? I could have called them if no one else had, I could tell them that I did not mean to kill him. I just wanted everything to stop. I wanted him to be alive but just away from me; that was all, just away from me and my home. They might have understood? There may have been a caring officer who would put her arm around me and tell me it was all over.

Or, I could have cleared the room myself? I could have dumped Mark on the compost and mopped the room until my French Renaissance wallpaper shone. But Mark was a big man and he would be too heavy for me to budge even with half his head missing. Also, I had no idea where my cleaner kept all the cleaning materials, I didn't even know where the mop was kept.

Or, I could run, which is what I should have done if my devil hadn't grabbed me for that one last conversation. So, I scrambled onto my bare feet and ran to the front door. Outside, the air held the weight of a forthcoming night storm: fresh and cold. The strong storm breeze whooshed up my nose and stole one breath from me. I closed my eyes momentarily, and when I opened them again I ran towards the burgeoning storm. I ran from my house, over fields, crossing country lanes and through gaps in hedges. In the middle of one farmer's field I felt the first splat of rain. I stopped to look up; I could feel the wind swirl around my body. I shut my eyes as huge drops fell heavily on my skin.

By the time dusk came I was shivering from my wet skin and hair. The rain had stopped but dark towering clouds still policed the sky. The light remained low as night slipped into the cracks between the black clouds. I retreated to the woods which bordered the field and I snuck into a natural cave inside an old tree.

This oak tree must have been decades upon decades old. It was far older than me and it will still be there long after you or I have gone. It had stood silently swaying in the breeze for many a lifetime, without any care. It would have existed at times of great social unrest: during both world wars, world depression, loss of towers and it would have grown during many different parliament elections and not cared about the outcome. Its leaves would have sprung out in the spring and fallen in the autumn, year after year after year. Its bark was weathered from the different seasons and cracked down the centre to deform the trunk and create a hollow for me to eventually hide inside.

It didn't care for me, who I was, what I wore or where I had run from, as it didn't care for anything. I sat within its belly and hugged my knees close to my chest and I shivered from the cold. My teeth chattered involuntarily and at times I shook violently, waking myself from my thoughts. These thoughts plagued my mind and they flitted from panic about what I had done, to calm acceptance of murdering a man. When the panic raged in my head then I crawled further into the tree and when it was calm I poked my head out to look at the pearl white moon that shone upon this part of England; this moon was like a search-light when I was scared, or a white sun brightening the land all around me when I felt calm.

As the night progressed the periods of calm were more frequent and I was able to lie on the ground resting my head upon a clump of fallen leaves. The sounds of the forest were a comfort to me; even the screams from the Muntjac deer calling for a mate gave me solace that I was not alone. I hugged my body and I watched the night floor itch with minibeasts within the soil. I remember squeezing some leaves against my face just to feel the wet dew upon my cheeks. I desperately wanted to crawl in amongst the worms, beetles and centipedes, I wanted to plant my limbs alongside the tree roots and watch England through the years the way the trees did season after season after season, not moving, not caring just existing upon God's green land.

Finally, I fell into a deep slumber until beams of morning sunlight pierced the sky and fell upon the earth where the ground held my head. My eyes eased open and my body shivered from the morning chill but I was relaxed, dare I say Jason, the most relaxed I had been for many years, right up to the point that my mind twisted away from its gentle sweet dreams and back to taking in all the weight of the day that had passed just twenty hours before, and the onslaught of the days that I must face from now on, starting with this day. I screamed in response to this and then I cried out to all the oak trees standing all around me. They towered above my puny body, the wind played amongst their leaves and their sound was like a child laughing at my cries.

'You're on your own,' the trees smirked. 'We have no interest in you or your troubles; leave us be to enjoy the sunrise and the wind and then the sunset of today and for many beautiful days to come.'

Their smug superiority snubbed any hope of further refuge so, like an urchin in a shop doorway, I crawled out before the shop owner brushed me away.

I returned to the field where a crop was growing and I walked in the gullies between each long line of winter green vegetables. I was not sure what the farmer was growing to feed the supermarkets' profits, but the green leaf heads reached my fingertips. I dragged my hand from crop to crop as I wondered who would eat this one then who would eat the next. These dull thoughts spared me from the hysteria that was rumbling in my body. My next distraction was the beautiful pain from my bare soles. I had been running upon my naked feet from house to road to field to wood, and they were now torn in places. Blood had oozed from my feet from the first moment they encountered a sharp stone but I would not allow myself to tend to these wounds, instead I wanted to feel this pain to the point that I sought hard ground within the gully and each time I winced I thanked the ground for the distraction of this agony.

Ahead of me was another field separated by a road. This wild flower field dipped down into the valley where my town had grown. Within it was the exclusive avenue and within this exclusive, 'sought after road', was my house. I stood on the hard concrete that intersected these two fields and looked down into

Stoning Town. I stretched my hand out to my eyeline to where the tops of the trees surrounding the town came. I stroked the air to stroke this bubble world which had its residents just waking to their alarm to start their day. Some would be rising for work, some would be rising to wake their children for school and some, as I would have been, would still be asleep waiting to wake before lunch. How easy all their lives are, I mused. How sweet that they have so little to fear from their society; no one will hurt them and they can enjoy their day and many other days to come. I continued to stroke the rooftops then eased my hand back to stroke the wild poppies swaying in the morning breeze. Each flower danced in unison, one way then the next.

Morning fog began to slide across the ground and swathed Stoning Town in a white steam as if it nestled in a hot bath supplied by a nurturing Mother Nature. I envied all those who were waking inside this happy cosy scene. I did not belong there or anywhere and Mother Earth was not interested in comforting away my loneliness.

Above the earth, the sun was crawling up into the sky, it was a raging red and, as it rose, this colour seeped into the morning blue. The haze from the ground smudged the horizon and diluted the red rays on the ground to a burnt orange colour. The bright sunshine stung my eyes. I closed them as I crossed the field to the busy A3 which separated this piece of green and flowery England to an English exclusive town on the outskirts of London. The road was beginning to fill with commuters and I wondered how many would see a ghost walking down the sloping field above them. How many would be calling the police to add their observations to the pile of other observations, of a woman in white with blood across the base of her dress billowing in the wind. She looks lost, one may report; she seems disorientated walking along this busy road; she's likely to get herself killed in her clearly deranged state, another would complain. Could she be missing from a care home somewhere? She's not wearing a coat, not even a shawl to keep her warm on this cold autumn morning and she's not wearing any shoes! Someone needs to grab her and take her back to the asylum. Has she been reported as missing? Is she the one on the news? Is she the woman in white who the police wish to question in relation to the shooting yesterday?

I could hear the news in my head.

The police are hunting for the wife of a revered business man who was killed yesterday morning. They are treating the death as suspicious and wish to speak to Mrs Olivia Hopkins whom they fear is armed and dangerous. The public are warned not to approach her and advise anyone who sees her to call the police for armed back-up.

I walked across the motorway bridge which took me back into the town. I could hear the commuter cars whizz past me and, with the whine of the cars beneath me, I again wondered how many were calling the police to say they had found me. I looked out for the police hiding in the woodland and blackberry bushes on the other side of the bridge. With each rustle of the leaves I flinched believing it to be the armed response unit waiting to pounce. I strode on, focused on returning to the house. I suspected that they were not going to grab and tackle me to the floor because they were waiting for my return, when an arrest for murder could be discreet, thus not upsetting the good society over their cornflakes.

As I got nearer to the pristine, perfect street where I once lived, I again mused over the gossip buzzing from one person catching sight of the police cars surrounding the Hopkins' house. Maybe it would be Cynthia Mason who caught sight of the police flashing lights on her morning jog or Pricilla Atkins on her walk with her yapping poodle? Either way, one word from one would be spread across the commuter town by breakfast and all across London by lunch.

As I neared my driveway, I felt the familiar twisting of my

torso as I envisaged the police cars surrounding my house. There would be an ambulance waiting to carry Mark's body out in a white body bag and policemen taking evidence inside and outside my home. I anticipated a fleet of police cars racing towards me down the drive then throwing me upon the shingles with my arms locked behind me in handcuffs as my rights were read.

But there were no sirens or police dogs or policemen in bulletproof vests stalking around my house. There were no ambulances to carry my husband away or people passing by to deliberately witness the humiliation of a couple torn apart by one bullet fired twenty-one hours ago.

Instead this seven-bedroom building with mock Georgian pillars and a double car port with swimming pool in a sought-after location sat peacefully in its two acres of land. To anyone looking in then the expected envy of the grounds and the house of a perfect, wealthy, socially elite area would remain intact as it has since the day I moved here. The house was magnificent and manicured to display a model house in a model village. Yet, for me, every step closer to the front door increased the amount of bile floating to my throat. I no longer felt smug about living here but nauseated that I had to open the front door to my white hallway with sweeping stairs and white marble floor. As the door closed behind me and I smelt the cold air infused with iron from the blood of Mark, this bile squeezed my stomach and opened my throat to make me retch. I grasped the French Renaissance display table to steady myself, which made the china white lilies topple over.

Like a ghost I floated from room to room looking for signs of help, but no one had noticed the gun shot killing my husband and so I knew I was alone to face Mark once more. As I approached the breakfast room the air felt like a frosty iron bar across my face. I saw the dark splatters of bloody footprints I had made last night from running in the opposite direction to where I was walking now. I was making new footprints, but this time it was wet dew mixed with new blood from the cuts made from walking barefoot across a wet autumn morning field.

I stopped just before the entrance. I could see the smashed window from the bullet escaping the room where it had killed Mark. I could see the congealed dried blood across my butterfly wallpaper. The sweetness of my birds were now dyed red and the peace of this room was now shut away as dark blood stained the room like a lid across the coffin.

I couldn't enter any further and see any more of the body, that lay inside it, so instead, I turned around and ran back to the hallway. There in in front of me was the telephone where I could call for help; I grabbed the receiver and dialled James' number. I screamed when James' voice told me he could not answer the phone right now but please leave a name and number and he'd get back to me as soon as he could.

'James, James! Help me,' I cried. My lips were shaking and my voice was tinged with the remnants of the scream I had given when I first fell to my knees, 'Help me James, help me, I've killed him. He's dead. There was a gun and a bullet and it killed him. I didn't mean to, I just wanted everything to stop, I'm sorry. Help me.'

I hung up the receiver and stared at the phone for an eternity, but my James did not ring me. I shuddered and thought of calling again but instead I grabbed my mobile phone and car keys and left my home for the last time. I drove my sports car that had been given to me on my birthday earlier in the year. I had used it only half a dozen times since the day the keys were sent to me and placed in my hand by a Porsche delivery man.

I raced away without any clue of where I was going. I figured the M25 would tell me when I got on it, so I turned left out of my drive and drove, still barefoot, towards the motorway. It was the morning rush hour and every turn I took was met with traffic but eventually I got to the M25 and headed anticlockwise.

I flitted from lane to lane to try and budge my way through the herd of cars I was caught in. I crawled along the slip road onto the M23 but I was met with more traffic tiptoeing along this stretch of road. I remained in first gear for nearly half an hour and in that time my mind was able to refocus away from the shuddering quivering panic I had when I got into the car, and towards a calm, gentle, stroking hand as it focused on the commuters surrounding me. Bizarrely, I felt comforted and protected by them and for a brief moment I was also just a driver on my way to work.

I was once more the young red-head on my way back to Liberty of London to sell rugs to different people. I was going to see my work friends and laugh about the night before and then discuss the next evening out. I was going to meet James for coffee later in the morning and chat about the future and, in particular, where we were going on our next diving holiday. I smiled when I remembered that just before I met Mark we had made a pact that no matter what happened we were going to work hard to save up to go diving in the Galapagos Islands. It never happened as Mark did not approve and James did not insist that I kept to my promise.

Dear wonderful James, a man who had loved me for who I was. Something my naïve youth rejected and my penance for trying to love the wrong man was a miserable life. My marriage was a slow execution and I was buried many years ago in my house, but nobody really noticed and very few came to my funeral or visited my grave. Except for James, he was different; he still reached out to me even when I had rudely ignored him since our beautiful days in Australia. My skeletal hands reached for my phone and once more I rang my James; again it went to answerphone:

'I wish you were here James,' I began. My voice was a waspish slow rasp, like my mind, it was tired and it was now deadened to the sadness from the last twenty-two hours.

'I'm sorry for everything, I'm sorry for picking up the gun and I'm sorry for shooting Mark, but most of all, I'm sorry for ever meeting him; but I did and now he's dead.'

I paused and allowed his answerphone to fill with the grey noise of the motorway. I was approaching the A27 towards Eastbourne.

'Do you remember the weekend walks we used to take together? Just you and me walking side by side watching God's English canvas being painted as the day progressed around us. How we loved watching the changing sky; with its mauves and pinks in the evening and sharp reds in the morning. You would love the sky around me now – the horizon is an orange band stretching across the fields either side of the road towards Beachy Head. Above this panel, and spreading across the morning sky, is a rose colour; it's so soothing, so peaceful.

James, do you remember the day we wandered across the cliff top then sat to have a picnic whilst watching the sun sink into the sea? I was happy then with you beside me.

I have to go, the traffic is picking up now that I'm approaching Lewes. I like this town. I wonder if they'll have their firework parade this year? I hope you get to go with your family. It's a fun night watching the guy burn. Bye-Bye my sweet man.'

Eventually the morning commuters dispersed around me to their respective jobs and left me to drive alone towards the edge of England. For the final half an hour I was a sole driver cruising through the countryside. I don't remember the fir trees lining the road nor do I remember the tree tunnels I drove through, but I knew they were there because I noticed their absence when I neared the white cliffs. The road was now bare save for the cliffs to my right and empty rising fields to my left. The cracked road swept round the cliff top until it reached a National Trust car-park.

There was one other car which I assumed belonged to the owner of the café in the far corner, overlooking the cliffs.

287

I could see a stout lady preparing for the walkers who would undoubtedly arrive throughout the day. She had short curly hair and a striped apron. Like all the commuters I shared the road with, she too had a purpose to her day; she needed to rise each morning, prepare her restaurant and serve the cakes and soups she had made for her guests. Then she needed to close her café and most likely, return to her warm and loving husband, reeling off happy tales to him about her day and the people she had met. One such couple passed me whilst sitting in my car. They did not notice me as they had their head to the ground and I briefly caught their discussion about breakfast before their voices tailed away: one was to have a bacon sandwich and the other a fried egg sandwich with tomato sauce.

Oh, Jason, how my body swelled with jealousy for each of these people. I craned my neck to watch them enter the café, chat to the waitress and then enjoy their earned breakfast. I yearned to be them, just to be leading a simple, gentle morning with no frustrations or fears that plagued me. I wanted to be a middle-aged lady who had aged gracefully and who was loved and who shared her life with someone. Instead I was a mannequin sitting in a white sports car in a white blood-stained dress.

My mind was weary and my body felt cumbersome as I finally left my car. I did not look back as I walked away because I did not want to feel the pit of fear at abandoning the final part of my life. There was a path ahead of me which took me up the slight incline to the very edge dividing England and her seas. I was still barefoot but I deliberately looked up from where I was treading so that each large stone that dug into my soles stung me, allowing me to soak up the living sensation of pain.

As I reached the cliff top the wind picked up and at times, along the cliff's edge, my dress whipped around my legs making me unsteady on my feet. Ahead of me stretched long white chalk cliffs which led to the narrow, pebbled beach far beneath me. I found myself giggling at the competition I had set for myself as I walked this path towards a lighthouse in the distance: I forbade myself to look down to steady myself, so each successful step I made was an achievement to celebrate with another step. I mused that should I slip and topple to my right, down to the beach, then God was merely bored of the competition I was playing and had decided to throw me away from life's board game.

Finally, I got bored before God did, so I elected to stop and sit with my bare legs and bloody feet dangling over the edge. I know that I was a bizarre sight and I wondered what a walker in their walking uniform would make of me. I didn't wonder for long as I watched a man in a bright yellow walking jacket and heavy grey walking boots with a tall staff, walk along the undulating path, starting from as far off as the lighthouse. I prepared myself for his intrusion over my welfare but as he finally passed he nodded my way.

'Lovely day,' he said,

'Isn't it!' I replied.

How quintessentially British we were? Two strangers politely ignoring the social misfit dangling over the edge of Beachy Head, in favour of a comment about the weather. Yet, how comforting for him to see a fellow human to comment about his day while how lonely for me to, again, be ignored.

I don't know how long I sat, but it was long enough to admire the sun clear the sky of any cloud and calm the sea beneath it. Throughout the morning the sky got progressively blue, so richly blue that I wondered whether, if I threw a stone high above my head, would it not splash and spread sleepy ripples across the sky?

The warmth of the sun made me feel dazed, it helped to ease the spasms of panic that sporadically gripped me each time my mind wandered away from the tranquillity of this beautiful spot, looking out to sea and back to the destruction left in a grand house far behind.

The hairs on my neck and the senses in my back eventually felt the movement of that massacre moving towards me, creeping slowly at first then deliberately striding to where I sat.

'Olivia!'

I resisted looking behind me as I wanted to keep hold of the beauty of the sea and the gentle warmth of the sun. How easy it would be to leap forward; I wondered how hard I would need to push off the cliff to dive into the calm waters and become part of the ocean.

'Olivia!'

I smiled at the knowledge that however hard I pushed I would never be part of it and I could only reach the sharp, stony beach separating me from the sea.

'Olivia!'

It was the dear voice of my beloved James.

'Olivia, I'm here,' he said, 'I'm here to help you.' His voice was as gentle as the sun, but still I did not have the courage to respond. I sensed him approaching me.

'Olivia, I promise everything will be okay. I've spoken to the police and they have agreed that I can speak to you first. I reassured them that you won't do anything stupid but please, Ol, please come closer to me.'

'Are the police here?'

'They are, we know what's happened and, Ol, I'm so sorry.'

I heard his worry and, for the first time since James said his first 'hello' to me, I heard a weakness in his mellifluous voice as it changed into a sad and scared tone.

'And I am sorry. I'm so sorry. if I truly knew how bad things were, I promise, I promise I, we all, would've saved you earlier... instead of being here now.'

My heart cracked as I heard James begin to whimper and so I rushed away from the edge to hold my James in my arms.

I burrowed my head into his shoulder and he squeezed me tightly. The man I have always loved held me for the last time on a sunny day on top of the cliffs of England. We were surrounded by policemen who were waiting for me but I didn't care as I held onto James for as long as he would allow. I truly believe he would have held me forever, but the police broke our union, leaving me with just a memory to hold.

I was walked back down to the car park by a young policeman. I was not handcuffed until we reached the police car. I was read my rights then ushered into the car to be seated between two policewomen. As we drove away I saw my abandoned Porsche; the luxury goods I had favoured above my James. And James stood close by watching me being driven away flanked by a fleet of cars which, even then, I thought unnecessary as surely I was not a danger to society? But then what do I know? I was the mannequin who had murdered her husband.

CHAPTER TWENTY-ONE

JASON

My aunt was taken to a holding cell somewhere near Eastbourne. It was twenty-four hours before we heard that she had been arrested for the murder of my Uncle Mark. I vaguely remember the news that evening.

'A man has been found dead in his home in Stoning Town earlier today; the police are treating his death as suspicious.'

The reason I remember it was because I placed greater prominence on hearing Stoning Town, on the radio than to the death of a human being. The next day, the novelty of hearing a place I knew well on the news slipped to shock when my mum rang early in the morning;

'Olive has killed him. She's killed him.'

'Who?' I innocently asked.

'Mark, your Uncle Mark of course! It's all over the news, it's everywhere Jason,' my mum screamed.

It was not everywhere. The death of a wealthy business man only earned a one-line sentence on the radio on the day the murder happened. Then, once the camera crews were in place,

Mark's death was featured on the television with a view of the house in the background whilst a newsreader added a further sentence to this family's' tragedy, to inform the nonchalant public that, 'His wife has been arrested on suspicion of the businessman's murder in their multi-million pound house in the wealthy suburb of London… the investigation is on-going.'

It was never mentioned again to the public's prying eyes until the trial, but from that phone call, it dominated all family and friends' discussions to the point that I began to resent my aunt's actions; not because of her taking the life of my uncle, but because I could no longer have a conversation with anyone I knew until I had fulfilled the obligatory:

'There's no update on the trial date; all we know is she's now at Holloway prison. Her lawyer is looking into the diminished responsibility route due to the stress of an emotionally abusive marriage, but we're not confident as she deliberately went away to get the gun and returned to shoot him, so the prosecution is going for first degree murder.'

Mum churned over the same facts seeking some solace in trying to find an explanation for why her little sister could kill someone. I watched Mum change throughout the winter months from sheer panic and shock about my aunt to raging anger, and in all that time she refused to see her sister. It was Dad who visited her and tried to do all the negotiations for the right lawyer and also trying to bolster Aunt Olive's spirits for preparation for the forthcoming trial.

I could see the strain this was placing on him as he struggled to keep up with his teaching and marking, appease Mum's fears for her sister each time he walked into the house, liaise with the lawyers for Aunt Olive, find the money to pay for these lawyers and finally try to find time to see his sister-in-law; all of which he found harder to cope with as each week passed.

I visited my parents as often as I could at the beginning to try and unburden the load from Dad.

'I just don't understand it Jason,' Mum spat one evening, 'she shot him, she went out of her way to find the gun then returned to kill him!'

'She just saw red, Janet,' Dad interjected on cue to the same conversation they had most evenings.

'Oh, I grant you, my brother-in-law was an evil, cruel nasty little man who deserved divorce papers and to be stripped naked by a wolfhound of a lawyer vying for his blood, but Colin, not to be killed...'

It was a rehearsed speech but Dad obliged by saying the same thing over and over to try and calm Mum down:

'The man crippled her; he used to beat her and when he couldn't get away with that he became emotionally toxic: he belittled her at every opportunity; he bought prostitutes back to the house, and he was a conman who was about to go bankrupt for dodgy business dealings!'

'I know. But she wouldn't leave. And now? How am I going to help her now? How am I going to get her off for murder?'

At this part in the script Mum would start crying and either Dad or I would comfort her until she finally calmed.

'What will be, will be, it's in God's hands and we have to wait it out... Now stop these tears, all of us and stay strong... I won't cry, I mustn't...Who's for tea and a bourbon biscuit?'

Just after Christmas, in the month burdened with the reputation for being boring, depressing and lacking in charisma, Mum finally agreed to see her little sister. So, on January 8th, I drove her to Holloway prison with visiting orders in her hand. I accompanied her through the security checkpoint and after being fully searched, scanned and interviewed about who I was seeing, I was ushered into the visitor's waiting area. The walls were a pale blue with blue plastic chairs linked in three rows for people to sit and wait on. It was cold with a smell of disinfectant hanging in the air. Large mock windows separated the waiting room from the corridors surrounding it. In the background were sporadic entrance and exit buzzing noises, clanging of doors and inaudible shouts.

Mum remained stoic throughout, staring firmly at her lap until our names were called and we were shown to another cold room with white tables which reminded me of my school canteen; except there were no rushing children scrambling to sit next to their mates carefree or munching on sandwiches, instead just a gentle hum of whispered voices from inmates. In amongst them all was Aunt Olive, gaunt, scared and with a distant stare across her face. Her hands were on the table and throughout the one hour meeting they were permanently squeezing together like two scrawny twins hugging one another.

'I have a trial date,' she whispered after an awkward greeting hug from her sister. 'March 18th, two days after your birthday.'

'That's good,' Mum replied, 'at least we can er, look forward, well no, not look forward, but perhaps find closure, well no, a result I mean. Sorry, I don't know what to say.' Mum lapsed back into silence.

'You're doing well, Aunt?' I asked, to fill in the silent hole.

Aunt Olive's once bouffant hair was scraped back into a pony tail, and grey roots were taking hold. She wore no makeup which highlighted the 'swollen allergic reaction' look she had adopted over the last fifteen years. Her eyebrows were still marker-pen dark stripes as she'd had them lasered off and then tattooed back on a few years ago. Sitting with her head bowed in front of me, she reminded me of a 1950s' cinema Martian with a tiny weak body and a huge swollen head. But unlike the little green men designed to scare earthlings she just looked pitiful.

At the end of the meeting we all stood up and then Mum grabbed her frail sister and hugged her.

'You'll be okay, sis, I promise.'

'I know,' she replied and, on the instruction from a nearby guard, they released one another.

Mum remained silent throughout the journey home except for: 'So, March. March it is.' I dropped her back home and apologised that I couldn't stay as I was taking my girlfriend out for a meal. It was a lie as she was at a training course in Nottingham but I couldn't endure another twisted evening of questions about the outcome of my aunt so I raced home leaving Dad to comfort Mum.

January left us, followed by a snowy February and finally a cold wet March arrived. The 18th knocked at our doors and we left our homes for London for the trial between the Crown and Mrs Olivia Hopkins. The trial was held at the Old Bailey and we were taken to a side gate to avoid the cameras at the front.

'They're not just for this trial as there's the Beckett case in courtroom number four. However, they do seem a permanent fixture these days I'm afraid. They seem to cover every trial, I believe in the hope that their day's effort makes the news. Not allowed in my day but times have changed; times have changed – more channels and whatnot and I suppose we all have to make money some way or another. Best we take the side entrance and not the school gates as I like to refer to them.'

My aunt's barrister was a Mr Partridge, a tall thin man dressed in the stereotypical dark blue pin-striped suit under his court gown. He had an autocratic, dismissive air which I found comforting. We reached outside the courtroom where he introduced us to my aunt's lawyer, a Mr Thomson. In contrast to Mr Partridge, he was an elderly, large man in a drab ill-fitting grey suit with a stained brown mud-coloured tie.

'We need to go in soon,' Mr Thomson said meekly. 'I'll be in there but my colleague, Mr Partridge, will be doing all the talking, maybe referring to me from time to time but er, that's it. Er, you need to sit in the spectators' gallery.'

Mr Thomson was an uninspiring lawyer who appeared not just bored of the proceedings, but slightly irritated by the fact that he'd have to endure watching my Aunt Olive's trial when he would rather be anywhere but here; preferably in the pub.

'Good God,' Mum said as we sat down, 'the lawyer, Mr Thomson, seems incompetent. Look at him Jason, he looks like he needs a good dusting. That suit couldn't be revived even if a good medic got hold of it. Look at the paperwork he's holding; it's all falling out of the folders and he hasn't even noticed!'

'I'm sure he's done a good job Mum, don't focus on that. Can you see Aunt Olive?'

She's coming in now,' said Dad. 'Dear almighty she's aged; her hair is completely grey. Was she always that thin?'

'I should have picked up the green suit; that black one is too big for her or is it because she's now walking with a stoop? The front is all baggy,' replied Mum.

'All rise for Lord Justice Banner,' interrupted the court clerk.

'She looks ghostly white; her eyes have sunk into their sockets; they look like they haven't experienced sleep in years,' continued Mum.

'They probably haven't,' I whispered.

The trial lasted far longer than the one day we ignorantly assumed it would take. I tried to attend most of it but it was seriously boring. Even though the trial was about a member of my family I found it difficult to stay interested as the defence and prosecution thrashed out every intricate detail about their marriage and the circumstances leading up to the murder. This was not helped by the heavy dark and musty wooden-panelled courtroom, which gave an oppressive, claustrophobic atmosphere.

The defence focused on years of emotional abuse but this was counteracted by the prosecution who forcibly demonstrated that there was no abuse.

'Mrs Hopkins led a lavish lifestyle and she enjoyed a wealthy jet set life, indulging in many holidays which her poor husband paid for to keep his beloved wife happy...'

They also claimed that she had plenty of opportunity to leave the marriage but she was inherently:

'...*a greedy woman who pushed her husband away to the arms of others as all he was looking for was love. This love he finally found in the arms of another who had stood by him and given him a son, and it was Mark who finally found the strength to leave this woman. However, this rejection caused Mrs Hopkins to snap and murder her husband, as she could not bear the idea of losing any of her wealth to another woman... So she found a gun and, with an evil calculating mind, she callously planned to murder him then escape undetected. However, her plan didn't work and she was finally apprehended by police before she had the chance to run away...*'

Throughout this trial Mum would tut.

'This is not the case, it's just not true Colin.'

'I know dear,' Dad would say.

'The jury will see through it Mum, don't worry,' I would say.

And the courtroom remained silent.

The jury listened and their body language didn't waver in favour of any side. There were no nods of agreement or murmurs of disgust; just twelve men and women sitting patiently through the trial. The only hint the jury were listening to the prosecution or defence was when a few members recoiled at seeing the pictures of the murder scene.

Occasionally, the focus was on my aunt who remained slumped in the dock; she appeared smaller as each day and hour passed. Her defence was disappearing and her barrister was beginning to appear as disinterested as Mr Thomson who, by now, was periodically nodding off; probably dreaming of the beer he was going to enjoy once this "pesky trial" was finally over.

Nearing the natural end of the trial our confidence in obtaining a fair outcome had disappeared. The prosecution had successfully painted Aunt Olive as an evil, greedy, manipulative woman and the defence seemed unable to disprove it; after all, the indisputable evidence was that a man was dead due to the trigger of a gun being pulled by his avaricious wife.

The benefit of watching Aunt Olive's defence crumble away was that we were prepared for the verdict. She was found guilty of murder and sentenced to thirty-five years. My aunt did not quiver when this sentenced was passed. All she did was to hang her head low when the judge described her.

'...You are a truly evil woman who abused your husband throughout your marriage. ...You did kill, with evil intent, a man who had supported you for over twenty years... You not only killed a man in cold blood but you destroyed the hopes of his son ever knowing his father... all in the pursuit of protecting your riches. Take her down.'

The court room watched a frail old lady totter to the prisoner's exit door. Before she left she was stopped by a guard to place handcuffs on her wrists. It was then that she briefly looked up to her family where she would have seen her sister crying whilst being supported by her husband, she would have seen me with pity etched across my face and she would have felt the court room audience bustle as they gathered their things after the final curtain of the case had fallen. Some were already standing, some were chatting amongst themselves reviewing the show and others were secretly checking their phones for any messages they had missed throughout the case. But there was one member who remained rigidly watching Olivia leave. He was a tall thin man with a full beard. He seemed lost, unable to fathom the outcome of the trial. He too looked frail as he tentatively, quietly stood and nodded at Aunt Olivia when she deliberately turned to look directly at him. She smiled with eyes swollen by tears then she disappeared through the door.

Outside the court room we were met by Mr Partridge who hurriedly made his prepared speech.

'I'm sorry 'he said, 'we did our very best but the evidence was stacked against us.'

'No, Mr Partridge,' my mother began between tearful rasps, 'no, this isn't fair, she led a miserable life, why didn't you call for more witnesses? Why didn't you ask her more questions about her mental state when you called her to stand? You used me as a witness but asked puerile questions that displayed nothing about her life or how worried we were for her such as; 'what was my favourite memory of my sister as a child!' – what use is that? Also, you could have shown to the jury that she tried to leave so many times but he wouldn't let her. So, no, Mr Partridge, you did not do your very best!!'

In an insincere, obsequious tone, Mr Partridge said, 'There there, I know it is hard to take in, but all I can do is to give the jury the evidence as we all see it. However, as I said, this was stacked against us and however hard I tried, and I did try hard for you, dear lady, the verdict comes down to the jury.'

I suspect Mum would have screamed at him a little longer but instead she turned and cried into the comforting hug of Dad who in contrast was quiet but firm.

'You did not defend my sister-in-law. She was a used and abused woman. Perhaps you would agree that to kill takes independent thought, but as Olivia was controlled in every way by her husband then, surely, he plays a part in orchestrating his own death? This may appear a tenuous link but it demonstrates that she may have pulled the trigger but it was not entirely his wife, no, let me explain… there were reasons as to why Olivia did what she did and these were not explored. So, no, Mr Partridge, the verdict is an unfair one.'

'Again, I am sorry for the outcome but despite all my efforts, society has judged Mrs Hopkins. Good day.'

And with that he swooped away like a black cat in the headlights of an oncoming car leaving my family mourning the final loss of their Olivia.

CHAPTER TWENTY-TWO

Today

JASON

It's a bright, spring Friday, the type of Friday in the year I love. For me, this day is even brighter as the weekend has begun at 5.45pm with the first pint in my hand at the Hare and Hound pub in Holborn. Work has slackened temporarily to let me leave on time and walk out into the remaining part of the day. It welcomes me with evening sunshine as the days get longer and people reach out to the pub as a prelude to the oncoming summer. It has not rained in days and the trees are as green as the grass, making any Londoner grateful to be right where they are in the heart of the capital. I sit on my own outside, on a wooden pub bench, waiting for Jess who has texted:

'Won't be with you until 6.30 and Sarah and Mike will join us for dinner by 7 – if it is ok for them to join up as well?'

It's not okay as I know they'll ask me more inane questions about my murderous aunt, such as. "Did you ever suspect she would become a murderer one day?" and "Were you subconsciously scared of her when growing up?" I was friends with them by default, for dating Sarah's best friend. Nevertheless, as with all relationships, there'll be difficult parts and great parts; today the difficulty was Sarah and Mike but the great part was I now had forty-five minutes to myself with a pint of London Pride as company under the summer sun.

It was a perfect opportunity to open the letter I received yesterday from Aunt Olivia. I'd got home late on Thursday and it was waiting for me on the door mat. I knew it was from her as there was a Durham prison postal stamp across the top. I resisted the temptation to open it then as our lives had finally slipped back into normality after the trial. Mum and Dad were planning a holiday to Tenerife to celebrate their belated twenty-fifth wedding anniversary and Dad's sixty-third birthday. These celebrations were some time ago but they used them as an excuse to upgrade their hotel to the Sensetori.

I'm seeing Jessica daily and we're already discussing moving in together. I've thought about Jess on every absent moment and I've missed her company throughout the day. She's given me purpose to finish work as soon as I can to pursue a life outside the eleventh floor of a London office block.

Aunt Olivia paused our lives for nearly eighteen months and now we're claiming those lost months back. So, seeing another letter from her was actually easy to resist. I didn't want to be dragged back down to where she had fallen because with the death of Uncle Mark she had inadvertently tried to pull us all down to the depressing pit she had lived in for decades.

However, out of a feeling of warped family loyalty, I at least picked it up in the morning and put it in my jacket pocket. If it was not a Friday and if a pint of London Pride had not bolstered my spirits then the likelihood would be the letter would have remained in my jacket until I discovered it when I needed to clear out my suit pockets on the drycleaner's counter some time later.

OLIVIA

'Dearest Jay,

I was moved to Durham maximum security prison a little while ago and I know that the distance is too far for you to visit, hence, another letter from me. I hope the last letter found you well and that it explained why your aunt would take the life of another. I'm deeply ashamed of my actions but although I will most likely see the rest of my days here, I now possess a sense of peace; a peace I don't remember ever feeling.

Let me explain this flippant remark: I'm receiving counselling and we're exploring the idea that I have held my emotions in a box and, throughout my life, inferiority was my jealousy's best friend; they colluded with one another to stop me accepting others, but urged me instead to scrabble around for any feeling of superiority over people, and this led me to Mark and the riches he offered.

I was scared of Mark and I was scared of how depressed I was, living in his hands. This led to feeling inferior, which led to jealousy, which led to Mark's credit card, which led directly back to Mark and hence this box was never closed until I killed him.

I know I have no right to be jealous of others; I accept I am inferior to everyone outside these walls as I have committed a terrible crime, but this fact gives me peace. I rejoice that I'm not scared anymore and my devil has not returned for a chat since the day I picked up Mark's gun.

I admit I was scared when I was first arrested. The police said nothing to me in the car and when I was at the police station I was strip-searched and made to squat in front of a policewoman just to prove there was nothing hidden inside me; it was humiliating but I accepted it without a quibble.

The cell was grey with a green plastic bed at one end and a stainless-steel toilet without a lid in a corner. The toilet was full as it was blocked, I tentatively complained, but there was no one to fix it. The surprising benefit to this was I was escorted to use the staff toilet; it meant I had a break in the long hours of sitting on this bed waiting for something to happen, so the need to pee bought a tiny bit of control and it refreshed me from the pain of boredom.

Within this first cell, time had left me and it was replaced with pure silence – empty and long, very long – which teased my internal sense of time: a minute was no longer a minute but an hour, and an hour was no longer an hour but a day. There was nothing to distract me from this confusion as all that was on offer to me was to sit on the green plastic bed and wait. But wait for what? A lawyer who didn't arrive for an eternity, meal times and, of course, toilet breaks which I utilised as often as I could just to be able to move and stop thinking about what I had done to have led me to be sitting on a green plastic mattress.

It felt like many lifetimes, but finally the administration of bagging and recording my possessions, which consisted of a pair of earrings, a wedding ring and a watch, was complete. I then saw a nurse who patched up my bloody feet and I briefly saw a psychiatrist who merely wrote a few notes then left me to be interviewed by the police. The police questions were not confrontational but there to clarify certain parts of my story. The lawyer that had been instructed to sit by me said very little as the case was straightforward: I had already admitted to intentionally murdering my husband then running away. The only request this young lawyer gave on my behalf was to ask for further psychiatric assessments but there was a problem with a staff change over, so I had to wait for another psychiatrist when someone came available.

The next part is hazy as all I can remember was the overall feeling of long waits, followed by long interviews, followed by long waits. I remember I was confused and scared but I'm ashamed to say, I was also thinking about what others were making of my actions and how all my lunch friends would be reading about their friend murdering her husband. If I listen hard enough I can still hear their gossiping and it was these voices that distracted me in the interview room, hence I found it very difficult to concentrate:

The sun shone through a high, dirty, sealed window, lighting up the dust floating in the stale air. These beams created lines of fog and one of them covered half the face of my interviewer; I could make out his loose brown tie on top of his cream shirt; I could make out his grey beard and his left ear but everything else on his face was camouflaged by the dusty rays. Jason, I was exhausted and because all I could see was the inspector's mouth, it meant I missed many questions which had to be repeated. After a while I sensed his frustration at having to repeat yet another question.

'I'll say again, were you aware your husband owned the gun used to kill him prior to the morning of the 15th?'

'Er, I think so. I'm not sure really but I remember seeing it, yes,' I said.

Before the bearded officer could re-word the question to gather a definitive, 'yes', a lady officer entered the room. She was no more than thirty with long black hair tied into a bun resting on the nape of her neck.

She looks like Lorraine when she was younger, I thought.

Lorraine was a lunch friend who had many affairs with prominent wealthy men and finally caught a futures' trader and married him two years ago. She continued to have affairs and so, within eighteen months of marriage, Lorraine gets to enjoy her country house whilst her new husband enjoys his Battersea house and they meet occasionally to keep up the pretence of the perfect social couple for the sake of their friends. These friends are fully aware of the masquerade but are too polite or disinterested to jeopardise this farce, thus allowing the marriage to remain intact.

She's celebrating her fifty-fifth birthday soon; in fact isn't it her girls lunch today?

'Mrs Hopkins, I'll ask again, have you ever used your husband's gun prior to the 15th?' the inspector said sharply.

It's 14.03 pm, I wonder if they're onto the canapés yet after the champagne reception?

I wonder how many times my name has been mentioned? I bet they're all laughing still. I wonder how many times they've said they knew I was strange: 'Yep she had murderous eyes,' they'll be saying,' I never trusted that one...'

'Would you like a break Olivia? I can ask for a break for you,' my young lawyer interrupted, which bought me back to the dusty interview room.

'No, I'm fine,' I said. 'Er, yes, I've used a gun before. My husband sometimes wanted me at a hunt, but I don't own one myself. Sorry was that your question? Sorry, I've forgotten what you said.'

'Let's take a break,' said the interviewing officer, 'this interview is suspended at 14.09...'

The officer leant back and I could now see his face; beyond his beard I saw his blue eyes sinking in a bag of wrinkles, but I could also clearly see the pity wallowing within him; pity for a foolish vulnerable old woman sitting in front of him apathetic to the carnage she had caused for herself.

I was refused bail and a day later I was bundled into the back of a police van where I sat inside a small cage and was driven to Holloway prison. On the way there I caught a glimpse of life still continuing whilst my life now stood still. There was the little old man walking his dog, the housewife hurrying her two daughters to school and the milkman finishing his rounds.

I slipped into prison life, which was a daily routine of conforming to rules. I received a psychological assessment which graded me as having moderate to severe depression, but I was not considered a danger to myself or others and, therefore, I remained in Holloway instead of being moved to a secure hospital. The drugs I was prescribed helped me cope with the sadness of no longer being able to move freely about my life.

I was an inmate of the British prison system who resided alongside all other of her country's social rubbish; rubbish thrown away and out of sight of her good citizens. Knowing I was one of them was harder to cope with than the lack of freedom. I couldn't relate to other inmates who were either angry or, like myself, scared and moved from shadow to shadow.

I rarely spoke, mainly because I was too intimidated by everyone in there and also because I couldn't understand the confused ramblings of many of the inmates who seemed to have led the same life as each other. Most of these women were neglected by their family and ignored by society. Their only escape was found in drinking and doing drugs which in turn led to isolation from any social norms; they didn't work, but instead signed up to crime or prostitution. They were arrested at a very young age to start their career cycle of drugs, crime, prison, more drugs, release from prison, more drugs then more crime and back into prison. For many women this was all they knew and anything outside of this was unknown and too difficult to attempt. So, some, like Trish, knew the prison guards on a first name basis.

Trish was a big woman with short cropped hair, baggy jeans and football tops. She would shout from across the canteen to either greet or swear at someone. Depending on their response it determined whether she would express deep love for them or threaten a fight if they didn't show respect. My eyes were permanently glued to the floor and I would pray the guards would intervene before another fight erupted around me.

Occasionally I saw your father who was there out of a sense of duty and love for my sister. He was awkward and he had very little to say to me other than the obligatory, 'How are you doing?' and updates on my case from my lawyer. I was grateful for his visits; Colin is a kind man and I'm sorry I sent this tsunami through your family. It's a shame I had to put you through the agony of the trial. If I could have skipped trawling through the details of my actions in front of twelve men and women and instead elected merely to hear my sentence from the judge then I would have. I knew I was guilty when I pulled the trigger, I should have just been shuffled away to Durham prison the moment I was arrested.

So here I am, my dearest nephew. I am currently sitting at a desk with a small wardrobe to the side of me, a small thin single bed behind me, a small window high up the ceiling in a small peach-coloured cell at Durham prison where I have been since the day I was sentenced.

I've settled well into the routine and, unlike in Holloway, I've actually made a friend, Sue. Sue has taught me how to survive the boredom of living in a peach box.

She is helping me in many ways to remain calm and to shake away the depression I feel. It's still there and when it comes it's overwhelming and crippling to the point I cannot get out of bed, but Sue ensures I don't leave a body mark in my bed the way I used to as the wife of Mark Mathew Hopkins.

But, today is a good day; today I'm writing to my nephew and later I have a visit from my James who has ventured up with his family. He has two daughters, his eldest, he says, may be bright enough to come to Durham University to study maths. I hope she'll make it here then I could look out and imagine, in the very far distance, a pretty blonde girl in an undergraduate black gown, and I will smile for Rae.

On the wall in front of my desk are speckled flecks of old blue-tack from past residents. I've picked most of them off to make use of it to stick my pictures on the wall. There are five in total: one of my parents, another of Janet and Colin on their beautiful wedding day, one is of you Jason, wearing a blue sailor outfit on a beach in Cornwall. You were no more than three at the time and I can still hear the swell of the tide behind as you ran in and out chasing the waves. I can also hear your laughter, your sweet happy giggles that still mesmerise and soothe me even though, now, this holiday is a mere memory.

Another picture is of my James in Australia when we went to a concert in Adelaide, he's raising a beer in the picture and, happily, I can clearly hear the words of love he declared to me on that day.

The final picture is of a plump ginger-haired girl. I'm sulking in the picture but around me are my parents looking at me adoringly, Janet is sitting in front of me with a huge smile and she is holding my hand. I see now that my sister was my support and she loved me but I wanted more than my family had to offer. What that 'more' was I didn't know back then, but I found a possible answer in my magazines, which pointed towards happiness in the arms of riches. I felt loved by society but ignored and ridiculed by the people I shared this life with. If I had just accepted that I had everything I needed in the love of my family then maybe I would have been part of your life a little more and I would have recognised the love from James and realised that I loved him, and I would be visiting Durham as the mother of an undergraduate and not as an inmate of one of England's prisons.

So, my final words to you are to love; recognise where it is and hold onto it. Love is not found in a bank balance, fine clothes, fast cars or large houses but it's found in the quickening beat of your heart that tells you the person you are with is the person who will help to make life happy without the need to wear a smile but instead, to feel a smile.

Be happy sweet nephew and love.

My love,

Aunt Olivia

P.S. Please visit!

I've finished my beer, folded my aunt's letter and returned it to my pocket. She talked of the society she lived in but I don't recognise the people she spoke about. She was like a peacock amongst ducks. Her plumage was grander than anyone around her but she stood alone with her feathers and gold shining in the river reeds.

Around me are various members of London society: two men laughing over an incident in their office; there's an old man deep in thought whilst enjoying his one pint of Guinness a day; and there's a labourer in orange overalls napping in the afternoon sun with his pint of beer on the pub bench beside him. I'm watching this stranger sleeping and my mind drifts to the promotion that I'd been working towards for nearly a year. I'd laboured for months in front of my computer. I had a greater relationship with my desk than I did with Jessica. I missed seasons as I went to work before sunrise and left work after sunset. But today I learnt that the company I worked tirelessly for had chosen an outside candidate over me.

'It was a tough decision,' said my boss. His foot continuously tapped the floor causing his knee to bob up and down. Every so often his hand would rest on top to try to still it. But it pounded away.

'We just decided that you weren't quite there yet, Jason. There will be other opportunities. Consider this a time of reflection, as although your work is excellent maybe, and I'm only saying this to help you, maybe there are areas you can improve on.' His knee pounded away. 'There is the head of statistical accounting that maybe you could consider?'

This job was a side-step; the same grade and money just a different department, it's known in the industry as flat-lining.

I was initially angry that I'd sacrificed a year of my life all for a humiliating refusal from a boss who cared as much about me as I do for him. But as I stare at the man sitting in front of me, content and asleep, and I think about the letter from my aunt, then maybe the loss of this job is not as crap as I initially thought. Fate was somewhere in that room; he'd not let himself known to me but I was confident he was there.

Dad told me from an early age that the secret to happiness

was to find the right woman and, "when you've found her son, look after her and never think that there is something better under another woman's skirt."

I know the right woman for me is Jessica.

I spied her in the distance walking towards me. As she neared, my heart beat faster and I felt my smile grow across my face. I stood to greet her and when she was close enough my beautiful girl came into my arms.

'I'm quitting my job,' I burst out.

'Seriously?' she said.

'Just decided it… Come travelling with me.'

'…Why not!' she replied. 'Where to?'

'Australia,' I said and I felt her smile.

Society expects us all to conform to what it dictates is a suitable life, where we work to add pounds into our bank to buy the right house and ideal car and fill our wardrobe with what it tells us we should wear – regardless of whether it suits us. We're each just a person living on this planet for the briefest of moments; just a blink in the history of time and we are gone, our possessions are thrown away or given to another without a thought for their origin. But if we're lucky, whilst we're here, enjoying the air we breathe, then perhaps we will recognise that the only people who truly care about who we are as a person, are not society, but the ones who love us and whom we choose to love in return. For me, they are my parents, my good friends and my beloved Jessica whom I will cherish and care for until the day I return to stardust.